MINIONS
OF THE
MOON

MINIONS
OF THE
MOON

Richard Bowes

A TOM DOHERTY ASSOCIATES BOOK
NEW YORK

MINIONS OF THE MOON

Copyright © 1999 by Richard Bowes

Edited by Delia Sherman
Designed by Nancy Resnick

A Tor Book
Published by Tom Doherty Associates, Inc.
175 Fifth Avenue
New York, NY 10010

Tor Books on the World Wide Web:
http://www.tor.com

Tor® is a registered trademark of Tom Doherty
Associates, Inc.

Library of Congress Cataloging-in-Publication Data

Bowes, Richard.
    Minions of the moon / Richard Bowes.—1st ed.
        p.   cm.
    "A Tom Doherty Associates book."
    ISBN 0-312-86566-X (acid-free paper)
    I. Title.
  PS3552.O8735M56   1999
  813'.54—dc21   98-43981
                                              CIP

First Edition: February 1999

Printed in the United States of America

0 9 8 7 6 5 4 3 2 1

For Vincent Tracy
1910–1975

When it gets bad, you're what I remember.

ACKNOWLEDGMENTS

Sometimes in fiction the deeply personal can be read as auto-biography. My actual family, my parents, brothers, sisters, nieces, nephews, in-laws, godchildren, grandparents, uncles, cousins, aunts, and grandaunts, would be a different tale indeed.

No one needs editorial assistance more than I do. Especially on a book, like this, which appeared over a period of six years in the form of ten stories.

Two gifted editors who also happen to be wonderful writers were decisive in the creation of *Minions.*

Kris Rusch showed me how to write short fiction, then bought the first Kevin Grierson story and six of the ones that followed. She saw the book more clearly than I did and began the process of shaping. She was the ideal reader for whom this was first written.

Delia Sherman took the disparate parts, excised repetition, reconciled discrepancies in names, ages, dates, motives, and physical features, suggested that I fill a gaping hole in the narrative with what may be the best of the stories and showed me how to turn a book into a novel.

Algis Budrys, Gordon Van Gelder, and the crew at *Full Spectrum 5* each bought a Kevin Grierson story. Ed Ferman provided my first and favorite short-form home. Terri Windling opened the Flatiron doors. Linn Prentis, my long-suffering agent, Mark Rich, Dave Truesdale, John Brizzolara, Jim Minz, and so many others gave vital help on the way.

I thank you all.

MINIONS
OF THE
MOON

PROLOGUE

MY NAME IS Kevin Grierson. If this were a twelve-step program for mortals haunted by doppelgangers, I would stand up now and say, "Hi. My name is Kevin. I'm fifty-four and I've been stalked by my own Shadow for as long as I can remember." Then you'd say hello and we'd exchange stories.

In fact, I long ago learned to see my Shadow as the embodiment of my addiction, my will to self-destruction. The wise man who taught me to do that also showed me how to stay aware of the one he called my Silent Partner without dwelling on him.

After long mastery of that high-wire act, I grew confident, even, God help me, proud. Then the other night, I saw a kid get on a streetcar in Boston over forty years ago. The sight gave me pause, made me wonder if my time of grace was running out. And in that moment of uncertainty, I felt my Shadow close in.

I'd had a warning a week or two ago when Gina Raille, an old friend, said she had seen a guy around who looked like he might be my evil twin. But I had other things on my mind and things like this happened every once in a while. Not until last Saturday night and Sunday afternoon was I shown signs I could not ignore.

A toy merry-go-round on Ozzie Klackman's work table was the first of those. Other business had brought me to his blowsy old apartment slightly above the riot that is Avenue A in August. Ceiling fans rotated. Decades worth of East Sixth Street curry hung in the air. Sirens wailed in the East Village. A boombox car bounced sound off the buildings. "LOCK UP THE FUCKING BANJA BOYS!" yelled a hoarse voice, a woman, or maybe a drag.

Ozzie, red faced and unshaven in paint-stained shorts and T-shirt, said, "You tell 'em, honey," and drained a tumbler of fruit juice and vodka. Then he went back to demonstrating a Chatty Cathy. "I reworked it for this rich fetishist down in Pennsylvania." Cathy still had her dippy smile. But now instead of inane talking-doll phrases, she uttered a string of obscenities in her dippy little voice. "It's costing him plenty," said Ozzie self-righteously, like overcharging the guy made him an agent of justice.

Every trade has its skullduggers, resurrectionists, procurers. Old toys is no exception. Ozzie Klackman is all those things and more. It's why I had business with him.

Years of cruising and of buying antiques have taught me to nod, smile, and look with bland indifference at what interests me. The carousel was worn, wooden, American-made by my guess. The condition was better than I would have expected in a toy that old. The detail work too, with each horse a firebreathing stallion, and the decorative motif of smiling suns and frowning moons was suspiciously bright. Not one of Klackman's master forgeries.

But it was its accuracy that made the hair on my neck stand up. To paint this, Klackman must have seen the real one as I had. He stopped talking. When I looked up, his small clever eyes were on me, measuring my reaction.

"You saw the original?" he asked. "I did. Years ago out in East Asshole, New Jersey. I was working for Augie Dolbier and he heard about this merry-go-round for sale. So he took me along and we barged right in. Real creepy scene. Like it was some kind of con game or rip-off. The carousel was the lure. The ones who had it weren't interested in selling. Not to us. Recently I got reminded. I took this old beat-up toy and did it from memory."

He waited like he expected me to ask questions. But I cultivate an attitude of professional disinterest and right then I was preoccupied with the present. "I've had a long day," I told him and turned to go.

"Sorry I haven't been to see George," Ozzie said. My partner, George Halle, was at Cabrini Hospice in a terminal coma. I indicated the visit wasn't necessary.

At the door, I handed him fifty dollars in tens and said, "Here's your retainer. You'll be at Masby's Monday at eleven sharp, right? And you know what I want you to do?"

"Don't worry, Kevin me lad," he said in a Long John Silver voice. "Nighty night."

Downstairs, yuppie couples scuttled home with Sunday papers and Kim's videos. Over on Second Avenue, old guys with hats and cigars hung around newsstands eternally waiting for that final Brooklyn Dodgers score and a few hookers still operated in the shadow of the St. Mark's-in-the-Bowery baptistery.

But mainly it was kids. From New Jersey and the Bronx, by car and subway, they were outfitted like 1950s nerds, like cybersluts and MTV stars, in shorts and baseball caps, miniskirts and high heels, striped boxers and sneakers, souvenir T-shirts and envelope-shaped bell jeans, sporting crew cuts, beaded pigtails, wisps of Day-Glo green and blue hair that caught the streetlight like glaucoma auras.

I walked through them, middle age making me as invisible as a ghost at a tropical carnival. It amazed me that with everyone out of town for the weekend, the city could still be so crowded.

A bus rolled downtown. That summer they displayed Calvin Klein ads on their sides. Each was a row of photos of the same well-defined young man clad only in various undershorts. His expression varied from defiant, to dazed, to blank. It looked like the draft physical for the clone wars.

Actually getting force-stripped is disturbing, not sexy, a sub-species of rape, as I could testify. Fantasy, though, is something else. Klein's genius is the exploitation of hustler poses, and August in New York gives everyone a horny itch. Normally I satisfied that itch through safe, clean call services.

Ozzie and his carousel had me thinking about the past when I stopped to pick up *The Times*. Just then, I noticed what looked like any club boy in his early twenties. His slightly glazed eyes met mine and held. The kid was for rent. Then his face lighted slightly. "Fred?" he asked. And I understood the kid had dealt with my Shadow.

Chilled but curious, I replied, "I have been. You and Fred are friends?" He indicated they were. I took the bait. Negotiations were fast. We were both pros. I said what I wanted and made an offer. He agreed and gave his name as Matt. I stuck with Fred, which had served my Shadow and me well enough in the past.

When we got to my place on Seventeenth Street, Stuyvesant Park across the way was still unlocked. Beneath the new moon, dogs and people moved under the lamp-lit trees, sat on benches waiting for love.

My building was quiet. Everyone else in the co-op is middle-aged too. My apartment is on the third floor and comfortable. On the living-room mantel I have assembled an antique toy zoo, animals behind bars, visitors pointing their articulated metal arms, an expensive whimsy. "The Heineken's is cold." I opened one for my guest and was not tempted. Once or twice in my past I have been touched by a grace so rare that it carries me through sordid passages and empty years.

I sat on the couch. Matt was cute in a dark buzz, shorts, and sneakers. I could remember when having to wear that particular outfit was a sentence to dorkhood. Of course, way back then we didn't have the option of silver earrings and leg tattoos.

Matt swallowed some beer, stood in the center of my living room, and stripped when I asked him to. Ralph Lauren, Gap, Old Navy, Tommy Hilfiger—the layers fell away and revealed how skinny he was.

He glanced at my front windows and noticed they were uncurtained. He made an involuntary gesture as if he wanted to cover his crotch and eyes, then thought he shouldn't. I felt a key turn in my heart even as I knew it was all part of the act.

Because of age and scars and a sense of aesthetics, I kept my shirt on. In the bedroom, the air conditioner played on our skin. I stroked his hair, which was as short and smooth as I imagine an otter's to be. He smelled of smoke and booze, Obsession and sweat, the scent of nightlife. Wings were tattooed over his left nipple, a snake wound up his right calf.

Then we got down to business and for a time, with my cock being licked and tickled, my hand on another's head, my mind sailed free with not a thought of who he was or who I was or what were the circumstances of this happening. It was like being a kid again.

To work completely, commodity sex should be emotionally self-contained and anonymous. Too much involvement makes that impossible. Matt had aroused my curiosity. And my empathy. Never underestimate a doppelganger's subtlety. This kid evoked my past.

When he got up and went in the bathroom, I looked through his clothes. Except for the sneakers, they had all been bought or boosted that day. Tomorrow, if all went well for him, these clothes would be in the trash and he'd have a new outfit. He carried no wallet, seven dollars in change, a couple of pills I couldn't identify, and slips of paper, most with names and numbers, one with just a Hell's Kitchen address.

In a small shoulder bag he had underwear and socks, Vaseline, polyurethene and latex condoms, plastic gloves, dental and tongue dams, skin salve, and nonoxynol-9. My guess was that these were all his possessions.

When he was ready to leave, I gave him a card. The name and number of my shop were on the front and my name and home phone number were on the back. "Call me soon." He nodded as I would once have done. "Since you used the name Fred, you must have met my imaginary friend," I remarked.

He gave me a look that said my Shadow was at least as real as I was. Then the kid was gone. And since nothing of any consequence was on my answering machine, I lay down on the bed and started leafing through *The Times*.

The next thing I remember was a kid getting on a Boston streetcar. An ordinary enough child, blond and small, a very young twelve, he walked like he was wary of being hit. He sat at the back of the car and turned his face toward the window. Someone once said that when the Irish get hurt they stay hurt. He might have had in mind something like the way that kid moved and avoided eye contact.

The last streetcars in New York ran long before I arrived here. But deep in the night, I started awake. The Week in Review and Arts and Entertainment sections fell on the floor and it seemed as if I'd just heard a trolley bell clang at the end of my block.

ONE

SUNDAY DAWNED BLAZING hot. Matt and the kid on the streetcar had faded as tricks and dreams do by light of day. Still, they left me aware of my Shadow. I hadn't slept well. The same wise man who compared my double to a Silent Partner had told me he was like an embezzler stealing my soul bit by bit.

That Sunday morning, I went by George Halle's apartment to take care of his mail and make sure the place was still intact. A quick look around was all that I could stand. Wooden louvers shaded the windows, cut the sound of the far West Village to nothing.

My memories of the place were wondrous. Over the past couple of decades, George and I had been lovers, business partners, friends, and, finally, patient and caregiver. The furniture is old, modern stuff from the forties. The art is American illustration and cartoons. Polished and mellow, the rooms awaited the return of George, who had now been taken off life support.

Ducking out of the place, I locked the door, walked down to the street, and stopped. George's block stood empty except for a scavenger. His garbage bags half full of bottles and cans, he rummaged in the trash with his back to me. He was gray haired and about my build. But his face, when he turned, was not mine.

The incident made me decide to stick to public places. Over on Hudson Street with a whole afternoon to kill, I idly cruised amid clusters of guys and women sauntering back from brunch, the gay Sunday service.

For the first time in years I seriously considered my early past. Ironic that it took Ozzie Klackman and my Shadow to do it, since antique toys and books, the compost heap of childhood, are my business. Those things, however, are nostalgia, memory in costume and party hat. Real recollection, as I was about to find out, is something else.

Memory, the word itself, evokes for me an image of bright lights and green grass, a night game at Fenway Park in, maybe, '48 or '49. If so, I am four or five, up way past bedtime, dozing against my uncle Mike, the cop. Suddenly everyone stands up and he lifts me onto his shoulder.

I see figures in gray, running. Then out of the left-field darkness sails a white ball. At third base, a man in white, his back to me, takes two steps to his left, nabs it, pivots, and fires. The catcher, his scary mask abandoned, comes up the line toward third, catches the ball, crouches, braces, tags the sliding runner. The game ends. The crowd roars in triumph, able for a moment to forget that they are Red Sox fans and thus doomed.

For the rest of the afternoon, as fragments, disjointed, incomplete, drifted from my subconscious into my awareness, I thought of the ball flying out of the darkness into the light. As I walked away from George's I recalled this line of a poem:

FOUNTAINS IN SUMMER

It evoked images of sunlight on green leaves and my mother leading me by the hand in the Boston Public Garden. My guess is that I was about three.

No trip downtown at that time was complete without a visit to the Swan Boats. So, at some point we must have floated on the shallow pond under low bridges with a Boston University undergraduate pedaling away in the great white bird at the back. But for the moment I couldn't say for sure. Nor could I remember more of the poem or where I had heard it.

On that summer day fifty years later, I walked north and east, unaware of my destination until I arrived at the Sixth Avenue Flea Market. In those aisles of jumbled tchotchke and kitsch, sprawling through empty parking lots and garages, trawled by every boomer who somehow forgot to get invited to the Hamptons for the weekend, Warhol once assembled his million-dollar cookie jar collection.

My eyes refused to focus on tarnished brass door knockers and plastic place mats with pictures of Italy. Then a couple turned and smiled and seemed to share their smile with me.

She, it appeared, was a young part-Asian woman, blue eyed and black haired, slim in a green silk blouse. He, I realized, was misshapen. But his face was delicate, his smile beautiful. Turning, he replaced something on a table.

A damsel and a dwarf, I thought as they moved away. I should have been able to spot my Shadow's hand. But right then, all I was aware of was what he had put back on the table. Amid a collection of distressed *Humpty Dumpty* magazines, coverless copies of *The Pokey Little Puppy*, was my face on a decaying dust jacket.

Actually, it was just a drawing of a little boy in a striped jersey and shorts. An Eton cap perched on a blond head almost as big as his trunk. Eyes wide with wonder, he stared at an Indian chief in full regalia. The title was *Go West, Jelly Bean!*

Others modeled before and after. But for several books, I was Jelly Bean. In truth, JB was sort of featureless. He was Everykid back in 1950 when they thought that meant a white boy.

The books weren't quite up there with Dr. Seuss or Curious

George. But more than a dozen titles got produced between the late forties and late fifties. If you were a child then and read, you probably had a Jelly Bean or two and may remember the gimmick, the running gag.

Jelly Bean never spoke. But this silent kid had so vivid an imagination that he turned into whatever attracted his attention. You knew just by looking at the cover, for instance, that he would end up as an Indian chief. He could only be brought back to himself by his parents' call of "Jelly Bean, where are you?"

Always there remained some evidence of his shape shifting, like the streak of war paint left on his face at the end of *Go West*. His parents, however, never caught on.

Dealing in antiques, I had encountered better copies of *Go West*, had bought them, sold them, even mentioned my connection with them to friends and customers. But that afternoon, almost like Jelly Bean, I found myself trapped in the thing that had hooked my attention. I became my own six-year-old self on a glorious spring weekend I spent dressed as an Indian chief.

"You buying or dreaming?" the dealer asked. "Ten dollars."

Being treated like a civilian aroused my professional pride. "For this beat-up copy? A first edition, preserved by some lonely maniac for forty-eight years in a state of mint purity, will fetch ten. Maybe."

So he backed down. But not all the way. Because he had spotted my weakness, I paid four dollars for something I would have said was only worth a buck. "I can get you all of that series," he called, going for the kill as I escaped.

A block east of the market is Madison Square Park. On a reasonably sound and isolated bench, I examined my find. The cover had two names, Helena Godspeed Hewett and Max Walter. Mrs. Hewett created and wrote the Jelly Bean books. I had a single memory of a big woman in a huge hat who pretended to adore kids, but was obviously annoyed when I asked if the foxes on her stole were kittens.

Max Walter's name evoked a lot more. I remembered him sitting at his easel, pencils in hand, sketching me, saying again and again, "It's perfect. Just one more minute, Kevin." He was catching Jelly Bean's look of goggle-eyed wonder. Max's goatee was what held me. He was the only person I'd ever met with a beard. It fascinated me that it moved right along with his mouth when he spoke.

Max's wife, Frieda, and my mother were friends. The two of them sat in the studio drinking wine, talking. "What's great about Sandra," my mother said, "is that with her you don't need a second opinion. She's so two-faced. I'm surprised she's never run into herself."

Max and Frieda laughed. Uneasily, I wondered if people often met themselves. "Okay!" Max told me, chin and beard wagging. "Take a break, Kevin." I walked over to the window. Max's studio was on the top floor of a house in Jamaica Plain. In the distance were the Arnold Arboretum's acres of trees, hills, and ponds.

But I stared at a weed-filled lot right across the street. There, two chains of boys and girls, aged five to ten, faced each other with hands linked, playing red rover. I watched as one small boy ran at the opposite line, threw himself on a pair of joined hands, and bore two kids almost to the ground. But he couldn't break their grip and he had to be on their side. I wanted so much to be down there.

With her uncanny timing, my mother brought over a glass of ginger ale and distracted me. "See what we have now," she said. I turned back toward the room and there was a feathered headdress, moccasins, a fringed vest and pants, a tomahawk, a bow and quiver of arrows. She pointed to an array of bright tubes. "War paint!"

The headdress went on even before I shed Jelly Bean's stupid clothes. On that glorious day, they let me go outside in my regalia. Down I went, two flights to the street. And there I stood on the porch with my arms folded in front of me. The game across the way came to a halt. The kids approached slowly. Before they reached me, I turned silently and marched back into the house.

All that day and the next, they called outside for the real Indian to come out and play. I would show myself at the window. On my breaks I'd go downstairs and walk among them. I said nothing. I thought that if they knew I was just an ordinary kid, they would ignore me. I wanted to play, but I didn't know how.

The next time I remember modeling for Max, it was cold out, the trees were bare. But I wore a bathing suit and stood under a bright light. The book must have been *By the Sea, Jelly Bean!* which came just after *Go West!* It's the one where Jelly Bean gets taken to the beach. By then, Helena Godspeed Hewett had gotten the series down to a dull routine.

At the sitting, the costumes, even the uniforms, were a pain. It was raining. No kids waited to ask for the real marine. My mother sat without talking much. Things had begun to change for her and me. For Frieda too. She had just had a baby. I was fascinated.

Then Max said, "Okay Kev, take a break. Let's get into the sailor suit next." Bored and tired of this game, I began to whine. I guess my mother was bored too. Sighing, she put down her glass and started getting me changed.

Turning to protest, I saw Frieda and her child and was oblivious to anything else. Frieda and Max were bohemians. She nursed in the studio. The baby, her eyes wide and unblinking, was attached to her mother's breast. In perfect harmony, the breast bobbed gently to the rhythm of the baby's mouth. An instant later, the tiny throat would swallow. The baby kept one hand curved in the air, fingers splayed as if she were maintaining her balance on an invisible high wire.

I don't know how long I stood. But at the same moment I realized two things. Max was sketching intensely and I was naked. Betrayed, I tried to hide myself. Max said, "The end of innocence."

That was the last time I had to model for Jelly Bean. It was also around then that my mother got married again. My father had died in the war and I never saw him. My childhood playmates were my mother's friends, actors and artists, poseurs and lallygaggers. As time went on they drifted away. My mother's smile would disappear if I asked about them. Above all else, I wanted that smile.

One last memory of my mother and Frieda remains. It happened at the very end of their friendship, in high autumn, in the Arboretum beside a pond just off the road.

I believe my mother and Frank had just gotten married. That means we had moved to a house in Dorchester near my grandmother's and I was the new kid in Sister Gertrude Julia's third grade at Mary, Queen of Heaven School.

Frieda and my mother talked behind me as I fed a flock of mallards that had paused on their way south. With the accuracy and blindness of childhood, I knew that my mother was angry, but did not yet connect this with her drinking. She said in too loud a voice, "I thought with my father gone it would be different. But nobody wants me to be happy. They don't want me to live like everyone else."

"Of course they do, Ellen," said Frieda, and I knew that my mother was arguing without anyone arguing back. I wished as hard as I could that I would turn and find my mother smiling.

"People are jealous about Frank and me."

"Not at all." By their voices, I could tell that my mother and Frieda were walking slowly up to the benches by the road. "Just rest for a minute, El."

That's when a hand lightly touched my neck and I turned. Two figures sat about thirty yards away with their backs to me.

My mother's querulous voice was indistinct. But that mother was just a Shadow.

Right beside me was my real mother. Instead of showing anger, she had a wonderful conspiratorial smile at the joke we were playing. Off we went, the two of us, on a walk around the pond, both watching our feet churn the leaves, turning suddenly each to catch the other's eyes and laugh.

When we had circled the pond completely, my mother led me to the bench. She and her Shadow merged. Frieda seemed tired, concerned. But my mother winked at me, reached out her hand for mine. If it was a dream, I must then have awakened.

That was as much of my past as the beat-up copy of *Go West, Jelly Bean!* would give me. Looking around Madison Square Park, I saw an impersonal space, somewhere for office workers to eat lunch on weekday afternoons. Standing up, strolling toward Fifth Avenue, I thought again of the line *fountains in summer.*

As if it were an invocation, my Shadow appeared before me. In a dirty white jacket, ragged jeans, and old sneakers, he crossed my path heading south on Fifth. With him were a bunch of kids with the marks of the street on their faces and clothes, each a bit skinnier than seemed possible.

Before my Shadow's eyes could meet mine, my heart gave a little warning kick and I stopped. He was as thin as any of the others. His cheekbones showed, his belt gathered in his pants. He had a three-day growth of beard and a wild, tangled mane touched with gray. My own hair is going back in what I hope is a graceful silver halo. He wore no glasses. Mine are gold rimmed, perfect for a twinkly little dealer in old toys.

Not wanting to get too close, I stopped at a pay phone and dialed my answering machine. Once or twice the caller had hung up and I wondered if that was Matt. One call, quite peremptory, was from an important client who wanted to discuss an auction to be held the next day. Then came a message from Addie and Lauren reminding me that dinner was at their place at eight. Dinner is a regular Sunday thing, half a dozen old friends entertaining each other.

Nothing from the hospice about George. His sister and family were on duty that day. It would all be over soon. I was unable to think past that.

Hanging up, I watched my double and his vagabond band pass through the crowds browsing the bookstores around Eighteenth. Trailing discreetly down to Washington Square, I thought of a reason to stop by my shop rather than follow them into the park.

Half Remembered Things is in the middle of a block of Italian bakeries and butcher stores just off Sheridan Square. We're closed Sundays during summer, but out front stood a forty-plus couple with their arms intertwined. She wore a tolerant smile, he a look of quiet rapture.

Something in our display window had grabbed him. That was the last one George had been able to do. It had been up for a couple of years and I knew we would never change it. With my help, he had put together a boy's bedroom circa 1955, one with everything other kids always seemed to have and you never did, like the rotating night lamp on which a rocket ship floated forever toward the rings of Saturn.

The fifth-grade geography text lay open on the desk to reveal the Scrooge MacDuck comic book inside. On the shelves, beside the lead marines in full dress, the junior football and the windup tin robots, Lone Ranger and Tonto bookends enclosed *The Arabian Nights, The Boy's Book of Pirates, Dave Dawson with the Flying Tigers, The Martian Chronicles.*

Roller skates, a cap pistol, and a Lionel yard engine lay on the floor near an interrupted Monopoly game. A Davy Crockett hat hung on the post of the bed, which was made up with

Howdy Doody sheets and a Hopalong Cassidy blanket. On the foot of the bed, a Little League baseball with busted seams was nestled in a worn third baseman's glove.

When George Halle and I opened this place, Carter was in the White House. More lucky than smart, we despised the yuppie '80s. But we were in place when all the financial managers in New York decided to buy back their childhoods at inflated prices.

As a business person, I should have crossed the street, found out what the guy liked so much, given him my card. Instead, I waited until the lady dragged him away before going over and slipping the book through the mail slot. The first thing Monday, a place would be found for *Go West* on the bed near the baseball. Together, the book and the ball were the story of my life as a kid.

That done, I headed back to Washington Square. In my mind was the idea that it was better to encounter my Silent Partner now in a public place than to be taken by surprise when I was alone.

Walking, I remembered my mother after her remarriage, after Frieda and Max and Jelly Bean, bringing me to a department store photo shoot as a favor to a friend. She had promised me that this would be the last time. They had a whole bunch of us, babies, a girl my age and another around eleven who were sisters, and their big brother Steve, who told me, "I'm going to be a freshman at BC High next year." I was awestruck. He had to be twelve at least.

The girls and babies and a couple of the mothers went to one of the two dressing rooms. Steve scooped up the sample clothes, put his hand on my shoulder, and said, "Let's go, Kev," before anyone could think to go with us.

"This modeling stuff is stupid," he told me as we shed our jackets. "I gotta do it to save for tuition. BC has a great baseball team. You know about baseball?" I nodded yes because I had seen games. "I was in Little League three years. I'm starting Junior CYO ball. Third base. The ball comes on like a bullet. I'm working on my throw to first."

Reaching over to his discarded clothes, he took a scuffed baseball out of a pocket. "This is just Little League size but I can throw a curve. Kind of." He showed me the grip. "What position do you play?" I didn't know what to tell him. "You should play third." Pulling on a sweater, he asked, "You talk, Kev?"

Hypnotized, a smile plastered to my face, I said, "Yes!" And he laughed. All that day, between people adjusting our clothes, brushing our hair, between waiting and posing and changing and waiting again, he explained to me about playing third base.

"The important thing is that you stop it getting by you," he said. On a break, he bounced the ball toward me and I couldn't lay a hand on it. "No, you gotta move as soon as you see it come off the bat. Get in front of it. Once more."

When the shoot was over and we were parting in the lobby, he reached into the pocket of his jacket. I could see from his face that this tore him. "Here, Kev. You're gonna play, right?"

I nodded as hard as I could and reached out for the baseball. "What do you say?" my mother asked. I managed to croak out a thank-you. Steve waved and disappeared in the forest of adults. Maybe all he wanted was someone to listen to him talk baseball. Maybe too he was a good kid and smart enough to sense another's aching need.

On that blazing Sunday, years after Steve, I took a seat in Washington Square Park and watched the show. There is poignancy spiced with danger when summer's more than halfway gone and those attitudes that haven't wilted have gotten extra sharp.

The fountains threw jets into the air. Dashing through the

spray were small, dark children, a large copper dog, a spacey white kid with a red kerchief on his head and his pants rolled up. Stretched out on the stairs leading down to the water, young people in gym bodies sunbathed with their heads thrown back.

On the circular plaza around the fountain, kids black and white and Asian circled on skateboards, bikes, roller skates. Along the raised outer rim of the plaza, dealers and trade tattooed and strung with pet snakes lounged. On the walk around the plaza, a police car sat with its windows open and its radio spitting static.

On the benches beyond the walk, I sat amid German tourists, undercover narcs, teenage hicks from the suburbs, and ancient Italian couples. In the sonic wash of rap and wheels, of crowd noise and the fall of water, I breathed the perfume of mown grass and piss and meat incinerating on shish kebab carts and waited to see what my Shadow would do.

Beyond a fence near the north side of the park, small children swarmed over the free-form jungle bars and slides. Parents, nannies, au pairs stood by. All this was a long way from my first and only playground.

Curtis Park in Queen of Heaven parish in Dorchester in Boston had jungle bars, slides, seesaws, and a brick building with rest rooms and the offices occupied by Charlie, the crippled caretaker. But mainly it was a big open space that was dusty ball fields in summer, a skating pond in winter.

That was where my Little League ball got me into a game with some kids from my third-grade class. We played off to the side on a diamond marked out by stones. The game was tossing the ball up and hitting it and lots of pushing and yelling and nobody ever caught anything. Then one day, Murph came by and took over.

A couple of summers later, the magic baseball was long gone. But its work was done. Hands in jean pockets, dirty and triumphant in the late setting sun, we strutted from a sandlot game, a gang of desperados in black high-tops. One by one kids reached their houses and peeled off until there was only Murph and me.

The Murphys were a dozen kids ranging from age four to twenty, a drunken, truck-driving father, a wispy-thin mother and her retarded brother who all lived in vast disorder at the corner of my block. All the male kids were called Murph by their friends. The one I knew was Jimmy, a crucial eight months my senior and the toughest kid in the fifth grade at "Queena Heaven" parochial school.

We reached his house first, lingered for a while. "And when he tries to tag me, he falls down and you run all the way home." Murph was doing a play-by-play of the game. I was laughing hysterically. Then Murph's mother yelled from inside and he said, "See you, Grierson." We only used last names.

"See you, Murph." No guys on earth are tougher than ten-year-olds. The streetlights came on and I was all alone. I wanted to hurry home, yet didn't want to go there at all.

As a child, I was expert above all else in navigating by the double star of my mother and her Shadow. I was never certain which one would be around. On that particular night, I heard the Shadow's voice, sharp and mean. "I beg your pardon. You brought this up!"

I froze for a moment. Sometimes my mother's Shadow talked to herself. Those were the worst times. Then I heard Frank say, "Ellen, for Christ's sake!" And I relaxed a little.

My stepfather never got the hang of my mother and her Shadow, never even understood that there was something to be learned. Frank and I kind of passed through each other. But he had his uses. With Frank to keep her busy, the Shadow would leave me alone. "You were so pie-eyed, you were—"

They shut up when they heard me come in. "Kevin," said the Shadow. "Where the hell have you been?"

"Down at Curtis."

I tried to get past her, but she blocked the way. "Who were you there with?" The Shadow's eyes, wide, unblinking, bore right into me.

"A bunch of guys." It did no good to lie. "Murphy. . . ."

Both my stepfather and the Shadow snorted. They disapproved of the Murphys in general and Jimmy in particular. "A bunch of drunken Irish trash," she said. Of course, we were Irish and the two of them drank quite a bit. Why the Murphys' Irishness and drinking were bad was a mystery deeper than any concerning the Blessed Virgin or Resurrection. "I don't want to see you with that crowd anymore," said the Shadow as I hurried upstairs. Then she and Frank went back to arguing.

What they didn't understand was that Murph was more important in my world than both of them put together. I just had to hope that next time I went out, my mother would be the one there when I got home. Or at least that the Shadow would forget what she had said.

I only went inside the Murphys' a few times. But Murph was fascinated by my house, with just the three of us living in it, by my room so well stocked with toys, and by my mother. I remember her appearing carrying a tray with glasses of milk and peanut butter and jelly sandwiches. We were scuttling over the floor directing a column of metal tanks and cars through a mountain of animals leaking stuffing. Murph looked up at her with an expression of adoration.

Of course, he wasn't there those times she stayed in her room and nobody could come by because any sound was too much. Or the times when the Shadow was up and angry, which I didn't want anyone to see.

Sometimes my mother and Frank would go off together and I would stay with my grandmother and grandaunt Tay who lived up the hill. Those times I loved. My mother's mother and aunt, with their white hair and soft brogues, were always exactly the same as my earliest memories of them. And my mother's Shadow, which seemed to fear nothing else, stayed clear of Aunt Tay.

On some occasions, like when I ran into the house on a dead of winter day with the sun silver behind clouds and iron snow on the ground, with my shoes squishing and my pants frozen to me, I was just as happy my mother wasn't present. While skating, I had stepped on thin ice and gone up to my waist in the water.

The Shadow did not bother to emerge from the bedroom and find out what I was doing. So I dashed upstairs, changed, and got back outside. My mother would have had me in pajamas and bathrobe drinking hot soup as soon as she saw that my skinny legs had turned blue. As it was, all I had to fear was the terrifying slow breathing from the closed bedroom.

My stepfather was the sales manager for a company that did business with the city. My grandfather had been in politics, and my uncles still were somehow. So the marriage made a kind of sense.

The reason Frank never learned to deal with my mother's Shadow, I discovered, was that he didn't have to. When things got bad, he left on business. When they stayed bad, he left for good. It was just my mother and her Shadow and me in the house. I was eleven years old and hung out with Murph in Curtis Park a lot.

That summer I remember a pair of bums, one an old guy maybe thirty, the other a lot younger. Both were filthy, their sneakers held together with tape. Bums and kids have a lot in common. They are powerless, without homes of their own, left to conduct private lives in public places. As my friends and I watched, the older guy drank from the water fountain, made a face, and spat. "Tastes like rust." The younger guy, seeing us, put two fingers to his mouth like he had a cigarette. "He wants a smoke," said the old bum. "You kids got some butts?"

About that time, a cop car appeared and the two guys faded.

Maybe because it was on the same day, or maybe just in the same summer, I connect those vagrants with a night I stayed out really late. It's almost magic the way you can lose all thoughts of home. It was pitch dark.

Coleman and Leary and Mackie and Murph and myself were now old enough and, with allies, numerous enough to show up after supper and hold onto one of the dusty diamonds in the park. The game started in twilight and held us entranced. We had three bats, I remember, a pale one with Ted Williams's engraved signature, a kid-sized Little League item and one that looked like a club and was dark wood and scarred, like something long lurking in the lower depths of baseball.

Smaller kids played, other guys' little brothers. But they were in the outfield. I was the shortest kid our age and I was at third. Stuff could sail way over my head but nothing got past me. Once I tripped and tore my jeans and cut my knee, and a couple of my fingers got mashed on a foul tip, but I couldn't feel it.

We played nine innings and people were watching. The score was close, something like 17-15. But we were ahead and Charlie, the park keeper, had already flicked the lights on and off three times, which was the five-minute warning and meant that if we could hold on we had won.

They had guys on second and third. A big kid named Billy Healey who thought he was tough was up and he was mad because people were yelling things about his mother. Murph was behind the plate. Mackie was pitching. Healey swung and the ball hit the bat. It was on the ground, bouncing wildly. As I moved forward, it caught a pebble, jumped up, and bit me on the left shoulder.

But it came down in front of me. I pounced and trapped it with my bare hand. As I did, something moved on my right. Some kid named Greg who had an actual Red Sox cap was running home. Murph behind the plate was yelling at me and I tossed right from where I had caught the ball.

Murph got it in his glove and Greg was still coming. Murph ran up the line to make sure he didn't get past and stuck the ball right in his nose, which bled. Then there was a lot of pushing and yelling. But the lights went out and we had won.

Walking home, kids dropped out as usual until there was just Murph and me. He had the great dark bat and a glove slung over his shoulder and his hat still on backwards. "I can take what my old man's gonna dish out standing on my head because we won."

Punishment at the Murphys' was a given. Mr. Murphy whacked kids at random. Once, not noticing I was a guest, he had even clipped me. Knowing what to expect almost seemed attractive. That night, adrenaline carried me all the way home. Our house was silent. My stepfather and mother's divorce had gone through. The light was on in the living room. I let myself in quietly.

I could have sworn my mother was asleep on the couch. Her form was there. But as I put my foot on the stairs, the Shadow appeared at the kitchen door and said, "Kevin!"

And I was so scared that I wanted to vomit and piss. She had a half-empty glass in her hand. Her eyes were wide, curious. Like I was a bug and she was a bird. Outside of that, the Shadow's face was blank. That expression didn't change. "I thought you were kidnapped. I just called the police."

Now, my mother would have called some other kids' mothers and pieced together what had happened to me. But her Shadow didn't do stuff like that. "I thought some stranger took you in his car, did something bad," she said very evenly. Then, "You're filthy. Get into the tub. Now."

From upstairs, I heard her get on the phone and say, "Terribly sorry to disturb you, Sergeant," in a weird, remote voice.

On the second floor, the door to her room was open. The bottles and jars from her dresser lay smashed on the floor. Clothes were everywhere, thrown around, all of them torn, slashed. A bright red stain spread where nail polish had spilled on the rug.

In the bathroom, everything from the medicine chest had been broken in the sink. The tub was full of lukewarm water. Locking the door, getting in the bath, I had to be careful how I stepped because of broken glass where the mirror was smashed.

The water stung my scraped knee, my mashed fingers. I heard the Shadow in my room. Things were getting broken, ripped. "On my own," she yelled, "I could go where I wanted. Do what I wanted. Without that runt." I was too scared to face her.

Then it seemed another voice was speaking, softly pleading that she be quiet. It seemed maybe my mother was awake. But when I crept out wrapped in a towel, it was only the Shadow and me. I stood and looked at the wreckage of my room, all my clothes and toys in a pile on the floor. "All this junk goes out tomorrow." She said this coldly, staring me down. "Stop crying."

"I got soap in my eyes."

Somehow, being a kid, I fell asleep. I awoke in the morning to the sound of weeping and quiet voices. More cautious than the night before, I listened to make sure that it was my grandmother and grandaunt. Then I heard my mother, not her Shadow. In a choked voice she told them that she wanted to kill herself. They said she shouldn't let me hear.

Shortly afterwards, the house got sold and my mother and I went to live with my grandmother and Aunt Tay. Around them, she kept her drinking quiet. And her Shadow kept its distance from Aunt Tay.

At the same time, her brothers got to meddle in my life. Uncle Jim brought me to his war buddy, Moxie the barber, for crew cuts long after I decided I didn't want them. That fall Uncle

Bob enrolled me in his alma mater downtown. The school was cold and merciless, I barely skidded by.

Uncle Mike signed me up for swimming classes at the Y. At the physical, he joked with another boy's father as I waited in a line of scared, sullen kids in our underpants. At the Y, the kids were tough. Tricks they showed me made it hard to concentrate on the *Aeneid.*

One spring evening in my junior year, I passed Curtis Park on my way from the MTA station to my grandmother's. In the supper hour dusk, the place was almost empty. A lone figure perched on the jungle bars smoking a cigarette.

By then Murph had turned sixteen and dropped out of school. I had found a sympathetic barber and imagined I was coming into my own. We didn't even nod as I passed.

That afternoon, I'd done my first modeling work in years for a guy with a camera who had seen me in Park Square. I sat on a couch in his studio gulping a double scotch while he patted my bare knees and talked about Rimbaud. On the walls were nude pictures of other young guys. I felt real cold and jumpy but very adult.

Going up the hill to home, I chewed gum to mask the booze. As I came in the front door, my mother stood on the stairs and looked right in my eyes. "Kev, it's after six, where have you been?"

For a moment, my heart went cold. But it really was my mother. Her smile was tired, sweet, like we were fellow truants. I remembered that day when the two of us kicked leaves behind her Shadow's back.

Right then, I would have told her what had happened to me. But things about myself confounded me so much that I couldn't find words. That's when a voice whispered, 'We can do this standing on our head.' And I heard myself say, "School play. Rehearsal. I told you."

If I was an expert navigator, my mother had limned the heavens. She knew I was lying and I knew she knew. But instead of making her mad, the lie made something go out in her eyes. Unable to stand seeing that, I went past her and up the stairs.

At the time, I thought that she had gotten a whiff of the booze. Much later it occurred to me that she had caught a glimpse of my Shadow, was more aware of him than I was. All I know is that for the remaining time she lived, we trod carefully around each other.

In Washington Square Park, I awoke from my memories and looked around. The place is a playground of the demimonde. Street and aristocracy mix, kids from nice families dress down to mingle with hustlers and runaways.

As I watched, my Shadow crossed my line of vision. He prowled the plaza around the fountain, gazing intently, like he was cruising for drugs or sex. It seemed he took no notice of me as he spoke to a group of dazed, sun-soaked kids with matted hair and a pet ferret crawling over their bare shoulders.

I stood up and found myself facing the damsel and dwarf. On second meeting, it was obvious that the blue-eyed Asian damsel was a boy in drag. The dwarf was a dwarf. But the angelic smile he flashed as he handed me a worn piece of drawing paper was junk-blank and unfocused.

On the sheet was a sketch of an enraptured putto. It took a moment, but I jumped when I recognized Max Walter's work and myself. What looked like wings were, in fact, my mother's hands resting protectively on my shoulders. Before I could wonder how my doppelganger had gotten hold of the sketch, I saw a file card and a scrawl much like my own: "This should be an illustration from the book old Helena never got around to writing, *It's the Sistine Chapel, Jelly Bean!*"

Despite myself, I grinned, which hadn't happened too often recently. On the card, in that same hand, was the poem I'd been trying to remember. It read like sampler verse but, as if a tape in my head had been jogged, a blocked memory began to run.

My mother and I were in the Public Garden and she was taking me to the Swan Boats. Maybe I was three. I let go of her hand and ran a few paces ahead. Then I heard her say, "Get away from us!"

I turned and saw my mother and another woman who looked just like her. Except the other's face was mean, angry. For a moment, she stood staring at us and then seemed to disappear. My mother took me by the hand and we sat down beside a fountain that had turned green with age and weather. After a moment, my mother told me, "There's something Aunt Tay taught me when I was little." And she recited,

> PRAISE ORCHARDS IN AUTUMN
> WARM KITCHENS IN WINTER
> WIDE MEADOWS IN SPRINGTIME
> AND FOUNTAINS IN SUMMER

We were quiet for a while. Then, like she knew that trying to change the subject would do no good, my mother said, "Kevin, I don't want you ever to be frightened of me. No matter what you see that one do or what she says, I love you with all my heart. Remember that."

'Don't say I never gave you anything,' murmured a familiar voice. When I looked up, my Silent Partner was already walking away with kids trailing after. Again I noticed how thin he was. There was nothing to him but his ragged clothes. In Africa, they call AIDS the slim disease.

This, I realized, was his way of showing me how deeply he is embedded in my past. Knowing him, I understood he wanted us to get back together. I wished him all the things we could never have: long life, calm seas, and prosperous voyages. I wished him far away and knew that wasn't going to happen. My continued existence is a tribute to the moderate life. With him around that would not be possible. He disappeared into the crowd.

The fountain was on across the way when I got home. Stuyvesant Park shows up a lot in movies. That's odd, since with iron fences, the Friends' Meeting House, the statue of old one-legged Peter, and the flowers planted around the fountain by the ladies from the Episcopal church, it looks like something from a more quaint and quiet town.

The police academy is in my neighborhood. At the end of my block, cadets in overseas caps, cop shoes, and paramilitary outfits flowed in clumps down Second Avenue. At a bad time in my youth I'd had to wear a uniform almost like that, and I can still get angry at the memory.

In my silent apartment with Caldecott prints on the walls and the air conditioner on, I examined the drawing and the note. Now that I had started, there was no way for me to stop remembering.

It was going to be a while before I had to go out. Music is evocative. I put disks of Glenn Gould's Bach and a Thelonius Monk solo into the CD player and went back to when I was sixteen and heard them for the first time.

TWO

THE AUTUMN OF my senior year of high school, my Shadow stepped forward for the first time and grabbed control of my life. The summer before, John F. Kennedy had been nominated for president and my mother died behind the wheel of a car.

Until then, my Shadow had been vague, hard to pinpoint, and I was happy to leave it that way. Sometimes I wondered if anyone outside our family had them. The only Shadow I'd ever seen was my mother's and it disappeared after she was gone. Her death hardly gave me pause. Since she had been drinking, I was convinced that, as always, my mother would show up sweetly apologizing for being late for the funeral.

Naturally, I told no one any of this. The code of silence for the Boston Irish was simple. Certain things you didn't tell other people. Lots of things you didn't even tell yourself.

When he came to the wake, my stepfather had little to say. His divorce from my mother had been a disaster for us. Not that Frank was all that great. Usually he ignored me. What I appreciated about him in retrospect was that while he was around we had looked like a TV family.

All around me, aunts and cousins broke down. Gramny, my grandmother, aged visibly. Even Aunt Tay was badly shaken. I alone was dry-eyed.

On one occasion or another at the wake, each of my uncles, Bob the lawyer, Mike the cop, Jim, who had the bar in Field's Corner, got lit and talked to me about Ellen, their little sister. She had been their father's favorite. I was the first and favored grandchild. Thomas "Terrible Tom" Malloy, my grandfather, had founded the bar and the family fortune, such as it was. His sons had gone in fear of him.

Jim, the eldest, shook his head sadly. "They had hopes for you, Kevin. School and all. When you have time to recover, we have to think about your future."

My plans included college, but otherwise they were vague. I thought sometimes about a .38 revolver that rested in the upstairs hall closet.

The day of the funeral, Aunt Tay hugged me. I don't think anyone else has ever been called Tay. Teresa was her given name, like the saint's, and she was very proud of it. But when, as first grandson, I called her Aunt Tay, it stuck. Even her sister Gramny began calling her Tay.

This thin, white-haired lady with great blue eyes looked at me and said:

BY FELL NIGHT

When I was small and down or scared, we had recited this verse. Tay Fallon was a storyteller, a poet. I tried to slip by her saying, "Come on, Tay, I'm fine."

BY FELL NIGHT

She repeated the line and stood in my way. With a bored sigh, I gave the response:

WITH STICK AND BONE

"Dilleachdan," she said in Gaelic, which I didn't understand. "It's hard for those of us with the gift." It wouldn't have surprised me if she knew I was thinking about the revolver upstairs. Tay had been born with a caul and claimed a kind of second sight.

She insisted that I too had a gift, though what it was she never said. All I knew for sure was that I lived under a kind of teenage curse. I was too smart to be a tough kid and too crazy to be a smart kid. The high school drama society was where I hid out.

Maybe the ability to see and to believe two completely different things is the very basis of second sight. My mother had always said that she wanted her effects to be given away to charity. That fall her sisters-in-law turned what had been her bedroom into a faceless guest room. Still, I managed to believe in one corner of my mind that she was still alive.

In an Irish household of my grandmother's generation, the eldest male, whatever his age, was Himself. His wishes might not be law, but his every failing would surely be ignored for as long as possible. My grandfather had died before I could remember, so when my mother and I moved in with Gramny and Tay, I became Himself.

That fall, I strained against the ropes and found there were none. At my all-boys school, the dress code called for jacket and tie. But away from school, I dressed like a street punk, cultivated my hair, carried cigarettes and even smoked a few. I snuck sips of whiskey at home and found winos willing to buy me half-pints. At the downtown Y, I showed up regularly but not to swim.

My grandmother's house, a gray Queen Anne on the hills of Dorchester, was a minefield of memorabilia. My favorite was the .38 hidden in the upstairs closet. Oiled and cleaned and wrapped in a piece of chamois, it was something I wasn't supposed to know about.

At first, all I did was take it to my room and spin the cylinder. A box of ammo was wrapped with the revolver, but at that time, I had never loaded it. Once, I put the barrel to the side of my head and pulled the trigger. When I did, I felt that someone was with me. But when I looked, I was alone. That time, I was careless about putting the revolver back.

Tay noticed. Had I been a few years younger, she might have whipped up some dark and special tea to snap me out of it. Instead, feeling I needed help, she leaked word discreetly to her nephew Bob, the lawyer. Bob's wife, Aunt Alice, who had gone to college, had a friend who recommended a shrink. Money was found to send me to him twice a week.

Tuesdays after school and early on Saturdays, I went over to Kenmore Square and talked to Dr. Charles Petrie, a fat middle-aged guy with nubby sweaters. Tuesdays, in blazer and slacks, I told him about my school problems.

"The drama society, remember sir, I mentioned that they're doing Shakespeare's *Henry the Fourth*, Part One? I told Mr. Royce the faculty advisor I wanted to be Hotspur, a great part, this rebel who stutters when he gets excited." Petrie nodded like he knew the play. "Yesterday, I found out I'm Poins who's, like, this minor accomplice. And he's not even in the last act."

A pause followed until it occurred to Petrie that I had stopped talking. "What"—another pause—"was your reaction to this?"

"I got real pissed."

"Yes?" He wrote that down. "Go on."

His office was part of a suite shared by a half dozen other analysts. Tuesdays there was a receptionist and the place was full of patients: unhappy fat ladies, tense guys clutching briefcases. The entire building was busy.

Saturdays, the halls were quiet, the waiting room empty when I'd come in wearing a short jacket, black chinos, taps on my loafers. Petrie and I never talked about my mother or the gun or what it was I did after leaving the office.

One Saturday I told him, "I'm in this long hallway, a sort of gallery with this soft kind of light and these middle-aged guys standing there. One of them looks at me and says, 'You're twins.' "

The phrase "middle-aged guys" seemed to interest the doctor. He nodded and wrote that down. "Do you remember any more of your dream?" he asked.

Back then, I almost never remembered dreams. The week before, in the place I described, a guy who called himself Joe had actually said that. Looking where Joe had, I glimpsed a horribly familiar kid giving the special hard smile I sometimes practiced in mirrors. Then the kid was gone and Joe shook his head, saying, "Just seeing double."

While I wondered how to explain that to him, Petrie said, "Time's up, Kevin. See you Tuesday at three."

Emerging from his office, I found the waiting room no longer empty. A patient with long, strawberry blond hair sat on a couch leafing through a *New Yorker*.

She wore pants and ankle-high riding boots. One of them rested on the low table in front of her in a way that was absolutely cool. With the dead accuracy of a kid, I realized she was a crucial few years my senior. I also knew that skin and bones like hers were expensive.

When she looked up, it was right into my wide eyes. From my limited experience of lovely girls, I was prepared for her to realize our differences in age and sophistication, frown, and go back to her magazine. Instead, she nodded like she understood what she saw. That was a feeling I never got from Petrie. Smiling she asked, "Is your shrink giving you anything good?"

Not sure what she meant, I shook my head. She nodded toward one of the offices. "I'm seeing Kleinman, a dullard but occasionally useful. My name is Stacey Hale." Stacey held out her hand.

I took it and told her my actual name, a thing I didn't always do. She left something in my palm. "Next time, have him give you those." I looked down at a green, heart-shaped pill. "Dexedrine," she said. "You're here on Saturdays?" Dr. Kleinman's door opened as I nodded.

Out in the hall, I still saw her face. The pill was a little bitter when I washed it down at a water fountain. At first, I felt nothing. But by the time I reached the Y, I was sailing and ready to play what some kids called the Game.

Saturday mornings and a couple of weekday afternoons they gave kids swimming lessons. We swam bare ass and counselors not a lot older than we were got to wear bathing suits and carry whistles and yell at us. Instructors and other adults could stay fully dressed if they wanted.

After a while, another kid showed me how to wrap myself in a towel and go through a door behind the locker room. It led to a place I thought of as the Gallery. There, instead of getting yelled at, boys were treated with respect and generosity. Going there always felt like I was on a quest and about to discover something.

Part of the Game was staying cool and keeping your clothes. The guy at the lobby desk was used to seeing me. He didn't even look at my card or watch to see if I went to the locker room. Going there meant I stood a good chance of spending a miserable morning in the pool. I turned down another corridor.

The Saturday I met Stacey, kids shouted far off in the water. In the gray-lighted Gallery, middle-aged men whispered. None of my regulars was around. Some guy I didn't know said, "Ten dollars."

He led me to a far alcove and murmured commands: "Open your clothes. Slowly. Shirt and jacket off your shoulders. Let the pants fall. Pull down your drawers. Yes! Hands behind like you're cuffed. Look tough."

I gave the practiced hard smile. "Yes!" It was creepy standing with my all-American jockey shorts around my knees and him all clammy and cold. But the danger was a turn-on and all this seemed to be happening to someone else.

Afterwards, I bought a milk shake at a luncheonette with my winnings from the Game and couldn't finish it. Inside my head, something crackled like the blue sparks on trolley wires. Gray and dowdy streets slid by around me until I found myself standing at a fence watching an engine shuttle cars in the Boston and Maine yards. In the distance, slanting October sun hit the John Hancock tower and I thought about Stacey.

Tuesday, in blazer and tie, I looked at Dr. Petrie and said, "You know sir, there's this kid in school who was having trouble like I'm having. His doctor gave him a certain prescription and it seemed to help."

The drug never again worked like that first time. But by Friday when the cast read through *Henry IV,* I already knew all my lines and most of everyone else's.

Saturday morning, tingling from speed and anticipation, I came out of Petrie's office and found the waiting room empty. Stacey's doctor didn't even seem to be in his office. I was stunned. Out at the curb sat a red MG with its motor running. Only when the horn blew did I focus. "Hey!" I said.

Stacey smiled. "Can I ask a big favor?" Anything, she must have seen that. "This is a no-parking area. Could you find a place for it? Oh, do you drive?"

I shook my head, ashamed to let her down. She turned off the engine. "Then, can I ask you an even bigger favor?" Any plan imaginable could be canceled. "Wait here and if the cops come by, turn on the motor and pretend you're going to pull out." She tossed me the keys and went into the building, saying, "I'll buy you lunch. It will be a chance to talk."

Conscious of the immense trust, I sat vigilant in that front seat. Once or twice, I turned on the ignition and ran the motor, looking front and rear for the police car that never showed.

Later that day, in some town like Needham, we stopped at a drive-in and sat in the car nibbling hamburgers. Neither of us had much appetite. We giggled about that, then each took out a green pill and washed it down with the last of our Cokes. "How did you end up seeing Dr. Petrie?"

Wanting to make an impression, I told her, "Playing with guns. That made them think I'm suicidal."

She looked at me, nodded, and said, "Yes, it would."

That afternoon, we drove out into the country. The leaves were changing. We parked on a road overlooking a gold and red valley and she told me, "I have to see a shrink to fulfill a probation requirement. There was a little party at school, kind of an orgy actually, and I ran amok. You know how it is." Only able dimly to imagine, I nodded.

"Kleinman at least understands that it's all a game. He gives me prescriptions, collects his fees, and doesn't interfere." She laughed. "The only trouble I have with speed is that once in a while, out of the corner of my eyes, I see this snake dart."

Emboldened, I told her, "Sometimes, just for a second, I see this Shadow beside me. He has my face."

She stopped laughing. "There's someone you might want to talk to. He's called Dr. X. I'll mention you to him." She started the car. "It's getting late. Where do you live?"

In Dorchester, neighborhoods went by the names of the Catholic parishes. "Queena Heaven. You can drop me at any MTA station."

"And miss seeing a place called Queena Heaven! Just give me directions."

It was dusk as we arrived in Mary, Queen of Heaven. Stacey glanced at Snyder's Market and the Woolworth's, the bars, the Shawmut bank, and the elevated station. We drove up the steep hill past the brick Gothic church.

The street I lived on ended with a cement wall. Beyond that, row after row of wooden three-deckers marched down to Boston Harbor and ten thousand diapers flew like banners from their back porches.

Seeing my grandmother's house with Stacey was like seeing it for the first time. I noticed how gray and spooky it looked in the dying light. "Hey," I said, "it's haunted, but what the hell, it's home."

She leaned over and ruffled my hair. Sunday morning at Mass, I could still feel the touch of her hand. Her interest in me was a mystery I didn't want to unravel.

Next Saturday, I watched her car again. Afterwards, Stacey found a deserted stretch of road and gave me my first driving lesson. Several times, our hands touched and a jolt went through me. When she dropped me off at home, I said, "Dr. Petrie isn't doing me much good. What about this guy Dr. X?"

Stacey kissed me on the mouth and said, "We'll see." She must have known that she owned my soul.

Inside, my grandmother, in a flurry of flour and white hair, was busy in the kitchen. "Jimmy, my love," she said, mistaking me for her son the bar owner, "run down to Snyder's for some baking soda before he closes."

The following Saturday, very tense, Stacey asked, "Do you have any pills?" Feeling I'd failed her because I'd left them home, I shook my head. It was cold sitting in that little car. When Stacey came out, she was crying.

She sat for a moment before saying, "I've got a 'scrip. But I'm broke." Desperately, I searched my pockets and came up with sixty cents. "This is bad, Kevin. I need something or I am going to flip out."

By that time, I'd probably had sex with a hundred guys, always for money. I didn't know their names and I didn't dream about them as I had about her. My heart leaped at this opportunity to rescue Stacey. I had her drive me to the Y.

On that day when everything had to work, a stranger in a sweat suit was at the desk. When I said I was going to swim, he asked to see my card, took it and said, "You get this back after class. Pool roll call is in five minutes. I'll look for you there. MOVE IT!"

This was a crackdown with a vengeance. Before I could think, I found myself herded into the locker room and issued a towel. "GRIERSON!" One counselor, a gym bully named Ridley, was in my year at school. He pointed to a locker and said "GET NAKED. PRONTO!"

He wielded a wet towel. A tough kid I'd seen strut through the Gallery in a leather jacket ran to the showers like a plucked chicken. He yelped when Ridley whapped him on the ass.

That was about to be me. My morning was going to be spent trying not to look at someone the wrong way or get hard at the wrong moment. Stacey would be long gone by the time I got my clothes and card back.

Stunned, I opened the locker and found my clothes already inside. A voice in my ear said, 'I can do this standing on my head.' My Shadow slammed the locker, snatched Ridley's towel out of his hand, and gave a yell that attracted everybody's attention.

I slipped to the back of the locker room, went through a door and down a hall. I was excited. My heart beat like a trap drum. In the Gallery, frosted windows set in deep alcoves let in a pearly light and older guys stood around. When I came in, one of them whispered, "Fred." Everyone always whispered like it was church. Fred was the name I used. This was the guy who said he was Joe and once thought that I was twins.

Joe was deft and generous. He made a little gesture indicat-

ing the two of us. We stepped into one of the alcoves and he positioned me on the window ledge. My belt buckle clinked as he
arranged my clothes the way he wanted them and showed me
his bald spot. Far away, someone whistled the theme from *The
High and the Mighty*. My eyes went out of focus.

"You're a good kid, Fred." I liked being told that. He patted
my arm, handed me the money. "Where do you live?"

"Inna projects," I said, zipped up, and waved good-by.

When I proudly handed her the money, Stacey regarded me
curiously. Innocent in a strange kind of way, I couldn't imagine
why. A few minutes later, she came out of a drugstore already
looking much better and said, "You are definitely ready for Dr.
X. You can learn a lot. But watch out for him. And remember
you come there as my friend."

That struck me as odd. "Is he a psychiatrist?"

"No. He hasn't let that happen to him." She took Beacon
Street out of town.

I remember asking, "His name is Dr. X?" as she turned off
Beacon and down a curving suburban road. Ponds lay behind
stands of trees. Victorian mansions spread over the tops of the
hillocks.

"He needs to protect his identity. There are a lot of things society just doesn't understand."

Without slowing, she drove through a set of open iron gates,
went up a curving driveway, and parked under a portico. "He
has a nice house," I said.

"Actually, this is my mother's place. He practices here while
she's away." Before getting out of the car, Stacey slipped some
of the pills from the bottle into her pocket.

She called "Hello?" when she opened the front door. The
place was quiet, dark, with the curtains mostly drawn. On the
hall table was a used Kleenex and a coffee cup filled with half-
drowned cigarettes. In a corner lay an empty glass. Wine had
dried into the rug.

To our left was a book-lined room that I identified as the library. A figure in a black suit stirred on a couch, a small man with a round face and fringe of gray hair. "A new communicant?" he asked in the voice of a testy troll. For a bad moment, I thought this was Dr. X.

"Hello, Max," said Stacey. "Max was once an Episcopal priest," she explained as she led me through a big kitchen. It stank of garbage and dirty dishes. On the table lay an open dictionary with pages hollowed out to create a pocket. On a sideboard, a silver bowl had been polished till it shone in the gloom. Upstairs, someone put on a record, jazz piano.

Lonely notes echoed through the halls. Stacey opened a door and motioned me down a flight of stairs. At the bottom was a low, windowless room. Walls, ceiling, floor were all painted a dead white. Bright lighting was set in the ceiling. The only furnishings were a white table and two chairs.

At the table facing the door was a guy, older, maybe thirty. A black beard made it hard to tell. "Dr. X," said Stacey, "this is Kevin." He was big and looked like he had once been fat. He wore a blue oxford knit shirt outside his pants.

"Hi, Kevin." Dr. X rose to shake my hand. "Stacey's talked about you."

"And look what he bought us." She held up the vial.

"Oh boy, vitamins! Thanks, Kevin!" Grabbing with the impulsiveness of a kid, he washed down a couple of the pills with the contents of a huge pewter stein that he picked up from the floor beside him. "Stacey said you were acting. What play?"

Self-consciousness seized me. "*Henry the Fourth*. It's pretty stupid. Just school."

"It's a great play!" He put the vial in his pocket. "It's about the demimonde." He waved his arm to indicate the house, the three of us. "About the street and rich people slumming. Wonderful lines! Falstaff says, 'Let us be Diana's foresters, gentlemen of the shade, minions of the moon.' "

"I just have a small part. Poins, he's a—"

"Poins!" Dr. X slapped his hands together. "Terrific! Poins is the knife, the street trickster. Even Falstaff is wary of him. Poins is some kind of disinherited son. He and Prince Hal are very young. Boys are natural street people, powerless, disposable. Poins disappears from the play because that's what happens to people like him."

Dr. X in his exuberance walked over to Stacey, put his hands on her breasts, and kissed her. He looked at my sudden jealousy, smiled, and put his arm around me. She excused herself and went back upstairs. It occurred to me that Dr. X may have known what play I was in and read up. If so, that was more trouble than Petrie had ever taken.

I sat in one chair with Dr. X opposite me and we listened to distant music. "Thelonius in San Francisco," he explained, taking out the vial and offering me a pill. He handed me his stein and I washed it down with warm beer.

Soon, my attention to detail became more intense. The only thing on the table was a blank prescription pad. I noticed the name Kleinman at the top. In a far corner of the floor was a bolt lock. It took me a moment to see the outline of a trapdoor. The music from upstairs changed at one point. Dr. X's mouth moved like he was tasting the notes. "Gould playing Bach's Goldberg Variations," he said.

That first Saturday, we talked for hours. Some of the insights that bowled me over were true of any unhappy sixteen-year-old. "Half the time you feel like an alien in this land. In this world."

Other things he saw were phenomenally accurate. "You have, let's see, three uncles," he said, staring into my eyes with his intense, pinned ones. "The youngest one's a pries— no, a lawyer. The middle one's a cop, of course. And the oldest one does what? Runs a bar?"

Never had I discussed my mother's family with Stacey. Dr.

X smiled at my surprise and said, "What makes this an Irish joke is that the bartender has all the money."

At that moment, someone knocked on the door upstairs. Dr. X rose, shook my hand, and said, "See you next Saturday?" as if he looked forward to it. I nodded eagerly.

A fox-faced man with red hair, the next patient, brushed past me on the cellar steps. Stacey was not to be found on the first floor and I was shy about going upstairs. Max still lay on the library couch. "Go in peace," he said as I left.

Outside was cold drizzle. That didn't bother me. My pulses skipped. Lights were on in other houses. But Stacey's, when I looked back from the end of the driveway, was dark. Then I saw her at an upstairs window. My heart bounded with speed passion. She saw me. Or rather, she saw the one who stood beside me smelling faintly of pool chlorine. Because he blew her a kiss and she returned it.

Too excited to let that worry me, with a Bostonian's sixth sense I headed for the nearest streetcar stop.

In the play, Falstaff says about Poins, "If men were saved by merit, what hole in hell were hot enough for him?" Monday, at rehearsal, remembering all Dr. X had told me, I bounced on my toes and talked like Fred who lived inna projects.

"Easy does it, Grierson," said Mr. Royce, the faculty advisor. "This is Shakespeare, not the Untouchables."

Over the next couple of weeks, I saw Dr. X regularly. Like amphetamine, he was never as good as that first time. When there were pills on the table, he'd give me an upper or a downer. If there weren't, he borrowed some of mine.

I came to understand that there were ways he was a fool. Sometimes he said stuff like "I'm a quarter Irish, a quarter French, a quarter English, with a bit of German and a smattering of Jew. Blood boils in me." He called speed vitamins and claimed it enabled him to read other people's minds.

Despite that, he had his moments. "Who is the third who always walks beside you?" he once asked. "When I count, there's just you and me. But when I look, there is always another walking beside you." Later, I realized he was paraphrasing T. S. Eliot. But right then, the words hit home.

So did his follow-up. "Everybody's got another self, Kevin. Most people—the dull, the mundane—never show it. But some get to let that dog run."

The next few Saturdays, I drove with Stacey out to her house. That became the center of my life. Everything else, school, family, Dr. Petrie, fast visits to the Gallery, was backdrop to those rides. Yet, each time she seemed a little more distant. We talked, but any mention by me of Dr. X and she became silent.

Max was always present when we arrived and there were usually others: college guys in tweed jackets clustered around a lady who smoked a pipe, a man in a turtleneck who played guitar, girls wearing leotards, a very light-skinned Negro man with a much older white woman.

One week when we came in, Max sat in the library with a plump, pale girl close to my age. Stacey grimaced and muttered, "Slug," under her breath.

Max introduced her. "Lisa. An acolyte, undergoing the process of finding herself." He added, "We have an oubliette, you know," as if he couldn't imagine my not wondering about that.

Everyone, but especially Dr. X, needed more and more drugs to function. When I went downstairs after meeting Lisa, he waved a prescription at me. "Kevin, there's a druggist in Coolidge Corner. A careless guy. I want you to go over there and break this. No one will suspect that choirboy face of yours."

It struck me as a bad idea. I shook my head and Dr. X told me, "You refuse because your mundane persona still holds sway. There's a little treatment I recommend. Isolation. Once you're alone, the strongest part of your personality can take over."

Suddenly understanding, I looked toward the trapdoor and repeated the unfamiliar word, "Oubliette."

Dr. X smiled like I was a prize pupil. "From the French, *oublier*, 'to forget.' Don't worry about our doing that. You won't be in there long. Maybe a couple of days over the Thanksgiving weekend." At the time, nothing more was said.

The Saturday before Thanksgiving, Stacey and I found Max and everybody else downstairs in Dr. X's office. "Just in time to witness a graduation ceremony, Kevin," said the doctor, unlatching the door to the oubliette.

He opened it to reveal a wooden ladder leading down to pitch dark. From below, a tiny voice cried, "It's cold down here. I've come to terms with myself."

Dr. X descended. Max waited at the top of the ladder. He extended his hand to Lisa. Her eyes were empty. All she wore was one of Dr. X's big oxford weave shirts. "Lisa was bold enough to want to confront herself," said Dr. X, glancing at me. Max and the others smirked as I backed away.

When Stacey and I went upstairs, she looked at me, really looked at me, for the first time in weeks and said, "Kevin, this is no place for you. I thought you could handle Dr. X, but my judgment was off, maybe my timing. You're almost ready, but you're still a kid. He sees your potential too. Get out of here before he hurts you."

We walked to the front door where she kissed me on the mouth and said, "When I need someone, I'll call and you'll be ready." On my way home, I managed to forget the warning and the brush-off and remembered only the kiss.

The first thing I did when I got in the door was turn off the fire under the pot in the kitchen. Tay still worked part-time as secretary to a professor over in Cambridge. That day she was helping him sort out his papers.

My grandmother was present, but not totally accounted for. She sat in the living room in the midst of boxes of photos and papers. With a bright smile she said, "Here's one of you, Jamey." From a faded photo taken before the turn of the century, a baby stared, wide-eyed in the midst of a vast christening gown.

"Nah, this is me, Gramny." I was in a snapshot of three generations, my mother, my grandfather, and myself on the front steps of the house. My mother stood looking up at Terrible Tom Malloy, saloon owner, ward heeler, legendary terror. He looked like a meaner, smarter version of his sons.

He stared right at the camera with clever, cold eyes. One arm he had around my mother. I was a blurry bundle in the other.

I remembered when I was about nine my mother telling me about her father. "Your uncles are still afraid of Daddy. If the old man came back and told them to, they'd all line up to get hit." We were speeding away from a family gathering like it was a getaway. She had suddenly pulled me away from my cousins and loaded me in the car as her brothers stood there looking stunned. "When I want, I make them afraid of me too," she laughed. "I just did it now." The laugh scared me more than the driving. It meant that my mother was drunk and her Shadow was at the wheel.

The next picture I found was a familiar one of my parents' wedding. It was wartime. In the background, girls with flowers, guys in uniforms smiled at the couple walking arm in arm. In a spring dress and wide hat, my mother, beautiful as some half-remembered forties movie star, leaned on my father's shoulder and smiled at the camera.

My father in his navy blues stared bewildered and adoring only at her. He came from New York, met and married my mother while waiting to go overseas. With hundreds of others, he died when the cruiser *LaSalle* went down in the South Pacific. He had almost no family. Once I had imagined I was secretly the son of a hero, the Lone Ranger, maybe, or Ted Williams. Now I saw too much of myself in his eyes to fantasize.

"Poor lamb," said my grandmother, looking at my father. "He hadn't a piece of meanness in him." She put out her hand and I helped her upstairs for a rest.

Back on the couch, I found photos of my mother from childhood up to the time of her second marriage. For a long while there was nothing. As she got older, she hated to have her picture taken.

Then at the bottom of the box I found one I had never seen. A few years before, Aunt Alice had taken candid photos with her new flash camera. Alice was no artist; the shots were unfocused, feet and head were cut off, radiators were centers of attention.

But in one, she had caught my mother walking into a room with a glass in her hand. At first, the photo appeared to be double exposed. Two mothers looked up. But instead of being identical, one wore a tired smile. The other, partly eclipsing the first, looked angry at being caught.

That night, after the TV stations had left the air, I sat sleepless at the kitchen table staring at papers. Some documents had my name on them. Every time there was a creak or bump in the house, I half expected the front door to open and my mother to come in. Once I looked up to find Tay watching me.

"Ah Kevin, you're so wise and owl-eyed lately. And you haven't been eating. There's ham and eggs in the icebox."

"I'm not hungry."

"Cocoa then. You always liked to make cocoa." Tay moved to the sink to fill the kettle. She looked over my shoulder at a picture of my mother at her junior prom. "She was her father's favorite." I nodded, interested.

Then she said, "Remember the story I told when you were small? How once there was a king with three sons who did not suit him and a daughter who suited him very well indeed? And as it happened . . ."

Impatient at what I saw as bedtime stories, I said, "And she gets cheated and gets turned into a magic hawk or something. I remember, but I'm a little old for that. There's stuff about me, Tay . . . I need to figure things out."

She waited, but words could take me no further. After a long pause, she reached out and patted my head. *"Faileas,"* she said.

It didn't occur to me that she recognized my trouble and was also struggling to put words to it. Sullen, I turned away from her. That Monday, I took the double photo of my mother and the papers with my name on them to school and stuck them in my locker, intending to study them later.

That year, family Thanksgiving was at Uncle Jim's house in Milton. Crying "God bless us," Gramny and Tay were lost in the flurry of little cousins as soon as we came in the door.

Thanks to the speed, I ate almost no dinner. But I drank whatever they offered me. Afterwards, kids laughed and screamed and the women washed the dishes, while in the den my uncles leaned on the furniture with their glasses.

As the oldest nephew, I was allowed in their presence. They were talking about Kennedy. "Sure it's a great day for the Irish, his election," said Bob with a phony brogue.

"The black Irish," said Mike.

"That's niggers to you," Jim said and they looked my way, noticed my distaste.

Uncle Bob poured me a beer. "From what I see, you're not much interested in school. College has gotten really expensive. Maybe you should think of the navy. Three years, see the world."

"My boards and SATs are fine. I can get into BU or MAS."

Jim said, "Bob went to college and law school and is broke. Mike graduated from high school and has finally got his head above water. Me, I got an eighth-grade education and I'm the one everyone comes to for dough. The thing is, now there is no dough." We were sitting in his ten-room house. Neither of his brothers seemed to be hurting.

The conversation then took an even more uncomfortable turn. Bob said, "Kevin here is good with money. Ma says he hardly needs an allowance."

Jim said, "He doesn't spend much on haircuts. He needs to visit his old friend Moxie."

"Money got put away," I said. "My mother—"

"Your mother raised an aristocrat," said Bob, sounding aggrieved. "Boot camp would be a change for you."

"Kevin never listens to anyone. Maybe he's in love," said Mike, giving me the dead-eyed glance cops reserve for outsiders. "You got a girlfriend, Kev?"

How to explain about Stacey and myself? I just shrugged. But I started thinking of her. Then I heard Mike remark, "Dad used to say, 'Whip a young dog who's too big for his britches and all of a sudden puppy drawers fit him fine.' "

"Then he'd take off his belt," Jim said. They all laughed, but not their eyes. They all looked at me. They were big and I was not. "You and Ma and Tay are staying over tonight. Tomorrow we'll talk about your future."

All this was news to me. Then a voice in my ear said, 'Let's show them what they're afraid of.' For a moment they choked and stared silently at the one who stood beside me.

That's when I got my coat, told Tay I was going home, and left before anyone could stop me. My thoughts ran to Stacey as I made my way by slow transit connections. It was just before one when I looked up at dim lights flickering in her second-floor windows. I had to knock for some time before Max appeared, his pupils small as BBs. He waved me in like I was expected.

"Stacey?" I wanted to know. He ignored the question.

Lisa sat in the kitchen with a trace of drool beside her mouth, sorting pills. "Once my inhibitions got broken down, Dr. X was able to show me that I'm the woman of situations. Yesterday, for instance, the situation was that everyone needed to get sleep. So I cashed prescriptions for these." She handed me a pill shaped like a torpedo.

Thelonius Monk was being played upstairs. "Isolation and realization," said Max, and poured me a Johnny Walker. "Drink up." I marveled at how little effect any of this had on me and my Shadow.

A time later, I found myself upstairs knocking on a locked door. After a while, the music and voices inside stopped. In the silence, I called, "Stacey!" The door swung wide and Dr. X stood in an open bathrobe. He was semihard. Behind him, a slab of moonlight or maybe streetlight fell on a slim figure on a wide bed. "Stacey?" I stepped into the room.

"Don't let him see me," she said. Immediately, Dr. X turned on a lamp. Stacey was covered by a sheet. Her hands were tied before her with the bathrobe cord. Instead of getting mad at Dr. X, she said to me, "What the hell are you doing here? Did I invite you?"

Dr. X laughed. "Look how confused all this makes him! The boy has no idea what he wants. Wait downstairs, Kevin. We're going to resolve these psychosexual dilemmas." I knew what he intended. But I obeyed.

My heart should have been crushed. I should have staggered and fallen down. Instead, remote and cold and wide awake, I moved with great purpose. Down in the kitchen, Max gave me another pill. I yawned and pretended to lose my balance when he led me down to the white room. I slid down the wall and lay on the floor with my coat as a pillow.

Max watched me for a while and then went back upstairs. I slept open-eyed the way sharks do. Everything was red and grainy and I could see myself lying on the floor. 'Like you're in the eye of the storm,' a voice whispered in my ear.

It was a while before Dr. X appeared. He held me up while

Max emptied my pockets. I watched from above as they guided me toward the open trapdoor with my head lolling, empty pockets hanging out like dogs' ears.

As Dr. X opened the trapdoor, I made it as easy as possible for Max to hold me upright. When they brought Lisa out of the oubliette, Dr. X had gone down to help her. As I watched from above, he descended again.

That's when my Shadow and I made our move. Max, stunned, looked from the zombie he held upright to the figure who grabbed him. Dr. X, wide-eyed, breathed, "Doppelganger!"

Then my Shadow swung Max over the trapdoor. I planted a shoe on his skinny ass and shoved him down on top of Dr. X. I slammed the trapdoor and locked it shut. On the table were my keys, wallet, and cigarettes. There was also a prescription pad. Everything went right in my pockets.

From the oubliette, Dr. X said calmly, "I thought you were more mature than this, Kevin. Just undo the latch and we can talk." Upstairs on the kitchen table were many pills, which I gathered up. Only then did the booze and drugs start to hit me. My stomach lurched. Blood banged in my head.

On the second floor, Stacey cried out that she was still tied up. I waited, but she didn't say my name. I needed fresh air. "Don't forget to call me!" I yelled and headed for the front door. She started to wail.

In the library, the situation was that Lisa snored with her mouth open. "Don't do the thing that will get you killed, little boy," Dr. X yelled while pounding on the trapdoor. "I see death around you. Cold nights and bad days, Kevin!"

In the first light, water trickled in gutters, the air smelled of wet, dead leaves. A voice beside my ear said, 'We got plenty of vitamins.' I didn't turn to look. The face of your Shadow is always closer to your fears than your hopes.

Tay and Gramny hadn't returned when I got home. A red torpedo from the cache put me out. I made sure to stay that way when Jim brought them back. Late in the day, I stared at the foot of the bed and saw a guy with a slightly banged-up face and hair that looked like the army had gotten him.

It took me a moment to recognize my Shadow. He smiled like that hurt him and spun the cylinder of the revolver. 'This is one sport you'd be good at,' he said as he aimed at his temple. 'Mom liked to play roulette too. Only she did it with a car.'

He pulled the trigger. I jumped as the hammer clicked on an empty chamber. 'People kill themselves when they don't have the nerve to kill someone else. Like Mom with her brothers. Her Shadow could scare them. But it scared her too. And she had a soft heart. I know they screwed her out of money. So instead of getting mad at them, she killed herself.

'Don't make that same mistake. You don't have to kill. All you have to do is show Uncle Jim that you aren't afraid. Take the gun and visit him today. I'll be there. We'll talk about our future. And his. Do it, or you'll end up looking like this.'

There was more, but all of it scared me and I woke up dry mouthed, soaked in sweat. More drugs kept me half awake and distracted. Till dawn, my thoughts were scenarios of Stacey, Dr. X, and me. Somehow I was older, taller, more dangerous, and driving a big black Thunderbird. The details were jumbled, but Stacey found ways of expressing her gratitude when I saved her from Dr. X.

Later that morning, nerves pulsing in my skin, I went to Petrie's office on the chance I'd meet Stacey. It turned out to be the last time I saw him. At one point, I tried to ask what the word *doppelganger* meant. But he looked up at me squirming in my seat and said, "You seem to be suffering side effects. I'm canceling your prescription."

Afterwards, as I should have known, there was no sign of Stacey. Not wanting to be alone, I headed for the Gallery, hoping Joe would be there. He had once seen my Shadow and I wanted to talk to him, to have him tell me I was a good kid.

Things had started to jump like they were on a bad TV and I saw the red MG out of the corner of my eye as I went up the Y steps. When I looked, it was gone.

They were still cracking down, but the lobby was busy and my Shadow slipped us past the desk. The Gallery was jumping. Most kids wore towels. Ridley, in trunks, glared at me. I spotted Joe and he seemed amazed, as if he saw my double again. But he made the gesture indicating him and me.

As I stepped forward, Max appeared on my left. He had a bad gleam in his eyes. His hand was in his pocket. At my right side was Dr. X, who lisped, "Say, we have a prior date!"

"Joe!" My shout got the Gallery's attention. Guys peered out of alcoves. Dr. X got his hand over my mouth. Max snapped something and stuck it up to my nose. It smelled like sweaty socks.

"Amyl nitrite," I heard Joe say as my head spun. Guys zipped their flies, boys grabbed their towels and edged away. "You're hijacking the kid!"

"I'm a licensed psychiatrist," Dr. X told him. "This is a dangerous patient." Their voices sounded like I was under water. Then their hands were gone from my face.

People started to run. Someone opened a fire door. An alarm began ringing. Someone yelled, "Raid!" Fresh air rushed in and my head cleared a bit. Max was on the floor with a bloody lip.

I saw that Joe had slammed Dr. X against a wall. "Get out!" he yelled. Like a rabbit, I bolted down the fire escape.

For a while, I just put distance between that place and me. Finally, pain stabbed my side and I lay behind an empty loading dock in an alley. My heart would not stop pounding. My nose bled. I passed out wondering what had happened to Joe, the only one who had ever fought for me. My Shadow said, 'None of this would have happened if we had gone to visit Uncle Jim.'

Later, I was awake and dry heaving through the fence around the train yard. A cop car raced by and I tried to shrink into the sidewalk. My Shadow said, 'Stacey told X where you'd be.' All I wanted was to die.

Then I stood beneath an el with a steam whistle screaming inside my ears. A hand was in my pocket. Said my Shadow, 'Take a red. Steady your head.' I tried to swallow dry mouthed and choked on the pill. If Dr. X didn't kill me, I thought my Shadow would.

From a bridge, I tossed every pill and prescription onto a busy expressway. To exorcise my double, I chanted over and over, "Stay away from me. Stay away from me."

Blood pounded like something was busting out of my brain. He whispered in my ear. 'You'll miss me while I'm gone.' Later, huddled and aching on a park bench, I spotted a flash of red. When I turned there was no MG. My Shadow was gone and I felt empty.

On the roaring subway home, I frantically searched the faces visible amid bags and boxes from Filene's and Jordan's, from Raymond's and R. H. White's. A woman in the first burst of Christmas shopping formed the word *disgusting* as she and her friend stared at me.

At Queena Heaven, it was cold and dark. My head spun as I tried to be sure everyone else off the train had left the station ahead of me. Across the avenue, bodies glided, streetlights gleamed off the ice at Curtis Park. They had flooded the playground for the first skating of the year.

Crossing the street, I sat not far from a small fire on the shore. People warmed their hands. Little kids whose parents had forgotten about them slid by on their shoes. One old couple skated arm and arm. At the center of the ice, guys played free-form hockey.

It was important to pull myself together. I promised God a lifetime of monastic devotion if He would just make my head stay still. After a bit, my breathing slowed, the ringing in my ears died down, my brain slipped a cog or two.

Before me, goalies crouched in front of improvised nets. Pucks hissed and jumped on ice bumps. Bodies collided. Murphy shot a goal, got checked hard, and skidded twenty feet on his ass.

Seeing him evoked hot afternoons crouching shirtless waiting for grounders at third. More than memory, it was a dream that smeared time and circumstances. I was eleven years old and on another world when I rose from the bench. Walking up the hill, I was going home to my parents.

Not my stepfather, my real father. He and my mother and I lived in my grandmother's house. Just the three of us. I knew they would be standing outside in summer sunlight, she in her picture hat, he in his navy uniform. I would tell them about my Shadow. They would explain that it was a nightmare and I would rest easy in their arms.

Not even the sight of that house in darkness stopped my dream. Lights were on in the living room. From the front hall, I saw my grandmother sitting on the couch with all the lamps lit and the family photos spread out before her. She had made tea, laid out three cups. "Here he is after all!" she exclaimed like she and my parents had been worried.

I stepped into the room. "Kevin," she said, "Dr. Exelmen has been waiting for you."

"Hi Kevin," said Dr. X as he moved between me and the door. "Did you forget about our overnight seminar?" He wore horn-rimmed glasses I had never seen before. They helped mask the swelling of one of his eyes. His smile was vitamin enriched.

A battered suitcase from the upstairs closet stood next to the couch. "Dr. Exelman helped me pack a change of clothes and your toothbrush so you'd be ready as soon as you came home." My grandmother smiled brightly as I stood paralyzed.

"We had a long talk about you, how bright you are," Dr. X

remarked. "About your amazing family. Now, Mrs. Malloy, I'm afraid we're late and have to hit the road." He picked up the suitcase and stepped forward to put an arm around my shoulder.

"First, let me use the bathroom." I ran upstairs. My thought was of the .38. The door to the closet was ajar. I fumbled with the light cord and heard Dr. X behind me. Reaching up, I pushed aside the imitation alligator binocular case, the bag full of Christmas ornaments. I tore through the shelf.

"No, the gun isn't there," said Dr. X. "I remembered your prattling on about it, so I looked. I also tried to find my property that you stole." He stood at the head of the stairs. "You caused me considerable professional embarrassment, Kevin. Are you going to summon your imaginary friend? I'm ready."

"Get out of the house!" I stood all alone.

Dr. X advanced slowly, speaking hypnotically. "You bad little boy. First, you are going to return the vitamins and minerals that you stole. Then, you and, I hope, your doppelganger are going to go for a little therapy."

The back stairs were at the end of the hall. I edged toward them. "Stand still, Kevin," Dr. X said softly. "If you run, I will do something very regrettable to Granny." He stepped forward and grabbed my arms.

Below, the front door opened and a voice called, "Mary? Kevin?" It was Aunt Tay. "Mary, do we have guests?"

"Mr. Axelroad came by to take Kevin on a trip. They're upstairs."

Dr. X didn't hesitate. "Stacey's the one who told me how to find you here. Told me to bring you back." My body felt weightless as he propelled me down the stairs.

Before us, in overcoat and suit, a hat set on her head, stood Aunt Tay. "Yes?" she said in a voice that had quelled generations of graduate students.

"Pardon me, madam," said Dr. X. "But young Kevin is due at an overnight seminar the school has organized. And I—"

"Indeed?" She looked at me. "Kevin?" I tried to speak. No sound came out. "Let go of him," she said. "I'm his guardian."

"Ah, his Aunt Tay! He's mentioned you. His grandmother and I have already discussed this." He started forward. I bobbed with him like a balloon. My grandmother stood at the living-room door. These two women were so frail. I didn't want anything to happen to them. "If you will excuse me, madam," said Dr. X, trying to move past her.

Aunt Tay did not step aside. Instead, she looked at me and said, clear and steady:

BY FELL NIGHT

My mouth wouldn't work. She repeated:

BY FELL NIGHT

Again, I couldn't speak. "An interesting folk rite," said Dr. X. "Perhaps I can return some day and record it." He made to move past her. Tay said:

BY FELL NIGHT

And what sounded like my mother's voice back when I was a little kid answered:

WITH STICK AND BONE

Tay said:

BY BLACK LIGHT

And I turned to see my grandmother answer, her voice young:

DOWN NARROW ROADS

Tay said:

BY CAT'S SIGHT

My grandmother responded:

THROUGH TIMES HARD AS ROCK

Dr. X said, "This young man has prostituted himself. He stole pills and prescription pads. He needs treatment."

BY OWL'S FLIGHT

said Tay. My own voice way at the back of my throat was more a moan than anything as I answered along with my grandmother:

PAST FEAR THAT FREEZES BLOOD

"Ladies," said Dr. X, "Kevin here is a most rare and fascinating case. Doppelganger syndrome. In other words, he has a double."

Giving no sign that she heard, Tay chanted:

BY MAIN MIGHT

Dr. X tugged at me, but I had the strength not to move. "Let me work with Kev—" Something cracked like ice breaking. Dr. X choked. My grandmother and I answered:

OVER NIGHTMARE'S DARK BRIDGE

Tay never raised her voice:

I WILL COME TO YOU

A silence followed. Dr. X tried to speak and couldn't. My grandmother could. "My son is a police officer," she said. "Get out of this house, or I'll have you arrested."

Tay stared stony faced. It took a long moment, but Dr. X finally let go of me and backed out the door. He made certain signs with his fingers like he was warding off evil spirits.

"Who was that?" my grandmother asked as the door closed. Then she felt tired and went upstairs to rest. The last few days and the weeks before that and the months all the way back to summer caught up with me. I slumped against the wall.

Tay led me out to the kitchen, fed me bread and butter, hot soup and cocoa, like I was a little kid. She sat with me and said, "The things that man said can't be so. But even if they are, I love you."

I couldn't reply. "With your mother too, I called it *Faileas*. It was too much for her, poor pet."

"*Faileas*." I got out the word with difficulty because my throat was so tight.

"A Shadow. Such as you have. Sometimes you should pay a little attention to what old women say. Not always, mind you. At my age, words whiz about like bees in the head."

I looked at her, wanting more. She asked, "Remember the story I used to tell about Prince Caoimin? How at his birth all the gentry, the fairy folk, stood over his crib and hurled wishes good and bad at him? One side wished him happy days, the other grievous nights, one side great wealth, the other bitter poverty, one the hand of the princess, the other lonely death.

"Now, I know you feel too grown up for such things. But

think how it could be that there were just too many wishes for one tiny baby to handle. Maybe in their trying to win the wishing they put too great a burden on one small head."

Once I would have grown impatient. But this lady maybe had saved my life with a poem, so I listened.

"When your mother was born, your grandmother knew she would have no more children. Your grandfather had won her with his brains and charm. But he had his black side, all drinking and violence. His sons were well enough but they feared and respected only that black side of him.

"Mary wanted something better for her Ellen. She tried with my help to give her blessings. We thought we had succeeded. But your grandfather had his hand on her too. She was his favorite, and deep in her lurked the very essence of him. It was the same when you were born. We wished, but he touched you."

The teakettle whistled and when she rose to take it off the flame, her step was a little unsteady. "All of us from myself to the pope have two selves, good and bad. It's the way we are. What was sad was to see your mother as pained as one who's been cut in two, unable to be at peace until she died."

When she sat back down, the house was absolutely silent. Maybe it was my Shadow's being absent, maybe the drugs and terror were shock treatment. But at that moment, I realized that my mother was never coming back. I remembered the two faces in the photo, smiling and apologetic and scowling and malign. Good and bad, both halves of her were dead.

That night, finally, I was able to cry for her. Right then, I cried for all poor souls who find themselves cut in two. I cried for my grandmother and for Tay and myself. I cried for drunks and abusers, for the crazed and scared of this fucked-up world. Sweet Jesus, that night I cried for us all.

THREE

FOR THE NEXT week or so, I was stunned by grief. The world was a distant rumor. At school, kids talked about applying to Harvard and MIT. My mourning was so delayed that no one but Tay recognized it. No Shadow dogged me, no red MG flickered at the corner of my eyes. Common sense should have kept me away from the Y, but gray loneliness led me back.

Nobody stopped me in the lobby or the hall. Everything was oddly quiet. The Gallery stood empty. As I paused, an iron hand grabbed my arm. Turning, I saw a raincoat and a long Irish face. A cop. "Here to swim, son?" I nodded eagerly, believing that was an escape.

He led me in lockstep and said, "I might have thought you were loitering with intent. Your family know you're here?" I shook my head. He propelled me into the locker room and said, "Another bathing beauty." A couple of guys in sweat suits looked at me with sadists' smiles. The room was empty except for us. The trap was sprung.

Classes had been canceled. Only those who didn't swim wouldn't have heard that. Voices jeered, someone howled down at the pool. The guys dragged me to a locker. "STRIP DOWN, PUNK!" They made sure I did.

"FRONT AND CENTER!" I was just a scared kid shivering before them, my hands over my crotch, unable to meet their eyes. "This small, we throw them back," said the cop and they all laughed. "Next time we meet, you get booked, son."

"MOVE IT, LITTLE GIRL!" I ran to the piss- and chlorine-stinking pool. I saw a kid, maybe fourteen, huddled in a corner. A hunting party of counselors in trunks formed a gauntlet. They knocked me into the water and held me under. They cheered when I choked and stamped my hands when I tried to get out. Ridley and a couple of others I recognized from the Gallery. They were the worst.

Then they were gone. I heard their shouts as they turned the showers on a hysterical Gallery kid who wouldn't strip. He saved me, maybe others. Slipping, gasping, I got to the locker, shimmied wet into pants, shoved on loafers, grabbed my jacket. Abandoning everything else, I ran.

Coming home frozen and half drowned, I felt I could fall no lower. I was wrong. Uncle Jim stood in the kitchen washing dust off his hands. "Here he is," Gramny said brightly. I was glad she didn't notice how messed up I'd gotten.

But Jim did. "Enjoy your swim?" he asked. All I wanted was to get to my room and lick my wounds. Sensing weakness, he followed me into the hall. "Your Uncle Mike tells me they got a vice sweep on." He saw me wince.

His breath was boozy as he said, "We got some matters to discuss. Like your future." Noticing I was still damp, he added, "Maybe you should go in the navy, you like water so much."

The navy sounded like three years' worth of what had just been done to me. I was still shaking. "Let's talk later, Jim."

Angry, he always got quiet. But he never lost his smile. "Is it the dope that makes you not understand me? You think you're too old to have to listen? We're going to have a little walk and talk." As with the people at the Y, I saw he meant me harm. And again, I folded.

My uncle shoved me out the backdoor. His Caddy was parked at the end of the driveway. "You look like shit. I see you wasting your time in school. I want you to preenlist before graduation, not wait for the draft. I want it settled today."

"My college boards are good enough. My mother said there was the money her father left." I sounded pathetic.

We paused next to the fence at the end of the street and he said, "Like we've been trying to tell you, there is no money. It got used up. On your mother. On other stuff. Understand?"

Not knowing what to say, I just stared at him. Fast as a snake, the back of his hand caught the side of my face. My head bounced on the chain links. He hit me again. Far below, Boston Harbor spun. I tasted blood.

"Understand?" he repeated. This time I managed to nod. "You stupid bastard, it's about time someone took you down a few pegs." He hit me again. My head jerked back.

"You think I don't know about your personal habits? The goofballs? About how you earn pocket money? I look at you and I know." With each question, he slapped me. "Understand?"

Instead of nodding, I dodged. He hit me left handed on the side of the head. My ear rang. "Big commotion here last week," he said. "Mom let it slip about some guy looking for you. Shithead, keep your freak friends away from her and Tay. Understand?"

I nodded, but he smacked me anyway. "Understand?"

"Yes. Yes, I understand . . . please don't!"

"And while you live in this house, which won't be for long, you keep your hands off what doesn't belong to you. What did you do with that .38?"

"Nothing." I braced for another blow.

It didn't come, though he didn't believe me. "There's other stuff missing. Papers. Mom . . . she forgets. Mom took your mother's death hard. Me too. I'm not letting you get like your mother." Reflectively, Jim banged my head against the fence a couple of times.

He pushed me toward the car. "Get in. We got to do something about you." I noticed Mrs. Reardon next door, a delivery boy from Snyder's among others, observing with interest my public fall. Word would get around Queena Heaven.

The afternoon seemed flat and metallic, unreal even while it happened. Jim drove to Field's Corner and brought me into his bar. We went back into his little office. "You could save us both trouble, if you knew about those papers." My mind was broken. I really didn't remember taking them. He gave me a whiskey and made me sign a document. The whiskey numbed the pain in my mouth. "You got nothing on under your coat. What the hell's wrong with you?"

Later at Moxie's, my uncle announced, "Kevin's going into the service." The afternoon crowd watched me sit rigid on the chair in a T-shirt several sizes too big as Jim's old army buddy ran clippers over my temples.

Afterwards, Jim stopped in another joint to drink and place a couple of bets. I sat beside him in shock. The face in the bar mirror was no longer mine.

Jim's beating was professional. The skin was unbruised. But swelling had turned the eyes into narrow slits. The hair was gone except for a half-inch high swath on top of the head. It was the face my Shadow had worn in the dream the week before.

Jim saw my expression. "Any further thoughts on what happened to the .38?" Once I remembered the dream, I guessed where the gun was. But I just shook my head and he didn't press me.

Instead he took me to the recruiter's office where the sergeant, another of Jim's pals, said it was good doing this now and they'd take me right after school ended. I signed papers there too. The sergeant gave me something for Tay to sign as my guardian. By then, none of this mattered.

To make sure I had nothing to live for, Jim said as he dropped me off, "You've been hiding behind women too long. Next weekend, I'm moving you out of here to somewhere that I can keep an eye on you. Get Tay's signature on those forms. Any whining to her and I'll kick your ass good." Jim knew just how to put someone over the edge.

Tay was home when I walked in the door. "Oh, Kevin," she said, and other stuff. But my ears hummed and I didn't hear. What had happened hurt too much to tell her. My future was hell. But it didn't matter. I wouldn't be around for it. I fell face down on my bed and passed out.

When I awoke, it was deepest night. Confused, aching, I got up and took off the unfamiliar shirt with prickly hairs down the back. Guys from school had seen me that morning. Nowhere in the city could I hold up my head. But I had the cure.

On my desk was a note from Tay, a plate of sandwiches, and a glass of flat ginger ale. The note read:

> BY ALL RIGHT
> I WILL COME TO YOU

It meant nothing to me. I couldn't eat. But my thirst was intense, so I drank the soda.

The house was cold, silent. In my grungy jeans, I padded down the hall and opened the door of what had been my mother's room. In the dream, my Shadow had said, 'Her brothers are still afraid to go in there.'

Remembering, I lifted the mattress. There was the .38 and the ammunition. All I had to do was load the revolver and blow off the side of my head. Picking it up, I saw a vial of pills.

'Shoot yourself,' said the voice behind me, 'and you finish

Jim's work for him. Like our mother did. He set you up for this. Look, I laid something aside. A couple of those codeine will cut your pain.'

The magic my Shadow brought was black. But it was magic. 'How's life been without me?' he asked. 'Pool parties? Manly outings with Uncle Jim? Going to send me away? No, huh.'

Back in my room, stoned, I held the revolver at the ready and looked in the mirror again. Instead of a face I didn't know, I saw a face that could be anyone: all-American boxer, army recruit, hired killer. And this time, I saw it twice.

I slept most of Sunday. Tay tried to talk to me. "I've spoken to Jim and he understands that he's to stay away from you from now on." Since I couldn't begin to describe what had happened or what my Shadow and I were going to have to do, I didn't say much.

Monday morning, on my way in to school, I saw a familiar face. Ridley and I met on a corner. Hate twisted me. Standing in his path, I looked death into his eyes. All alone, he was frightened. And he should have been. Along with the coolest clothes I still owned and the pills, the loaded .38 was in my schoolbag.

The kids who went to the Gallery called what we did the Game. But the guys at school had another name for it. The invisibility I had cultivated in my years there was gone. In class, they stared at my haircut and whispered a story that was going around.

Angry and scared, I realized that my next class was gym. 'Unwise, possibly fatal,' said the voice in my ear. I slipped into study hall, dropped Dexedrine, and looked at the papers from my locker. I didn't understand much, but documents mentioned me and money. There was a paper naming Tay as my guardian. 'The enlistment papers are worthless without her signature.' I tore them up.

That afternoon, several kids looked at me like I troubled

them but they were afraid to speak. I kept wanting to leave. But my Shadow whispered, 'Stick around. I got a feeling.'

The drama society rehearsed after school. Grebesky, a forward on the hockey team, was Mistress Quickly, the tavern keeper. Grebesky had the moves down surprisingly well, but he couldn't remember his lines. Nobody laughed as Mr. Royce, the faculty advisor, kept prompting him. In my ear, the voice said. 'We have time. We don't visit Uncle Jim until later.' The thought made me uneasy.

Then I realized there was a stir on stage. "Take five," said Mr. Royce. "Grierson, get down here."

At first, I thought I'd missed a cue. Wondering what the big deal was, I came off the stage into the gloom of the auditorium. And my eyes bugged. Royce stood in the center aisle. Stacey was with him. "Nothing to worry about, Grierson," he said. "Your cousin assures me it's just a minor family emergency."

"They were really nice about letting me in," said Stacey in an unfamiliar, bright, chirping voice. She had on a blue dress with a Peter Pan collar. "When I called, Grandmother said you were here." She smiled girlishly. "Sorry to take Kevin away, Mr. Royce. It was fascinating watching you direct."

Royce stared at her enchanted. Girls hardly ever entered the school. I could hear the guys on stage behind me panting. It turned out the two of us were from an affectionate family. "Hey, Cuz!" I said and kissed Stacey on the mouth.

"Very good, Grierson, you can go. Try to pay more attention," said Mr. Royce. As I picked up my coat and book bag, he added roguishly, "You never told me you had such a lovely cousin."

"Right," I muttered as we walked through the rotunda and out the door. "I can just imagine that coming up in conversation. 'Please don't give me detention, sir. I have a lovely cousin.'"

"He's a filthy pervert," Stacey said matter-of-factly. Out on the street, she glanced around. Then she looked at me, assessing. "I need your help."

I was looking too. Now that she wasn't putting on an act, Stacey seemed tense, desperate. I stayed cool. "What's wrong?"

"Dr. X. He's up in New Hampshire, collecting money, drugs. He's coming back tonight. Then he's taking me to Mexico." She took my hand. "Kevin, he's crazy and I'm scared."

My desperation was as big as hers. I was afraid that the rest of my life was going to be a continuation of the last few days. Stacey seemed like a way to ease that terror. But I just said, "Don't go with him."

She shook her head. "It isn't that easy. Things are slightly out of control. My mother and stepfather are coming back next week. Dr. X threatens to stay in the house and confront them. My father has wanted to hospitalize me all along. If I can't straighten this situation out, my mother will let him."

Because of how she had helped to wreck my life, I said, "You told me to get lost. You told Dr. X where I lived and about the Gallery."

"No. I said you weren't ready yet. And he forced me to tell. I was stuck in the goddamn oubliette. In my own house. You humiliated him and he took it out on me. Today he locked me in the bedroom but I got out. Kevin, I recognized something in you the first time we met. Seeing you now, I know you can get rid of Dr. X."

I hesitated, but my Shadow whispered, 'Dr. X is a punching bag. Tell her about your fee.'

"Before I get rid of Dr. X," I told Stacey, using the same gesture as Joe in the Gallery to indicate the two of us.

She said, "You're a creep." But the deal was made.

Looking up and down the block, I asked, "Where's the MG?"

"Dr. X has it. He says it's his now. That's another thing. You have to get it back." She started walking toward the streetcars and I followed. "When I first met him, he seemed brilliant. After what you did to him, everything dried up, the drugs, his power. Everyone who hung around deserted. Even that toad Max."

We didn't speak much on the steamy, crowded streetcar to her mother's house. Anticipation kept me on edge. I watched Stacey. She was beautiful. I know now that there is a brief time in youth when depravity does no more than refine the features.

By night, her stop looked like something out of a European spy movie, gleaming tracks, frosted breath, figures walking in overcoats as faces at light windows moved past in the other direction. 'In case this is a trap,' said the Shadow, and I slipped the revolver out of the bag into my overcoat pocket.

The house, it turned out, was dark and silent. Stacey picked up a half-empty bottle of J&B in the kitchen and carried it up to the master bedroom. We both had a swallow. I took deep, sleeping breaths and watched Stacey as I fumbled with the buttons of my shirt.

In soft light, she stepped out of her dress and her shoes, undid the stockings and slipped them off. She took off her bra and slid out of her panties. She sat on the bed and beckoned.

And I froze. All of my experience was guys doing things with my body. Now that it was time to take the initiative, I heard the laughter and taunts of Saturday morning. I smelled piss and chlorine and felt crippled.

'It's easy. Maybe even fun,' my Shadow whispered. My hand brought up the bottle and I took a swig. My feet had trouble finding the rug. But Stacey had reasons for wanting this to work. She got me undressed quickly, put one hand on my waist and another on my ass and guided me gently. When I came, it was a relief and a wonder. 'Something else you know how to do,' said my Shadow.

After that, she let me play. At one point, I felt like we were a pair of beating wings. I remember running my hands over every inch of her skin because I felt I was entitled to. I wanted, as I never had with anyone, to make Stacey want me. Caught in the moment, I forgot there was a meter running.

But Stacey didn't. The last thing she did was kiss me long and hard on the throat just below my chin. "Something for those gorillas at school to see," she whispered. Then she rose and I noticed that exactly half an hour had elapsed.

We smoked a cigarette and had some more whiskey. "Sorry to spoil things," Stacey said, "but he's going to be back soon." We dressed and she got busy.

Dr. X had already begun to pack. She moved a suitcase and a cardboard box full of papers down to the front hall. "He can take his things. What I want out of him is all the keys. And make sure he knows he can't return. Ever."

We put most of the lights out and Stacey went back up to the bedroom. After a few minutes, she put on a record, the Goldberg Variations. I sat on the stairs with the .38.

Dr. X drove up fast. The car door slammed; his key was in the lock. For an instant, I panicked. But my Shadow whispered, 'This will be fun, too.' My hands steadied as I cocked the piece.

Dr. X flicked the switch in the front hall and the first thing he saw was his belongings. He looked flabby and flushed like he had been drinking. Out of the darkness, I said, "Good evening, Dr. X."

It took him just a moment to recognize my voice. "You little pussy. She let you fuck her. Now she thinks you're going to save her? No witches to help you? Weird kids like you disappear and nobody is at all surprised." He made a move. I stood up and leveled the gun. Dr. X faltered. My pulses leaped. "Stacey wants the keys back. Lay them down on the table and you can take all of this you can carry. Understand?"

"I'm taking the car," he said and turned to leave. For a moment, the gun was leveled at the back of his head. Then I raised it and squeezed hard.

WHAM! The revolver jumped like a snake. The explosion and the impact of the bullet in the wall over his head were simultaneous. I had never fired a gun before. But I heard myself say, "That felt good!"

Dr. X stood frozen. "Empty out your pockets. Understand?" He didn't jump fast enough. "UNDERSTAND?"

When Stacey came out of the bedroom and stood at the head of the stairs, I had Dr. X lying facedown on the floor. She went and called a taxi.

"I think you and your doppelganger have made a remarkable synthesis," said Dr. X. "But I also see you turning that gun on yourself when you realize you're just his puppet. You see, I know what you're really into, Kevin. Forget that spoiled bitch. You need a man like me."

For a while, I listened appreciatively. I really had learned stuff from him. And he talked a great show. But he began to whine and I had to press the gun into the back of his head to shut him up. When the taxi came, I let him take his belongings.

As the taillights disappeared down the driveway, Stacey descended and looked at the hole in the wall. "Firing that gun was really stupid," she said. "I hope I can get all this fixed up before Mother gets back."

I unloaded the revolver, stuck it back inside the book bag. "I don't even know his real name."

"Botley, Herbert Botley. I had him for freshman psych." Stacey sounded like she had already dismissed him from her mind.

It occurred to me that it would be nice to be close to her again. Reaching out, I suggested, "Let's go back upstairs."

"That wasn't part of the bargain. Do you let your customers have extra goes for free?" Startled, I was silent. She showed me to the door without a kiss. "I'm leaving right after you. Repairmen will be here in the morning. Do you need money to get home?"

I shook my head. "Maybe I could call you."

"I don't think so," Stacey said, closing the door.

That just about broke my heart. At the same time, I kind of admired how she had carried everything off. It was cold. I stuck my hands in my pockets and listened to my Shadow.

'Pretty soon we visit Uncle Jim. We wait outside the bar until he's alone or he comes outside. Then we step up and show him the gun, let him know the family curse is still in operation. We want money and we want him to leave us alone. But I don't think that will be a problem. A bullet or two in the dashboard of his Caddy and he'll cry real tears.'

It sounded more possible than it had a little earlier. But I still wasn't happy. "What about school?" As we approached the station, a streetcar swung out of the dark a few hundred feet down the track. We picked up the pace. "What about Tay?"

"Forget her. Forget school and Boston. We take the train down to New York tonight. Find girls who make Stacey look like Grebesky. Sugar daddies. Guys like Joe but rich." Running away sounded less impossible than staying put. We crossed the outward-bound tracks as the streetcar stopped. My Shadow boarded the car right behind me.

An hour or so later, at the foot of the stairs of the Field's Corner elevated station, my Shadow held the pill vial upside down. I yawned, trying to find enough air to breathe, and gazed across the street at the neon Malloy's Bar and Grill sign.

He said, 'I'll check it out.' From behind one of the iron el pillars, I watched him cross the street, surprised at how small and skinny he looked. Then a voice in my ear said, "Rest easy." Uncle Mike the cop patted me down, took the piece out of my pocket.

"In the car, Kevy boy. Your friend keeps his distance if he

knows what's good for you." We sat in the front seat of his Chevy. "You running away? I'm not going to stop you." Mike broke open the .38. "You fired this, asshole! Hit anyone? I'm asking you." I shook my head. "Coming back here to shoot Jim?"

"Just scare him." I saw my Shadow start to cross the street toward us and signaled him to stay back.

Mike seemed amused. "You with a gun is scary. But the sight of your playmate there is what'd do him in. Jim takes things hard. He's the oldest. He took the brunt of the crap from our old man. Him and your mother. Jimmy loved his little sister. Even when it turned out she had, what is it Aunt Tay calls them? *Faileas?* Shadows? And now you. It kills him. It kills me too. I look at my kids, I think what if that happened, what would I do? Shoot myself? Shoot them?"

He let that sink in. Then he said, "You're leaving, you need money. It's not a great bet, but I'll put some dough on you not coming back. Jim will too. How much do you want? One hundred?"

I said. "No. Make it two." That seemed like big money. I was a stupid kid. And my Shadow was no more than a step ahead of me. He had a kind of foresight. He knew some of what I would later discover. Like he saw us in New York, probably. What he didn't see until he got here was that in New York things happened fast. What we found was a lot of people smarter and tougher than both of us put together.

After a few days, drugs and money gone, we sat on the stairs at Grand Central Station. Messed over body and soul, I turned to the dirty, tense face that was also mine and said, "This was your idea. What are we going to do?" All I got back was a duplicate of my own baffled expression. "Get lost," I said. "Get lost!" As he faded, my Shadow whispered with real surprise. 'Guess we can't live on my brains and your ass.'

That night, without him, I wandered around Hell's Kitchen.

A guy smiled in passing and seemed okay. By then all I wanted was someone to talk to and a place to be warm. Down an alley we went and through a door. In a cellar room, he put his hands on my shoulders, ran me up against a wall.

The side of his face he'd kept away from me was so creased by a thick scar that it looked like it had been crumpled. "Don't be scared, little boy," he said. "I'll make sure this *never* happens to you. Now let's see what you got." Scarface and his friends had me in handcuffs for the next few days. I didn't know if I was getting out of that apartment alive. I lost virginity I hadn't known existed.

A week or so later, owning nothing but the clothes on my back, I blubbered on the skinny shoulder of Veronica, a Spanish drag no older than I was. We stood in the lobby of a hotel. Veronica hooked some change out of her bra and asked, "Anyone you can call, honey?"

There was. Certain of my family were not anxious to see me again. But my grandaunt Tay begged me to come back, wired the money. Lots of kids like I was don't get that grace. And even Tay seemed angry when I came limping home.

"Don't you be mad at me too, Tay. I couldn't live if you didn't like me."

And she said, "I'm not mad at you, Kevin. I'm afraid for you." She recited a poem. At the time, I mostly didn't understand it. The first verse went:

> Just we three go sailing
> Me, Myself and I
> Over walls and fences
> Through the night we fly

My future got decided that Christmas as I lay in bed too sick and numb to care. I didn't want to show my face in town. The family house was going to be sold. Gramny was going to live with my Uncle Jim. Tay was getting an apartment in Cambridge.

In that time and place, a young man in trouble with God and the law was treated to a dose of military discipline. Since Tay wanted me to finish school, my share of the sale of the house sent me to St. Sebastian, Soldier and Martyr, in New Hampshire. That winter, I marched, went to morning Mass, exercised, got cropped, prayed, studied, and took cold showers.

For all but the last activity I was in some variation of a uniform much like one the police cadets in my neighborhood wear. At St. Sebastian's S&M, no one knew anything about me, which was the one good thing. Beer, let alone drugs, was unobtainable and the brothers of the Sacred Cross made sure even sex with yourself wasn't easy to arrange.

One of my roommates prepped for West Point, another prayed in his sleep. My grades were as bad as they had been for quite a while. I couldn't focus. The face in the mirror seemed to be a huge distance off. I thought of ways of dying, hid razor blades, tested pipes to see if they could hold my weight.

That's when the dreams began. In them, I woke up in apartments I'd never seen before, talked to people I didn't recognize. Once, I snapped open a knife almost like a switchblade. When someone made a heavy pass, I heard my voice whisper, 'I'm not real good at close body work.' My Shadow woke as I slept, lingered in my waking memory.

Around then I turned from thoughts of offing myself to reading science fiction—*Childhood's End, Twilight World, Citizen of the Galaxy.* Alternate worlds, mutant teens, alien conquerors, prison moons are an easy fit when a doppelganger cruises your dreams and a man in a dress lectures you about chastity.

The last day of spring semester, graduating seniors, guys who wouldn't be coming back, threw pieces of their uniform— hats, ties, insignia, and nameplates—in the air as they left St.

Sebastian's forever. I sat waiting for the charter bus to Boston, reading *A Canticle for Liebowitz.* I'd just done fifty push-ups because my brass wasn't shined. My high school credits were not complete. Summer term was the black hole, punishment detail.

Two weeks later Uncle Bob deposited me at the Park Square bus station. "This is your last chance, Kevin. Blow it and you have no place to go." He seemed as amused as a lawyer ever gets to be as I tried to hold my luggage so as to hide the fact that my knees were bare. In 1961, except for dorks, fairies, and social cripples, guys between six and thirty sported jeans, pegged trousers, chino slacks. St. Sebastian's summer uniform featured khaki shorts. It felt like I'd been publicly depantsed.

Uncle Bob drove off and a car full of kids came by. They honked, and when I looked their way, they gave me the finger. I was a scary and disgusting sight, a tamed teen with no control over his life. These guys were going to the beach, to visit their girlfriends, to parties.

My life was going to be barracks, mental hospitals, prisons. I was utterly worthless. Just then, I caught a glimpse of a familiar figure walking up to the Statler Hotel across the street. My Shadow had a slick haircut and hip clothes. He wore a great pair of shades. When I looked again, he was gone.

But I took that eye-flash as a kind of promise to myself. Summer term was a bit looser. I cheated, I flirted, I lied. I even studied. I'd forgotten I wasn't stupid. The brothers took credit for turning me around. I knew better.

My college boards had been fairly impressive. Aunt Tay arranged my late admission to huge, anonymous Mass. Arts and Science. College was good to me. Amid the general dislocation and chaos, I finally learned to play the role of a human child well enough to pass. A lot of that I owe to the kid I'll call Boris.

My first day at MAS was when I met him. A week out of

uniform, still crewcut and tense, I entered my dorm room. My new roommate was sprawled on a bed, already unpacked, shades pushed up on his forehead, hair like my Shadow had worn, a butt hanging from his mouth. One glance and he recognized me the way a former marine or an ex-con always knows another.

"At ease, cadet!" he barked like a drill sergeant. When that didn't work, he asked, "Where did you do your time, man?" When I told him, Boris nodded and said, "A Catholic delinquent!" He pointed to his own chest. "Jewish youth in disgrace. Truancy. Two years at Ticonderoga Military Academy, 'cause only hoods go in the army and only Negro kids go to jail."

I'd had plenty of time to edit and shape my adventures. I gave this guy the hard-ass version. "It was speed and booze. A lady stepped on my heart so I stole a gun, held up my uncle, and took off for New York. . . ." Certain details got distorted, other were omitted. My Shadow especially.

Without asking, Boris stepped over to the bathroom, brought out two still-chilly bottles of Carling's Black Label and opened them both. He handed me one and picked up an album. "You know Ray Charles?"

I shook my head and sank down on the other bed as "What Did I Say?" was played with aching joy. After a while he said, "I know they can twist you, but we got over on them, man." He gave me an assessing look. "It will be a while before you need to buy a comb. But try these." He tossed me his shades. After a while I looked in the mirror and smiled at the mysterious stranger.

That first semester, I took biology in a big amphitheater with six hundred other freshmen, a lecturer, and a slide show. Down front were kids who took notes. Up at the back, I skimmed past a dozen glazed stares, caught a young woman's gaze, rolled my eyes, and got a smile. I'd seen her at a drama department audition. She did costumes.

Like two souls awake in a sleeping world, we rose and went out to the hall. Naturally, we both smoked. But neither of us did it that well. We introduced ourselves. Sarah Bryce was lovely with dark eyes and rich auburn hair. And she didn't fully understand that yet. In high school only slam-bang good looks work.

Over the next couple of weeks, I discovered that Sarah's parents veered between periods of seeming prosperity and total bankruptcy. When she was twelve, her father almost went to jail. Her mother found Librium at about the same time. That, I would guess, was about when Sarah decided not to look too closely at the ones she loved.

She learned a lot about me too. It poured out. "Chicken hawks jump-started me before I knew what was going on. After my mother died, that side of me became a big school and family scandal. The only thing I could think to do was run. New York was bad. Since then, I've been afraid to let anyone touch me."

She stroked my cheek. My sex life seemed more like something I had witnessed than a firsthand experience. And getting to take the lead for the first time in my life with someone I cared for soothed me in a lot of ways. As we lay tangled together in the borrowed bed, though, I saw my Shadow looking on. He had been left out of this account too.

The campus was connected to Boston by a streetcar line. I loved the cars, the clatter of their wheels, the sway of their ride, like they were old friends.

One October afternoon, broke and hungover, I headed into town. We rattled through the wooded suburban landscape. Suddenly, I recognized Stacey's house. My memories of times there felt distant, almost legendary.

At that moment, a voice whispered in my ear, 'Found your life lacks a certain zest?' I said nothing. I had played this scene out in my imagination often. My Shadow said, 'I want to make up for what happened.' When I didn't reply he said, 'Without you, I don't even half exist.'

I'd rehearsed our reunion carefully. This time I would be in control and use my Shadow. I dictated terms. "You stay away from school and my family. Weekends, I'll come in town and we'll get together."

He kept his side of the deal for a long while. Going into Boston, I'd take the streetcar and he'd appear as the suburban landscape rattled past.

At school, I majored in English but hung around the drama department. I got cast as cadets, sons, younger brothers. Bland stuff. In town, I slipped into the life my Shadow had established and found a more interesting role. "Bad little boy!" giggled a fat john, slapping my butt. I flicked open what I'd discovered was my Shadow's gravity knife and put myself firmly back on top.

Booze and drugs made it possible for me not to wonder why I was doing this. It was the age of speed. Segments of MAS ran on it. In them I was a hero. Junior year, I stood in a pad in Cambridge as a fat lady in an orange muumuu counted out two hundred black beauties for me and my customers. Meanwhile, a skinny, shirtless guy with wild eyes and a knife stuck in his belt tried to focus on my Shadow who was lounging in the doorway. 'He's not her double,' my doppelganger murmured later. 'But he's something damn close.'

My transformation back to college student took place on the streetcar ride back to school. Once, as Saturday night turned to Sunday morning, I stood up in the infamous last car to MAS with a load of speed. As we passed the big house, it was ablaze with light. People stood on the porches, cars rolled down the driveway. 'Stacey's wedding,' my Shadow whispered as he faded and my eyes surprised me by tearing up.

Mostly I found MAS a good time. And good times don't get

measured as minutely as periods of torment. I turned twenty-one in the spring semester of senior year.

Early one morning, the phone in the hall of the residence house cut through my hangover. On the other bed, Boris snored in counterpoint to the ringing. It was right outside our door and nobody was getting up. Fumbling in vain for my robe, dancing on the cold floor, I went out to the hall. The phone stopped in midring.

And there he was, wearing my bathrobe and my face, speaking in my voice. "Oh my God! Thanks, Uncle Bob. I don't know what to say. I'll be over there as fast as I can."

As he hung up, I whispered. "We had a deal. What are you doing here?"

His eyes, when he turned to me, were unreadable. 'Aunt Tay died.' I doubled up like I'd been hit in the stomach. He put the robe over my shoulders. 'You'll need something to get you through this,' he murmured. 'There's a half-pint of whiskey in the pocket and some Dexies.'

"Fuck you," I said. But I didn't tell him to get lost. With Aunt Tay gone, we two were alone. I showered and dressed in what she and I called my confirmation outfit: blue blazer, gray slacks, and a rep tie.

My departure awakened Boris. "I'm really not such a bad monster," he said in the same Karloff voice that had seemed endlessly funny at the party the night before. His nickname, Boris, came from that shtick which, as he said, he could start and stop almost at will.

I held out the bottle and said, "Aunt Tay died."

"You serious? Sorry, man!" He took a pull. "Sorry." He pushed the hair out of his eyes, said, "Shit, I'm seeing double," and collapsed again.

Over the years, Boris had found out nearly everything about me. But close as we were, and we were like brothers, cool as he was, and nothing shook him, I never explained my Shadow.

Right then, I couldn't even begin. Knowing they would be necessary, I stuck my sunglasses and the bottle in my pockets.

The next stop was softer and tougher. Seeing my expression, Sarah's housemother brought me into the front parlor. When I told her why I was there, she went upstairs. The Shadow sat beside me in the window seat. "Could you give me a few minutes?" I asked.

'She won't notice, Kevin. But if you want.' And he was gone.

Sarah was down in moments in her gray and rose robe, knotting an old towel in her wet hair. I never loved her more than at that moment. For the last couple of months, she had been a little distant, distracted, and I knew why. She put her hands on mine, felt them trembling. "Oh Kevin, she was such a sweet lady."

Sarah's house sisters came downstairs for breakfast, peered into the parlor. I got up mumbling about having to get into Boston. "Call me, Kevin. We'll be in for the service." Sensing my reaction to the word "we," she explained, "Boris and myself."

Not, thank God, Scott Callendar. He had appeared on the scene that fall. A big, blond guy a year or two older than the rest of us, he had dropped back into school to sidestep the draft. He lived off campus and hung out with motorcyclists. We had some mutual acquaintances. I met him first and was attracted.

But it was Sarah who fell. I had no rational complaint. By then I was using her as a comfortable refuge while I had a nice, sordid life elsewhere. "Call," said Sarah, hugging me as I left. "If there's anything you need."

My Shadow was at my elbow as I walked to the station. 'She likes you because you're cute and screwed up. But she naturally went wild for someone as handsome and demented as Scotso. I'll bet he's already knocked her up.'

Both my Shadow and I knew how much I was going to need him. So I kept silent. At that hour nobody much was around the campus. The streetcar, though, was full of commuters. We passed Stacey's old place. It looked deserted. Feeling utterly alone in the world, I put on my shades, got off at the next stop, and walked up to that familiar house.

Through the windows, I saw furniture covered with cloths. I went around to the back, found a porch, and sat on the stairs. The garden was overgrown, but flowers had started to bloom. Birds sang. A car door slammed a few houses down.

I took out the bottle and drank, a sip at first, then a swallow. 'Let me find you some more,' said my Shadow.

Alone, I thought of Aunt Tay. The last time I saw her, we talked about that poem she'd told me when I came back from New York. "What was it again?" I had asked, and she said:

> Just we three go sailing
> Me, Myself and I
> Over walls and fences
> Through the night we fly
>
> People half awaken
> Hear us pass and pray
> Out of fearing for our souls,
> Won't we rest and stay

And I said, "Gee, I thought I had problems and there are only two of me." Tay smiled then and so did I. That was the memory of her that I wanted to save.

FOUR

The August Sunday afternoon had gone without my noticing. I sat in the dark as Gould played the Goldberg Variations for the third time and thought of Tay, of Me, Myself and I, of the arc by which we return to ourselves. Then I remembered, jumped up, prepared my middle-aged face for the world, changed my shirt, grabbed a box of Italian pastry from the refrigerator.

Our Sunday night dinners are an old tradition. Addie and Lauren's place is a garden duplex up in Kips Bay. We ate on the lantern-lit patio, good food, half a dozen old friends. That night it seemed everyone was in a nostalgic mood.

My acquaintances, all slightly brittle careerists my age, had come to New York for school or their first jobs, and never left. They reminisced about their early days and I thought about that first desperate attempt in the city when I was sixteen.

But when the conversation came around to me, I edited that kid out in favor of a more conventional beginning. "I moved down here after MAS. A whole crew of us. Sarah Bryce Callendar and her husband. A guy named Boris and his girlfriend

Gina Raille, the actress. And along with me . . ." I realized I was about to mention my Shadow and paused. Across the table, Addie caught that and became alert. Over the years, she has found out more about my life than anyone. Instead I said, "All I had was clothes and graduation money, a radio, some books . . ."

"You didn't bring any toys?" someone asked laughing. I shook my head and smiled. Once again, the conversation passed me by. The wine and grass did too. No matter how often I turn down booze, it still gives me a tingle. And always I picture a figure in what could be a throne. His white hair framed by the silver light behind him, he sees me and asks, "How did you find me, my friend?" The image has become like a talisman rubbed smooth with use. Leo Dunn has been gone for over twenty years.

Most of my dinner companions probably attributed my being as out of it as I was to George's having just been taken off life supports. They were his friends as well as mine. But in this time of awful attrition, I was the one closest to him. Spouse, lover, relative, partner are all ephemeral ties, easily broken. In the age of AIDS only primary caregiver continues until death does us part.

At some point the other guests said goodnight, patted my hand, told me when they'd visit the hospice. Finally I sat in the ground-floor consulting room while Addie listened to her answering machine. Lauren massaged my neck. "Think about Christmas in Santa Fe," she murmured, generously including me in their plans. When her lover hung up, she said, "Talk to you during the week, Kevin."

Addie told her, "I'll be up in a little while." Then we two sat with the lights dim and the windows open on the backyard and midnight. There in the center of a block of five-story town houses, street noise was muted. A couple argued at an open window, a hundred air conditioners hummed, but Manhattan in August was quiet enough for us to hear a tug hoot on the East River, the rumble of a long freight train on the Queens shore.

For a few harmonious moments, we listened to each other breathe. Long ago, before she met Lauren, after I left George, there was Addie and me. One autumn we went everywhere: plays, leather bars, Hoboken, bed. In my relations with humans, that species whose Shadows don't speak to them, I specialize in six weeks of frenzy and a lifetime of exchanging casserole recipes.

Middle age helps reduce all our faces to professional expressions. Addie, for instance, radiates calm and compassion, a handsome priestess. I have the antique toy dealer's look of quizzical appraisal. But we knew each other before we had fully developed our masks.

"Let me show you what I found." Addie rose and I followed her into the blue room. She flicked a switch and a light came on over the sand table. Four feet square, three feet high, it stood in the middle of the floor. A construction was still intact.

Addie started taking it apart. I saw a hill molded in the fine, white sand, the sides embossed with seashells. Turrets and walls ringed the top. At its foot were a two-inch-tall bear dressed in a clown suit, a trio of jolly, fat Chinese men, a smiling lady rider on her circus horse.

My first take was that it was a happy scene. On second glance, I saw that the hill was armored: a closed, empty castle. And the figures all faced away from a small pit in the sand where the figurine of a little girl lay facedown. "The poor kid who built that," I said.

Addie nodded. "We made progress yesterday. I left this up so Laurie could photograph it." Addie is a psychiatrist. Children are her specialty, play therapy one of her tools. On white shelves, built at child's-eye level around the walls, sat miniature pagodas and stands of trees, African American wedding parties and elephant-headed gods, pirates and nurses, three-masted junks, Madonnas, yellow dump trucks, lambs, chariots, anything kids might need to recreate their interior landscapes on the sand table.

I'd helped her find a lot of these items. It's what had brought us together. We had both found jobs that let us play with toys. "See what's new?" she asked. I heard a collector's pride in her voice.

The streetcar stood, green and boxy, trolley up, between Saint Francis with birds on his shoulders and a family of giraffes. The color was wrong and the shape, but it made me jump. "You're uncanny! It's so long ago that I told you about the dreams. And I had one last night for the first time in years." She gave a smug smile as if this were an elementary trick of her trade.

When I was little, my mother and I lived in an apartment building near a trolley barn. I loved the cars, the old square orange ones, the new cigar-shaped model. I liked seeing them lined up in the yards, watching the sparks on the wires in the dark, hearing the rattle of the change box. I'd fall asleep to the clatter and scrape of wheels as the cars turned the corner toward the terminal. Streetcars had worked their way into my dreams. All this Addie and I had discussed over the years.

Now I rolled the car on the sand and said, "Last night for the first time in years I had the dream about the boy on the streetcar." Addie knew who he was. She was the one person to whom I had told everything. It all came out. "A couple of days ago, Gina Raille, who I've known since school. Remember we saw her in that Cole Porter revival? She asked me if I had an evil twin I'd never told her about. She said there's a guy who looks like me except in really tough shape hanging around the theater district."

I told her about Klackman and the merry-go-round and Matt. "Today, after the dream, my Shadow's path crossed mine. He wants to talk. He's very sick. It looks like AIDS."

"Oh, Kevin!" For a moment, I thought Addie was going to whip out a thermometer and take my temperature. Instead, she hugged me. None of this, not even my Shadow, had come up in a long time. She had always taken it well, though in psychiatry a belief in a double is the kind of thing that turns up in schizoids dying of cancer. "This is part of your dealing with all that's happened to George."

She's smarter than anyone I've met and able to set aside a lot of preconceptions. But, in the end, she wanted to think I was hallucinating. And I'm a friend, not a client. I was imposing. "Could be," I said, rising. "It's late. Sorry."

"It is absolutely nothing to be sorry about," she said as best friends do. When we kissed on her front stairs, huge apartment towers across the way made me feel like we were miniatures on her sand table. "Call me tomorrow, Kevin. Promise?" And she didn't let go until I did.

The way down from Murray Hill to Stuyvesant Park is less than twenty blocks. Mostly it's a gentle slope kind of like the path from youth to middle age. Instead of taking a cab, I walked.

The big Korean supermarket near Twentieth Street was full of police cadets just out of night class and stocking up on junk food. The uniforms made most of them, male and female, look boxy and sexless. One Hispanic guy, though, was tautly hand-some. He caught me looking his way and nodded with satisfaction and contempt.

A bunch of club boys were buying beer and cigarettes. Like rival tribes, they and the cadets eyed each other warily. I thought of high school corridors. For an instant, I saw Matt's earring and profile, glanced again, and saw it wasn't him. As I

bought a quart of skimmed milk, I watched the kid with the earring and the Spanish cadet lock gazes.

Stuyvesant Park, when I came home, was empty, gates locked
for the night, trees motionless by lamplight. On my answering
machine was a message. "Grierson. This is Sandler. I want to
talk to you about the Dolbier Collection." Edwin Sandler is a re-
markably wealthy toy collector. Dolbier's antique toy soldiers,
estimated at a million-plus dollars, were going up for auction in
New York the next day.

The voice after Sandler's was that of Miranda, my godchild.
"Uncle Kevin, I wish mostly for a doll with different dresses."
She would be six in a few days and had just mastered long dis-
tance. Her requests changed almost hourly.

Listening, waiting, I got into some pull-ons. The last message
was muffled, half lost, made from a street pay phone. "Fred?"
A long pause. Then Matt said, "Hey, Fred!" as if he'd just caught
sight of me. My Shadow always manages these chilling effects.

At the beginning of our second try at New York, he had
stayed deep in the background. Sarah was the first of my
friends to find a job. It was at Macy's. She even found one for
me at Darlington's Department Store. She and Scott got married that June and the baby was born five months later. Scott
stayed home with the kid.

Boris and I roomed together on St. Mark's Place just like
college. One day he said, "I gotta cool my brains a little, man.
Gina and I are heading to the West Coast. Want to come
along?" My Shadow told me to say no.

East Village apartments were cheap, entry-level jobs were
plentiful, all drugs from acid to speed abounded. The legal
drinking age was eighteen. That first year in the city, I still got
asked for proof.

Every time I showed my draft card I remembered Uncle Jim
banging my head against the fence on that cold afternoon. Se-

lective Service sent me a lot of letters. I'd tear them up un-opened. Each day my Shadow ran my life a little more.

Then, one Monday morning early in 1967, I stared at a glassy-eyed disaster in my mirror. A lump behind my ear was painful to the touch. It was eight-thirty and I wasn't dressed. 'Hey,' said my doppelganger, 'the choirboy from hell.'

He wore the very same neo-Edwardian suit and wide tie I'd worn on Friday night when I told him to stay away from me. 'The rent is two months overdue and you're very late for work,' he said. 'You don't have the nerve for a life in advertising or crime. So it's up to me to save our asses.'

As I watched, he gargled mouthwash, ran his hands through his hair, and wiped a trace of methedrine off his nose. We still didn't need to shave every day and at first glance he wouldn't look like someone who had slept in his clothes.

Over the last year and a half I'd gotten used to him whis-pering directions in my ear but out of sight. Nobody else seemed to spot him. It seemed he was under control. Now, sud-denly, he was trying to take my place.

As I moved to block his way, he pulled on my overcoat and asked, 'No word from the draft board?' The reminder paralyzed me. This revolution was well planned.

Long before I was taught to think of him as my Silent Part-ner, I knew what my Shadow was. So did he. 'I am all your bad habits,' he said, walking out the door. 'And you are mine. Get some rest.'

He had seen to it that I was medicated the night before. So though there had been a coup, I was relieved to crawl back into my dark cave of a bedroom. To lull myself, I invoked a memory of a laughing baby held up against the sky. It was a kind of magic charm as I rolled between sleep and waking, catching glimpses of the world through my Shadow's eyes.

Miraculously, he got onto the subway with a *New York*

Times in his hand. Had he paid? I watched him scan the pages. My stuff appeared in the daily papers.

He found something I'd had a hand in writing. It wound like haiku past elongated drawings of an ultramod young couple:

> FASHION KICKS
> AS 1966
> WELCOMES '67
> AT DARLINGTON'S
> . . . BUT YOU KNEW THAT!

By dark magic and luck, my Shadow got up to Herald Square before nine. Fresh-faced, bleary-eyed employees flowed out of the subway into Macy's, into Gimbels. He cut his way west against the tide from Penn Station, past porters loading the last turrets of Santa's castle onto a truck.

My view now, I realized, was the one he'd had when he lurked inside me. As he must have seen me do, my Shadow turned and passed under a sign:

> ON THE CORNER
> OF SEVENTH AVENUE
> AND THE WORLD
> DARLINGTON'S . . .
> BUT YOU KNEW THAT!

Inside the employee's entrance, a guy yelled, "Watch it, bub!" Technicolor stripes enveloped my Shadow. Black and red, blue and white, purple and gold, a psychedelic zebra herd. In a lyric flight tempered by a strict character count, I had written about these very miniskirts:

> ABOVE THE KNEE!
> BEYOND FASHION LAW!

Dodging moving racks, my Shadow stepped onto an elevator. A trio of salesladies practiced looking right through him as they got off on three. Assistant men's suit buyers walked off on six, talking basketball. Ten was Advertising and Promotion. My Shadow arrived there at the stroke of nine and I could not have managed that.

In New York it was winter, but up on ten it was spring. Easter promotion artwork was stacked in the reception area, along the halls. Umbrella-sized cardboard flowers, colored eggs that must have been laid by the roc were everywhere. But no people: the place was deserted, eerie.

In the copywriters' office, the phone on my desk rang. As my Shadow moved to answer it, a meeting broke up in the conference room. Then it occurred to me that this afternoon was the spring fashion presentation, a big deal with all the buyers attending. Everyone in Advertising was supposed to have shown up at eight in the morning with a bunch of punchy copy ideas. I had missed the meeting, had in fact no punchy ideas. I was doomed.

The phone rang again and my Shadow slipped out of my overcoat, grabbed the receiver, and said aloud, "Darlington's. Fashion copy. Kevin Grierson."

"Copy!" a man yelled. "I'll give you copy!" It was Wiggy Glickman, the Misses and Juniors blouse buyer, a middle-aged fanatic. "LODEN! I'm reading LODEN!"

The conference room door opened and everybody, copywriters, artists, stylists, began filing out. Some stared with curiosity and not a little malice.

"In the *Daily News* yesterday," Wiggy screamed, " 'Lovely flare-sleeved elegance in pearl, turquoise, ocean, ebony, and LODEN.' That was you left that in the copy?"

It was me. "Not really," said my Shadow very calmly.

"SCHMUCK! I told you. Loden is something guys wear when they're out in the woods. Ladies wear jade. JADE!"

Les Steibler, the art director, elegant, balding, all smiles and showbiz, came out of the meeting, caught sight of what he took to be me, and rolled his eyes in dismay. 'Good old Les here will help us,' my Shadow murmured and turned toward him with the look of a lost waif.

Glancing back to make sure that Jackie Maye, our boss, wasn't watching, Les gave brisk orders. "Randy, for one last time, a change of clothes for Baby Face Nelson here. We know his sizes all too well. Tell Barbara we need a complete make-over. Connie, could you make sure the studio isn't in use? Go Kevin."

Connie was the production assistant, the lowliest of the low. For my first six months of employment in New York, that had been my job. Tiny, cute, she led my Shadow to the studio at the other end of the floor. In the shooting area stood a dozen naked manikins, pink and faceless, arms akimbo. 'Luv Dolls,' my Shadow whispered and laughed when he felt me cringe at a certain memory.

Makeovers were a specialty of Advertising and Promotion. I had availed myself of them more than once. My Shadow knew the routine. The changing room had a shower. He undid his tie, unbuttoned his shirt, kicked off his shoes.

"Jackie Maye was furious that you weren't at the meeting," Connie was happy to say. She was after my job. "Jackie told me to work up an accessories presentation. But Les made excuses, said he was sure you'd come across with great copy ideas."

"Yeah, I was up till four last night working on them," said my Shadow and started to drop his pants as Connie handed him a towel and retreated.

"Disaster! We haven't got anything to show," I whined. "I'm going to be fired."

Undressed, my Shadow pulled a small package out of a jacket pocket, snorted some crystal meth, and put it away again.

Amused, he turned on the water. 'Poor little Kevin went all to pieces at a party. Remember?'

Suddenly, I did. That Friday night, I had wound up in a loft on a deserted street near Madison Square. The decor was black and white. Flickering lights gave everything a silent-film effect as the Garment District and Max's Kansas City, the world of fashion and the Warhol Factory, linked.

"They rounded up the usual crew of perverts," a thin guy in a flashy suit remarked. He seemed to be someone I knew. With no idea of what he was talking about, but aware that he was the current source of the speed, I smiled.

"Mr. Accessory-Before-the-Fact, that's me," the man in the flashy suit had said. "Yeah! Guilty as charged." He too was ripped. Something about his nose and eyes gave him the look of a falcon. All I was certain of in the world was that I had been drinking and snorting since lunch. Speed swam underneath the thin ice of gin. "Let's go see the Luv Dolls, Kev."

Then we were somewhere else, maybe an upstairs annex of that same party, maybe a totally different scene. Mr. Accessory-Before-the-Fact spoke to a guy on a landing, slipped him bills. We went through a couple of smokey places and into a hall. Halfway down, I peeked into a gauzily lighted room.

Inside, on a mattress, I saw slim legs, firm breasts, a fan of long black hair, a kid sixteen, maybe fifteen, with eyes so blown that light seemed to shine through to the back of her head. I was wired enough to get turned on.

Then the Luv Doll's gaze, empty as a manikin's, transfixed me. Suddenly I remembered Scarface and my first time in New York. This kid from, maybe, Ohio was getting passed around, with no place to rest and her body her only possession. Maybe she got told about a party and found she was the party. Maybe she had an old man who was acting as her pimp. Waking up tomorrow was not going to be nice.

Behind me, Mr. Accessory asked, "You like this one?" He and the room were as distant as the view through the wrong end of binoculars. I was in a remote, calm point. The scene revolted me. I turned to go.

'Oh, oh, Fred is in the eye of the storm,' said my Shadow, smiling, blocking my way.

Mr. Accessory did a goggle-eyed double take. "You have a twin brother, Kevin?" he asked my Shadow.

Before my clear, icy sobriety faded, I told the doppelganger, "Stay away from me," and headed for the stairs.

'See you soon Fred.' He didn't disappear.

Monday morning at Darlington's, fashion stylists and junior artists popped into the fitting room bright as elves. My Shadow emerged from the shower wrapped in a towel and asked teasingly, "Could I get some privacy?"

"No!" They clustered around, fascinated by this usurper as they never seemed to be by me. "How are you feeling, Kev?"

Les appeared, carrying a folder. "Are you feeling, Kevin?" He moved his hand in front of my Shadow's eyes to see if they tracked.

"Jockies and sockies, Kev. Nobody in second-day undies can look another person in the eye," someone said.

As he slipped into clothes, ran an electric razor over his face, people handed my Shadow Alka-Seltzer and Binaca, deodorant and talc. "Powder them buns!"

"Drops to take the red out of the eyes."

"But nothing on earth will get rid of the glaze."

"I want to see him in this striped Carnaby Street shirt."

"I'd love to see him in just black dress shoes and a bow tie."

"For surprisingly little cash up front, I'm sure that can be arranged," Les said. "Okay. Everyone back to work."

When the two of them were alone, he handed my Shadow a

folder. "This artwork I did for your accessories presentation? You left it on your desk over the weekend, didn't you? We were supposed to get together Saturday, remember?" Worse than mad, he sounded hurt. "I must have called you a dozen times."

'What is he, your wife?' my Shadow wondered. But once again he gave the lost-waif look. At home, I squirmed at the cheap ploy. Worse, it didn't work anymore.

"Get your coat," Les said as he turned and walked away. "There's an outdoor shoot. It was arranged that you go as my assistant instead of Connie. Mainly to keep you out of Jackie Maye's sight."

I was in despair. But my Shadow shot his cuffs and murmured, 'See the trouble I have to get you out of?'

When he went to my desk for the overcoat, Connie was working on an accessories layout. "Kevin," she said. "Message from Sarah. Lunch at twelve-thirty at Schlep's."

My fellow junior copywriters were amused. Sure that I was going to fall flat on my face, each of them was also doubtless working on accessories presentations. "Does Les know about Sarah?" asked one.

"Does Macy's tell Gimbels?"

"A ménage for every taste."

"At Darlington's . . ."

"But you knew that!" they chorused. Suddenly, everyone was very busy. My Shadow turned and faced Jackie Maye directly for the first time.

Almost six feet tall, a kind of goddess, Jackie had modeled for Chanel back before the war. She used an ivory cigarette holder and wore a hat in the office as if at any moment she might have to fly off to a fashion show. Twenty years before, she had coined the slogan, "At Darlington's . . . but you knew that." Les had told me the whole story, how it became a tag line, something that Milton Berle would say when a second banana asked where he got his dresses and picture hats.

Jackie's off-center smile could enchant and it was on full force for the pair of Italian designers who were with her. It faded slightly when she saw my Shadow. With the absolute courage that comes with being ripped, he stepped forward and made the gesture of handing her the folder containing Les's sketches as if it were his presentation.

My heart jumped. There wasn't a word of copy in there. But, just as he had gambled she would, Jackie Maye walked past him remarking, "Meshuganah!" For the benefit of her guests, she translated that from the Yiddish as "eccentric creative staff."

Amused, my Shadow told me, 'You got to keep them guessing,' as he headed for the elevators. Les awaited him, wearing a handsome topcoat and an unusually serious expression. 'This,' murmured my Shadow, 'is going to be painful.' Instead of taking an elevator, Les walked downstairs to the selling floors.

Nine was Linens, cloud banks of sheets, blue fields of bath mats, the scent of cedar chests. My Shadow gave a bored sigh as they went to the escalator. "We do this to see which of our ads are selling merchandise," Les explained, still trying to teach me the business.

'Les Steibler, the Rembrandt of ready-mades, Picasso of the Paris knockoff,' my Shadow said to me. 'He's been here so long, he really cares about this crap.'

They floated down through the post-Christmas aroma of stale candy canes in Children's and Toys, the leather and aftershave of Men's Wear, a mélange of fragrances from sachet to Chanel from the tailored Lady Shoppe, the Bridal Boutique, Lingerie, Misses and Juniors. "I know you don't make much now, Kevin. No one does at first. But you can in a few years."

'Yuck,' said my Shadow to me. 'Homilies from wise Auntie Les.'

That soon after the holidays, shoppers were few and feral. Salespeople called back and forth to each other as they arranged their shelves, an occasional bell bonged to summon a buyer, a porter, or security.

As they made the majestic thirty-foot descent to the main floor, Les said, "Saturday night, I spotted you over on Fifty-third and Third." At home, I tensed. "You were too far gone to notice me. I tell you this because I care about you. I'm a hardened New Yorker, but what I saw was disturbing."

My Shadow hung his head in what might have been shame. 'The cheap voyeur,' he whispered. 'What was he doing in that neighborhood except cruising for street trade?'

Their way out of Darlington's lay past slender gold pillars hung with jewelry, past tables on which marched serried ranks of single high heels. Les said, "You need some kind of help, Kevin."

With the bright insincerity that ends all conversation, my Shadow said, "I think you're right."

Les shrugged and said, "Well, I tried," and was silent on the short cab hop over to Sixth Avenue and Twenty-seventh Street.

Wiggy Glickman was already waiting at the curb. The moment he saw Les, he set up a wail: "PLEATS, Steibler. Fifty thousand blouses we got coming in. All with pleated fronts. The treatment today has got to be flowing, feminine, flattering."

"Ten in the morning and he's worried about pleats!"

"The artwork I've seen is like men's dress shirts worn by the Beatles. The models look like your friend here," he said, gesturing at my Shadow. "A nice boy, I'm sure."

My Shadow said quite clearly, "Tell the old pervert to buzz off."

"What are you on?" Les asked quietly. "Just so I can avoid it." Then aloud, "Wigs! Such poetry! Flowing, feminine flattery! Plus a set of knockers that'll give you a heart attack."

My Shadow muttered, 'Where does Les get off being self-righteous? He's peddling his ass hard right now.'

We were in the heart of the Flower District, blocks lined with wholesale florists. One of them had contracted to set up potted trees and hothouse blossoms on the sidewalk in front of his shop.

It wasn't frigid. But it was January and they were shooting spring fashions. Truck drivers honked and whistled at girls with goosebumps and blouses pinned up to emphasize the flowing, feminine pleats.

Even the plants shivered. To commemorate the vernal theme, a lamb had been hired. Between shots, its handler wrapped the animal in a wool blanket. A young lady with the face of an angel was supposed to hold it on a leash. She sneezed and exclaimed, "I'm allergic to that gawddamn sheep."

"Kevin! Kleenex!" Les yelled.

"This is a prize-winning Exmoor lamb," the handler snapped.

My Shadow was kept busy, which made him sullen. In a free moment he went into the store's rest room and snorted some more speed. When he got back, they were breaking for lunch. The florist was yelling because the lamb had eaten a fern. "Whose idea was the Extra More Sheep?" Wigs wanted to know.

"Kevin's," said Les. And it was certain that I couldn't rely on his protection anymore.

That's when my Shadow remembered his date with Sarah. He was flat broke. "Can I borrow two dollars?" he asked Les.

Handing it over without even looking his way, Les said, "Your usual fee, no doubt?"

My Shadow crossed Seventh against the lights in the midst of a fast-moving convoy of racks laden with women's coats. I told him, "You're wrecking my life."

'Me! Remember the dead drill sergeant Monday morning?'

. . .

Like a reflex, the lump behind my ear throbbed and I recalled the gray dawn light, an unfamiliar room, a guy in khaki sprawled motionless on the bed. All I knew was that Saturday night he had made a very bad mistake with me.

Memory of my path to that room was sketchy. Waking up on Saturday afternoon after the incident with the Luv Doll, I had used cheap vodka and tap water to nurse a gruesome hangover. The clear rational state I had known briefly the night before had passed. I was broke and my speed edge from the party had turned into black depression. My Shadow's absence felt more like an amputation than a release.

The only mail was a couple of very overdue bills. Nothing from the draft board. The phone rang a few times. I would have loved it to be Boris calling to say he was back in town. Sarah inviting me over. But there were so many calls I didn't want to get that each time I hesitated until the ringing stopped.

Then it seemed I could stay inside no longer. Without speed I couldn't do my presentation. Preparing to go out, I searched for the gravity knife, but couldn't find it.

The next thing I remembered happened a bit later on Third Avenue up in the Fifties, where I went a lot when drunk and broke. A voice called, "Fred!" He was a big, bald guy with a mustache. I didn't recognize him. But if he knew that name, we had done business in the past.

In my Upper East Side riff, I was Fred, on the run from high school troubles and a brutal stepfather who was going to put me in a military academy. It was a tale that could move me to tears. When I first came to New York, I had worked it for all it was worth. But time and poison took their toll. I noticed that bars didn't much ask me for proof of age anymore.

A blank period followed his picking me up. Then deep in the night, I emerged from an ambulatory blackout to find myself naked in a white tiled room. A shower ran. In the steam, a big, bald guy I couldn't remember, a stranger in khaki, poked my chest and shouted, "You're gonna get some military discipline, boy."

It was like he had pulled a trigger. This was the Y and St. Sebastian's all in one. My personal nightmare wasn't the Vietcong, it was being murdered in basic-training barracks. I threw myself on him. He yelled, "Fucking street trash!" and slammed my head against the door. Everything went red and all sound was an echo as I went for his throat.

Early Sunday morning, I came to, facedown on a thick carpet. The shower still ran in the bathroom. A shiver that turned into a convulsion passed through me. All of me hurt when I started to get up. But it was the back of my head that throbbed so much that my eyes watered.

When I finally managed to focus, I saw the bed. On it, all akimbo and dead still, was a big guy dressed in khaki. There were bruises on his neck. His head was at a weird angle. He must have decided to run a fantasy called drill sergeant and hippy recruit. Perhaps he had even tried to explain that to me.

Had I left fingerprints? Had anyone seen me? My clothes were on a chair. My head spun as I dressed. Something in the room moved. Another shiver seized me. When I looked, two eyes, red, startled, stared back, "Oh no!" He sounded scared. "Take what you want. But please, go!"

Monday, lying in my bedroom, I tried to block that memory with the image of a child laughing against an overcast sky. 'We're lucky I hid the knife,' my Shadow said. 'And lucky that I didn't really go away this time. I was what saved you from getting your face kicked in by that guy. You're a menace to yourself and others. We need another racket.'

With that, he stepped into the roar of Shactman's Kosher Dairy. By legend, the restaurant had started as a hole in the wall serving lowly schleppers, haulers of goods. Thus the nickname Schlep's.

Two generations later, it offered high and low, Jew and goy, generous portions and the rudest service in the Garment District. The place was a maze of alcoves.

Sarah Callendar wasn't hard to spot. In the dead of winter, her skin and hair seemed magically touched with the sun. Others noticed her too. In that neighborhood their attention was as much on the white and navy A-line Courreges knockoff she wore as on her looks.

As a fashion coordinator at Macy's she was several steps higher up the ladder than I was. We shared, though, the feeling of being undercover agents, spies from downtown. Besides, my claims on her predated husband and child. 'After all,' my Shadow whispered, 'you filled both those roles before they showed up.'

When she and he hugged, Sarah looked puzzled. She knew something was wrong, that this wasn't me. But as bright as she was, all her training at home had been in the art of ignoring scary truths. She was expert at it. I hated seeing my Shadow use that in exactly the same way I had.

"I thought we were going to look at your presentation this weekend." The anger and concern in her voice pleased me. Only one who still loves you can feel both those things at the same time. Les, for example, no longer felt concern about me.

"Hey, I saw the two Scotts out for a walk, Sunday," said my Shadow to change the subject.

It worked. At the mention of her kid, Sarah brightened immediately. "I wanted you to see. Yesterday, Scotty took six steps before he realized what he was doing and sat down."

I felt a deep twinge at missing that. She paused like there was something she wanted to talk about. But since she avoided mentioning trouble and since life with Scott Callendar Sr. was mostly about trouble, we never discussed him.

Just then, the waitress appeared. "This the one you were

waiting for, sweetie?" she asked with disbelief. "What will it be, mister?"

My Shadow's stomach and mine both lurched at the thought of food. Schlep's, of course, served no booze, doubtless one reason Sarah wanted to meet there. He managed to order tea and cheesecake. She produced an envelope. "I had some ideas for you."

"Thanks. Here's some of what I have." He spread Les's mockups of shoe, belt, hose, handbag, hat, jewelry ads, like they were his own.

Speed had put a tiny tremor in his hands and mine. Sarah simply didn't see that. "What's your theme?" she asked.

My Shadow gave her an idea that I had worked on the night before:

ACCESSORIES
AFTER THE FACT
ABOVE THE LAW

As soon as he read it aloud, he and Sarah shook their heads. She held up a pair of her own sketches, one of a Victorian lady encased in clothes. The other was a lithe young woman in a miniskirt. "The idea is that fashion used to be something permanent, leaden, immobile, unfun."

"Then came the revolution!" said my Shadow.

ACCESSORIES COUP D'ETAT
LIBERATING THE INNER YOU

It amused him that the talk about coups and the triumph of the inner self made me squirm.

"What are you going to say about belts?" she asked. All that I had thought of was:

A SOLID BELT

That line evoked for me a double shot of bourbon and my mouth watered. When I concentrated on Sarah and my Shadow again, they had a mock-up of an ad with the headline in the shape of an *s*.

"Something like, 'Sauve, sensuous,' " he said.

"Lithe," she said, "Gliding like a snake."

At its best, copywriting could be as amusing as a game. Her tuna salad and his cheesecake were delivered and eaten absentmindedly. They sat with their heads side by side. One of Sarah's sketches for hats had a very familiar face in it.

My Shadow saw it too. "Sketch in a cigarette holder," he said. "The headline is, 'THE HAT CAME BACK!' "

She said, " 'LIKE MOTHER SWORE IT WOULD!' "

" 'AT DARLINGTON'S! . . . BUT YOU KNEW THAT!' " said my Shadow. "We need one more line."

Suddenly, a familiar voice asked, "What's a nice Irish boy doing in a place like this?" The tall thin man with the nose and eyes of a falcon. Mr. Accessory from the Friday-night party stared at Sarah while asking me, "You're keeping that offer in mind?"

My Shadow smiled and nodded. Mr. Accessory turned away saying, "See you at the presentation."

Sarah looked at his back with distaste, and asked, "Who was that sleaze?"

"Stephens," said my Shadow and I remembered the name too. "The hottest buyer at Darlington's. Big man in leather." Before she could ask what offer Stephens was talking about, my Shadow said, "We need to get back to work."

Besides, he needed to go take more meth. I knew that, maybe Sarah did too. "Give my regards to the Scotts," said my Shadow when the two of them kissed and parted. On his way back to the office, he said, 'It's too bad that in return for all her love and understanding, we betray her the way you did yesterday.' And I remembered Sunday afternoon.

My head had rung right along with the church bells. I was over on Avenue B. Spanish families walked home from St. Brigid's Church. In my pockets were bills scooped off the drill sergeant's dresser and a pint of Smirnoff's vodka bought out the backdoor of Old Stanley's.

My nerves twitched, but my brain was still numb from the slam to my head the night before. With chemical energy, I told myself, it would be easy to do my presentation. But the dealers, it seemed, had all gone to spend Sunday with their mothers. Then a familiar voice called, "Hey, Grierson! Kevin!"

Turning, I saw a big, handsome blond guy pushing this beautiful baby in a stroller: Scott Callendar, father and son.

The father's looks were the first part of what Sarah and I had seen. And he could generate a lot of excitement. Scott had turned out to be a kind of preppy hood. He liked to ride other people's motorcycles and couldn't hold a job. His appetite for booze and drugs amazed even me.

But the son! I had never really been around a baby. I crouched down face-to-face with him and he smiled. I would have loved to see him walk for the first time, just so some little piece of that weekend could have been soft. The kid touched my face and gurgled. The father asked, "You looking?"

Like I didn't want the kid to see me say it, I stood up. My mouth didn't work very well. "Yeah."

Then he said, "Twenty-five bucks for a spoon and I'll take a third." Scott Callendar was also a thief. Desperate, I nodded yes. Foggily, I thought I would mind the kid and he would make the run.

Before I could make that into words, he asked his son,

"Scotso want to take a ride?" The kid clapped his hands. As Scott turned the stroller, I remembered it was an article of faith on the street that cops would not bust anybody who had a kid with him. Knowing Scotty should not be touched by this, I still went along.

It was a damp chill day and overcast. Scott turned down a tenement block. Ahead of us, a skinny guy with long, lank hair went into a building. Scott lifted the stroller onto the stoop.

Finally, I managed to speak. "Man, this is not cool." Scott looked questioningly. "I'm staying down here with the kid."

As soon as his father disappeared inside, Scotty looked around and started to cry. As I crouched down to him, a woman, Polish or Ukrainian, wearing a babushka and overcoat like it was cold in her apartment, stuck her head out the ground-floor window. She looked at Scotty, then stared at me like I was dirt. "Maybe he's wet or something," I suggested.

"He wants to be held." She had a voice like doom. "Pick him up. What kind of a father?" Then she ducked back inside. She was right. When I picked him up, Scotty stopped crying. But he stared at me, wide-eyed, ready for a howl.

"Here. This." The woman gestured us closer. With the fingers of one hand, she broke a lump of sugar, reached out the window, and put a piece on the kid's tongue. The sweetness calmed him. I held Scotty up in the air, against the gray sky, and he looked down on me and smiled.

At that moment, I felt the most intense love. Suddenly, it seemed a simple thing to walk away from my tangled life. Before his father came back, I would take Scotty away, call Sarah and ask her to meet us somewhere. I'd tell her the awful thing that her husband had just done. Of course, I'd have to tell her my own lousy part in it. But at least it would be the truth. I had the stroller down on the sidewalk when Scott Sr. reappeared.

'But,' said my Shadow, amused at my stupidity, 'once he

waved the speed, you handed the kid right back to him.' He was doing pasteups, working fast. 'Nice intentions burn away when you got a habit like ours.'

The presentations were given in the conference room. Each copywriter stood up in turn before Jackie, Les, and the merchandise buyers involved, showed their ads, and read their copy. Afterwards, the audience offered comments. That afternoon, artwork, pictures of miniskirts, silver boots, striped bell-bottoms with fringed cuffs, got hauled into the room and carted back out.

Accessories came last. As my Shadow rose, Mr. Stephens walked past with a half wink. 'The fix,' said my Shadow, 'is on. But you've put us on such shaky ground that only that and luck can save us.' He strode in front of the audience, strung taut as a wire on the last of the meth. He set up his boards on a display easel, looked around the room, and said:

> DARLINGTON'S AND YOU,
> ACCESSORIES BEFORE THE FACT
> . . . AND AFTERWARDS

It was hard to tell how this was going over. Jackie Maye sat to one side of my Shadow. Les looked right through him. Mr. Stephens had a smile so bright it was radioactive. Jewelry came first. At one point my Shadow said:

> A FASHION COUP D'ETAT
> UNLEASHES THE INNER YOU

Old Jess Gambelian the jewelry buyer seemed to like that. At any rate he woke up and nodded, though English was not his first language, probably not even in the first five. Hosiery, handbags, scarves, shoes all got dealt with. Every trick we knew, my Shadow used. As part of the belt promotion there was the snakelike shape that read:

SO SMOOTH
&
L
I
T
H
E
SO SLEEK
&
S
U
A
V
IT'S SUEDE

He delivered the lines with a hiss. Jackie's eyes gleamed, amused either by the act or at the fool he was making of himself. Mr. Stephens, whose department included belts, nodded approval.

Hats were last. My Shadow put his final art up on the easel. This was a gamble: Sarah's sketch of the woman in the hat with the cigarette holder was a good-natured caricature of Jackie Maye herself. The copy read:

THE HAT CAME BACK!
LIKE MOTHER SAID IT WOULD!
AT DARLINGTON'S . . . BUT YOU KNEW THAT!

People understood, looked toward Jackie to see if she found it amusing. My Shadow paused and delivered the punch line:

EVEN UNCLE MILTY KNEW THAT!

Finally, people chuckled. That was the finale. Jackie looked Les's way. He grimaced. "Amusing, I guess. But what's he selling?" It was clear to all that Les had written me off.

There was a moment's pause when everything hung in the balance. Then, Mr. Stephens spoke. "Great! Punchy copy! Nice look to the handbag and belt pages!"

He turned to the other buyers. A couple of them shrugged. It was a presentation like a thousand others. But Jesse Gambelian suddenly awoke again and said in his unique accent, "Good. Good! I like the Cadillac tie-in. Darlington's is a Cadillac store."

Even my Shadow seemed baffled. "You said, 'A fashion Coupe de Ville,'" Gambelian explained. "You gotta work the car into the art, though." My Shadow nodded vigorously and made a note.

It was well after five. The other buyers were willing to go along with Stephens's opinion. People began to leave. My Shadow picked up the artwork and started to follow them. "Hold it a minute, Mr. Grierson." And he was alone in the room with Jackie Maye.

She gestured for him to put up the last sketch again. While fitting a cigarette in her holder, she looked first at the caricature and then at him. When she spoke, her words flowed out on a cloud of smoke. "Your presentation was light on substance, but the buyers seemed to okay the format. For whatever reasons. And in this business, the client is always right."

Barnard and Brooklyn mingled in her voice. "You've been around here long enough to know what chutzpa is?" He nodded and she said, "Well, I have had precisely enough of yours. Come in here one more time like you did this morning and you're out on your ass." She indicated the sketch. "Change the art. Nobody outside the business knows me. It's too inside a joke. But keep that Milton Berle reference. Goodnight."

We had held the job. I was dizzy with relief. Advertising and Promotion was almost deserted as my Shadow walked out. Down the hall, someone working late typed briskly. Mr. Stephens, aka Mr. Accessory, waited at the elevator. "Give you a lift?"

While the two of them caught a cab downtown, I was back at the apartment full of plans for my recovery. I wouldn't use drugs. Or booze. I'd be at work at quarter of nine. I'd apologize to Les with tears in my eyes. "You thought over the deal we talked about?" Mr. Accessory asked my Shadow.

"Yeah," said my Shadow. "I need to supplement my pay-check. I'd like to take my share in product. In fact, I could use some tonight." Mr. Accessory nodded.

"What deal?" I wanted to know.

'We have speed connections up in Boston,' my Shadow told me. 'He's got the money and friends around the country. We can do the transporting.'

"I could get busted!"

'Very unlikely. In a suit we still look respectable.'

Mr. Accessory was saying, "You could walk through any airport in the world with your bags crammed full of speed. And everyone will think you're a nice kid visiting his family."

My Shadow smiled and said, "A guy from a nice family would have matching Louis Vuitton bags." As his new partner thought that over, my Silent Partner told me, 'If worst comes to worst, Scott Callendar can unload those along with some of the speed.'

As the cab barreled nearer, I told my Shadow, "Stay away from me. This time I mean it." I heard him chuckle like it was a joke. My telling him to get lost had no effect this time, because, as we both knew, there was no truth in it.

The same thing had happened Sunday night when he came back and took control of both our lives. After I had left the two

Scotts, I spent that afternoon and evening snorting speed, drinking beer as I wandered my apartment in a frantic haze trying to get my mind fastened on ad copy. The place was strewn with scraps of paper on which were scrawled stuff like:

DARLINGTON'S AND YOU
ACCESSORIES
AFTER THE FACT

When the drugs ran out, memories of the Luv Doll and the dead drill sergeant bobbed around in my head. Only little Scotty laughing against the sky didn't make me wince. I held on to that magic image.

But just before dawn, not even that worked. I had no conscious memory of asking him to come back and save me. But when, deep in the night, the doorbell rang, I knew who it had to be and buzzed my Shadow up. He seemed amused when he appeared. 'I got something to make you relax.' It was heroin. I shied away.

'Cool out, man.' His tone was soft, coaxing. 'The worse the addiction, the surer the cure. There are more guys walking around who have shed drug habits than ones who have stopped biting their nails.' The next thing I knew, it was Monday morning and he was going to work in my place.

Monday evening, from my bedroom, I heard the apartment door open. "I can make the first run this week if you want," my Shadow said. He turned the radio to a rock station. A bunch of English saps sang about Winchester Cathedral. He said, "Let me get changed."

My Shadow came into the room as I pulled on jeans and a sweatshirt. "Disappear," I whispered. "Out of my life. And take Mr. Accessory with you." It was bullshit. He ignored me.

In his hands were opened letters. 'You want to be Kevin Grierson? Good. Here's a notice from the landlord. But don't worry, you won't need an apartment. Or a job. Here.' His tremor made the paper rattle. 'Nine tomorrow morning, preinduction physical at Whitehall Street. Followed by a bus ride to Fort Dix. Bring a toothbrush. Decide where you want them to mail your civilian clothes.'

The news froze me. 'You'll be too scared to resist. And this time you really will end up dead, in jail or in a padded cell. By this time tomorrow. . . ." He ruffled my hair like he was clipping it, then walked over and sank down on the bed.

He said, 'You're dumb enough to deserve all that. But it would be the end of both of us. I can take care of tomorrow. Like I did today. But it's not true that evil never sleeps. Right now, I need a rest. Make yourself useful. Go talk to our friend about his plans.'

Before I could reply, Mr. Accessory called, "Hey Kev, want a hit?"

Yes, I did. As I left the room, the voice behind me whispered, 'It will take more than babies in the sky to untangle us, Kevin.'

FIVE

THE TWO GUYS knelt on a mattress on the floor of a second-story room illuminated only by light from the street through the open windows. Even so, I recognized the tattoos. Matt Daniels, his body made liquid by junk, arched his back, leaned into the one behind him.

My Silent Partner wore only a sweatshirt and that hung loosely. His legs were like sticks. I saw lesions. He stroked his partner's back and got ready. Then he sat down and drew Matt to him.

It wasn't the clang of the bell or the rattle of the wheels on the tracks that brought my Shadow's eyes back into focus. It was the burst of sparks from the trolley wire right outside the window. In that brief flash I saw his look of surprise, even of alarm. And I knew, as one does in dreams, what he would have seen had he gone to the window to watch the passing streetcar.

Then I lay half awake on my couch and knew why Matt would not be coming by that night. I thought about him and the Luv Doll and myself when I was as young and dumb as they. Mostly, though, my thoughts were of my Shadow and our time together after he took my place that day at Darling-ton's.

We somehow managed to hang on there for many months. But when it was all over, my doppelganger and I were left to do what we called our "freelance gigs" in a landscape blighted by bad choices and ill fortune. That period of my life lasted almost exactly seven years. It's with me now only in vivid flashes, like the ones that remain after a troubled sleep.

Scott Callendar Sr.'s last night in this world was one of those flashes. He called me, his voice hoarse and wild, and asked that I bring him something to get off on. "Sarah's working late on some fairy fashion show. I got to mind the kid and I'm going crazy," he told me.

'This is what we can spare,' my Shadow told me and held up some tabs of acid cut with speed which even we wouldn't touch.

"Things are dry, man," I heard myself tell Scott. "All I got to sell is some really bad acid." He wanted it. I warned him several times. I didn't want to do business with him.

'He asked for it. Sell it to him,' murmured my Shadow. 'We're a connection, not his mother.' Then, because he knew I was a sucker. 'Besides, you need to check on the kid.'

When I arrived, Scott Sr. was playing a very nasty game and singing a song to his son. One line seemed to be:

I came, sir, in flame, sir

The game involved lighted matches. They looked like flam-ing death heads. I gave Scott the drugs and convinced him not to take his son with him when he stormed out into the night for the last time. Narcotics masked any remorse that I might have felt. My Shadow knew what we had done but I managed not to.

Lucky was another matter. Unlike Scott Callendar who died offstage, he screamed "MAN!" and OD'd in my apartment. Lucky was a pusher, a classic junkie, emaciated and filthy. But my Shadow and I called him the Avon Lady because he made house calls.

A young punk named Carl, who loved my Shadow, was staying with us. Boris came by shortly afterwards. He had a van. Lucky turned out to be no more than cold bones in thin denims. We put him in an oversized garbage bag and loaded him into the back of the van long after dark.

Carl wanted to be up front with me. Boris shook his head. "No. Kevin rides alone. We get in back. One Irish guy, minimum suspicion. He still looks like every Irish cop's fucked-up youngest brother."

I drove Lucky down the deserted streets of what would become TriBeCa. Boris was wrong, I didn't ride alone. I was about to roll through a red light on a deserted corner when a hand pointed. A cop car sat motionless at a curb. My Shadow whispered, 'Relax, the fuzz are glassy-eyed. Just don't wake them up.' When we left Lucky on a loading dock, the bag fell open, and his empty eyes stared right into mine. When I choked on my own spit, I alone heard my Shadow's laugh.

One autumn day sometime after Lucky, I stood in a kitchen in Cambridge, Massachusetts. The woman in the muumuu watched me zip up my fatigue jacket. We had been doing business together since I was in college. I was now so thin that there was room in my clothes for me and for several pounds of methedrine. She stopped mumbling chemical formulae long enough to tell the skinny guy, "Okay, okay, okay. This one is full."

The skinny guy still wore no shirt, but now had a Colt automatic stuck in the waistband of his bell-bottoms. He had grown a big mustache and his skin was so taut that every rib looked ready to burst out. He pushed open the backdoor and said, "All clear," in a crazed chipmunk voice.

Outside the kitchen, an alley ran between wooden houses. Where it opened onto the street, my Shadow stood in a jacket and tie. It made the pair inside too jumpy when they saw both of us together.

'Walk easy,' he said. 'The heat is only interested in the Commie commune.' As we headed for the Central Square subway, Sisters' School kids, home for lunch, ran past us, past a three-story house with red trim and pictures of Che Guevera in all the windows, past the detectives in their car.

Two hours later, I walked through Logan Airport, dressed in the jacket and tie, my overnight bag stuffed with crystal meth. The idea was to look like a student, or the bright, young copy-writer I had been a couple of years before. I caught sight of myself in a mirror and clenched up. I was minus an overcoat on a chilly day, wearing the shades it was best never to take off, with hair down to my shoulders because barbers gave me the same feeling dentists did. I looked like nothing on earth so much as a speed courier.

Guys in uniform moved toward me, blocked the exits, called to each other. I bit my tongue hard, got ready to bolt. The voice in my ear said, 'Off-duty pilots, chauffeurs. Nothing to do with us. Take a deep breath.'

Northeast Airline's 3 P.M. New York shuttle was full enough to give me cover but not so crowded that my Shadow couldn't have the seat next to me. Salesmen bent over reports. A silver wing shone outside the window. I had just snorted junk in the bathroom and was serene.

Then I glanced up and saw two stewardesses staring at me. 'Buy your ticket,' my invisible friend told me. I drew out the crisp tens I'd put aside and realized too late that one was still rolled up from my bon voyage blast.

The last leg down from Cambridge was by cab. 'We split with the crank,' my Shadow told me. 'Burn everyone before they burn us. Leave no forwarding address.'

Ahead of us, the setting sun balanced on the towers of Manhattan. Behind us rose a sickle moon. "Where would we go?" I asked.

'Anywhere. We are about to earn fifteen hundred bucks for delivering sixty-five grand worth of crank to these guys. Lift the shipment and we can go anywhere.' I shook my head. This was my Shadow's idea and I mistrusted it. 'Their luck is overdue to run out,' said my Shadow. The Spanish cabby paid us no mind. We got out in the fragments of streets that are all that's left of that neighborhood where the Queens Midtown Tunnel empties into Manhattan.

Angie's loft was upstairs in a two-story building on one truncated block. No one else lived amid the garages and small factories. We'd been introduced to him by Mr. Accessory-Before-the-Fact before old Mr. Accessory suddenly lost his job and disappeared into thin air.

Behind us, rush hour traffic flowed out of the city like a river. I rang the bell and waited where I could be seen from the window. I had a talent for not thinking about what I was doing.

'No wonder they call drug couriers mules,' my Shadow muttered. But when I shivered uncontrollably and had trouble stopping, he shut up. Sometimes I scared us both.

Finally, the buzzer sounded. Inside was a flight of stairs. At the top was a door with a peephole. Again I waited as they looked me over. It hit me that something was wrong. 'Run!' my Shadow suddenly cried. And I almost did.

The door flew open. A guy put an automatic to my forehead and gestured me inside. His eyes were dead, cold pins, his mouth a slit. But on his throat was a long curved scar like a smile. Other hands grabbed the bag and yanked me into the room.

Angie and Lars, his partner, lay facedown on the Persian carpet in a pool of blood. I got shoved onto the floor near them. My Shadow started talking. 'We know the connections, man.'

Facedown on that bloody carpet with a gun at my head, I felt my heart beat under me as my Shadow cut a deal for both our lives. Lots of what followed did not stick with me. My next clear memory is of a summer night. My Shadow and I sat in a booth at the Eatery, nicknamed the Speedery, across from the Fillmore East. We were dealing.

At our table was Carl, a hip, stylishly androgynous neighborhood kid. I loved him. He grinned as the voice that could have been mine murmured, 'You need a gimmick that will keep a john's attention. . . .'

Outside the window, a black Charger pulled up and beeped its horn. My Shadow nudged me, whispered, 'Smiley Smile.' I got up, walked past boys thin and brittle as wineglasses, past twitching, toothless old crank heads and the girl in a witch's hat who revolved slowly outside the door. The guy with the slit mouth and dead eyes sat in the front seat of the car. I found it easier to look at the smile on his throat as we exchanged drugs and money and then parted.

Back inside, I found my Shadow whispering to Carl, ". . . Russian roulette. You must know about that. Your folks being Ukrainian." The kid listened to him with such fierce devotion that it twisted my heart.

Another night, we walked, my Shadow and I, through the cavernous, deserted Newark train station. In a far corner, lights shone in one ticket window and above the single active gate. I had no clear idea how we had gotten there or where we were going. Then I saw a figure standing in the dark but all silvery and flickering like a silent film. I felt my Shadow suddenly snap awake.

'Sojourner,' he whispered. I turned to ask him what he was talking about and saw for an instant a deep, fresh gash on his forehead. I looked twice and it was gone.

Later, but how much later I don't know, I was paralyzed by junk and riding through wintery streets slumped in the backseat of a big car. My coat and shoes were gone. The heads of the driver and the man with him in the front seat flickered.

Smiley Smile shivered in a T-shirt beside me. This time, his eyes weren't dead, they were wide and scared. When I looked, he screamed at me, "What the fuck are you staring at?"

The Sojourner beside the driver was half turned toward us. That let me see the butt of the automatic in his jacket. I didn't know the make and didn't want to find out. "Shut up. Now," he said and nothing more. I knew that Smiley Smile was in big trouble because my Shadow had gotten away. And I knew that if I thought about it, I'd remember that my troubles were deeper than his. So I sat back and left everything to my doppelganger, wherever he was.

My next memory is of a white room and a guy around my age in a white tunic asking me my name. I tried to answer but found my mouth hurt too much. Besides, I didn't remember. Then he asked, "You know where you are?" I shook my head and he said, "Roosevelt Hospital. In Hell's Kitchen. In New York. Does any of that mean anything to you?" It didn't.

"You were found with damaged nose cartilage, a couple of broken teeth, and a three-inch gash above your left eye. Your skull was exposed. We practically had to close you up with bailing wire. It won't be pretty. You have a concussion. And amnesia. You know what that is?" I wasn't even curious.

Afterwards, a gray-haired man in a baggy suit read from notes. "We found you two days ago in the basement of the Atlantic Shipping and Transfer building on Twelfth Avenue. You know where that is?" I shook my head.

"Someone called the police to say there was trouble. The first officers on the scene found you facedown in the elevator. The door was opening and closing on your head. You had no wallet, no ID, no coat, no shoes. You had opiates, amphetamine, and alcohol in your system. Any idea how any of this happened?"

Faces flickered in my memory. "Sojourners," I told the detective. He waited. "Silent-movie people," I added. But when I could tell him nothing more, he shook his head and closed his notebook.

A little later, someone said, "Kevin!" Sarah and Boris had found me. Carl had gotten upset when my Shadow and I went missing and he had alerted my friends. Seeing them brought back a lot. Some relatives called and more memory returned. But not everything.

Boris bought me shoes so I could get out of the hospital. In the shuffle, I lost my apartment. And without the apartment I lost touch with Carl. I stayed down in SoHo with Sarah and Scotty in a mostly raw loft. She and he were pioneers. A paper jobber had his business on the floor above her. There was a machine shop on the first floor. We were the only ones living on her block.

Sarah had started doing well. Her store was already getting mentioned in *New York Magazine* and *The Times*. Life should have been sweet: waking up beside her, taking a five-year-old to the park. But memories of Scott Sr.'s last night made life with his widow and child more than slightly haunted.

My nose was only a little bent, my teeth got fixed at a clinic. But the scar was an angry red gash. The street had reached out and marked me. I thought of Scarface and my first time in the city, of old Smiley Smile. What I saw in the mirror was a mug that would not look out of place in a gutter.

Life was flat except for a tantalizing sense that part of me was missing. One night on an East Village block lighted by a silvery city glow, a figure in a doorway said 'Hello, Kevin.' And I remembered my Shadow and lots more. But not everything.

"What happened in that cellar?" I kept my distance.

'The Sojourners had nasty plans for us. Life in a cage. I got us out.' He stepped closer and I saw a scar just like mine. 'You really want to know the bloody details?'

It seemed we'd had a close call. I had a certain curiosity. But when he held up a sheaf of glassine envelopes and said, 'I got works,' I forgot my questions. In the few days after our reunion, I made short work of life with Sarah and Scotty.

Her store in the West Village was called Callendar Days. On the Saturday afternoon right after my Shadow had found me again, I staggered in there with a bloody nose. I had been supposed to take Scotty to the zoo. But gin and junk and destiny play funny tricks. "I have people I'm trying to wait on," Sarah said, and managed very expertly to maneuver me into the storeroom at the rear of the shop.

At a little desk in the corner, Scott sat doodling with magic markers. "Your mother is pissed off at me," I remarked, amazed that she couldn't accept my simple gift of myself.

"That's because you're stoned," he said, like an adult explaining something to a child.

I begged to differ. "She's afraid that everybody she gets involved with is going to kill themselves like your father did." Scott looked at me wide-eyed. His father's death was an unspoken event in the household. Since this seemed like the perfect moment, I asked, "You know what happened to your old man?"

When he shook his head, I was pleased to tell him. "One winter night a few years ago, he dropped five thousand mc's of methedrine-laced California acid and took a motorcycle ride on Roosevelt Drive. He hit an ice patch and plowed into a bridge support. The gas tank blew up and he went over the side in a ball of flame. The bike was borrowed and the first thing your mother had to do was repay the owner."

Scott ran past with his face down so I couldn't see his tears. On the desk was a beat-up old book that I hadn't noticed before. The title was *A Garland Knot for Children*. I was leafing through it when Sarah came into the storeroom and said, "I can't stand to see you this way, Kevin." I told her a few things about herself. The next day, I moved out.

My Shadow stole the following years with my eager collaboration. It was a stretch of time when I lost all idea of past and future and lived in one hard, endless present. My doppelganger seemed natural and inescapable.

In my late twenties and really strung out, I lived with him in a fleabag hotel, the Victoria, up on the Square, pulling stupid, dangerous, penny-ante stuff. My Shadow ran my life and I was like a zombie. Then, like a miracle, I walked away from this bad deal, this unwise arrangement.

One night, I was in the stench and jangle of the Seventh Avenue IRT station. Right near the Grand Central shuttle, I took a turn I'd never taken before, went down some stairs, and found myself getting on a streetcar. I did not question how that was possible. We rolled through a tunnel and out into what looked sort of like Queen of Heaven Parish in Boston. Compared to Times Square, it seemed open and hilly with lots of trees. It was so easy to get to, I wondered why I didn't live there and commute.

Then I saw this kid, maybe twelve, across the aisle, staring out the window. The kid started to turn and I realized who he was. I was jolted awake to find my Shadow looking at me strangely. He asked me what I'd been dreaming about. And I realized there was one small thing about me that he didn't know.

The dream repeated itself over the next few months. Having a secret from my Shadow was important to me. At times it felt like the Streetcar Dream was all I had in the world.

SIX

MY LIVING ROOM was awash in sunshine, the sign that I had fallen asleep and forgotten to set my clock radio. My voice said, "This is Kevin Grierson . . ."

My answering machine delivered its message. After the beep, a familiar voice asked, "Grierson, where the hell are you?"

"Ah, Mr. Sandler," I babbled, trying to figure out what day it was. "How are things in California?" Edwin Sandler is the fat kid who owns all the toys. Malcolm Forbes probably had more. But Forbes is dead, while Sandler walks among us still.

You may have seen him on the news when he bought an old Southern Pacific roundhouse to accommodate his vintage electric trains. George and I have acted as his New York agents for almost twenty years.

"Did you look at the Dolbier Collection? You were supposed to call. Is lot ninety-eight authentic?"

It came back to me. We were talking toy soldiers, fifty-four millimeters tall, hollow cast, old. Intensely desirable, at least to Sandler and a limited number of other people. "I had someone look at the lot," I lied. "He says yes. But I'm on my way up to Masby's for the preauction viewing."

"Well if it's authentic, I want it. Don't let that little fart Jonesy get it. He's beaten us out a couple of times recently. You have the list with the other lots I'm interested in. But Ninety-eight is the important one. I want it, however you have to do it. The usual bonus applies." Sandler is cold-blooded when it comes to toys and employees. With no change of tone, he said, "I hear George isn't doing so well."

Some days I was able to spend twenty minutes or half an hour before getting wrenched by a reminder of George. "That's right," I managed to say.

"It's a shame. You and he are young men." All things are relative. Sandler is in his seventies. He hasn't come near either of us since George's illness became general knowledge. I thanked him for his concern and said good-by, very tired of Sandler and this whole business.

It was well after ten o'clock. My mind was a blank as I sat up and looked at the catalog again. On the cover, under the title, *The August Dolbier Collection, Antique Toy Soldiers 1885–1920*, I had written, "Ozzie Klackman. Masby's. 11 A.M."

I put a kettle on the stove, showered, shaved, had tea and granola, and changed into blazer, slacks, and rep tie. I believe that outfit inspires trust. It also reminds me of Tay.

The phone rang again. It surprised me that the one I wanted it to be was Matt. Instead it was Ozzie Klackman.

"Hey, Grierson, you said be at Masby's at eleven sharp, Monday morning. I'm here with my meter running. Where are you?"

"At home, Ozzie, otherwise you wouldn't be speaking to me."

"Sharp, sharp. Everyone's always saying, 'Old Kevin G. is going soft.' But I tell them, 'No, no. He's still got all his marbles and he's selling them at twenty bucks a pop in that swank little Greenwich Village boutique of his.'"

"Hang on. I'm on my way."

It had taken Klackman to remind me about my own store. I dialed Half Remembered Things. After many rings Lakeisha answered, sounding out of breath. "You just got a UPS delivery," she said. "From Maryland someplace. Gettysburg?"

"Gaithersburg?" Vaguely I remembered purchasing a load of 1950s tin windup cars. "I'm not going to be in until late this afternoon." Remembering myself at seventeen, I had qualms about leaving her in charge. "Will you be okay?"

"There is no doubt in my mind." She was offended that I would question it.

It was already steamy when I hit the street and hailed a cab. On my way to Park Avenue, I reviewed the catalog, checked off lots for Sandler, marked a few items for myself. There was a small collection of turn-of-the-century miniature circus figures. A photo of the horses and clowns made me think of a carnival and that reminded me of Klackman and his merry-go-round.

Uptown at Masby's, I looked the crowd over. Despite the auction being on short notice and in the off-season, most major collectors or their agents had gathered. I was willing to bet that none had my exact business background. The auction house staff assigned me paddle 163.

Stepping into the showroom, I nodded to the big white mustached guy who's a retired colonel, to the Trasks, a husband and wife team of gnomes, and to Maxwell Jones, a shiny-faced child of sixty-five. Klackman, my hired accomplice, lounged against a display case. We pretended not to see each other.

Recorded marches played. Tiny conveyor belts drew hand-painted guardsmen in red coats, hussars on plunging horses, through display dioramas of castles and battlefields. American Indians in wild, impossible costumes galloped forever around a wagon train. The figures were eighty, ninety, a hundred years old. The kids for whom they had been bought were aged or dead. But here perpetually was the bright, savage world of childhood.

Everyone knew I represented Sandler. Eyes followed me as I approached lot ninety-eight. Rare, maybe unique, it stood in a display case by itself: French army medical figures, horse-drawn ambulances, supply wagons, hospital tents, stretchers, patients, nurses, doctors. It was attributed to William Britain Ltd., the famous English toy company, made in its Paris office circa 1910. The estimate was twenty-two thousand to twenty-six thousand dollars. This was the one that Sandler wanted. I wanted it too. And cheap. My bonus with Sandler was that if I brought the item in for under midestimate, in this case twenty-four thousand, he and I would split whatever I saved him. It would not be easy, but I had a plan.

Madge Brierly, the decayed gentlewoman whom Masby's has employed ever since I can remember, asked if I wanted the case opened. I nodded and asked, "Are you working the phones?"

"But of course."

Examining a two-inch-tall hand-painted doctor, I tried to remember all George had taught me. The uniform, once brilliant red and blue, the bright cheeks and black mustache, had in age acquired a nice patina. It showed no signs of retouching or repair. The crucible for toys is their passage through the hands of their young owners. Unworthy, at first, of adult attention, few survive intact. "Much prebidding?" I kept my voice low. Such information is confidential.

Her shrug indicated that preauction bids were less than the estimate. "Collectors are curious but wary. It seems August Dolbier's reputation wasn't the best. Everyone wants to see firsthand."

Right on cue, a voice called, "Grierson!" Heads turned. Madge stepped away as if to avoid contamination. Shabby, grinning, in need of a shave and doubtless a drink, Ozzie Klackman approached. In a loud, hoarse whisper I hoped everyone caught, he told me, "Anybody can have old antiques. But how many can have brand-new ones?"

Value in an antique depends on rarity and integrity. Repairs, repainting diminish the worth. Fraud and forgery are not uncommon. Those are Klackman's specialties. Everyone suspected that and knew that Klackman had worked for Dolbier.

"So what do you think?" Ozzie asked proudly as if the medical corps were his work.

The figure looked authentic to me. I replaced it in the case and went on to view other lots. Ones I wanted for the store I listed on an order bid sheet. Next to each item on my sheet I placed the top amount I was willing to pay. I handed Madge my sheets. If nobody topped my bid on a lot, I would get that lot. I had left lot ninety-eight off my list.

The crowd began to buzz. The auction was ready to start. Usually I stayed at the back of the hall. Today, I was up front in plain sight with Ozzie right beside me. It would appear that I was buying with his advice.

Hillary Westall, chief auctioneer, bright and stiff as a toy soldier himself, stepped to the podium. Madge Brierly stood at his left, receiver to ear, ready for phone bids. All attention focused on Westall as he said in clipped tones, "Lot number one, Britain's set number six. Boer Cavalry. Original box. Circa 1902. Bidding will start at one thousand dollars. It is with the room."

Klackman said nothing. I raised my paddle to establish my presence. "One thousand. Do we see twelve fifty?" Madge signaled that someone on the phone had topped my bid. The phones were my opportunity and the greatest uncertainty in my plan. Madge listened with her gaze fixed on the front window.

Westall looked my way on each lot. I raised my paddle regularly. Klackman said, "Hey, you got that one!" a few times.

"Lot number seventy-one. Lucotte Napoleonic General Staff.

Thirty pieces. Circa 1890. Bids start at twelve hundred dollars," said Westall.

A moment later Klackman whispered, "That asshole Jonesy got it for twice the estimate and the only part of it that's authentic is the tail on Napoleon's horse!" I made like I was very annoyed at having lost.

A few minutes later, timing it carefully, I rose and walked up the aisle followed by a grinning Klackman as Westall said, "Lot number ninety-eight, Britain's depose. Medical . . ." Jonesy glanced at us sharply and immediately turned his attention back to the podium.

More than face or paddle number, location is identity. An auctioneer looks to the place where she or he last saw the bidder. Giving up the place I'd established signaled to the room that I had no interest in bidding on lot ninety-eight.

"We start at sixteen thousand five hundred." Immediately, a phone bid came in and Madge relayed it to Westall. Only those in the room had witnessed Ozzie Klackman's fouling the authenticity of this lot. A phone bidder might still be willing to shoot for the moon.

Phone bids came in for $17,000 and $17,500. But those on the scene congratulated themselves on their firsthand knowledge.

As I reached the front window, Westall said, "We stand at eighteen thousand for a unique artifact. Going once . . ." I stood behind all the other bidders directly in Madge Brierly's line of sight. She gazed off thinking, perhaps, of better times. I smiled and lifted my paddle. She listened to a phone bid and looked right through me as she relayed it to Westall.

"Eighteen thousand five hundred. The bid is with the room. Do we have nineteen thousand? Going once, twice . . ."

I waved my paddle frantically. Madge squinted, perhaps her eyesight was bad. Then she nodded imperceptibly and signaled

Westall. "Nineteen thousand dollars. Thank you," he said, and everyone present assumed it was a phone bid.

Then people actually on the phone raised it to $19,500 and $20,000. Again I waved my paddle. Again Madge looked my way but couldn't find me. "Going once, twice . . ." I handed the paddle to Klackman who waved it back and forth like he was guiding a dirigible in for a landing. She nodded and spoke to Westall. "Twenty thousand and five hundred. Going once. Twice. Sold to paddle one sixty-three who has chosen to migrate."

Jonesy turned around amazed. "Hey, my meter is running!" said the voice in my ear. Ozzie and I retired to the foyer where, very discreetly, I passed him three hundred dollars in tens and twenties. "Very slick, Mr. G.," he said. "Especially the part where you became the Invisible Man."

We both knew there was another piece of business. Since I didn't mention it, he did. "You had your eye on that merry-go-round last night," Ozzie said like he was trying to sell me the toy. "I can offer you a good price."

I shrugged and as if it were idle conversation I said, "You mentioned that something reminded you of the original."

Klackman looked around and it occurred to me that he was nervous. "Not something. I haven't seen it recently. But the other week I ran into a guy who was one of the ones selling it last time." I made a throat-cutting gesture that duplicated Smiley Smile's scar. "Yeah. Him. That one. Al's his name."

Someone stepped out for a smoke and we heard Hillary Westall say, ". . . Hannibal at Carthage, including six elephants in fair condition."

We moved away from the smoker. Ozzie said, "All he told me was the merchandise is available again. Asked if I knew you. It's what you might call a weird scene." This was Klackman's way of giving me fair warning that the procedure might not be entirely legal or safe. "You interested?"

"Interested in what you can find out. I'll talk to you, Ozzie."

Klackman left promising to get back in touch. His voice in my ear that afternoon, confidential, boozy, criminal, had reminded me of my Shadow. I was stung by how much I missed it.

Next I arranged payment and shipping on Sandler's lots and mine. Then Madge Brierly and I slipped off to a little place around the corner. There I had iced tea and chicken salad while she polished off a surprising number of vodka and tonics and dished the auction world establishment.

I mentioned having been afraid that she wasn't going to recognize my bid and Madge said, "It was odd. I could see that oaf Klackman all too clearly. But you, somehow, kept getting lost against the sunlight in the windows."

Before we parted, I surprised myself by saying, "A good-sized collection is about to come onto the market. Toys of all kinds." The collection I had in mind was the inventory of Half Remembered Things. Until that moment, I hadn't known we were going out of business.

When I was fourteen, I gave away my toys because I thought I was grown up. Actually, all that had happened was that a guy a few times my age gave me money to let him blow me. I remembered that as I paid the cabby on the corner of Bleecker across from the store.

Inside, framed by Howdy Doody drinking glasses, a mint Fun on the Farm game, and a brace of Sergeant Preston of the Yukon lunch boxes, Lakeisha was on the phone. She buzzed me in without hanging up. Lakeisha is the daughter of one of George's nurses. Just out of high school, she is, like it or not, on her way to St. Regis College in Rhode Island this fall. George wanted very much for her to go to school outside the city.

She might have done something with her hair since Saturday. But I wasn't sure, so I said, "You look wonderful," which is always safe and true. The curves of her chin, the lines of her cheek, are flawless in the way Black faces can be. I looked at the register and saw that we had done seventy-four dollars and ninety-five cents' worth of business that day. That wouldn't pay the rent.

"That German man from Saturday came back and bought the dollhouse chair. Some people left messages," she said after hanging up. "Are you going to visit George tonight?"

"Yeah."

"I want to say . . . to see him before I go away." Lakeisha and I got along fine but it was George she loved. She looked past me out the window.

Turning, I saw her confidante, Claudia of the three-inch green nails with smiley faces painted on them, and Claudia's boyfriend, James, a chubby, good-natured kid. Standing behind them on the corner was Lakeisha's latest, Lionel, a wiry little snake. Lakeisha is unlucky in love. "You want to go?" I asked. And as the words left my mouth, Lakeisha asked, "We can see George tomorrow?" and was out the door.

My shopkeeper neighbors don't like seeing African American kids around. I watched Lionel, almost lost in his baggy clothes, put his arms about Lakeisha. The gesture was clumsy with self-consciousness. Suddenly she and he seemed so young and vulnerable.

In the two years I've known her, a couple of Lakeisha's friends have been killed. Claudia's arm was slashed on the subway. Even Lionel I recognized as a fellow changeling trying in all the wrong ways to be mistaken for a human child.

The first couple of phone messages were routine business. The landlord wanted to talk about a huge rent hike. A lady asked if we sold sex toys. Some guy wondered if we had Mr. Potato Head *with* his pipe.

After that, I was left to think about Smiley Smile and my Shadow, to wonder what the next move would be and who would make it. I looked around at the French puppet theater by

Maison Lillibon, the red American Flyer wagon filled with ABC blocks, and made a note to begin an inventory. Outside, tanned, half-clothed bodies cruised past. With my eyes slitted, I pretended I was lounging in the shade, scanning the boardwalk at some sun-soaked resort.

Then I was aware of an unfamiliar room pale as a daytime moon. On the floor was a mattress with my Shadow lying on it. His skin was tight over bones, his eyes hollow. Like a death mask. My nerves twitched. What I felt wasn't pain but its ghost.

Just then Addie called and said I should come by that evening. And soon it was closing time and I shut up Half Remembered Things. The store's time was past. I walked across town thinking how much of my life in the human's world had been connected to the place. It seemed that time too was passing.

My destination was Cabrini Hospice. Like so many in the plague years, I had a part-time job as an angel of death. George's sister Corrie was leaving as I arrived. "He had a small seizure just before I got here. I cut his nails." We hugged, dry-eyed this close to the end. Corrie is his older sister. She and her husband are going to retire to the Yucatán. Their plans are on hold. I had made no plans.

In the course of twelve years, I had seen George through clinics and wards, support groups and marches, through hopes for a last-minute cure and final disappointment. His will to live was a wonder. Now, finally, emaciated, small as a monkey, he lay on his left side with his eyes closed. Single, wirelike hairs still grew out of his head. Treatment for fungal growth made it look as though his face had been scoured by fire.

I took his hands and rubbed them. I'd been told that patients in a coma, with only tubes connecting them to the world, retain the sensation of touch. He had been shaved. A tiny fleck of blood had dried on his chin. I was reminded, despite wanting desperately not to remember, of the time a few years before when George had coughed a mouthful of his deadly blood directly into my face. He deserved so much more from me than the look of horror and revulsion I showed.

Beside the next bed, an Italian woman in her sixties murmured over her dying son. Maybe she was saying the rosary, maybe she was talking to him, saying things she couldn't while he was conscious. It's what happened with me. That evening, I sat with George, speaking softly.

"I never told you about my Shadow and the life he and I had. You would have listened. But I wanted to forget. Maybe that secret was part of what came between us. Another thing I let my doppelganger wreck.

"I keep wondering what would have happened if I had even just bothered to pretend I was faithful. Would we have stayed together? Would that mean you'd have stayed healthy? Would we both be dying or dead now? Should I have warned you about me that first time?

"All I'm sure of is that my life got saved by my bad heart and your good one. It was my heart that got me out of circulation when AIDS was still a mystery. After my bypass when all I wanted was to die, you dragged me back to life, smuggled in tiny bites of forbidden desserts, took me to see *Sunday in the Park with George.* A very serious evening. Lots of times we were the only two laughing.

"You did all that knowing that you had started to die. When you got sick, I tried to do the same for you. But my magic wasn't as strong as yours."

It was late. The Italian woman had left. Rising to go, I suddenly was certain that I wasn't going to have another chance to say farewell. I leaned over and kissed George. "Back when we first met, I felt that all this, you and me, the store, the city, was a stop along the way. And I guess it was. Just longer than I thought. And better. Because you are the very best. I hope what I've felt for you is what humankind calls love."

.   .   .

Addie had invited me over. But when I arrived, only Lauren was there. "She's held up at a meeting. Come on in." Laurie was in the blue room with her lights set up. The sand table construction she had just shot involved a labyrinth and cars and trucks, dozens of them. Laurie mostly does fashion work. She also photographs each sand table creation of Addie's patients. And she did the photos for *The Eternal Child,* George's last book about toys.

We disassembled the web of roads. "This kid's subconscious looks kind of like New Jersey," Laurie said. As I put a tow truck back on a shelf, I noticed Addie's streetcar and placed it on the sand. Laurie was about to take down her lights. She stopped as I ran the car back and forth on the sand.

"You know about my Streetcar Dreams?" I asked.

"Addie told me something." Lauren grinned. "I grew up in Greenwich Village. So I heard a lot stranger stuff." I took toys off the shelves, boats and buildings at first. I set the buildings up close together like New York blocks on one side of the tracks in the sand. On the other, I set up the boats as if they were docked.

"Back when I was in my late twenties my life was seriously rotten. I was living on the margins. I had this kind of partner. He had me under his thumb."

Lauren nodded. She knew that I thought I had a Shadow. "When things were at their worst, these dreams started. They were always the same. I'd go into one of the armpit Times Square subway stations, take a passage I'd never seen before, and go down a flight of stairs. Instead of trains, I'd find a streetcar. I'd get on board and it would roll out of the tunnel and into my past."

As I spoke, I took figures off the shelves, marching sailors and soldiers, civilians of all kinds, and set them up on either side of the tracks. "One time I burst out of the subway onto these

World War Two–era city streets. Guys in uniform, women in hats, Buy Bonds posters. Brilliant sunshine. Spring light.

"We rolled down the West Side past Hell's Kitchen, all kinds of warships and transports and sailors and girls. My father got killed in the South Pacific. He sailed from New York. My mother came down to see him off. I remember thinking that this is where they did the deed that resulted in me." I put a U.S. sailor in blues and a woman in a pink dress together waiting to cross from the buildings over to the ships. As I did, Addie came in and stood quietly in the doorway.

"What happened after the dream?" Lauren asked.

"The next thing I remember clearly is giving my Shadow the slip just after my birthday. That had happened before. Always I'd ended up crawling back to him. But this time, my life changed. It was like an explosion of light."

Both Addie and I watched Lauren for her reaction. She checked her cameras and equipment, gestured me away from the table. "So, it's a lucky dream," she said. "My Italian grandmother used to play the numbers. She had these dream books."

"My Irish grandmother did too! I'd forgotten about dream books," I said. "They still have them. Each dream has a three-digit number. You had the dream—"

"You played the number. Streetcar Dreams. My advice is play it, Kevin."

We laughed. Addie hugged her. "On matters like this, she's uncanny. While you two were in here, I had the time to whip up sesame noodles and broccoli with mushroom and rice. I even stuck them in Chinese restaurant take-out containers so you'd be comfortable with it."

When I got home that evening, lights were on in the windows of the big apartment houses across the park. I stood for a moment in the vestibule scanning my mail: bills, auction catalogs, GMHC fund-raising appeals.

Up in my silent apartment, the phone rang. When it turned

out to be Mr. Sandler, I was disappointed. Old Edwin, though, seemed happy at my news. "Your bonus check will be in the mail." The thought left me numb.

On my message tape, my godchild said, "Uncle Kevin, what I need very much is a horse. An alive one with a gold . . ." In the background, her mother could be heard asking, "Miranda, what are you doing?" And the connection abruptly broke.

The next message was a voice from the past that made me sit up. Gina Raille and I go all the way back to Mass. Arts and Science. "Kevin? Remember the evil twin I asked you about? The guy who looked like a really raddled version of you? He's back and I think I need to talk to you about him." The number Gina left was an answering service, one of the last still operating. I left a message.

Finally there was Klackman. "Grierson? That matter we discussed? Those people want to talk to you. Tonight." That was what I thought they'd want. I didn't return the call.

Waiting for the phone to ring, I channel surfed. I turned the TV sound off and sampled CDs. Jimi played at Monterey as Larry King talked to a woman senator. The slow movement of a middle symphony by Antonín Dvořák, who lived down the street from my building a hundred years ago, accompanied the Atlanta Braves at St. Louis. Ella Fitzgerald sang Cole Porter to the liquid bodies on MTV.

As I did that, I thought about betting and dreams. I remembered the time when my only refuge was in my dreams. It was back then, very late on a night when it would not do for either of us to be seen on the streets, that my Shadow and I were in a bar called the Dublin Green.

'Stay here,' he told me, thinking I was too drunk and stoned to move. 'I need to speak to this guy.' He and a dealer slipped downstairs. And like I was acting on a plan so secret I wasn't conscious of having formed it, I was out the door as soon as he was gone.

All this led me to an encounter a few days later. I was seated before a shining figure in a place of silver light. I could hardly focus my eyes. "How did you come to me?" he asked.

It took me a moment to get my mouth to work. All I could say was, "By streetcar."

Clear winter sunshine framed Leo Dunn. He gave a wide smile, poured me some hot coffee, and said, "It must have been one hell of a ride, my friend." When that image, those words caught me, I hit the remote, killed the TV and CD player, sat in the dark, and let memory take me.

SEVEN

My Shadow found me again, of course. I'd known he would. But it was a couple of weeks after that night in the bar before I saw him again. And in that time everything had changed.

I was holed up in Hell's Kitchen where an old lady of no charm whatsoever named McCready and called Mother rented furnished studios in an underheated fleabag on Tenth Avenue. Payment was cash only, by the week or month, with anonymity guaranteed whether it was desired or not.

Looking out my window on a February morning, I spotted my Shadow heading south toward Forty-second Street. He was already past me, so it was the clothes that caught my attention first. The camel hair overcoat had been mine. The dark gray pants were from the last good suit I owned. That morning, I'd awakened from a drinking dream and was still savoring the warm, safe feeling that came with realizing it was all a nightmare and that I was sober. The sight of that figure three floors down filled my mouth with the remembered taste of booze. I tried to spit but was too dry.

In the last couple of weeks things had changed for me. My Shadow now had a new name. I had learned to call him my Silent Partner. And I saw things differently. Before it had been me and my Shadow against the world. Now it was Leo Dunn and me against my Silent Partner. This attitude, though, was still new and fragile.

Hustlers called Forty-second Street the Deuce. My Silent Partner paused at the corner of Tenth Avenue and the Deuce. I wanted to think that my spotting him was just a coincidence. So naturally, just before heading east, he looked directly at my window. He wore shades. Though the face was mine, I couldn't read his expression.

Seeing him made me too jumpy to stay in the twelve-by-fifteen-foot room. Reaching behind the bed, I found the place where the wall and floor didn't join. Inside was my worldly fortune: a slim .25-caliber Beretta and beside it a wad of bills. Extracting six twenties, I stuck the rest in my boots, put on my thick sweater and leather jacket, and went out.

At that hour, nothing much was cooking in Hell's Kitchen. Two junkies went by, bent double by the wind off the Hudson. Up the block, a super tossed away the belongings of a drag queen who the week before had gotten cut into bite-sized chunks. My Silent Partner was not the kind to go for a casual walk in this weather.

Looking the way he had come, I saw the Club 596 sitting like a bunker at the corner of Forty-third. The iron grating on the front was ajar but no lights were on inside. As I watched, a guy in a postman's uniform squeezed out the door and hurried away.

In that legendary era not twenty-five years ago, the Irish still terrorized that tenement neighborhood between the West Side docks and Times Square. I knew that inside the 596, the Westies, last of the Mick gangs, short, crazed, and violent, sat in the dark dispensing favors, collecting debts. I also knew what my Silent Partner had been up to.

But I went to breakfast, pushed the incident to the back of my mind, and prepared for my daily session. The rest of my time was a wasteland, but my late afternoons were taken up with Leo Dunn.

Mr. Dunn lived in a big apartment house over in the East Sixties. Everything seemed bright. The outside of his building gleamed white. The lobby was polished marble. Upstairs in his apartment, sunlight poured through windows curtained in gold, hit a glass table covered with pieces of silver and crystal.

The first time I went there was in the stunned aftermath of a major bender. My eyes wouldn't focus. All I could see was this tall, white-haired man. I stood in my grubby street clothes and he was a figure of light. I could barely think, let alone speak.

That's when he asked me how I came to him and I said, "By streetcar." When he said it must have been a hell of a ride all the warmth and the joy in the world were in his smile. I wanted to sit in its radiance. He gave me coffee and I warmed my hands on the cup. I knew he was watching me, assessing my chances. "I haven't gotten high in almost two days," I said. "I want to stop. I'll do whatever you say. Help me. Please." I had never asked anyone this before.

"My friend, this is not a charity. I wish it were. But it's how I make my living." He told me his fee. I stood up and pulled bills out of my jeans pocket. He stopped smiling then and asked me about the drugs and booze. He told me that my addiction was like a Silent Partner stealing everything from me and I nodded my head and thought of my Shadow. But I said nothing about him right then.

Two weeks later, on the day I saw my double again, Mr. Dunn stepped forward smiling and shook my hand. "Kevin, my friend." He led me into the apartment. "Every time I see you come through this door, it gives me the greatest pleasure."

I sat down on the couch and he sat across the coffee table from me. The first thing I thought to say was, "I had a drinking dream last night. The crowd watched like it was an Olympic event as I poured myself a shot and drank it. Then I realized what I'd done and felt like dirt. I woke up and it was if a rock had been taken off my head."

Amused, Dunn nodded his understanding. But dreams were of no great interest to him. So, after pausing to be sure I was through, he drew a breath and was off. "Kevin, you have made the greatest commitment of your life. You stood up and said, 'Guilty as charged. I am a drunk.' "

Mr. Dunn's treatment for alcoholics was a talking cure: he talked and I listened. He didn't just talk: he harangued, he argued like a lawyer, he gave sermons of fire. Gesturing to a closet door, he told me, "That is the record room where we store the evidence of our mistakes. Any booze hound has tales of people he trusted who screwed him over. But has there ever been anyone you knew that used you as badly and that you went back to as often as you have to booze?"

We had been over this material a hundred times in the last couple of weeks. "You're a bright boy, Kevin, and I wouldn't repeat myself if I hadn't learned that it was necessary. We go back to the record room." Again, he pointed to the door. "We look for evidence of our stupidity."

My addiction and my Shadow had been with me for so long that I had been unable to imagine existence without either of them. Shortly before I met Mr. Dunn I had turned thirty. That was ancient on the street. I'd lost a lot of my immunity. Cops took to tossing me, throwing me against the sides of buildings, over the hoods of their cars, patting me down for drugs and weapons. My Shadow noticed that too. He talked about a big score that would let us leave the city.

He was only marginally less confused than I. My Streetcar Dreams slipped past him. On a Saturday morning I found myself almost broke and standing at a bar reading the *New York Post* while my Shadow concocted a desperate deal in a back booth. In the paper was an article about some guy called Dunn who cured drunks. I tore out the page and stuck it in my boot. My Shadow didn't notice.

In less than a day our fortunes reversed themselves. In the small hours of Sunday morning I stood at the same bar with a loaded .25 and several thousand dollars in my pockets. I was at the apex of a bender, what my Shadow called the eye of the storm, that fine moment when mortality is left behind and the shakes haven't started. My double had just taken a couple of hundred dollars and gone downstairs with a junk dealer. 'Supplies for our journey to place or places unknown.' The door had no sooner closed behind them than I bolted from the place.

Tuesday afternoon, I came to, empty, sweat soaked, and terrified, in a room I didn't remember renting. At first, it seemed that all I owned was the clothes I had been wearing. Gradually, in jacket and jean pockets, stuck in a boot, I discovered the vaguely familiar pistol, the thick roll of bills, and the page torn from the *Post*. The choice that I saw was clear: either shoot myself or make a call.

My newly sober brain was blank and soft. Mr. Dunn remolded it relentlessly. On the afternoon two weeks after our first meeting he saw my attention wander, clicked a couple of ashtrays together on the table, picked up the gold lighter, and ignited a cigarette with a flourish. "How are you doing, Kevin?"

"Okay," I told him. "Before I forget," I said, placing five of the twenties from my stash on the table.

He put them in his pocket without counting and said, "Thank you, Kevin." But when he looked up at me, an old man with pale skin and very blue eyes, he wasn't smiling. "Any news on a job?" He had never questioned me closely, but I knew that my money bothered Mr. Dunn.

Behind him, the light faded over Madison Avenue. "Not yet," I said. "The thing is, I don't need much to get by. Where I'm living is real cheap." At a hundred a week, Leo Dunn was my main expense. He was also what kept me alive. I recognized him as a real lucky kind of habit.

He went back to a familiar theme. "Kevin," he said, looking at the smoke from his cigarette. "For years, your addiction was your Silent Partner. When you decided to stop drinking, that was very bad news for him. He's twisted and corrupt. But he wants to live as much as you do.

"Your Silent Partner had the best racket in the world, skimming off an increasing share of your life, your happiness. He is not just going to give up and go away. He will try treachery, intimidation, flattery to get you back in harness. It will take every resource you have within you to stop him."

He paused for a moment and I said, because I had to talk about this, "I saw him today. Across the street. He saw me too. He was wearing clothes that used to belong to me. I've known about him since I was a kid. I always called him my Shadow. My mother—"

"What did he look like, Kevin?" I guess nothing a drunk could say would ever surprise Mr. Dunn. But he seemed wary too.

"Just like me. But at the end of a two-week bender."

"What was he doing when you saw him?" This was asked very softly.

"Coming from a mob bar up the street, the Club 596. He was trying to borrow money from guys who will whack you just because that's how they feel at the moment."

"Kevin," said Mr. Dunn. "Booze is a vicious, mind-altering substance. It gets us at its mercy by poisoning our minds, making us unable to distinguish between what is real and what isn't. Are you saying that you had to borrow money?" I shook my head. Very carefully he asked, "Do you mean you remembered some aspect of your drinking self?"

"Something like that," I said. But what I felt was a double

loss. Not only did my Shadow haunt me, but Mr. Dunn didn't believe what I said. My Silent Partner had broken the perfect rapport between us.

At that point, the lobby called to announce the next client. As Leo Dunn showed me to the door, his eyes searched mine. He wasn't smiling. "Kevin, you've done more than I would have thought possible when you first walked in here. But there's what they call a dry drunk, someone who has managed to stop drinking or getting high but has not reached the state beyond that. I don't detect involvement in life from you or any real elation. I respect you too much to want to see you as just a dry drunk."

The next client was dressed like a stockbroker. He avoided looking at my street clothes and face. "Leo," he said, a little too loudly and too sincerely, "I'm glad to see you." And Dunn, having just directed a two-hour lecture at me, smiled and was ready to go again.

Outside, it was already dark. On my way across town, I went through Times Square and walked down to the Deuce. It was rush hour. Spanish hustlers in maroon pants, hands jammed in jacket pockets, black hookers in leather miniskirts, stood on corners, all too stoned to know they were freezing to death. Around them, commuters poured down subway stairs and fled for New Jersey.

Passing the Victoria Hotel, I glanced in at the desk clerk sitting behind bulletproof glass. I had lived at the Victoria before my final bender. It was where everything I owned that I wasn't wearing had been abandoned. Without trying to remember all the details, I sensed that it wasn't wise to go inside and inquire about my property.

Back on my block, I looked up at my bleak little window, dark and unwelcoming. Mother's was no place to spend an evening. Turning away, I started walking again, probably ate dinner, maybe cruised the movie houses. Without being stoned, I couldn't connect with anyone. I wasn't ready to face my old friends.

Mostly, I walked, watched crowds stream out of the Broadway theaters. *A Little Night Music* was playing and *A Moon for the Misbegotten.* Then those rich tourists and nice couples from Westchester hurried into cabs and restaurants and left the streets quiet and empty.

In Arcade Parade on Broadway, goggle-eyed suit-and-tie johns watched the asses on kids bent over the pinball machines. Down the way, a marquee announced the double bill of *College-Bound Babes* and *Bound-to-Please Girls.* Around a corner, a tall guy with a smile like a knife gash chanted, "Got what you need," like a litany.

Glancing up, I realized we were in front of Sanctuary. Built to be a Methodist church, it had gotten famous in the late sixties as a disco. In those days, a huge Day-Glo Satan had loomed above the former altar, limos idled in front, a team of gorillas worked the door.

Now it was dim and dying, a trap for a particular kind of tourist. Inside, Satan flaked off the wall, figures stood in the twilight willing to take money for whatever you wanted. I could remember in a hazy way spending my last money there to buy the .25. My trajectory on that final drunk, the arc that connected the pistol, the money, the absence of my Silent Partner, wasn't buried all that deeply inside me. I just didn't want to look.

At some point that night, the rhythm of the street, the cold logic of the Manhattan grid, took me way west past the live sex shows and into the heart of the Kitchen. On long dirty blocks of tenements, I went past small Mick bars with tiny front windows where lines of drinkers sat like marines and guys in back booths gossiped idly about last week's whack by the Westies.

I walked until my hands and feet were numb and I found

myself over on Death Avenue. That's what the Irish of the Kitchen once called Eleventh because of the train tracks that ran there and killed so many of them. Now the trains were gone, the ships whose freight they hauled were gone, the Irish themselves were fast disappearing. Still, rounding a corner, catching blank blue eyes and flushed cheeks, a look of regret, a touch of a brogue embedded in the talk of someone born in this country, I was for a moment back in Queena Heaven.

On Death, in a block of darkened warehouses, sat the Dublin Green Tavern. It was just before closing time in the dead of night at the Dublin Green that I had found myself in my moment of utter clarity with a pistol and pocket full of money and a newspaper article about Leo Dunn. I stood for a while remembering that. Maybe the cold got to me or the bar began to look too attractive. I started walking again. What happened next I don't remember. But I know I ended up back at Mother's. And apparently I was tired enough to fall asleep sitting in a chair.

Sometime after that, I found myself staring at a ship outlined in green and red lights. I was intensely cold. Gradually, I realized I was huddled against a pillar of the raised highway near the Hudson piers. One of the last of the cruise ships was docked there and I thought how good it would be to have the money to sail down to the warm weather.

In fact, it would have been good to have any money at all. My worldly wealth was on me, suede boots and no socks, an overcoat and suit and no underwear. In one pocket was a penny, a dime, and a quarter. In another was a set of standard keys and the gravity knife I'd had since I was seventeen.

Then I knew why I had stolen the keys and where I was going to get money. And I recognized the state I was in, the brief, brilliant period of clarity at the apex of a bender. My past was a wreck, my future held a terrifying crash. With nothing behind me and nothing to live for, I knew no fear and was a god.

With all mortal uncertainty and weakness gone, I was pure

spirit as I headed down familiar streets. A block east of Death and north of the Deuce, I looked up at a lighted window on the third floor. I crossed the street, my overcoat open, flapping like wings.

Security at Mother's was based on there being nothing in the building worth taking. Drawing out the keys, I turned the street door lock on my third try and went up the stairs, silently, swiftly. Ancient smells of boiled cabbages and fish, of damp carpet and cigarette smoke and piss, a hundred years of poverty, wafted around me. This was the kind of place where a loser lived, a fool came to rest. Contempt filled me.

Light shone under his door. Finding a key the right shape, I transferred it to my left hand, drew out the knife with my right.

The key went in without a sound. I held my breath and turned it. The lock clicked, the door swung into the miserable room with a bed, a TV on without the sound, a two-burner stove, a table. An all-too-familiar figure dozed in the only chair, in stockinged feet with his jeans unbuttoned. Sobriety had made him stupid. Not even the opening of the door roused him. The click of the knife in my hand did that.

The eyes focused then widened as the dumb face I had seen in ten thousand morning mirrors registered shock. "I got a little debt I want to collect," I said and moved for him. Rage swept me, a feeling that I had been robbed of everything: my body, my life. "You took that goddamn money. It's mine. My plan. My guts. You couldn't have pulled that scam in a thousand years."

For an instant, the miserable straight-head in front of me froze in horror. Then shoulder muscles tensed, feet shot out as he tried to roll to the side and go for the .25. But he was slow. My knife slashed and the fool put out his hands.

Oh, the terror in those eyes when he saw the blood on his palms and wrists. He fell back, tripping over the chair. The blade went for the stomach, cutting through cloth and into flesh.

Eyes wide, his head hit the wall. The knife in my hand

slashed his throat. The light in the eyes went out. The last thing I saw in them was a reflection of his humiliation at dying like that, pants down, jockey shorts filling with dark, red blood. His breath suddenly choked, became a drowning sound. An out-stretched hand pointed to the loose board and the money.

"I was just cut down," I told Dunn the next day. "It wasn't even a fight. I was just some stupid mark killed so easily. I left that knife behind when I had to move and the Silent Partner had it and just cut me down. I looked like a fucking fool dying in that stupid room." It was hard to get my throat to work. He had never managed to do anything like that to my head before.

"It was a dream, Kevin, a drinking dream like the one you told me about yesterday. It has no power over your conscious mind. You went home and fell asleep sitting up. Then you had a nightmare. You say you fell off your chair and woke up when you hit the floor. The rest was just a dream."

My eyes burned. "The mood my Silent Partner was in when he walked into my apartment, I recognize. It's like the eye of the storm. Moments when it was like there wasn't anything I couldn't do." Then I was crying.

Mr. Dunn pushed a box of Kleenex across the table. "Nothing else I've seen has reached you like this, Kevin."

"Sorry. I couldn't sleep."

"Don't be sorry. This is part of the process. I don't know why, but this has to happen for the treatment to work. I've had de-tective sergeants bawl like babies, marines laugh until they wept. Until this, you haven't let anything faze you. Our stupid drinker's pride can take many forms."

"I won't be able to sleep as long as I know he's out there."

"Understand, Kevin, that I'm not a psychiatrist. I was edu-cated by the Jesuits a long time ago. Dreams or how you feel about your mother don't mean much to me. But I hear myself say that and spot my own stupid pride at work. If dreams are what you bring me, I'll use them." He paused and I blew my nose. "What does your Silent Partner want, Kevin? You saw through his eyes in your dream."

"He wants to disembowel me!"

"The knife, even the murder, were the means, Kevin. Not the motive. What was he looking for?"

"My money. He knew where I had it."

"You keep money in your room? You don't have a job. But you pay me regularly in fairly crisp twenties and hundreds. It's stolen money, isn't it, Kevin?"

"I guess so. I don't remember."

"Earlier you mentioned that in the dream you went for a gun. Do you own a gun? Is there blood on the money, Kevin? Did you hurt anyone? Do you know?"

"The gun's fully loaded. It wasn't fired by me."

"I assume it's not registered. Probably has a bad history. Get rid of it. Can you return the money?"

"I don't even know who it belonged to."

"You told me that he was in a calm eye when he came after you. That was his opportunity. You described having that same kind of clarity when you decided to leave him. You had the money with you then?"

"The gun too."

"Kevin, let's say that some people's Silent Partners are more real than others. Then, let's say that in a moment of clarity you managed to give yours the slip and walked off with the money the two of you had stolen. Without him holding you back, you succeeded in reaching out for help. The money is the link. It's what still connects you to your drinking past. I don't want any of that money and neither do you. Get rid of it."

"You mean throw it away?"

"The other day you said your Silent Partner was borrowing from the West Side mob. If he's real enough to need money that badly, let him have it. No one, myself above all, ever loses his

Silent Partner entirely. But this should give you both some peace."

"What'll I do for money? I won't be able to pay you."

"Do you think after all this time I don't know which ones aren't going to pay me?" I watched his hands rearrange the crystal ashtrays, the gold lighter as he said, "Let's look in the record room where we will find that booze is a vicious mind-altering substance. And we have to be aware at every moment of its schemes." I raised my eyes. Framed in the light from the windows, Dunn smiled at me and said, "Keep just enough to live on for a couple of weeks until you find work. Which you will."

Afterwards, in my room, I took out the pistol and the money, put two hundred back in the wall, and placed the rest in a jacket pocket. The Beretta I stuck under my belt at the small of my back. Then I went out.

At first, I walked aimlessly around the Kitchen. My Shadow had terrified me and made my life seem worthless. Now my choices were to give him money or to keep the money and give up Mr. Dunn. The first I thought of as abject surrender, the second meant I'd be back on the booze and drugs. Then a third choice took shape. Payback. I would do to him just what he had tried to do to me.

Searching for my Silent Partner, I followed what I remembered of our route on the last night of our partnership. It had begun at Sanctuary.

Passing by, I saw that the disco was no longer dying. It was dead. The doors were padlocked. On the former church steps, a Black guy slept with his head on his knees. No sign of my Shadow.

But I finally recalled what had happened there. Sanctuary was a hunting ground. Tourists were the game. That last night, I had run into four fraternity assholes in town with seven grand for a midwinter drug buy. Almost dead broke, I talked big about my connections. Before we left together, I bought the Beretta from someone I knew slightly.

Following my trail, I walked by the Victoria. That's where I had taken them first. "Five guys showing up will not be cool," I said, and persuaded two of them to wait in my dismal room. "As collateral, you hold everything I own." That amounted to little more than some clothes and a few keepsakes like the knife. With the other two, I left the hotel that last time knowing I wouldn't be back. I recognized my Shadow's touch. He walked with me at that point.

Turning toward an icy wind off the river, I took the same route that the frat boys and I had taken a couple of weeks before. At a doorway on a deserted side street near Ninth Avenue, I halted. I remembered standing in that spot and telling them this was the place. In the tenement hall, I put the pistol at the base of one kid's head and made him beg the other one to give me the money.

Standing in that doorway again, I recalled how the nervous sweat on my hand made it hard to hold onto the .25. When those terrified kids had handed over the money, I discouraged pursuit by making them throw their shoes into the dark, take off their coats, and lie facedown on the filthy floor with their hands behind their heads.

They were victims, dumb, shivering marks. I was in total control. The one I'd put the pistol on had pissed his pants. He wept and begged me not to shoot. Remembering that made my stomach turn. Right then my Shadow had been calling the shots and I was a faithful minion.

Long hours of that night were gone beyond recovery. Just then, they weren't important. I knew where the search for my Partner was going to end. Death Avenue, north of the Deuce had always been a favorite spot for both of us. The deserted warehouses, the empty railroad yards made it feel like the end of the world.

Approaching the Dublin Green bar, I spotted a lone figure leaning on a lamppost watching trailer trucks roll south. Only a lack of funds would keep man or Shadow out on the street on a night like this. Touching the pistol for luck, stepping up behind him, I asked, "Watcha doing?"

Not particularly surprised, not even turning all the way around, he replied, 'Oh, living the life.' I would never have his nonchalance. His face was hidden by the dark and masked by sunglasses. That was just as well.

The air around him smelled of cheap booze. "We have to talk." I gestured toward the Dublin Green.

As we crossed the street, he told me, 'I knew you'd show up. This is where we parted company. When I woke up days later, all I had was these clothes and a couple of keepsakes.' That reminded me of the knife. My Shadow knew as soon as that crossed my mind. 'Don't worry,' he said. 'I sold it.' And I knew he had. He went through the door first.

The Dublin Green was a typical Hell's Kitchen joint with a bar that ran front to back, a few booths, and beer and cigarette-soaked air unchanged since the Truman administration. The one distinguishing feature of the place was the facilities. The rest rooms lay down a flight of stairs and across a cellar/storage area. You could organize a firing squad down there and the people above wouldn't know.

Or care. The customers that night were several guys with boozers' noses, an old woman with very red hair who said loudly at regular intervals, "Danny? Screw, Danny," and a couple of Spanish guys off some night shift and now immobile at a table. The dead-eyed donkey of a bartender looked right through me and nodded at my Silent Partner. In here, he was the real one. We went to the far end of the bar near the cellar door where we could talk. I ordered a ginger ale. My companion said, "Double Irish."

As we sat, he gave a dry chuckle. 'Double Irish is about right for us.' At no time did I turn and stare my Silent Partner in the face. But the filmed mirror behind the bar showed that he wore the rumpled jacket over a dirty T-shirt. The camel hair coat was deeply stained. When the whiskey came, he put it away with a single gesture from counter to mouth. Up and in. I could taste it going down.

It was like living in a drinking dream. I touched the back of my belt and said, "You found out where I live."

'Yeah. Billy at 596 told me you were staying at Mother's. Of course, what he said was that he had seen me going in and out. So I knew.' Indoors, my partner smelled ripe. The back of his hand was dirty.

"You owe them money?" The last thing I needed was to get shot for debts he had run up.

'Thanks for the concern. Not even five. My credit's no good,' my Shadow said. 'You left me with nothing. They locked me out of the hotel. Ripping off those kids was something you never could have done by yourself. You needed me.' He signaled for a refill. The bartender's eyes shifted my way since I was paying.

I shook my head, not sure I could have him drink again and not do it myself. "I've got most of the money on me. It's yours. So that we don't attract attention, what I want you to do is to get up and go downstairs. After a couple of minutes, I'll join you."

'Pass the money to me under the bar.' He didn't trust me.

"There's something else I want you to have." For a long moment he sat absolutely still. The TV was on with the sound off. It seemed to be all beer ads. "When you come back up here," I told him, "you can afford enough doubles to kill yourself." That promise made him rise and push his way through the cellar door.

For a good two minutes, I sipped ginger ale and breathed deeply to calm myself. Then I followed him. Downstairs, there were puddles on the floor. The rest room doors were open. Both were empty. One of the johns was broken and kept flushing. It sounded like an asthmatic trying to breathe.

The cellar was lighted by an overhead bulb above the stairs and another one at the far end of the cellar near the rest rooms. Both lights swayed slightly, making it hard to focus. My Silent Partner had reached up and bumped them for just that reason. It was the kind of thing that I would not have thought of. He stood where the light didn't quite hit him.

When I reached the bottom of the stairs, I reached back and drew the .25. He seemed to flicker before me. 'Easy does it,' he said. 'You know how jumpy guns make you.' His tone was taunting, not intimidated. 'And killing me might well be suicide.'

I could read him as easily as he could me. My Shadow wanted me to try to shoot him and find out that I couldn't. After I had proved myself helpless without him, we could both go upstairs, have some drinks, and resume our partnership. Carefully, I ejected the clip and stuck it in my pocket. "You bought this, you get rid of it," I said. "My guess is it had a bad history even before we got hold of it."

'You'll never have another friend like me.' His voice, my voice, had a whine to it and I knew this was getting to him. I reached into my pocket and took out the money and a piece of worn newspaper. 'You thought about what it's going to be like to be broke?' he asked. 'It's not like you've got any skills.'

I'd had those thoughts and they scared me. I hesitated. Then I noticed that the newspaper was the page with the Dunn article. Taking a deep breath, I riffled the money and told my Silent

Partner, "Almost six grand. Just about everything I have." I put the cash on the stairs beside the Beretta and turned to go. "So long. It's been real."

'Oh, I'll keep in touch,' he said in a whisper. Looking back, I saw nothing but the blur of light from the swinging bulb.

On the stairs, I felt light-footed, like a burden had been laid aside. This was relief, maybe even the happiness Mr. Dunn had mentioned. From his perch near the front, the bartender gave me a slightly wary look like he wondered if the next one going down to take a leak was going to find a nasty surprise in the basement.

But just before I went out into the cold, his gaze shifted, his hand reached for the pouring bottle, and I heard the cellar door swing open behind me. Then I went back to my room, packed my possessions in a shopping bag, and fled into the night.

EIGHT

JUST SHORT OF a quarter century later, I sat at a window with
the lights out and waited for either the Sojourners or my
Shadow to make the next move. For a moment I wished I had
a gun or a container of mace or even a gravity knife. But my
Silent Partner was right: things like that just made me nervous.

In the park below, a police car making a midnight circuit
shone its light in dark corners. Human forms rose up from
benches and drifted toward the gates. I looked for flickering
heads among them. But all I saw were the lonely and desperate
hitting the street, some with their belongings under their arms,
as the park gates were locked behind them.

The call came just after that. The voice on the line quavered,
"Kevin?" It took me a moment to recognize Matt.

"Most of the time, I am." I waited. A long pause followed.

"Fred said for me to talk to you. I need...," Matt trailed off.
"I need help."

"You know my name now and where I live." The connection
broke and I heard a dial tone. Oh, my Silent Partner was clever.

He knew how to catch my attention, to jog my memory. Along with reminding me of myself, Matt reminded me very much of Carl Valleck, the punk who had loved my Shadow.

Carl came back into my life that first spring when I was struggling to stay sober. The place I moved to right after Mother's was another fleabag across town. I was broke and desperate. Almost anyone whose name and number I could remember got calls.

Some were saints. Les Steibler invited me to lunch at Schlep's. Jackie Maye had retired, Les had her old job and a new boyfriend. My clothes, my appearance embarrassed me. The waitress gave me an especially sour glance. Les just smiled and said, "Kevin, I think that Darlington's has one last makeover left in it." Someone else gave me a freelance research job. Boring, but it was work and there was plenty of it.

Boris and I had parted on bad terms a couple of years before. But when I called, he jumped in a cab, drove uptown, and hugged me. He was living with Gina Raille, who was singing in a revue that ran on weekends in someone's loft. He was dealing still. But once he knew I was clean, he never discussed business. He also came through with a basement apartment in the furthest reaches of Chelsea. Gina found me some broken-down furniture and a bed.

Even I wasn't dumb enough to think that running from my Shadow would do any good. As Mr. Dunn told me at that time, "There's a secret court inside each of our heads where we are defendant, prosecutor, judge, and jury. And from that court there is no escape."

As winter faded, I began to get itchy. Alone and unsure of myself without the props of drugs and alcohol, I sought the intimate anonymity of the decaying West Side piers. There my past and anything I might have done were irrelevant. Hands reached out, clothes got peeled away, and only a carefully timed match flicker revealed my partner as a goblin or a god.

My trial began on a soft spring night in that year when Carter and Reagan were still just out-of-work governors and AIDS was unknown. I was about to cross West Street when a Checker cab pulled up beside me and a voice said, "Kevin!" Startled, I turned to see Carl Valleck smiling as he got out of a backseat. "Kevin, I need to talk to you."

Back in the East Village of Smiley Smile and Lucky, Carl's hair was as long and lustrous as Jim Morrison's. Now it was shorter than I had ever seen it. He had muscles that hadn't been there before. But the brown, slightly Slavic eyes were the same. So was the attraction he held for me. Indignant cruisers stepped around us and wondered why they hadn't been chosen.

Sobriety had distorted my memories of Carl and me. Otherwise, I would have remembered that it had never been me that he loved, and passed up the invitation. Instead, I replied, "It's been a long time."

A man and a woman in dark glasses followed him out of the cab. The man paid. Carl made the introductions. "Kevin, this is Judith and Michael." Neither of them reacted at all. Carl just winked at me.

We were in front of Cape Fear on West Street. "Join us," said Carl. The other two said nothing. I felt bad about the time when he and my Shadow and I had been together. Thinking maybe I could make it right this time, I followed him inside.

Entering Cape Fear was like going from a darkened wing onto a bright stage. What once had been a warehouse was now a restaurant, all exposed brick, polished wood, and photos of great ladies and talented young men. On the stereo, the Velvets sang the concert version of "New Age," the one with the line about waiting for the phone to ring.

Judith was the only woman in the place. She looked around avidly like she wanted to implant it on her retinas. Along with the glasses, she wore a black sheath dress and long black hair. As we got seated, she fixed on two guys walking past. One wore a wide, scarred belt with several feet of chain attached. The chain ran into the half-opened zipper of his partner's jeans. They moved in tandem and you had the feeling the friend was very tightly secured.

"This place is a theater of the eye. Brilliant!" said Michael. He looked kind of delicate, his hair was mostly gone. He wore a beard, a watered-silk vest, and the only suit in the house.

Carl sat opposite me and ordered a double Wild Turkey when the waiter came. "The same," said Judith. It was the first time I had heard her speak. The voice sounded remote.

When I ordered a club soda and lime, Carl gestured toward Michael. "Drink up. Daddy Big Bucks is paying, man." But I just shook my head. My instinctive take on the situation was that Judith had Michael, Michael had money, Carl was for hire, and they had rented him. I guessed that he was a tour guide and I wondered about the other terms of the lease.

"What are you doing these days?" Carl asked me.

"Oh, a little acting." This was a perfectly acceptable reply in that time and place. Were we not all actors in the dramas of our lives?

Judith and Michael paid no attention. Carl winked again and lighted a cigarette. As he did, the sleeve of his leather jacket fell back, revealing a series of cigarette burns on his wrist and arm. Some were old, some fairly new.

My stomach turned, but I couldn't help looking. He told the other two, "Kevin was the one I talked about on camera last time." The attention of the pair of voyeurs was on me, their expressions calculating but respectful. Suddenly, I was somebody, but I didn't know who.

A big, gray-bearded guy with a beautiful half-Asian kid in tow stopped to kiss the top of Carl's head and say in an awed whisper, "The boy in the white room." He continued his grand exit. But what he had said and the sight of Carl's scars left me with a twinge, a memory I didn't much want to probe.

When our drinks came, Michael looked around the room and said to Judith, "Half the people here would be delighted to be in our little project."

She spoke again. "Asshole, we have the one we want." She stared at me raptly. I looked to Carl for an explanation.

"Kevin and I have to talk," he said. Shortly, he swallowed his drink and got up. We left the two of them gorging their eyes.

Outside, I cast a glance at the dance of the silhouettes across the way as men singly, men in pairs, outlined by streetlights, passed under the ruined highway and headed for the Hudson. I could have joined them, but by then curiosity, and maybe boredom, had gotten the better of me. "Carl, who were those two geeks?"

"Judith is a videomaker. Michael is, like, her producer, puts up the money. I guess they're an item. I'm the star of the thing they're doing now. Let's take a walk." He gestured uptown. "I live at the Landing."

That was a couple of blocks from where I lived. As we walked, I had a million questions. "What did you tell them about me? What was it the old chicken hawk said about a white room?"

"That's why I got to talk to you." The Landing was an old riverfront hotel way west in Chelsea. Carl lived on the top floor. We went up wide, worn stairs that stank of piss and mold. "You disappeared, Kevin. I guessed you were dead. Then I got involved in this project that was, basically, your idea, and I started seeing you around. Like fate, man."

His room was bigger than I expected. White paper covered the windows. Walls, floor, the bureau, table, and two chairs were all painted white. The only intrusive items were a stand of lights in one corner and five bullets on the table. The paint job was recent and hastily done, intended for immediate effect and the camera's eye. "The white room all set up for shooting." Carl emphasized the last word.

I sat on a chair. Carl sat on the bed and stared at me with his fixed half smile. Painful memories of a certain night at the Speedery wanted my attention. To continue avoiding them, I asked, "What are you doing with your time? No TV or radio, I mean. . . ."

"Your amnesia still bothering you, Kevin? When I was just a kid you told me how to set this scene. The room had to be white, a complete blank. Nothing to identify yourself. Hide anything personal away, you said. Maybe leave one item out, an open switchblade, a pair of handcuffs, a needle. Something to grab a straight's attention. You were like nobody I ever heard. Sometimes there were two of you. I saw it. Now you're going to tell me you don't remember any of it?"

What I recalled more clearly than I remembered sex with Carl was watching my double play with the kid's mind. And I remembered that I had let him do it. "That's past," I told him. "I've got a lot of apologizing to do."

He shook his head. Slowly, he reached under the mattress and drew out a revolver. It looked like my uncles' old .38. Still smiling, he broke it open, showed me there was one bullet in it. "The straight won't be able not to look, you said. Just sit and watch the straight's reaction, you said. Well man, I am watching."

"That was booze and drugs and my Shadow's bullshit. I was only about the same age you are now and scared at what deep trouble he and I had gotten in. Scared that you'd see how scared I was. Wanting to impress you with how tough I was. I let my Shadow talk a lot of dangerous crap. Please don't . . ."

Carl locked the pistol. The sharp snap of metal made my heart lurch. He spun the cylinder. "Do something like this, you said, and the straight can't look away."

A pulse I hadn't seen before stood out on Carl's forehead. It started throbbing as he brought the gun up behind his right ear.

Trying to keep my voice steady, I said. "You play this game often, your number is going to come up."

"I have done this a lot, man. And it's not a game. It's a test. If you got to think of it as gambling, then, you get five to one odds. This is a test." He spoke softly, looking right at me. And I was unable to move or look away.

In the instant before he pulled the trigger, his eyes glazed and lost contact with mine. Had they bulged and rolled back into bloody sockets, my own brain and heart would have stopped along with his.

Instead, the hammer clicked on an empty chamber and the breath rushed out of my lungs. Carl's hands hardly shook as he offered me the revolver. "Want to try it?"

The hotel, the streets, the whole city, was silent at the moment, transfixed. I shook my head. Sirens cried in the east and music burst, then died as a door opened and closed. On the street, a man yelled for a taxi.

Carl's smile came on again. "I know what it is, you want to wait, save it for Judith. I talked about you on the video the other night before I rolled. Said how you were like this wizard. How your Shadow talked and you and him taught me. Then I saw you tonight and thought what a great film it would be. Think about it, man. Two good-looking guys in a white room. They discuss old times. Then first one rolls and the other. People will watch that video."

"We're supposed to die just so those ghouls can film it? How did you get into this?"

Carl rolled up a sleeve so that I could see his whole scarred inner arm and said, "Love bites. What you don't see is even better. Remember one time you held matches next to your hand to see what it was like?" I had managed to forget. "That got to me and I thought it would do the same for other people. I was right.

"Of course, things kind of escalated. I was so drugged out I didn't even feel it. But after a while, not enough people dug my act to pay for my medicine.

"Without this"—he indicated the gun and room—"I would have ended up peddling my ass out of some bang-and-walk-up on the Square. That's what happens to kids with no daddy to send them money. People play with our bodies, play with our minds. Then they discover Jesus or something. Forget about us.

"Kevin, nobody is going to forget about me. Weirdos and perverts, that is to say everyone, will whisper to each other, 'I saw this shocking film you are just not going to believe.' If you weren't so numb, you could be in on it too."

He sounded disappointed in me. All I possessed of any value was my sobriety. So I offered that. "There's this guy I'm seeing who helped me out of drinking and drugs. Leo Dunn. He's real good. You can talk to him."

Carl shrugged. "You're clean. You're broke. Your magic is gone and you're nothing." He took a worn piece of paper out of his pocket and handed it to me. "When you change your mind, call the number where it says Judith." He said nothing more, just stared at me until I left.

Mr. Dunn was seeing me three times a week at that point. The next evening I went up to his place right from my research job. I'd had trouble sleeping the night before. That day summer heat arrived in New York. Leo Dunn met me in front of his building wearing a suit of pinkish tan and we walked over to Madison Avenue. A cop in his car said, "Hey, Leo!" The setting sun turned city browns and grays to bronze and peach.

"I'm just no damn good," I said.

"My friend, no one tells me that about a client of mine. Not even the client. As I've told you before, you are the best person in the world, the bravest, the smartest." Mr. Dunn reached into his coat for a cigarette, paused, patted his pockets a bit like an old actor, and walked into a place that smelled like a humidor.

"Leo! Good to see you about!" said an elderly pixie of a tobacconist behind the counter reaching for a pack of Marlboro's. "You're looking well."

"Pat, how are you!" Mr. Dunn patted his pockets again and the man put it on the tab. Mr. Dunn's silver lighter seemed to appear in his hand by magic. "What brought on this sudden blindness to all your good points?" he asked as we stepped onto the street.

"A guy named Carl that I haven't seen in a few years. We lived together. This isn't easy to explain." I'd never discussed my sex life with him. Or anybody else, really. Even Boris and Sarah only got bits and pieces of it. But he just nodded and we walked down the avenue.

"He was a kid I picked up when I was really crazed. I let him stay in my place. Look." I turned to face Dunn. "Sex was this stuff adults showed me when I was a kid. I never felt like I had much of a say. But a lot of it hurt me badly. So . . ."

"You used sometimes to hurt others." I nodded and wondered what it would have been like to have been able to talk to Mr. Dunn when I was a kid. That may have been all I wanted, someone to talk to.

"At first, I didn't even let him have keys. When I left for work, I'd give him a dollar and put him out on the street. Later on, my Silent Partner . . ." I saw Mr. Dunn shake his head. "No, I take responsibility, okay? It was my fault he got told stupid things." I took a deep breath and went on to tell Mr. Dunn about the white room and my previous night.

We walked a little further downtown before he spoke. "Even the cleverest of us can get caught in twisted logic," he said. "Especially when they have a Silent Partner ready to give them bad advice." Leo Dunn had a wide variety of roles, priest, fellow sinner, salesman. That evening, he was a wily old lawyer with a tough case.

"You say someone you knew in bad times made you an offer that leaves you with a fairly good chance of blowing your brains out. You refused, showing, I would say, very good sense. Do I understand that you are blaming yourself for his having tried to get you killed?"

"Eventually, he's going to shoot himself and I planted the idea."

"He drinks?"

"And does drugs. Junk."

"You want me to talk to him?"

I shook my head. "I asked."

"In other words, despite the great influence you had on him, he knows you stopped getting stoned and that doesn't make him want to stop too. Do you see the flaw in that?"

"He never had a chance. People think that guys like him and me are trash."

"My friend, I know what it's like to get the back of society's hand. I drank myself onto the Bowery, wrecked career, family, marriage when people believed only a born degenerate could do that. I'm not asking what others may think about this unfortunate boy and what may have happened to you in the past. I want your own unbiased judgment of yourself in the here and now.

"Kevin, we've talked about the secret court where each of us is defendant, prosecutor, judge, and jury. Like any court of law, it can be corrupt. I've seen the worst offenses get winked away. Other times it's harsh and unjust. Sometimes the death penalty gets dealt when the defendant was at most a bystander.

"By the look on your face, I would not care to come up before you at this moment looking for the mercy that human weakness always deserves. Fortunately, I don't have to worry about that because each one's secret court tries only him or her.

Its decisions can be biased, its methods suspect, its authority tainted. But its verdicts quite often get enforced."

We paused on a corner and were about to turn back uptown. Down the brownstone block, a car with embassy plates deposited a couple in evening clothes. On the other side of the street a hustler, thin, threadbare, no longer young, passed by. I could remember when the desperate and destitute all seemed a lot older than I was.

Just as I noticed him, he homed in on us, crossed in the middle of the block. "Sir," he said to Mr. Dunn. "You look like a good man. I haven't eaten today." Leo Dunn dug into his pockets, came up with a quarter, then a dime. I did the same.

"Thank you, Kevin," Mr. Dunn said when the guy had left. "I once was about where he is now. I pray to God I never will be again. I made a promise many years ago that I would never turn down any request for help. Assisting others has helped me much more than what I've done has helped them."

I nodded like I understood.

We turned and started back. "I plead," said Mr. Dunn, "for compassion for the poor drunk inside each of us, Kevin. There's a way in which our basic instincts play us false. Other people don't have that trouble. But a drunk's instinct is like a bad knee. He can't put his full weight on it. What seems to him a sure thing is just bad judgment. The young man you described can only be helped if he learns that. The same is true for you, my friend."

We walked back silently. I was lost in thoughts about the white room. A big reason for my sobriety was Leo Dunn's convincing me that saving my life was a worthwhile project. Carl's testimony had thoroughly undermined that case. I found myself wondering where my Shadow was and how much of this he knew.

Mr. Dunn sighed when we got back to his building. "Nice walking with you. This is Wednesday. I have a special client in from England all day tomorrow. I want to see you Friday at six. But call me sooner if there are any problems. This is important. Against great odds, you have stayed sober for months and I am very proud of you."

When I got home, sunlight still bounced off concrete and chrome, blazed on the Hudson at the end of the street. My block, all small trucking companies and decaying tenements, was a long-established whore run. That evening, the girls' halters were extra skimpy, their skirts mere slivers.

My apartment was at street level with the windows of its front room barred like a cell. The place was two tiny rooms and a bath. It was damp and impossible to keep clean. But it was cheap and not quite the gutter.

It was dark by the time I reemerged. Certain girls I thought of as regulars. One, a Black called Rosie, had a sweet, round face. "You want a date?" she asked.

When I smiled and shook my head, her friend Carla laughed and said. "Don't bother with him. Where he's going, they're giving ass away."

Down on West Street, guys flocked like pilgrims to a holy place. Then someone dropped a heavy set of keys with a sound like a hammer hitting an empty chamber. Suddenly, the warmth drained out of my night and the scene lost all appeal.

A drink seemed very tempting at that moment. Drugs were easily available. Carl was the one I had to see. His life and mine had tangled together again. It seemed to me I could save myself by saving him. But he wasn't at the Landing. I spent hours circling the hotel waiting for the lights to be on in his room.

The girls were busy when I gave up and came home. Across the street, Rosie bent over to talk to a taxi driver, exposing her ass to the world. Compared to me, she was so innocent.

My apartment was an oven. The bedroom was a crypt. Finally, I dragged my mattress out near the front window and fell asleep to the music of the car radios of the cruising johns. Then deep in the night, a familiar voice called, "Kevin? Kevin we got to talk."

I awoke and recognized Carl crouched outside. Only when I rose and went to the window did I see that his eyes stared empty and unfocused. The white of his right eye was dark red. The entrance wound on his right temple still throbbed with blood.

I closed my eyes so as not to look at his ruined face. But I could still hear him. "Kevin, I talked about you again tonight. I held the gun and faced the camera and told how when I was a kid and scared you talked to me the way no one else ever had.

"You used to say how you weren't going to clear thirty because you didn't want to. You were going up in smoke, you said. The hustlers and queens and junkies were going to be amazed by what they saw. The important thing was to call the shots, to make it your own game.

"I told them how after, when we didn't have much to do with each other, I'd still see you around and it looked like you were right on schedule. When you disappeared, I thought the way you went wasn't that great. But at least your words meant something.

"All of a sudden I saw you again. And I thought that maybe you had problems with forgetting. Like forgetting it was time to die. But when I reminded you, man, you were afraid.

"That made me afraid. For the first time tonight, when I put the gun to my head, my hand shook. The magic was gone. When the gun went off, the sound of the explosion hurt worse than the bullet.

"It was weird. I could still see the room, but from high above. Like I can see us now with you too scared to look. Michael threw up, but Judith was so goddamn cool. She got her stuff and him out of there so fast that she stepped over me on the way. I could have been alive. They didn't even check for a pulse."

Carl paused. The thought of their leaving him for dead brought bile to my throat. "For years, my mother hangs up the phone when I call," he said. "You're the only one I can tell."

But, as if I knew what he was going to ask, I had stopped listening and turned away. Rage pounded in my heart. I was a hanging judge. I reached for Carl through the bars and felt nothing. I opened my eyes and saw only the first gray of dawn and a couple of hookers watching me from across the street.

In a kind of trance, I got dressed and went around to the Landing Hotel. Sometime after that, I called Mr. Dunn from a pay phone. "Carl who I told you about? He talked to me last night. It must have been when he died. The side of his head was all blown off. Just now, I saw the police take his body out of his hotel."

"Kevin, where are you?" Dunn was very calm.

"Everyone will think it's suicide. But those two bastards killed him with a lot of help from me."

"The older I get, the more sure I am that there is no great trick to becoming dead. Life, that's the hard part. For some poor souls it proves impossible. I have confidence that you aren't one of those. I want you to come up here and talk."

"He came to me asking for justice. For revenge!"

"They aren't the same thing," was the reply and I hung up. To the judges of my secret court, blame for what had happened to Carl was obvious and only one course was open.

For what had to be done, I needed fuel. In the first bar I saw, a nondescript place down the avenue from the Landing, I got a double bourbon, my first drink in months. Despite the heat, it was the only warmth in my body.

When I told Carl the part of me he remembered was gone, I was lying. I saw a figure, filmy, translucent, move behind me in the mirror and I knew my Shadow walked with me. He wasn't there when I turned so I ordered another double and felt myself in a place beyond fear and pain where I was judge, jury, and executioner.

I took out the piece of paper that Carl had given me. On one side was a faded number with a New Jersey area code. On the other, several numbers had been crossed out. One remained with "Judith" written beside it. The phone booth was at the back of the joint.

The line was busy. I returned to the bar and had a drink. Then I called again. I did that a few times until the phone was picked up. "This is Kevin, Carl's friend," I said and the person at the other end hung up. When I dialed again, the line was busy.

A delivery man wheeled a loaded hand truck into the bar. A couple of guys in coveralls came in for a midmorning snort. I finished my drink and dialed. The phone rang six or seven times before it was picked up. I said, "This is Kevin. I'm ready to play my scene." The other party hesitated before they hung up.

The delivery man needed to use the phone. I had one more drink and left. The vacation from booze had done me good. The stuff hit me the way it had when I was sixteen.

But now at thirty, I had better connections. In a narrow candy store on Eighteenth Street, I walked the length of the counter back to where the magazines were. "You got that racing magazine?" I asked the tiny woman with reddish blond hair. She looked at me empty faced and I held up five fingers.

"Twenty," she said. I had all my money with me. Without arguing, I gave her twenty dollars and took the five black beauties she dealt.

The amphetamine kicked in fast. My senses were acute. When I called from a street phone, I heard two receivers get picked up. Then I heard myself say, "What Carl did, he did because of me. I accept my guilt. I'm going to put myself on trial right in front of you. The penalty will be execution."

Around me, people were out of their offices for lunch. Michael said in a whisper, "We can talk about it tomorrow."

"The scene gets played today with you filming it or not."

"We can't," he said.

"Where?" Judith asked.

"I have a room that looks like a cell."

"When?"

"As soon as you can get to my place with a camera and a loaded revolver." I understood my plan only as I heard myself speak it.

"If you don't have a gun, how are you going to play roulette?" he whined.

But Judith grabbed at what I offered. "Call back in an hour," she said.

Ten minutes later on Thirty-first near Penn Station, my nerves jumped as I ran up two flights of stairs. I called, "Angel? Man, what you got?"

A peephole opened. "Motherfucker, who are you? I don't know you." But Angel let me in. The door clicked behind me. And I heard a hammer hit an empty chamber.

Once I had bought junk and taken some, everything became more like a dream. I asked, "When?" from a phone booth.

"A few hours. Hang on. I'm waiting for the guy to bring the piece."

I gave Judith my address and telephone number. "Ring three times. Hang up and ring again." Then I sat in a playground near the river and plotted the scene, saw in detail how Judith and Michael would arrive at my apartment and set up their equipment.

It's dark by that time and I move smoothly to draw the curtains against prying eyes from the street. I see Michael, looking sick and scared, hand me the unloaded revolver. It's a Smith and Wesson .38. Sober, I would never touch it. But as an agent of the court, I fear nothing. "Let me have six bullets so I can be sure."

"Five," says Judith. "There's no dramatic tension if it's six." Both of them are sweating but I feel cold. I don't argue. I just make sure that I'm seated between them and the exit.

She films me loading the piece. The junk lets me sit quietly until all is ready and I can face the camera and say, "The secret court condemns everyone who killed Carl: the family who abandoned him, the johns who used him. But they are beyond our control. Before us right now are prime murderers, the one who gave him the idea, the ones who stand to profit from his death."

Michael breaks and runs as soon as I level the revolver. The first shot catches him in the side and he falls through the bathroom doorway. My second shot hits the camera. Judith cries in a high-pitched wail as she backs into the bedroom. A shot in her face throws her against the wall. I finish off Michael as he writhes under the sink.

That leaves one bullet for me. I am careful not to waste it. The last sounds I hear are shouts and footsteps on the street and then a final explosion. There is an unbearable bulge behind my eyes. Then something snaps and all is black. Such was the movie that ran in my head.

When I came off the nod, I was still sitting on the bench. Before me, silent gray forms moved majestically from left to right up the Hudson. Rising, I saw that it was a tugboat hauling a string of barges.

On the street outside my place, Rosie and the night shift had just come on duty as I came home. "Honey, you look bad. Want a date? We can do it in your place." I shook my head. "Your friend the other night seemed like he was hurt bad." I looked at her. "The one talking to you at the window," she explained.

In my apartment, the phone rang three times, stopped, and rang again. I picked it up. "Yeah?"

"The gun took longer than we expected," said Judith. "We'll

be over within an hour. Just hold on." As she spoke, I glimpsed a face outside the window. Pale and fleeting, it was gone when I went to look.

At first, I thought it was my Shadow. Then I wondered if it was Carl reminding me. He didn't have to worry. All that remained was enacting what I had already seen.

While waiting, I nodded out. The phone rang and I came to in the light of the setting sun. It stopped and rang again. Knowing it was Leo Dunn, I ignored it. Having him plead my case would make it hard to maintain my remote calm.

It was dark when Judith and Michael appeared at my apartment. Things ran much as I had foreseen. They set up their equipment. I moved to draw the curtain against prying eyes from the street.

Against the city night, I saw a pale face. Reaching back, I turned off the lights. The two behind me protested. Then they saw and shut up.

"Kevin." Carl's voice was a whisper. "They got me in the morgue. I am more cold and lonely than I could ever have believed."

"He's still alive?" Michael said. "It's a trap!" I heard them scramble for their equipment in the dark.

This time, I looked at Carl. Evening masked the wound and he appeared lost, childlike. Once, when he first lived with me, before I trusted him, before I loved him, I had stayed out all night drinking and forgot he had no key. Coming home, I found him sitting on the stairs rocking back and forth with his head on his knees. When I called his name and he raised his head, it was with the same lost expression he had outside the window.

The memory tore my heart. Behind me the door banged as Michael and Judith fled. "Kevin," Carl pleaded. "Don't get angry and stop listening like last night. I have no ID, nothing to tell them who I am. My mom's number was on the back of the paper I gave you. They don't know who to call. You're the only one I can ask for help. See if she won't come get my corpse. All I want is some place to rest. That's all. Please?"

I managed to choke out, "Forgive me, Carl." Then the booze and drugs caught up with me. My head spun and everything went black.

Light hit my eyes like nails and all I could see was a tall figure looking down at me. "Jesus Christ," I said.

"No," replied Leo Dunn. "You're not even close."

I lay on the floor of my front room feeling very sick and criminally stupid. "How did you get in here?"

"I couldn't sleep last night thinking about you. I came down this morning and saw you lying in here. Two young ladies from the street picked the lock. Did it easily. In their way they were quite concerned."

Still confused, I saw, on the floor, the paper with Judith's number. I looked around expecting to see carnage. "What have I done? What the fuck have I done?" I crumpled the paper.

"Nothing that millions of others before you haven't. Wash your face and put on a clean shirt and we'll begin again." His voice held a sadness that I had never before heard there. And I was the cause.

My secret court was still in session. Judges, a whole panel of them, held that I didn't deserve to be in the same room with anyone who could still stand the sight of me. Instead of wasting Mr. Dunn's time, I should continue what I had started and kill myself. I could think of no redeeming aspect, nothing that would cause me to be allowed to continue in this life.

Then I looked down at my hand and remembered one slim possibility. Smoothing the paper, I looked at the Jersey number. It rang several times and I felt my life hang in the balance. "Hello?" a woman answered.

"Mrs. Valleck?"

"Not for years." She sounded tough but tired.

I took a deep breath. "It's about Carl." On the other end was silence. What could I say? I hesitated.

Mr. Dunn reached out and put his hand on my shoulder. It was the only time he ever touched me except to shake hands. I almost felt like I had dirtied him. Then I looked up and he smiled at me. "I'm sorry I have to be the one," I said. "But he wanted you to be told."

It wasn't easy. But Mrs. Valleck didn't break down and I hardly did. We agreed to meet up at the medical examiner's office. Mr. Dunn said, "Let's fix you up, Kevin." We drove uptown past the sprawl of the Port Authority to the Market Diner, the heart of Irish Hell's Kitchen. The Market was a place where the road met the city. Cross-country truckers and street thugs ate their steak and eggs, drank their shots and beer. Cops' radios blasted in the take-out line.

Anyone seeing us walk in might have thought we were a distinguished criminal lawyer saddled with some friend's black sheep boy as a client. I had the always painful look of a guy who has done himself damage on the street. Mr. Dunn, on the other hand, tall and smiling, wore a gray suit and a blue shirt that matched his eyes. As soon as we came in, a waitress in her fifties with a blond beehive and wing glasses spotted him and said, "Leo!"

"Dorry! How's it going with Jack?"

"Bearable, which is a lot more than I could say before."

"Dorry, this is Kevin."

And she understood why I was there. "Kevin, this is a great man. I got a son about your age who is only walking the earth because of him. Now, what can I do for youse?"

"Coffee for myself, but my friend here needs the works." Dorry nodded and departed.

My stomach lurched. I excused myself and went downstairs to the men's room, splashed water on my face, tried to get my insides to lie down. 'Hey,' came the whisper. I looked up and there twice in the mirror was the scar, the tangled hair, the two days' growth of beard, a fresh bruise on the chin. Only the bloodshot eyes were different. Mine were scared. His were clever. 'I guess,' my Shadow murmured, 'that you're ready to blame everything on me. In fact, I had nothing to do with your little spree.'

"Why can't you just die?"

'You might not like that, Kev. You might die along with me. Anyway, I miss you. You have any idea what life is like without you? I mostly float in what feels like a long junk dose. Then every once in a while the soles of my feet, my fingers, tingle. And that means that you're thinking of living enough for two. Without you, there's hardly any me. Without me you're a dangerous chump. But together? Together we make a pretty fair psychopath. Think of that, Kevin, in your dull routine.'

Before he could talk his way around me, I said, "Go." Just like that he disappeared. A trucker came out of one of the stalls and gave me a weird look. I left wondering how much of the conversation he'd heard. Only my side? Or that and the whispers of my Silent Partner?

At our booth, Dorry was saying, "Coffee *and* toast for you, Leo, since you look like you ain't eating. Coffee for you too, kid. But first . . ." She handed me a bubbling glass and a saucer with aspirin and a couple of other pills. The two of them watched until I had taken them all.

"What's wrong, Kevin?" Mr. Dunn asked when we were alone.

"I just saw my Silent Partner. I told him to get lost."

Mr. Dunn sighed, glanced out at the blank wall of the United Parcel building across the street. I knew it bothered him when I spoke of the Silent Partner as real. Psychosis was a problem about which he could do nothing.

"Sorry."

"Don't be. Don't ever be. You hired me to help you. If there's a failure, it's mine." Then he looked up and his eyes widened. "I believe you were sent by God to teach me humility. Forget my doubting the actual existence of your Silent Partner. Maybe we all have them. If so, here comes mine."

"Leo," said the little man under the battered gray fedora. "A word with you?" I caught the scent of stale cigars and fresh booze. "I hope I'm not interrupting."

"Indeed you are, Francis. I see that reports of your demise were sadly exaggerated."

Extending his hand to me, the other man said, "Francis X. MacLunahan, Esquire." Small, furtive, threadbare, he was a kind of reverse image of Leo Dunn. He looked at me closely and it seemed that he too recognized something. "Young man, it often happens in this life that one needs a lawyer. If that is your case—"

"I'll see you in a moment, Francis," said Mr. Dunn, cutting him off. It was the only time I ever saw him be rude to anyone.

As MacLunahan faded back, Dunn told me, "Your Silent Partner wants everything, your money, your health, your peace of mind. The further you give in to booze and drugs, the less of you there is and the stronger he becomes."

He glanced to where MacLunahan seemed about to blend into the diner doorway. "I contributed money a few years ago for his funeral. My guess is that on the strength of his having been a companion in my drinking days and later having de-frauded me, this particular Silent Partner wants a hundred dol-lars." He rose up saying, "I'll give him twenty, since that's what I can spare."

That afternoon, I went with Carl's mother to the morgue, stood by her when they showed the remains and while she filled out endless forms. His eyes had come from her. She was a good-looking woman. His father, Carl had once told me, was very handsome but violent.

When they said Carl's death was suicide, I said nothing. He

was buried out of the Ukrainian funeral home on Seventh Street in the East Village. The casket was closed. All Mrs. Valleck's old friends and relatives, people who knew Carl from when he was a kid in the neighborhood, came by. I was the only one in attendance who was part of his later life. Judith and Michael did not show.

The leaves on the trees in Tompkins Square Park whispered in the evening of the wake. When the funeral was over, I came back to my cellar apartment, packed my clothes, kissed Rosie and Carla good-by, and left.

My next home, the Abigail Adams Hotel on Lexington Avenue in the Thirties, was a horror. But not my own private one. Smashed faces did not call my name from the window, my double did not stalk the halls. Gina Raille found me a job weekends working the door of a club in the Village. It didn't pay all that well, but it and my research job meant I was at the Abigail Adams as rarely as possible.

Toward the end of summer, word found its way to me. Sarah Callendar was happy to hear that I was okay. It seemed she had a proposal for me and wondered if I would call her. The friends who relayed the message were as surprised as I was.

NINE

MY DOOR BUZZER yanked me back to the present. I went to the intercom and said, "What?"

"Kevin?" The voice was slurred, uncertain. "Can I come up? Please?" It sounded like Matt. But after ringing him in, I stood ready to slam my door on the off chance I found heads flickering like gaslights or my own mug coming at me.

The clothes and hair were a flash of the past. The good brothers of St. Sebastian's S & M had turned out to be fashion prophets. But the face was Matt's. In an unguarded moment as he turned on to my landing and before he looked up at me, I caught a glimpse of terror and exhaustion and saw the large, fresh bruise on his left cheek. His eye was swollen half shut.

"Kevin!" He looked at me warily and touched the bruise. "I fell and got banged up. It doesn't feel like it got broken. I thought maybe you'd understand. . . ."

"And not ask who hit you?" A disfigurement like that was going to make it very hard for him to earn his living. It reminded me of bad times when I was his age. I could tell exactly how my Shadow was trying to twist my head.

"I fucked up. I need a place to crash. Fred told me you try and help people sometimes." He shrugged to indicate that whatever happened would be up to me. His vulnerability was chilling. "I know what you think: 'A boy this careless isn't going to live long.' "

So the kid wasn't entirely stupid. I stopped trying to figure out my doppelganger's games, smiled, and let him in. Matt's body vibrated slightly as he hugged me. He smelled of cheap cologne and funk. The clothes were the same ones he'd worn the night before last. His bag was gone.

"You're hungry?" He shook his head. But in my kitchen over the next half hour he demolished bagels and eggs, orange juice and milk, pasta from the microwave, bananas and granola. At one point he told me, "Fred says you despise him because he's broke and because he can't stay sober and he's sick. He said you both have some magic."

In the back of my medicine chest was the remains of an old Percodan prescription left over from an episode of root canal. I gave Matt a couple. His head began to nod. I led him to the bedroom and got him out of his clothes. The kid turned me on. But when all I did was tuck him in, he smiled like a little child.

The phone rang and the answering machine came on. It was Klackman. "Grierson? Where are you? This deal isn't going to be here forever." I didn't pick up. He sounded more than a little desperate. I wondered what kind of threats the gas heads had made.

Then I sat for a long time and thought about my Shadow saying that we had magic. I wondered if magic, like sobriety, is evoked by remembering the past but not getting caught by it. I thought of what he said about me helping people and I thought of the second time I'd lived with Sarah and Scotty.

People had said she wanted to see me, but the warmth of her welcome was a surprise. Sarah Bryce Callendar met me at the door of the loft wearing a wonderful turquoise blouse. I could remember when the whole place was raw, unfinished wilderness with a small settled area around the kitchen and bedrooms.

Now, she threw open the door of the guest room and I saw a big bed with a soft comforter. A table and chest of drawers were set between two ten-foot-tall windows. "There's space for you here, Kevin. I'd like you to stay, if you think that's possible." Her auburn hair was worn long and loose.

Her offer was more than I'd been able to imagine. Unlike our last time together, Sarah and I would clearly not be lovers. My bedroom was all the way across the loft from hers. Still, her kindness almost overwhelmed me. "Thanks for being able to forgive," I managed to say.

"Kev, whatever else happened, we started out as friends. When I heard you had cleaned up and needed a place, I knew you were the only one I wanted here. I understand you have to hold two jobs to get by. I'd like you to quit the weekend one. Room and board will be free. Since I can't be here with Scotty on Saturday and Sunday during the day, I'd especially like you to be around then. How soon can you move in?"

Her making it sound like she needed me soothed the pain of being thirty-plus and scrounging for a place to live. "Tonight?"

"Great. You heard what this is about?"

"Something with your in-laws."

"They've made noises about wanting custody of their only grandchild."

Scotty was over at a friend's. His room was next to mine, its door open. I looked in on a eight-year-old's lair and said, "What about the kid? I was pretty rough on him."

"He still asks about you, Kevin." Out in the main living area, a phone rang and Sarah went to answer it.

I looked around Scott's room. A green plastic brontosaurus with bright red eyes was new to me. The diesel engine and battered cars, the handful of beat-up metal grenadiers, I recalled from my last stay. They were the legacy of Scott Callendar Sr.

The tall chest in the corner was Sarah's, come down from an ancestor who had been a ship's captain. In gold paint on its dark front, chipped and scratched Chinese men in robes and wide hats poked with long sticks at a large porcupine.

On the chair next to the bed were a couple of books open and facedown. One, a collection of rhymes called *A Garland Knot for Children*, seemed familiar and I didn't immediately remember why. Picking it up, I saw inscriptions on the title page indicating that it had been in the Callendar family for generations. *Garland* contained favorites like "Humpty Dumpty" and "Mary Had a Little Lamb" along with odd limericks, riddles, and fragments I'd never seen before.

The original artwork was woodcuts. But the book had gotten annotated over the years with crayon drawings and faded pencil scribbles by children now old or dead. My attention was caught by a brand new thumb-sized illustration in red, black, and yellow. I recognized Scott Jr.'s work. The poem on that page, strange and irregular, went:

I CAME, SIR, FOR FAME, SIR
THE SPOILS OF YOUR FAIR TOWN
AND 'TWAS STRANGE TO SEE, SIR
THE WHOLE WORLD WAS WATCHING ME

I DIED, SIR, IN FLAME, SIR
THE OLD DEVIL TOOK ME DOWN
IF YOU DOUBT 'TIS TRUE, SIR
YOU WON'T WHEN HE COMES FOR YOU

At first, I thought he had drawn a match head. It took me a moment to realize it was a fiery motorcycle and rider. I slammed the book shut and had a moment's trouble getting my breath. This had been on the storeroom desk the last time I spoke to Scott Jr. It felt warm to the touch.

The trail of memories the book evoked was one I would have preferred not to follow. But Carl had shown me that was impossible. I had to perform what Mr. Dunn called the balancing act: remembering the past but not letting it control me. I put *Garland Knot* down very carefully and left the room.

In the rolling main area of her loft, the couches were draped with quilts in Southwest motifs, samples for Sarah's store. She told me, "I'm advised not to let Scott go visit his grandparents for fear of not getting him back. It's hard to make him understand why he can't see his only grandfather. And even though I think they're mighty creepy, I don't like him to grow up hating them."

The front windows looked out on a cobblestoned street. "Recently," she said, "I noticed a black van parked across the street and a guy in it, just watching. A couple of times I spotted another man out back staring up at this place. I feel like I'm under observation."

The back view was a deserted SoHo panorama of faded brick and old wooden water towers. The roof behind was three floors down and separated from us by an alley. "Let's see what happens," I said, trying to sound wise and tough.

As she let me out, Sarah asked, "Remember Ian? You hated him, right? Well, he got real mean before he went back to England. Frankie you never met. Looked like a million bucks. Had a million bucks, said he loved kids. After two months, he was doubled over with back pain and screaming at us. I decided to take a short pause and think things over." She almost looked haunted as she told me that. Like she was beginning to wonder where she found guys like all of us.

Down on the street, I looked for the black van she had mentioned. In the September twilight, beneath the iron fire escapes, artists in work clothes smoked dope on loading docks, a cluster of Spanish women headed home from the Triboro Pinking Shears Company.

SoHo was no longer the frontier. By the midseventies, Manhattan south of Houston Street had started to boom, and the World Trade Center's twin towers were an eye-catching wonderment on the downtown skyline. But Fanelli's bar and the shops still closed in the evening. Despite grow lamps in loft windows, whole blocks of SoHo could still seem empty after dark. Riding the IRT uptown, I thought about Sarah's taste for guys who were flying off the beam. It was her only failing.

Mr. Dunn's number was like a charm in my wallet. That night, the evening of my reunion with Sarah, I called from a pay phone and told him what had happened. "That sounds like wonderful luck, my friend," he said.

That was my thought also. I returned to the Abigail Adams Hotel at Thirty-third and Lexington and packed my bags. As I did, some guy upstairs screamed like his teeth were being pulled out. Then I walked through a lobby full of hookers and took a cab downtown.

My first Saturday back in the loft was September bright. The TV was on in Scott's room when I made my way to the kitchen. The two of us hadn't spoken much since my return. Sarah went out the front door telling me, "This may be a late day."

The kitchen contained potentially dangerous things, sharp knives, a small box of matches. None of them could do harm if they were left alone. While the tea brewed, my eyes were drawn to the cabinet where Sarah kept liquor.

My last time in residence, it had been a shrine for the display of my totemic symbol, the empty booze bottle. Since then, it had been restocked with name brands: Johnnie Walker Red, Bombay Gin, Napoleon brandy, a few well-chosen wines.

The night I showed up again, Sarah had asked if I wanted her to clear it out. I shook my head. "Booze will always be there," Mr. Dunn once told me. "Get used to it. They won't reinstitute the Volstead Act just for you and me."

As I thought about that, Scott came out of his room and

went to the refrigerator without saying anything. Pushing the blond hair from his dark eyes, he pulled out a giant Coke bottle, spun on one sneaker heel, hooked a mug off the shelf, and poured in one continuous action. As I sat wondering how to begin to untangle things, he saw me watching him. "Kevin?"

"Yeah?"

"Mom says you're not drinking and stuff."

"That's right."

"I'm glad." Very solemnly, he came over to me and shook my hand.

"Me too," I said, full of wonder at kids' wisdom. "Listen, Scott, I'm sorry for a lot of things I may have said and done. About that last time you saw me in particular."

I was prepared to go on. But Scott nodded and said, "Okay," like the subject was closed and we were friends again.

That Saturday, we had two adventures. The first began in Scott's room shortly after our handshake. He held up a drawing of an Indian medicine man wearing a buffalo mask. The eyes behind the holes looked mean. "This is a Sioux," he said. "I'm doing it for school. You like him, huh?"

"It's great. Especially the eyes." I couldn't find *A Garland Knot for Children* and wasn't quite ready to ask. Suddenly, Scott turned toward the window and shouted, "There's the guy Mom talks about!"

Looking out, I saw a man with wild gray hair staring up avidly, eyes hidden behind thick glasses. His wrinkled face reminded me of an old sponge. I recognized a chance for an easy triumph. "That's TJ," I said. "Let's go talk to him."

Without hesitation, Scott ran for his jacket. As we walked around the block, I remembered TJ. He had been a drinking companion of Jackson Pollock's, a friend of de Kooning's. A couple of falls on the head had left him permanently dazed, a very abstract expressionist. "The guy's an old-time artist," I told Scotty.

On Greene Street, directly behind Sarah's place, was a one-story converted garage. From my previous stay in the neighborhood, I knew that a bored old lady sculptor gave life-drawing classes there on the weekends. She and TJ were a longtime item.

Everything worked perfectly. Scott and I arrived at a break. Students stood outside smoking, discussing art. Indoors, a young lady in a robe did flexing exercises to get her circulation back. I told the teacher, "Listen, we live on the next block. There's a problem at the back of our building and we'd like to get up on your roof, take a look."

She shrugged. We went up a flight of iron stairs, came out on the roof behind TJ. He was still looking up. Following his gaze, I saw what at first seemed like a stain on the wall next to Scott's windows and mine.

It took me a moment to decipher it. Pointing, I told Scott, "That's an old advertising mural of some kind. The words are worn away. All that's left of the ad is color, splotches of red and dying yellow, like a faded canvas."

The artist turned around looking confused, a little embarrassed. "Good morning, TJ," I said. "Looking at the mural?"

"I was." I started walking away. "Fucking tourists," he added in a toothless, Loony Tunes delivery. I felt bad intruding on him that way. But Scotty seemed fascinated. When we went back downstairs, the class had started again. He watched the nude model out of the corner of his eye.

Outside, Scott told me, "TJ is okay. Frankie always said he was going to talk to the guy, scare him away. But Frankie always got sick with a bad back. He was an asshole."

I had never met Frankie, but given what I knew of Sarah's tastes, that seemed not unlikely. We went home and had lunch: peanut butter and jelly sandwiches all around. "We can tell your mother that she doesn't have to worry about TJ." I felt like I was earning my keep.

Scott nodded, one man of the world to another, then asked out of nowhere, "Do you remember the Islands Game?"

"I'm the one who showed it to you." The kid amazed me. I had wondered how to bring up certain things that lay in Scott's past. The Islands Game was the perfect way. "Let's look at your toys. Got anything new?"

His room, with its wide expanse of floor, the light flooding in the windows, was the ideal playing area. Since I'd been gone, Scott had acquired a castle, a fine wooden structure with a drawbridge and some stalwart plastic knights to guard it. One knight appeared slightly fused—like he might have been the victim of an experiment with fire.

Also present were a garage, a train station, what looked like the cabin of an antique Noah's ark, toy trees, a train, and tracks and blocks. "Plenty of blocks," I said.

"Let's make three islands," Scott suggested. "And a boat."

The game was evocative. As we went to work, I thought of Uncle Jamey teaching me the game when I was about ten. A long and dapper man, his hair the color of gray sand, he was Gramny and Aunt Tay's youngest brother, over from Dublin for a family funeral. Stepping into my room, he saw me sitting alone among my possessions and said, "Ah, would you look at this!" Picking up a cannon, he asked, "Does it fire now?" We talked for quite a while about my toys.

As mysterious to me as the death of the relative I hardly knew was the hostile chill between my mother and stepfather. A few days later when my mother had to be away, Uncle Jamey came back and spent an afternoon playing on the floor with me. I remember his breath flavored with whiskey and cigarettes as he said, "Those you have in your hand are Highlanders. Fierce fighters but unwitting tools of English imperialism. Where shall we put them?"

"In the fort," I answered. "You can be their leader if you want."

"Thanks kindly. And where do we put the fort?"

"On this island. They're hiding there because of the Indians and animals."

"The garrison and I will hold against the half-naked savages and wild lions," said Uncle Jamey, who wrote for the newspapers back in Ireland. "And what will you be doing?"

"I'm this guy," I said, producing a cowboy on a rearing horse. "He's gonna lead the cavalry to rescue you. But he doesn't know you're in danger."

Mr. Dunn, who had taught me that I could never forget the past, also said that some memories were like bombs to be defused with great care. Kids are aware of everything and nothing. At ten, I knew that my mother and stepfather didn't get along and that it was getting worse and worse. But, as kids do, I accepted that, just as I accepted the existence of my mother's Shadow.

By the time of the funeral, my stepfather was never around and my mother's Shadow was around all the time. I had questions about what was happening and, in Jamey, an adult who could have answered them. But I couldn't find the words or the way to ask. That weekend, as their marriage wound up, I was slaying lions, defeating Indians, rescuing Uncle Jamey.

As Scott and I built islands out of blocks, placed the buildings and trees on them, made an African Queen sort of ship out of a shoe box, I remembered Jamey saying, "No one wins or loses the Islands Game."

"What about the castle?" I asked Scott.

"Ian made that the castle of the evil prince," Scott said.

Jealousy rose in me. "He knew the game?"

"I showed it to him. He had to be the good knight and win." He gestured toward the slightly melted figure. "He was an asshole."

Ian had been my immediate successor and I couldn't have agreed more. "Did you show Frankie the game too?"

"One time. He wanted to be the American soldier and shoot everybody, then he hurt his back and couldn't play." Scott laid out the figures: the metal English guardsmen—one or two of whom had misplaced their heads—the knights, a dozen or so plastic Indians, several West Point cadets, an outsize GI missing his rifle.

We even had civilians: a worn, ancient Mr. and Mrs. Noah, a silver ballerina, Mickey Mouse dressed as a Keystone Kop, an armless china shepherdess, a pair of small pipe cleaner dolls in Mexican gear. Animals also appeared, a wooden bear and tiger left over from the flood, assorted plastic cows and pigs, a camel from a nativity scene.

"The GI is on this island with the tiger," I said. "He doesn't know the war is over." As I picked the figure up, I noticed a welt along its back.

Scott produced a chicken that laid white marble eggs and was bigger than a man mounted on a horse. "Maybe that can be the roc. Its eggs are magic," I suggested.

"It lives in the castle on the big island," Scott added. He put the grenadiers in a boat. "These belonged to my father. This one is me." He held up the officer. "I heard about the legend. I'm sailing the boat looking for the roc."

"I'm the captain of the ship." I put a cadet on the bridge. "Whoever gets a roc egg can ask any question he wants and the roc will answer." That was my own contribution to the game: the chance to ask a question.

Half the afternoon went in setting up the islands. The rest we spent moving the boat a couple of feet each turn, deciding where to land and what happened then. Scott, as the grenadier officer, was brave yet merciful. I tagged along, uttering an occasional, "Avast there!" in my capacity as the ship's captain. Between us, we played everyone else from the camel to Mrs. Noah.

From a position flat on the floor, I discovered again that furniture could be mountains, the ceiling, sky. Holding a railroad engine in one hand, a cow in the other, I felt at once mouse and monster: in other words, eight years old.

As the sun faded, Scott pushed the guardsmen and the Indians who had become their friends past the ark cabin where the ballerina stood. "Because they helped her capture the bear," I explained, "the silver goddess tells them about a secret entrance to the castle."

With amazing ease, Scott polished off the knights who were doing duty as the slave robots of the roc. I sensed his great urgency. The final confrontation was anticlimactic. The grenadiers burst into the throne room, Scott pressed the roc's head and grabbed the egg.

"I get to ask it a question," he said, "and it has to answer correctly."

"Okay."

Without even taking a deep breath, he asked, "Are Kevin and Mom going to start making it again?"

Instead of pretending to be the roc, I answered him simply. "No chance at all. She's letting me stay here for old time's sake."

Scott nodded seriously.

Then I moved the cadet/naval captain up to the throne, pressed the chicken's head, and picked up the white glass egg. This seemed the right moment to ask, "What has become of the sacred lost book *A Garland Knot for Children?*"

Scott was startled. He shrugged and gave me a wide-eyed, baffled look like I had asked the unknowable. "Hey," I said, "the mystical and holy chicken has to answer."

Scott was quick. He spoke into cupped hands for an echoing oracle effect. "It's gone to the land of dust bunnies and lost socks." All I could do was laugh. Afterwards, I looked again under his bed and behind the radiator.

When Sarah returned, Scott leaped up saying, "Me and

Kevin talked to that guy on the roof out back. He's an old artist. He's cool!"

Next I decided to see about Van Man. My research job paid badly but was loosely structured. One morning at eight-thirty, I sat at a front window and watched Scott get picked up for school. Sarah bent to kiss him. He stood stock still. I had noticed the constraint before, like something stood between them.

No van was in sight. A bit after ten, just as Sarah left to open her store, the black van pulled up across the street.

Van Man was a beefy, sullen guy in his thirties. He sat at the wheel staring as Sarah walked up to Houston Street. It was hard to blame him. Living on the downside, I had forgotten that people could move with her grace. Van Man watched other ladies too. After a while, he got out, loaded boxes from the back of the van onto a hand truck, and headed down the block.

Very casually, I followed him over to Deluca's on Prince Street. These days, Dean & Deluca's is a huge, upscale emporium on Broadway that sells coffee for a dollar a bean. Then, Deluca's was a tiny shop offering the new residents of SoHo good breads, fine cheese, and countermen who made sandwiches while singing bel canto in the manner of Maria Callas.

From them I found out about Van Man. His name was Jay Imanella and he delivered farmer's cheese that his mother made. "Delivery days are the only time he gets away from her," said a tall, bearded diva. "We call him the Merry Farmer because he isn't. Usually we're his last stop. If you're really anxious to cruise him, he's probably down the street tying one on."

"Down the street," meant Fanelli's with its antique frosted windows and array of boxing photos. Jay Imanella sat at the polished bar amidst light sculptors and office supply salesmen. He drank in a joyless, determined way as I sipped club soda in a corner. Then he went back to sit in his truck and watch women go by.

This information I saved until its proper time. One night, I came back late from visiting Mr. Dunn and found Sarah sitting on the huge couch, her legs drawn up under a quilt, looking worried. She said, "The creep in the van was out front this morning when I left for the shop. He was still there when Scott came back from school."

"You think it's your in-laws?" I asked, knowing it wasn't, but curious about the Callendars.

"When they threatened to sue for guardianship, my lawyer warned me they might put the place under surveillance. To find something to use against me. She suggested they might try a snatch." Sarah sighed. "I joke about it, but I really think my mother-in-law is a witch. I don't want Scott to grow up hating his father's family. But they are so nasty and so strange. I can understand what my husband was trying to escape."

Sarah hardly every talked about him directly. "We were all pretty rebellious at that point," I said. But I remembered wondering when I really got to know Scott Sr. if my family was the only one with a curse.

"Every time he talked to them on the phone, he'd get angry, then he'd get stoned. And you remember how he got then, Kevin. Especially just before the end."

To that I made no answer. I recalled Scott Sr., blond haired, mad eyed, storming off to a fiery death in the ice and rain. I remembered many things. But all I said was, "Don't worry about Van Man."

Mr. Dunn would have said that what I planned was underhanded and more than a little cruel to a fellow drunk. So I never told him about it.

A couple of days later, I let Van Man stay in Fanelli's until he was sure to have a load aboard. Then I called the bar and asked for Jay Imanella. The poor, befuddled slob came to the phone. "Imanella," I told him in a dead, phlegm-choked voice. "I saw you looking at my wife. You know which one she is." Then I uttered the most terrible threat he could imagine. Two minutes later, I watched him hurry up the street, leap into the van, and speed away.

After a couple of weeks, Sarah said, "What did you do with Van Man?" and I just smiled enigmatically.

Maybe my sobriety was a new chance at childhood, or I was trying out what it would be like to have a kid. But in lots of ways that autumn, I was a perfect companion for an eight-year-old. I felt closer to Scotty than I ever had to almost anybody else. A couple of times we played touch football with some of his friends and their fathers. One Sunday I had to take him to a ninth birthday party for a beautiful little Asian girl whom he hated.

I began reading to him: *Treasure Island, Doctor Dolittle and the Secret Lake, The Thurber Carnival, Grimms' Fairy Tales, Nine Princes in Amber.* He liked most of them. I loved them all.

His hand-illustrated *Garland Knot for Children* was nowhere to be found. I searched the Fourth Avenue used bookstores for another copy. No one had ever heard of it.

On my way downtown from Mr. Dunn's one evening, I stopped at F.A.O. Schwarz and bought a fine plastic African elephant with an arched trunk and flared tusks. Scott was delighted when I placed the elephant at the center of the labyrinth we constructed in our next Islands Game. The way it looked pleased me too. But I regarded it as a kind of bait.

Once about then, I awoke with the fading memory of a dream. In it, I stood in the street outside the loft on a gray, overcast dawn. Looking downtown, I saw, instead of the World Trade Towers, the jean-clad legs of a gigantic child, disappearing into the morning fog. Nothing in the neighborhood stirred. The only sound was a motorcycle blocks away and approaching fast.

A Saturday or two later, we built a mountain topped by a ramshackle pagoda. Looking up from the floor, I saw the Chinese men on the chest tormenting a porcupine and said, "Those are the wise men of the mountain. Whoever makes it to the top of the pagoda can ask them a question."

When we took out the toys, I discovered that the elephant listed to the side. One of its legs was partially melted. Scott too looked surprised by this. I said nothing. In our game that day, I made sure that after some adventures and much imaginary mayhem, both Scott and I got to ask questions.

Scott asked first. He seemed a little anxious. "Can I get a skateboard for my birthday?"

In an outrageous accent, I replied, "This question is for wisdom even greater than that of the all-knowing porcupine pokers. We must ask Sarah, the mighty mother."

For my question, I held up the elephant and asked, "How did this get burned?"

Scott started to cup his hands for the echo effect but then thought better of it. Very hesitantly he said, "You know that book you asked about?"

"*Garland Knot?*"

"You saw the drawing I made?"

"The flaming cycle."

"That's what did it." He shrugged like I could believe him or not as I wanted.

Chilled, I started to ask him more questions, but he just stared at the elephant not with shame or regret but with a kind of savage awe.

When I looked, the matches in the kitchen were undisturbed. I found no others in the loft. The matter lay between us all week. Next Saturday, we sat watching TV. Scott, beside me on the couch, slouched down so his sneakers could reach the coffee table on which I'd rested my legs. Out of nowhere, he asked, "Kevin, remember what you said about my father?"

Flinching, I replied, "Whatever I may tell you, I'll never say that a lot of the time I don't act like an asshole."

"What you said was true. I asked about it. He's cool. If

you hadn't told me that, I would never have asked anyone. Mom wouldn't say much. But Grandma Callendar showed me a lot.

"She taught me where to draw the picture of him. That book was both of theirs. It's not around most of the time, only when Dad thinks there's going to be trouble or I'll need him. And the two of us can tell each other stuff. Like he was mad you were here but I explained you're cool."

I could think of nothing to say. In a couple of weeks, Scott was going to be nine years old, approaching the height of child-hood, a king among kids. I had loved his mother before she met her husband. And at first I had loved his father too for his beauty and style and appetites. Later I saw all of that translate into brutality.

Scott breathed a sigh, as if relieved that the message was de-livered. Did I detect some trepidation? A trace of the outlaw's kid who craves his father's secret, hurried visits even as he fears him? Before I could consider that, Scott jumped up and said, "Let's go and I'll show you the skateboard that I want."

Even though Halloween was past and everyone was thinking of family and Thanksgiving, that afternoon was lingering Oc-tober bright. Sarah was going to a dinner party after work and asked me to stay until she got back. "No later than twelve."

I took that to mean one. Maybe two. Plenty of time for me to seek my fortune over on West Street. Scott was long in bed when something called *Saturday Night Live* came on. Amaz-ingly, it seemed to be all drug jokes. An old TV movie followed that. Then I awoke to the sound of a key in the door. "Kev, I'm sorry," were her first words. "I just could not get away." Some-thing had not worked out for her that evening.

"It's fine." That came out sounding a lot sadder than I'd known it would. I threw aside the comforter and sat up.

She crossed the living-room area and gave me a cognac-flavored kiss. It was the first time we had kissed since before I'd moved away. "Scott's asleep?" she asked. I nodded. "I'm a lousy mother."

"You're just a party animal. He showed me the skateboard he wants for his birthday," I told her.

"What do you think?" Her tone said she saw it as a step on the road to the flaming motorcycle. She drew me up. Barefoot I was shorter than she was in heels.

"It'll be fine. I'm thinking of getting one myself." Sarah stood before me. She slipped her hands under my shirt. I said nothing, just waited to see what would happen. I'd come to realize that having a Shadow wasn't the only way I wasn't quite human. I never really understood what people wanted until they showed me.

She ran her hands over my skin and drew the shirt over my head. I kissed her. The taste of booze remained in her mouth. "Closest I can come to a nightcap," I said. She undid the belt and my pants hit the floor with a thud from the big brass buckle. We both paused. No sound came from Scotty's room.

City light shone through the windows and it was chilly in the loft. "Oh ho," she said. For cruising, I wore no underpants. Placing her jacket over my shoulders as I stepped away from my clothes, she led me to her bed.

Our being together was a surprise. I hadn't anticipated this. My recent partners had all been male and anonymous. This night was wonderfully familiar but upside down. For the first time I was sober and she was stoned, a creature of the subconscious. Her stockings down, her bra and panties off, her dress pulled up, she sat on my lap. She swam in my arms, brushed me like silk, bit me. And I responded.

Just as we climaxed, I saw us from above like I was a spider on the wall. I gasped and rolled flat on the bed. Sarah lay beside me. I looked up in the dark to see if I could spot my Shadow but Sarah distracted me. "Is what I did what it's like to pick up a hustler?" she asked, giggling.

"Well . . ." She'd never asked about that part of my life before and I guessed she was drunker than I'd thought. "Not quite," I said. But it bothered me that she thought of it like that. I fell silent.

A little later, Sarah asked, "Kev, you were so smug about it. How did you get rid of Van Man?"

"Simple. I just went downstairs and tipped his little truck over." She pinched my ass. "You really want to know? Promise you won't think less of me as a man?" She raised her hand like a Girl Scout.

"I asked around about him. Then I called him while he was at Fanelli's." Here I put on the voice full of phlegm and danger that I had used. "Imanella? I see what you're doing. I know where you live. I'm gonna tell your mother you're getting drunk and looking at my wife."

Even as Sarah laughed, I knew telling her was a dumb thing to do. A good magician doesn't reveal his tricks. A foolish one thinks the audience will love him anyway.

Abruptly, Sarah stopped laughing and asked, "Did Van Man have anything to do with my in-laws?"

"Not so far as I can tell."

"What I have is guilt projection. My anxiety leaking out. I did analysts, you know. All kinds. Because of my recurring feeling that my husband was somehow observing me. Haunting me because I didn't do enough to help him before that night. Rationally, I know there was no stopping him. I was afraid of him just before he died. He was demonic. My big worry with Scotty is that he'll turn out like his father."

That was the moment to tell her about *A Garland Knot for Children* and the singed toys. Just then, from somewhere uptown, louder than a backfire, came a single bang, an explosion in the night.

The sound startled me to full alert. But Sarah, as if she hadn't heard it, sighed and shifted away from me. A police siren ran north. Others, fire and ambulance followed. Clear and distant they were, as if far away or long ago. In the suddenly cold loft, in the suddenly wide bed, I looked to Sarah, but she was asleep.

When I picked up my clothes, the brass buckle was hot to the touch. Passing Scott's room, I noticed that his door was partly open. At the corner of my eye, a spark flared and was gone when I turned. Outside the windows, nothing stirred on the dark rooftops of SoHo.

Sleep was neither quick nor easy. Dreams and memories got entangled. Scott stared at me, his dark eyes pinned on his pale face. He sang a song of which I remembered the lines:

> I drove, sir, in flame sir,
> I burned like a match head

I woke up to drizzly Sunday morning. Groggy, I put on a robe Sarah had bought for me and staggered to the kitchen. There, Scott whined at his mother, "Then don't get me anything. If I don't get that board, I don't want your lousy presents!"

"Fine," Sarah replied, tight-lipped, slightly hungover. "Good morning," she said to me and left to get ready for work.

Scott looked up angrily and asked, "Were you out late?"

"Up late." It isn't wise, and probably not possible, to lie to a kid. But I felt that wasn't the moment to discuss the fact that his mother and I had been together again.

I showered and dressed and accompanied Sarah downstairs. The loading docks were bare, the streets empty. There were things about her son and her husband and about myself that I had to tell her. I didn't know how to start. Mist swirled around the World Trade Towers. She said, "I'm going to miss Van Man. If I have nothing to worry about, then why am I worried?"

"Sarah, there was something about Scott Callendar that last night. The drugs he took . . ."

She kissed me quickly. She didn't want to hear. "Kevin, thank you for last night. I broke the agreement we had and you were wonderful. I said some things to you that were really stupid and you were so sweet."

In the cold light of day, the night before didn't seem like a good idea to either of us. All that I had been going to say stuck in my throat. As she left and I turned to go back upstairs, I saw a figure on a loading dock down the street. My Shadow sat looking at me. Sarah didn't see him.

Riding back upstairs, I knew I couldn't stay there. In my maudlin self-pity, it seemed that all the good spots in the world were taken and there was no place for me. For the first time in many weeks, I remembered the liquor cabinet, pictured the bottles. Then I got angry at myself and decided to give Mr. Dunn a call.

But as I opened the loft door, I heard Scott in his room singing in a beautiful, clear tone. It was a jaunty marching song like Dixie or Yankee Doodle. Then I picked out the words:

> You brought, sir, I bought, sir
> Drugs that would kill me well
> You knew but said not, sir
> Ice paved my way to hell
>
> I drove, sir, in flame, sir
> I burned like a match head
> My bride turned to you, sir
> When word came I was dead

In his room, Scott sat on his bed with *A Garland Knot for Children* open in front of him. He ignored me standing in the doorway until I asked, "Where did you learn the tune?"

"Grandma." It seemed we were barely on speaking terms.

"And the new words?"

He held up the book. "They're different each time. It's how my dad talks to me."

"Scott, when I said there was nothing between Sarah and me, that was true." I sounded like a lawyer.

He regarded me with contempt. "My dad's real angry. I told him that it was going to be okay with you and Mom. He didn't believe me. He was right." Holding the book open in my direction, he riffled the pages. They flapped like wings. A bike bright as a spark sprang at my face. Its rider's hair was red flame, his face skull white, his eyes two black holes.

Flinching, I backed away. Scott slammed the book shut and we were alone in his room. The remnants of our last game lay on the floor between us. "Get out!" he said. Beneath his anger, I sensed his fear. I was very aware of my own.

"I'll be moving." Not, however, before I tried to finish what I had so stupidly started. "Let's play the Islands Game one more time."

Scott glanced around uneasily and muttered, "He doesn't want you here." But when he looked down at his toys, he couldn't resist.

It took just a moment to go to the kitchen and stick the box of matches in my pocket. Before fear and doubt got the better of me, I returned to the room. Scott was already building islands. The book lay open on his bed.

The last game was our most elaborate. Everything from the wooden Noah to plastic dinosaurs were used. Scott decided to be a drummer boy and I chose to be an Indian chief.

Then the game itself took over, and a most violent expedition it was. Our ship wrecked itself on the shore. A dragon/brontosaurus attacked a railroad bridge as the train we rode crossed it. As long as I was on the alert, paying attention to my surroundings, all was well.

But in a lull in the action, I remembered Scott Callendar Sr.'s last night. I had warned him about the acid. Several times. Like

I was covering my ass. Like I wanted him dead after seeing the games he played with his kid, but wasn't willing to take responsibility for doing it.

I wondered if it was a twisted remorse that had brought him blazing back to life. And, suddenly, I was back on the floor of the bedroom. Plastic Indians stood around me like statues and I was no bigger than they. The tiger peeked out from behind a tree. The flaming cycle rounded the corner of a hill and headed right at me. I shook my head, stood up with a cry. I was no longer small. The flaming cycle was gone.

Scott said, "He did stuff like that to get rid of Ian and Frankie. Ian had nightmares about fire. Frankie hurt his back trying to roll away when the cycle came after him." He didn't bother to add that they were assholes.

My advantage over those two was that I knew what I was up against. The game with Scott Jr. continued and he lost himself in it again. The elephant was the oracle. It stood on a hill in a grove of trees. It had been scorched again. The trunk and tusks were melted.

"Why did you kill my father?" Scott's question when he reached the grove was simple and direct. The book lay open in his lap. It felt like I was under the judgment of a god, remote and childlike and pitiless.

"It was the ice that killed him. The bike. The curse he lived under." Again I spoke the weasel words of adulthood. My answer angered the kid and I didn't blame him. Had I in some part of myself wanted his father out of the way so I could inherit his wife and child?

Quickly I pushed the Indian chief into the grove and said, "My turn to ask a question." Hands shaking, I pulled out the box and lighted a match. "Do you remember your father that last night?" Scott stared at the match, book frozen in hand. He shook his head.

"Yes, you do. It was in your drawing." The sound of the engine faded. I blew the match out and lighted another. "You were two years old. Your mother was working that night. Remember how your father played with matches? He stood over the crib throwing them so close that you could almost grab them. Each one got nearer. Every one had gone out on the floor. He hadn't yet managed to burn you and he hadn't set fire to the room. Yet. But there were plenty of matches left."

This was rough. Scott was rigid, expressionless, as I continued. "I gave him the drugs to get him away from you. I warned him they were dangerous. I suggested that he and I take a walk. When I got him outside, he wanted me to ride with him on this motorcycle he had borrowed. I didn't go, but I didn't try to stop him. Even though I knew he could be killed. To me, it was a choice between him and you. I wanted you to live. And you remember that night. It's why you're still afraid of him."

It felt like I was punching the kid repeatedly in the face. But the boy didn't blink. I said, "You have to drop him, Scott. What your father is doing is hurting you. But you know who he's hurting more?" No response. "Your mother. You can't let him do what he's doing to her. He's making her live in misery and fear. Do you want that?"

Scott wouldn't look my way. There was an endless pause before he slammed the book shut. Then we both heard an explosion distant but clear. Sirens screamed their way uptown. We sat on the bed and he leaned against me and cried. And I tried to think of ways to explain to Sarah what had happened. When Scott felt a little better, we put away the toys. *A Garland Knot for Children* was nowhere to be found.

TEN

CAUGHT IN MEMORIES of the past, I was surprised to find myself middle aged and staring out my bedroom window at four in the morning. Four A.M. is the devil's matinee. It's when human confidence is weakest, life is at its lowest ebb. Beside me, Matt lay defenseless, arms and legs akimbo, like a boxer who had been knocked flat. What I'd do with him when he came to was tomorrow's problem. Meanwhile he was company of a sort and I was glad to have him.

Over in the park, leaves shimmered, streetlights outshone the moon, gleamed off the back of one-legged Peter Stuyvesant's statue. On a bench a kid sat absolutely motionless. His expression, innocent and scared, evoked angels and runaways.

My heart jumped alarmingly as I recognized the boy from my Streetcar Dreams. A second glance revealed nothing but a trick of light and dark. I made a circle with my thumb and forefinger and thought about Matt and the kid on the streetcar and how the start and end of a life join together. In lots of ways, my own life started with Leo Dunn. I thought about Mr. Dunn then and about Celia, his granddaughter. I met her for the first time on the same day that Scotty and I played our last Islands Game.

That evening I had wondered what to tell Sarah. But when she came in the door there was no need to say anything. Scotty ran to her and she held him tight as they swayed together. All the while, she looked around like she felt something had changed. Maybe Sarah picked up the fact there was only the two of them now.

And me, of course. At that moment I was an intruder and my sobriety felt like a weight. So I went to the phone and called Mr. Dunn. "Come and pay a visit, my friend," he said.

He was at the door of his apartment when I arrived. A young lady who was leaving turned back and hugged him. She was still a kid, maybe sixteen, tall and fair, already a beauty. And there was something more. I found myself thinking about Stacey Hale for the first time in years and not knowing why.

"My granddaughter Celia," Mr. Dunn said. He looked at her with fond disbelief. She had his smile. Greeting her, I was momentarily light-headed. For an instant, as she said hello and slipped past me into the hall, it seemed that I was seeing not a young woman but her reflection in a dove gray mirror.

As Leo Dunn led me inside, I turned and found Celia was gone. I could have told myself the elevator had come. Instead I realized what had reminded me of Stacey. That first time we met in the doctor's office when I was sixteen, she must have caught the hint of an aura, a trace of my Shadow. Celia's magic was different, but that's what I had sensed as she stood in her grandfather's doorway.

But my mind just then was on Scott Callendar Sr. and Jr. I told Mr. Dunn as much as I thought I could about what had happened. "All I hope is that I wasn't too brutal, that I did more good than harm. I was trying to break the hold that a particular past had on all of us," I said.

Mr. Dunn looked out the window at the lights of Manhattan. "You've met Bob and Maggie." Leo Dunn's kids were nice people, a little younger than I was. I nodded.

"You've never met Diana, my oldest," he said. "She's managed to make a fairly stable life for herself. Hard to do when you have an alcoholic for a father. Worst thing for a child. Her mother and I separated when she was six. After I finally got sober, Diana and her mother were beyond wanting to have anything to do with me. I can probably count the times I've seen or spoken with her since. Once was at the death of her mother. Another was when she was expecting Celia. That was the last time I saw my oldest daughter."

He looked away and lighted a cigarette. "It's the great sorrow of my life." He turned back with an enchanted smile. "Then, one evening last January, I was here alone when I got a visit from an almost grown grandchild whom I hadn't seen since she was a baby. She's been by a few times since. Curiosity, maybe.

"Our past is always with us. Be aware of that without letting it engulf you, Kevin. That's all we're trying for. Celia redeems, at least a little, a lot of shame and regret that I have. My bet is that with Scotty you've managed that."

Suddenly, he clapped his hands together. "Sunday evening, you've doubtless noticed, is one of the great times for drunks and their self-pity. Especially Irish ones. My wife and Maggie are out visiting her family. I didn't feel up for in-laws. Are you hungry? Lct's see what they left for us."

While I ate cold chicken, he said. "I'm glad that you, of all the people I know, were able to be here and meet my granddaughter. Because you understand." He paused, then looked at me hard. "Kevin, mention nothing about this to anyone. Especially to my family." And I thought it was strange, but I agreed.

When I got back to the loft, Sarah told me that Scotty had a slightly high temperature. He was in bed with what seemed like a flu for the next couple of days. Sarah or I was with him most of the time. He told her about *Garland Knot* and the flaming cycle and she chose to think of that as fever dreams. I told her more or less what I had told Scott about his father's last night on earth. She shook her head and replied, "Well, that's been said. It would have to be sooner or later." Then she told me, "Whatever you did, Kevin, it seems different here. I can walk in and not feel I'm under surveillance."

Wednesday morning, I sat on the foot of Scott's bed, my back leaning against the wall, and read *The Times*. He sat up at the head, drawing. This would be his last day home from school.

"Kevin?"

"Yeah?"

"Are you going to move because of what I said?"

For this, I put down the paper and looked at him. His pajamas were a Mets sweatshirt and thermal long johns. "Not at all. I'm not leaving immediately. It's time. I need privacy and so do you and your mother."

"She doesn't believe what I told her."

"Not entirely. Most people won't. But she's really good. To you. And to me."

"But she's a mundane."

"Wow! Where the hell did you learn that?" He shrugged his shoulders, shook his head, and smiled. "Listen, Scott. I'll be around. If anything happens, if you see that book or he comes back, you tell me right away. And I'll be there. Okay?"

"Okay," he said, like that was something settled. I started to pick up the paper. He went on to the next matter. "Mom said she won't get me the board."

"She didn't tell me not to, though." Because of things that happened when I was young, I tend not to grab at kids no matter how much I love them. But if they yell and jump on top of me, like Scott did at that moment, it feels like maybe I did something right.

At Christmas, Scott got his board. He gave me a set of antique marching fusiliers. I hadn't owned any toys since I was fourteen. Sarah showered me with gifts. One was the deposit on a good, cheap apartment over on East Ninth Street (this was back when such a thing existed). Another was an introduction to a lady named Madge Hollings. Madge ran a decorating and antique business. She needed someone to help out in her store, Old Acquaintance, and she hired me.

One Sunday afternoon, I packed my belongings, which now filled several boxes instead of one bag. Sarah waited with me on Houston for a cab. Scott was out with friends. I heard a rumbling, turned, and saw him in a red ski jacket careening up the SoHo sidewalk toward us. He slapped me five and continued on his way. Sarah and I kissed and laughed in the face of time.

My new apartment was a block away from the building on St. Mark's Place where I'd first lived in the city almost ten years before. Most midmornings, I walked from my gritty tenement block in the East Village to a winding tree-lined West Village street and opened the store at eleven A.M. sharp.

In my old neighborhood, I began seeing familiar faces. Boris, for instance, walked west with me a lot, returning to Gina's apartment after a night in the after-hours clubs on Avenue A. We never talked about his business.

Back then, there was a huge bum with a dirty red beard and red-rimmed eyes who stood all day and every day in front of the truck rental lot on West Fourth Street.

At all those who passed from East Village to West or went the other way, he stuck out a filthy paw and yelled in a hoarse voice, "HEY SUCKER, HOW ABOUT A QUARTER!"

Because of what Mr. Dunn had told me, he got a quarter every time. But I didn't pay him much attention.

One morning, Boris walked with me, stoned and acutely aware of wonders. Seeing the bum up ahead, he told me,

"Kevin, they got a giant guarding the bridge! Maybe he'll let us by if we can guess his name."

As I reached the curb, the bum stepped in my path, stuck his hand in my face, and bellowed, "HOW ABOUT IT, SUCKER!"

My pal looked at him goggle-eyed and said, "I'm Boris. What do they call you?"

The man replied in an ordinary tone, "Spain."

"No shit. You don't look Spanish."

"I ain't. I'm Irish like your buddy." He gestured my way.

"So, how come they call you Spain?"

Spain paused, looked puzzled for a moment as if there must have been a good reason but he couldn't quite remember it. Then his eyes focused on me again. "HEY SUCKER, GIVE ME A QUARTER!"

That I did, gladly. Unlike Boris, I didn't need drugs to see magic. The bridge Spain guarded led to what was starting to feel like a magic land: sobriety. A quarter was an easy toll. "You didn't ask Boris here for money," I said.

"Cause he's one of us. BUT YOU'RE A SUCKER AND YOU GOTTA GIVE!"

Boris laughed as we walked on. He wore post-hippy high fashion, fine leathers soft as butter and sunglasses that probably cost more than my whole wardrobe. His long, black mustache was a work of art. "Hey, at least I can still remember how I got my nickname."

And I laughed, remembering the Karloff as Frankenstein's monster impersonation that he could start and stop almost at will. The nickname became in effect an alias when we moved to New York. Except for a couple of his girlfriends and the cops, I was probably the only one in the city who knew his real name. Eventually he would ask me never to tell it. And I won't, though we haven't met in years.

That morning, his day ending as mine began, Boris was like a time capsule. "Remember that junk connection, Mama? It used to be you'd never take anyone along when you went to visit her. Someone told me she's still in business."

"I'd forgotten about her." And didn't want to be reminded. Certain charms Mr. Dunn had taught seemed to make me invulnerable to the dark. But I'd been trapped deeper in addiction than Boris was now.

He slid past my reaction. "Remember Bonnie?" he asked. Boris saw everyone. "Bonnie Lewis, the chick who used to live with Jimmy Dace? I met her the other night. Man, she was real interested in seeing you again. There's a bunch of us going to an opening at the Public Theater tonight. Bonnie will be there. Some other good people. Come along."

"I have to see Mr. Dunn after work." We stood in Sheridan Square where we would go our separate ways.

"After the show, there's a party at Phoebe's. Stop by." I nodded and turned. A headless, snuffling shape that seemed to be made of dirty plastic and old paper came toward us. The smell of piss and garbage choked me. Then I saw an extended hand and recognized a bag lady. Realizing I had no change, I felt for a moment that a promise was at risk.

"Hey, you got to do your good deed," said Boris, and gave me a bill which I pressed into the dirt-caked hand. "I'm helping him stay holy," he explained to the woman.

My visit to Leo Dunn is the main reason I remember that day, just as he's the reason I'm here to remember at all. Though I didn't know it when I walked in, that evening a year after my last bender was sort of my graduation.

Mrs. Dunn opened the door, as unfailingly gracious as she must have been to every drunk, druggie, and deadbeat who crossed the threshold. She also did counseling work with alcoholics. Behind her, spring sunset turned the windows across the street gold. Light flowed into the living room, glanced off the glass coffee table, formed an aurora around Leo Dunn. He sat on his couch, smiling at me, the wizard of sobriety.

"Forgive my not greeting you at the door, Kevin," he said. "I'm tired today." Then he leaned forward and hooked me with those stark blue eyes and said, "We've done this a hundred times. But you remember the four virtues?"

As in catechism class, where I had once also excelled, the answer popped out, "Temperance, humility, patience, charity."

He nodded. "Temperance allows us to acknowledge our excesses. Humility allows us to subdue our diseased egos. Patience allows us to forgive ourselves for all trespasses real and imagined."

Dunn had dozens of routines. That evening, like a fusillade at the end of a fireworks display, he ran through all of them: booze the Silent Partner, the record room with its catalog of failings. My attention wandered. Dunn caught it by moving an ashtray on the coffee table, flashing his silver lighter. "Charity is the most important, Kevin. Not just writing a check, but real charity. Answering the call of others as your call and mine were answered.

"I've always understood pretty much what people wanted to hear. When I drank and had money, that insight made me very contemptuous of my fellow man. Always, I was able to see right through everyone else's fraudulence. Not my own, sad to say. That I managed to keep a complete secret from myself. Then one day, I woke up flat on my ass in a flophouse.

"Even when I found my way off the street and started trying to help others, my impatience destroyed all charity. So I swore to my God that I would give help to whoever came to me, without prejudice or favor, taking from them only what I thought they could afford. Otherwise, I wouldn't be available to whoever needed me and I wouldn't be available in the way they needed me.

"My reward has been the joy of doing something I love so much. Sometimes it takes a strength that doesn't really belong to me. Because of my promise, I feel as though I'm able to borrow strength from all the people like you who have let me help them."

He paused and took a long drink of water. Around us, the life of the household went on. A phone rang and someone answered it. Water ran in the kitchen. A cat's paw darted out from under the couch and darted back.

I told Leo Dunn about the Irish bum called Spain who couldn't remember why. He smiled and said, "When you're down there at the absolute bottom, you can feel it all slip away. Possessions. Life itself. Your identity is more a burden than a right. And at that moment when you need charity most, it is hardest for people to look at you as a human being. You give him money when he asks?"

"Yes. Because of what you've told me."

"Good. It may be the only thing standing between him and death. Or maybe he just needs a drink. You just do not know. It is not a judgment that is ours to make."

The sun had set behind him. Dunn was in darkness as he told me in a quiet conversational tone, "Alcohol is a vicious, mind-altering drug. It will tell you any lie you want to hear. But I will spoil all its lies for you. You can run from this truth, my friend, but once you have seen booze for what it is, you will never believe in it again." I remembered hearing these same words that first afternoon when I had come to him off the cold winter streets.

"Kevin, you have a good heart," Dunn continued. "I love you and have every faith in you. I have given what I have to give and I believe you will do very well. Just remember what I said about giving to those in need. It will be a source of enormous strength. Not just for you, but through you for me as well."

It's great to be praised, to feel yourself in a state of mystical grace. Especially if the means of achieving it seems as easy as this did. "I'll always try to do that," I said, really imagining I knew what had been pledged.

No thunder roll accompanied the oath. No blood had to be offered. A slight chill ran through me on that balmy night but I ignored it.

"Good. Now, I'm old and my children assure me I understand nothing. But I can tell that you're dying to get out of here. Go. And don't forget to keep in touch. Call me in a couple of days and tell me how you're doing."

After that, riding back downtown, I felt a thrill of expectation. That spring in what I thought of as the official start of my sobriety, everything about New York seemed fresh and newly minted. I hooked up with Boris for an opening night party at Phoebe's Bar. "This show was one more incoherent attempt to create the new *Hair*," Sandy, a funny gay guy with a sad face, explained to me. "It's been a few years, but no one wants to admit that the sixties are over."

Gina Raille was there with Boris. Tall and zaftig, she was up for a part in another show. As Boris had mentioned, Bonnie Lewis was also present. I recalled Bonnie as a round-eyed and long-haired blonde who got taken advantage of. She was now a fierce little silver fox who took no nonsense.

At one point, Sandy jumped up to dance and lip-sync with Smokey Robinson singing "Tears of a Clown" on the jukebox. Bonnie, his dearest friend in the world, told me, "Sandy just broke up with his boyfriend and he's doing a lot of coke. Too bad, but he's always got drugs on hand. He's one of Boris's connections."

We all left the party and walked through the bar area together. On the stools sat boys in shiny suits and wrinkled narrow ties, girls in tacky, backless cocktail dresses and high heels. The timeworn East Village which had once given us refuge was about to do the same for the next generation. At the sight of the fifties finery from the bins of Unique Boutique, all the stuff he had fled the suburbs to avoid, Boris reacted like a bull moose whose territory had been violated. "Fucking punks," he yelled. "Go back to Great Neck."

One of the kids cleared his throat and said, "Hippy scum," like he was trying out the phrase. Boris lunged. Sandy and I grabbed him, but he broke away. Then Gina put a very expert headlock on Boris and the four of us hauled him outside and got him home.

In an unnatural place like Manhattan, it's possible to lose touch with the seasons. Sitting one afternoon in Vaselka's Coffee Shop on Second Avenue, eating cold borscht and challah bread, I noticed kids buying candy on their last day of school and realized that summer had officially begun.

That season I saw other people. But Boris and Gina, Bonnie and Sandy were the regulars in my life, a self-contained unit, a box made of people. I was very young, not in years, but in the sense of being newly hatched. Waking up sober every morning was exciting.

Bonnie helped make my place livable with a telephone and my toy soldiers on a bookshelf along with Lou Reed and Mozart records. She lived with a couple of roommates, the remains of an aborted commune, over on Tompkins Square. We two hung out some nights with Spanish poet friends of hers in a cafe way to the east where sunflowers grew in the vacant lots amidst tinned-up buildings.

Sandy too invited me out. We went to an opening down in SoHo for a guy who did Donald Ducks on silk screens. Gina and Boris came in later. "Tell him about the show you're going to be in," Boris said to Gina.

"It's a takeoff on thirties movie musicals," she told me.

"Except it, you know, *is* a thirties musical," said Sandy. He and Boris turned away to talk and Gina told me, "I'm worried about Boris. It's not just coke anymore. He's doing a lot of junk."

Boris turned back toward us and said in his Karloff voice, "I'm really not such a bad monster." On impulse, I borrowed a pencil and wrote down Dunn's name and number. Boris stuck it in a back pocket.

About then, my boss Madge Hollings began spending very long weekends in the Hamptons and I understood that it was August. Since Old Acquaintance was open Saturdays and Sundays, that meant she left me more or less in charge. I liked pretending I was a shopkeeper and not a shop assistant.

Mondays and Tuesdays were my days off. One lazy afternoon, I sipped tea amidst sullen painters and toothless Ukrainians at Vaselka's while Boris made calls in one of the huge old wooden telephone booths in back. Returning, he slumped into a seat and remarked, "Summer, a lot of white people go away. Mostly only the serious druggies are left behind. The protective coloration is removed. We stand out. Easy targets for the old narcos."

That moment of quiet despair was my opportunity to insist he call Leo Dunn. But just then Bonnie walked in with a whole bunch of people and the chance passed.

That same week, Bonnie and Sandy each suggested we become roommates. Bonnie made the suggestion one morning in my apartment before I went to work. She was quite frank. "We get along. The situation where I am is impossible. Our not being totally compatible can be a plus. I know ways to make a space like this one work better."

"This loft is larger than the Starship Enterprise and not nearly as boring," said Sandy at his place as I got dressed a few mornings later. "I'd like having you here."

"I'm still not steady on my feet," I told one. "It's not that I don't think a whole lot of you and about you," I told the other.

Sandy shrugged, said, "It's lonely at the top," and smiled.

"You are a selfish son of a bitch," Bonnie remarked matter-of-factly.

The truth was that I felt invulnerable and liked the sensation. But maybe that's what selfishness is. I could hang around bars or watch Boris and Sandy deal drugs without feeling it touch me because of the enchanted quarters that I gave to Spain each time I passed him.

Mr. Dunn and I talked on the phone. Every couple of weeks, I would drop by and see him. He wasn't feeling well. His wife was worried. "Kevin, he simply will not eat," she said, handing him a milk shake. "Get him to drink this." He made a face and shook his head. "Leo, the doctor wants you to go in for tests," she told him.

"Not now," he said. "I have a client starting. A very difficult case. He doesn't think he has a problem. I know the the family and they persuaded him to see me."

On an overcast day with deadly humidity, a stormy Monday brewing, I awoke feeling tense. The phone rang and Mr. Dunn asked, "Could you come up here?" He sounded tired.

On the street a few minutes later, I barely saw the wolf-faced junkie until he said, "Kevin," and I recognized Boris. In the couple of days since I'd seen him, he had cut off his mustache, cropped and dyed his hair. He looked shaky and had obviously just thrown up. He said, "I need a favor. The narcs have shut everything down."

"Man, I know what you're feeling." In truth I only dimly remembered. "But what can I do?"

"Mama. I went by and she's still cooking. But she won't do anything for me. Only people she knows. Remember you never wanted anyone along when you copped from Mama? Take this hundred and keep what you want. But get something to keep me going."

The thought of that twisted me inside. "No, Boris."

"Don't look at me disgusted, man! Have I ever asked a favor

from you? You can call up and say, 'Boris, old friend, why don't you risk a jail term transporting a stiff in your van?' And I did it. I bought you fucking shoes so you could leave the hospital when you didn't even know who you were. I helped you go clean so you can stand here like this telling me to go fuck myself! Okay. So you're a prince and I'm a bug unworthy to be crushed under your shoe. Only do something for me before I die!"

Leo Dunn had said about giving Spain money, "It may be the only thing standing between him and death." But I was late and it was going to rain and the thought of buying drugs terrified me for several excellent reasons. I said, "I'm on my way to see Dunn. Come uptown and talk to him." As I spoke, I knew it was useless. In extremis all a junkie wants is heroin.

Boris screamed, "YOU THINK YOU GOT IT MADE? YOU GOT NOTHING, MOTHER!" Passersby pretended not to notice. I turned away.

Riding the IRT uptown, I felt not empty but dark, like some kind of light inside had been doused. As we pulled out of one stop, my eyes met those of a ragged figure sprawled on a bench. Despite the beard and dirt, the fresh cut on his cheek, I recognized his face. It was the one I'd have had if I still drank. My Silent Partner nodded to me.

Thunder rolled in New Jersey by the time I got uptown. The lamps were on in the Dunns' living room. The unfamiliar light helped me see him plainly. I remembered the first time I was there, blinded by winter sun reflecting off the glass table. From behind that aurora, Leo Dunn's eyes had looked into my heart.

Now he sat on his couch and his body was like a rig of wires inside the fine tan suit he wore. His head and his hands, unshrunken, appeared huge. He saw my reaction and said very quietly, "Yes, I took a good long look at myself in the mirror this morning. The doctor wants me in the hospital for tests.

But I can't. I have a new client, Damian. He's difficult, a hit-and-run drunk driver who won't admit he has a problem.

"Remember my telling you I draw strength from all the people who let me help them? Well, now I want to ask more than the usual charity from you, Kevin. You've seen a bit of life and understand things. Will you help me with this young man?"

Stunned by my encounter with Boris, I felt that my life had lost whatever grace and magic it may ever have contained. Unable to confess that, I just nodded yes.

Dunn gestured at himself and the room. "His first impression will be the most important one." He had me close the curtains partway so that he sat with his pale head dead center in the silver light. Then he told me to turn off the lamp next to him and put on a couple of smaller ones in the far corners. In that way, while sitting absolutely still, he could dominate the room.

The windows were closed. It was warm and stuffy. "I feel so cold," said Leo Dunn. "You know my appetite is off. When I was in my cups, I'd drink anything—hair tonic if it was all there was. But as to food, I had very discriminating tastes indeed. I ate nothing at all."

He paused for a long moment, then said, "Let me tell you the whole reason I need you here, Kevin. The doctor I'm seeing has his office in the Village. We were there earlier today, my wife and I. On the way back uptown, the taxi driver took us east over to the Bowery. It brought back a lot of memories."

The first drops hit the windows. "We stopped at a light and there was an old Black man down on the pavement with one hand out to me. I tried to open the door, but I wasn't steady enough. The cabby didn't understand or didn't want to and he drove on. I can still see that man lying on the sidewalk like a broken promise.

"Way back when I got the better of my own problem, I went

back to the Bowery and gave people money and put them up at hotels. I'd spent Christmas Eves down there and I knew what it was like for the ones who weren't able to make it out.

"My ability is a gift. I don't understand its workings. My wife and I tried once to count all the people I've been allowed to help and we couldn't. I've always known this was not my personal property. I'm only an agent, a custodian. But I'm happy to be that. And I'd hate to think I lost it through breaking my promise to do all that was possible for each person who came to me."

The house phone buzzed, the lobby announced the client. "I asked you up here because in your own way you made a similar pledge," Mr. Dunn told me.

My inadequacy was a gaping pit inside me. If Leo Dunn considered what he'd described as breaking an oath, then what was my walking away from Boris? Unable to meet his gaze, I turned to watch his wife open the front door.

"I hope you didn't get wet, my friend," said Dunn. The client shook his head. His name was Damian Greene and he came from Darien, Connecticut. To my eyes, Damian was a sullen rich kid who badly needed a kick in the ass. I know he didn't fall in love with me either.

I took a seat where I could watch them both. Mrs. Dunn also stayed in the room. Thunder rolled, rain drove against the windows, lightning flashed behind Leo Dunn's head as the client shook his hand. I saw the kid's eyes widen slightly at the effect.

Then Leo Dunn began to speak clearly, forcefully. "My friend, you are here against your will, maybe against your better judgment. Even if you never come back to see me again, let me just try to convince you of one thing. Alcohol is a vicious and mind-altering substance that has wrecked much of your life and will wreck the rest if you give it any chance at all."

After a long pause, Dunn said, "Kevin here can testify that booze is a Silent Partner. It is a partner who wants it all." He glanced my way and another pause followed, during which thunder echoed off skyscrapers.

Suddenly, Leo Dunn put his hands over his face. "My friend," he said, and his voice was muffled, "whatever your motive, you came here to be cured. What you found was an unworthy agent. I can't help you!" His body convulsed and I realized that he was crying behind his hands. We all heard his sobs. "After seeing that man today and failing to help him, I was afraid that I'd never be able to help anyone again. And I was right, the gift is gone, taken from me."

The client looked appalled. He was not used to having doors slammed in his face. I wonder what my own expression was. Mrs. Dunn came over and put her arms around her husband. She said, "I think Leo understands now that the doctor is right about his going into the hospital."

That afternoon, I watched Mrs. Dunn check her husband into St. Vincent's. By the time he was settled, the rain had stopped and I walked the streets scared and wanting a drink. Leo Dunn thought the loss of his power was all his fault. I felt I knew better. At least part of the responsibility was mine.

The phone rang as I came home wanting company for a quiet dinner. When I picked it up, Bonnie screamed, "Where the hell have you been? Hanging out with that turd Boris?" That's when I found out how the rest of my little world had fallen apart.

"Listen, Bonnie, I had a bad day," I began.

"Oh poor you! Did you know that Boris has dropped dimes on everyone he knows? Sandy! The cops busted him. I went to his place to have lunch and there were police everywhere. Sandy gets arraigned tonight downtown. I've spent hours finding a lawyer, raising bail. The one time I need your help, you disappear. You'll come with me to night court, right?"

"Jesus!"

"I take it that means yes."

When she hung up, the phone rang again and it was Gina Raille. "Kevin, where's Boris? Everyone's calling me."

"How would I know?"

"Didn't he go uptown with you to see your friend? Mr. Dunn?"

"Gina, Mr. Dunn isn't . . . he's not feeling real well."

"But Boris came home this afternoon saying he needed money for Mr. Dunn. He said you were both going up there. I gave him all the money I had."

"Gina, that was just some junkie scam. Boris stole your money to buy drugs."

I did not feel proud that I hung up so as not to hear her crying. At night court, Bonnie and I sat between some pimps in silk suits and a woman who smelled like rancid butter. Bonnie looked around and said, "Kafka was a chump, a hick."

She wanted something, support, maybe just conversation. None of that was in me. Poor Sandy, when we bailed him out, was hysterical. Since his house was a wreck, we took him to Bonnie's. She dug up some Valium and he quieted down. As I was leaving, Bonnie said, "Kevin, you're still warm to the touch, but you don't care about much, do you?" And I couldn't answer.

The truth was that my invulnerable shield was gone and it was my own fault. I wanted a drink badly and was glad the bars were closed and the streets clear of dealers. The night was cool. Passing Tompkins Square Park, I heard trees whisper in the predawn. Lights shone on a bench where a guy with my face sat all alone watching me.

Here was someone who would know where the after-hours bars were and how to get drugs during a police sweep. My Shadow, my addiction, raised a hand to beckon me. He grinned like a maniac when I backed away and hurried home.

That night, what sleep I got was tangled in dreams of being on a streetcar that rolled through a land of goblins and narcs to a black tower. I awoke full of dread, but knowing what had to be done. A quest awaited me, and not the kind you get sent on by the Queen of Elfland. Instead of donning my knightly armor, I shaved, showered, and put on running shoes, a hooded sweat-shirt, and worn jeans. Carrying no weapons since I owned none, I set out to redeem Leo Dunn's faith in me.

For those who disapprove of the action I am about to de-scribe, I ask you to consider the Orc. Faceless slave of the dark that he is, an Orc dies at the hero's hand and no one mourns. But what if, though now a hero pure and true, you had once run with the Orcs? What if one of the Orcs, whom you have come to recognize as a loathsome creature, was once as close to you as a brother? On a morning when you felt a touch of the old Orc in your bones, could you turn away from him?

With no idea of where to find Boris, I decided to raise him as I'd been used to doing. Though it was a day off, I walked from east to west. At Fourth and Bowery, two figures awaited me. Spain stood, as Boris had said, like a giant guarding the bridge. "HEY SUCKER, YOUR BUDDY HERE IS HURTING."

Beside him was Boris, shivering in the crisp air. "You do one good deed every day, I understand," he told me. "Yesterday, for instance, you warned Gina that she was getting ripped off by a junkie. She locked me out. Help me, man, I'm begging you!"

But I was the beggar, more desperate than he was. My peace of mind was gone. Boris and Spain were the instruments of my winning it back. "Let's take a little walk," I told my oldest friend and turned back the way I had come.

"HEY, WHERE'S MY QUARTER?" Spain shouted.

Boris, loping wary as a coyote beside me, asked, "Remember all the times you used to do this?"

Junk is just the high, copping is the habit. Memory guided me east to Avenue B where a faded thirty-foot mural of Satan played guitar and sported a huge erection. As we turned north, a couple of guys, impassive in an unmarked Chevy, watched us go. My anxiety began to rise. Like he could read me, Boris said,

"Don't fear the narcs. You'll have the stuff in your hand maybe ten seconds, five seconds."

"Nice job you did on Sandy," I told him.

"What would you have done, man? I got busted last month and didn't tell anybody. Some guy I knew around the bars turned out to be an undercover. I had two choices, jail or names. It used to be the cops were happy you gave them one name. Now you practically have to join the force. Sandy's got the same choices I had, that's all."

Where a car frame filled with charred mattress springs sat next to a fire hydrant dribbling water, we turned east again. On that block, lots of stuff had fallen down, but Mama's building stood, surrounded now by empty lots. I recognized the tower of my dreams the night before. A stray dog sniffed busted trash cans. From the far end of the street, two little kids stared at us.

While I had been away, part of the cement stoop had crumbled and the ground-floor windows had been tinned. The front door was a gaping hole into pitch dark. Past the light from outside, Boris guided me like he had night vision. On the second floor, a forty-watt bulb burned. Under it a sign read, "Take light and die," with a skull and crossbones.

The front door of one apartment looked like it had been broken down with an ax. Music came from somewhere not far off. Someone turned it down and listened as we passed. My stomach was tight and there was bile at the back of my throat.

"This next one's a mother," Boris muttered. Sunlight shone down on us. The top steps of that flight were gone. So was part of the wall and a chunk of the hallway. It was like a bite had been taken out of the side of the building. This was new. Boris pulled himself up onto the third floor. "Don't look out," he said.

Of course I did, and saw sun hitting broken glass next to a brick path that led through grass and goldenrod to someone's fenced-in garden. The vacant lot was empty. In the garden, tomato plants danced in the breeze.

The fourth floor was dark. Something breathed there, deep hibernating breaths. The music came back on downstairs.

On the fifth floor, there was a lighted bulb jury-rigged from a cable, and a familiar door. "Ten dimes," whispered Boris and handed me the money.

"Watch close," I said. "I'm not doing this again." At the door, I cried, "Mama," softly like I used to do.

Nothing. A truck went by in the street outside and the building shook. I turned to Boris and shrugged. Then, someone in slippers moved on the other side of the door. I said, "Mama, *por favor,*" my Spanish just as bad as ever.

There was a pause and a voice soft as a sigh asked, "You been in jail?"

"*Sí.* Like that. Listen Mama, I need ten."

"Six. For a hundred, six." Boris grimaced but nodded and I slipped the hundred under the door. When it disappeared, I felt the same moment of anticipation and dread I always had. Then, there was a rustling sound and I gathered up the six little rolls of aluminum foil.

"*Gracias,* Mama," I said. No reply. "Mama, I got a friend here, *un amigo,* Boris." The packages burned cold in my hand. The chill ran up my arm to my heart.

"Mama?" said Boris. "I'll be back, Mama." Dead silence behind the door.

Copping was the habit, junk the reward, immediate relief of all pain and fear. I remembered Leo Dunn as I had last seen him, the best person I had ever met, limp and despairing in his hospital bed. It occurred to me that I had earned a share of the spoils. Boris saved me. "Hey," he whispered. "Mine," and took it all away. The cold left my heart. I thought of Mr. Dunn and imagined him in his hospital bed. He was smiling.

"Had to think about it, huh?" Boris said and moved quickly to the stairs.

On the fourth floor, the deep breathing stopped. From the dark, a voice dark as sleep, said, "You gonna come back once too often."

On three, Boris leaped past the gaping hole to the stairs below. Again, I looked out. The lot was no longer empty. A tall, thin man in black leather jeans and vest, a classic rip-off artist, watched me scramble past.

Before I could say anything, Boris muttered, "Saw him." His hand went to a back pocket. As we walked under the lightbulb, the music faded again and someone listened. Then sun and the street lay ahead but the figure in black stood at the front door waiting to take us off. I froze thinking there was no way this wasn't going to be bad.

Boris, not missing a step, went toward the door. His hand coming out of his back pocket grasped a little semiautomatic. My heart stopped. The guy at the door melted away. "Must only have a knife," said Boris, putting the pistol back. He opened one package and poured junk under his bottom lip. "Just to hold me until I can do up."

Out in the sunshine we walked away fast. Relief made me babble. "I used to fantasize some Spanish Madonna behind the door but from the voice I can't tell. It might be a guy sitting there thinking the whole thing is a huge joke. Anyway, that's the connection. Listen, I've got a feeling Dunn is going to be able to talk to you."

Boris said nothing. Remembering full well the ways of junk, I knew I should have been able to hold onto the drugs long enough to talk to Boris about Leo Dunn. It probably wouldn't have done any good. An Orc with junk had no need for anyone else.

At Avenue A, he halted. His voice when he spoke was remote, like we had already parted. "Always at the back of my head was that I could get the cure like you. The thing is the cops want me to testify against guys who'll whack me. Do me a favor. Forget my name. Forget you knew me. It was a blast while it lasted. Good-by, Kevin." He turned and in seconds was gone.

If there is a god who cares for the likes of us, then what Boris did was between the two of them. And I will gladly answer for what I myself did that day. All I regret is never seeing my oldest friend again.

Mr. Dunn sat up in bed, his right arm attached to bottles and monitoring devices. He still looked weak but he smiled and said, "Damian just called asking if he could come talk to me. A half hour ago I couldn't have found the resources to tell him yes. I was still in the same damn funk I was in yesterday. Then lying here, I suddenly dreamed of you helping some poor soul in a very bad place. All my useless self-pity lifted. Thank you, Kevin, for being as true as you are."

All I could do was sink into a chair and look down at the floor so I didn't have to face him. "You think I'm true, Mr. Dunn. But when you asked for my help yesterday, I should have told you that I had just walked away from my best friend on earth. If I had kept my promise and helped someone who asked for help he might be talking to you right now. I keep thinking maybe my doing that is what made you . . . not able to do your work."

There was silence. Then Leo Dunn said, "Kevin, my sickness came from my own stupid pride. Your friend will get here under his own steam or not at all. The past has no power over the present. And present circumstances are that my client is coming here to see me. I can't handle him alone. Maybe he's not a favorite of yours, but will you stay and talk to him?"

I wanted to tell him how scared and alone I felt on a summer's day with all the wonder drained out of the world. I wanted to tell him that oaths are hard and dangerous things, and that the way to peace of mind lies through perils worse than dragons. But he already knew all that. It took a long moment, but, beggar that I was, I nodded yes.

"Good man. What was it that you said the first time we met? I asked you how you got there, meaning how you had found out about me. And you told me you'd come by streetcar. What did you mean?"

While we waited for Damian, I told him about my Streetcar Dreams and he listened as enraptured as a child.

ELEVEN

I RODE MY memories into the dawn. The screech of a streetcar at the end of the block brought me out of a light doze. The
telephone rang. My answering machine message came on. Long
habit made me think they were calling about George. I held
my breath and listened. Then I heard Klackman say, "Grierson!" I waited but after a short pause the connection broke.
Matt stirred beside me. On an impulse, I got up and called
Klackman. The line was busy. I turned back to the bed.

Seen in the first light, Matt's bruise looked angry. Another
person hurt by getting too close to me and my Shadow. I wondered what I was going to do with the kid when he awoke and
what he thought about my Shadow.

Klackman's call reminded me of the autumn when I last saw
Mr. Dunn. Those days had been full of wonders, but the nights,
like my current ones, were riddled with wrenching memories
and dreams.

Once back then, I found myself crouched in the chill dark at
the rear of a van, alone except for my Shadow and a corpse
called Lucky. 'Could be,' my Shadow murmured in my ear, 'if

we asked the stiff, he'd say he was here keeping watch on a dead man and doppelganger.' As that sank in, the van door opened and I reached for the .25 in my belt. What I touched was my bare hip which made me think I must be laid out in a morgue. Like Carl had been when his mother and I found him.

That brought me awake. I discovered my legs tangled in sheets and the city warm and silent at first light of a Sunday in September. The pistol, the van, and Lucky's corpse were bits of unwelcome debris from the place where memory doubles back on itself. I told myself, "The past has no control over the present," and repeated that mantra several times. Gradually, my fear faded.

Still, I remained motionless, held my breath until I was sure I was the only presence in the room. Because while the nightmare was out of the jumble of the past with no power to hurt me in the waking world, my Shadow was still very much with me. And since Mr. Dunn's illness, I could feel my Silent Partner circling closer.

Just as happened years later with George, on good mornings, I could go for as much as half an hour without thinking about what was happening to Leo Dunn. But the first memory of him would always put a bad twist on the day.

Shaking off the dream, I pulled on the prior night's cruising jeans and went into the front room. A pin of light still shone in the sky above Alphabet City, the last of Sirius, the Dog Star. At the end of the block, First Avenue was as empty as it only gets at that hour of that day.

Then the phone rang. My first reaction was that it was my Shadow calling. My second was that the hospital was calling to tell me that Mr. Dunn was dead. Not until the third ring was I able to pick it up. After that, it took a moment until I could croak, "Hello."

A guy, unrecognizable because he was unexpected, said, "Kevin? Hey, hope I didn't wake you."

"I'm awake." I was still tensed for horror or tragedy.

"I need to talk," said the caller and made it sound like my listening was a service to which he was entitled.

That's when I recognized Damian. Bad news, but not the kind I had expected. Damian of Darien, as I called him, was maybe Leo Dunn's last client. Mr. Dunn had told me, "You're only ten years older than he is, not fifty, closer to his experience. Speak to him, Kevin." But Damian aroused no kindness in me. I felt he'd had it too easy.

"What do you want to talk about?" I asked.

"I can't sleep, man." One night that June, Damian, home from college and drunk at the wheel, hit a girl, crushed both her legs, and drove off without stopping. Bad mistake. The story got into the papers. Her parents were more important in Connecticut than his were.

"People are saying I should be taught a lesson. Like their own kids are angels," he whined.

"Isn't Mrs. Dunn seeing you?" While Leo Dunn was in the hospital, his wife was working with Damian.

"It's so early, man. I mean she's been great, but it's Sunday and . . ."

With a twinge, I realized that in the midst of my own troubles the year before, I had not been much concerned about jolting an elderly couple awake. "What's the problem?"

"I didn't know she was there. I would have stopped." As I'd already heard him do a few times, Damian was reliving the crime, trying to establish his innocence in his own mind. "I didn't know until they busted me that it even happened. Now they say she won't walk again." His voice cracked. "They want to put me in jail. As an example."

It bothered me that this kid could cripple another human being and still reserve his most profound concern for his own white ass. My reply was pretty brutal. "I don't think they'll put you away. But if they do, it probably won't be for long, a few months. Cut that hair off and request protective lockup. Be careful in the showers. You'll be fine." I sounded like my Uncle Jim.

"I guess jail's okay if you're a faggot," he said and I wanted to slam the phone down.

Then I remembered the reality that lay behind my recent nightmare: Lucky dead in my apartment, poor Boris and doomed Carl risking prison to help me out of my criminal stupidity, my Shadow riding shotgun in the cab of the van. Nothing in my past justified any kind of self-righteousness.

So I took a very deep breath and told Damian, "The important thing is to stay sober so the judge can see what a model citizen you are. You've got no choice. Like me, you don't have a real talent for the criminal life."

"Did you ever get sent to jail?"

"No." I was about to say, "I was lucky." But that word brought back the image of my helping to slip an emaciated junkie into a king-sized garbage bag. So I changed that to, "Dumb good fortune." I couldn't resist adding, "The kind you don't seem to be having."

"Are things better for you now?" What the kid probably wanted to know was if there was a life after booze. I heard instead a question I'd been asking myself, "What are you doing with your new, sober life?"

"Things are okay. You staying straight, Damian?"

"Shit yes. My girl broke up with me after I got arrested. Everybody I used to hang around with thinks it's a bore that I don't get stoned. Why else would I be on the phone with you? I would have found something better to do if I was high."

As he spoke, I remembered driving Boris's van down dark streets, dumping Lucky on a loading dock, his empty eyes staring into mine.

"Kevin?" Damian was calling into the phone. "Talk to me."

This came out as an involuntary plea. "I mean I haven't been able to sleep all night. What do you find to think about?"

I looked out the window. At the end of the block a single figure pushed shopping carts. "Well," I told him, "right now, there's this bag woman walking south on First Avenue against traffic. She's pushing one cart, hauling another full of stuff. She's unstoppable. I kind of admire her."

"That's stupid."

"A smart person wouldn't have picked up the phone at six on Sunday morning." But it seemed stupid to me also. The woman was crazy. She was going to get run over.

"I think it's put me to sleep. Thanks."

"Good. See you." Hanging up, I knew I hadn't given the kid what he needed. I lacked Mr. Dunn's magic. I couldn't love Damian because of what he was or even despite what he was. Against all odds, Mr. Dunn had managed to do that for me. At times like that morning, I realized that such love was a miracle.

It had been sixteen months since I'd gotten high. As I bought *The Times* and some onion bagels, as I drank tea and tried to do the crossword puzzle, as I took a bath and dressed for work, I wondered what would become of me.

The streets at noon were alive with fall adrenaline and summer weather. St. Vincent's Hospital, by comparison, was serene, nothing but the hum of fans, the murmurs of the ladies at the reception desks. Long, cool Catholic corridors were lined with plaster saints and virgins in niches, paintings of powerful clergy and generous laity.

Upstairs, the cardiac ward was air-conditioned and the halls were chilly. Gentle voices came through half-closed doors. "So hard to believe this happened to me," a woman sighed. At Mr. Dunn's end of the hall, there was quiet commotion.

Staff clustered around Kendall Madison, Leo Dunn's private nurse. Elegant and Black in an immaculate white uniform, he held up a finger and said, "No. Only one is a bishop. The other is a monsignor, his secretary." Seeing me, he gave a wink.

The door to Mr. Dunn's room opened, revealing a movement of black cloth against white sheets and walls. "And now, Leo, I'm going to give the episcopal blessing," said a light, fruity voice. Mr. Dunn mumbled something that I couldn't hear and there was a low murmur, a sound like water going down a drain, a veteran priest running through a familiar formula.

"Good-by, Leo. I'm sure you'll be up and around by the time I'm back in New York," said the bishop in a normal speaking voice. "It seems that every day I use what I learned from you, the record room, the Silent Partner, the virtues." By this I knew that his Grace too had been one of Mr. Dunn's clients.

Out the door came two pink, well-nourished faces, two pairs of gold-rimmed glasses. Kendall Madison, it turned out, was a prelate groupie. "Oh, I'm sure this will be such a comfort to him, your Grace." When Kendall bowed to kiss the episcopal ring, bishop and monsignor exchanged delighted little smiles.

As the visitors were escorted to the elevator by a flurry of nuns, Kendall said, "Come in and talk to him, Kevin." I went into the room with a smile.

Mr. Dunn's problem was a simple one. His heart was bad and had to be operated on. But his kidneys were failing, so they couldn't operate. By then, I was used to Mr. Dunn's being so thin and so pale, with hands like dry bones when I grasped them and skin as white as his hair. But the eyes were alive. And that day they absolutely danced.

Kendall bustled around straightening the sheets. "Leo, you had a *very* important visitor."

"I know, Kendall. I am as stunned by it as you," and they both laughed.

Another nurse, his hair long and processed, wearing an earring, stuck his head in the door. "Was that a *cardinal?*" Kendall put his finger to his lips and ushered his friend outside to re-view the whole matter.

"Blessings from the Bishop of Syracuse," Mr. Dunn laughed. "Things must be worse with me than I had thought. Bill is an old friend. When I met him, he was a parish priest about your age."

"Getting ripped on the sacramental wine?"

"Every trade has its risks." Then he was serious. "Have you talked to Damian today?"

"Yeah. He's all right. Having trouble sleeping. You're look-ing great!"

"We're trying to get me out of here and back home. I need to work with people again. Damian needs our help. Even if he doesn't always know it. You're a good man, Kevin." He had told me that so often that I had, against all available evidence, started to believe it. "Do you work today?"

"I have to open the store at one. I wondered if you needed anything."

"Just to see you, my friend. My wife will be down shortly. And the kids." He looked at me carefully. "Bad dreams?" He knew. "Kevin, I was on the street for years and willing to do anything for the next drink. That comes back to me too in my sleep. But that is not who we are anymore. The past has no hold on us. We are free, you and I. Uniquely free."

Getting up to go, I said, "Sorry to be like this."

"Don't be. I need the work. It keeps me in shape."

As I handed in my visitor's pass downstairs, I noticed an old gray fedora. It was perched on the head of a tiny man with eyes bright as a malicious child's. But it was the hat, not the face that brought the name to mind: Francis X. MacLunahan. I remem-bered meeting him at the Market Diner in Hell's Kitchen and that he was connected with Leo Dunn. Tiny in a threadbare, striped suit, he looked thoroughly at home loitering in a lobby.

He placed me also, though we had met only briefly the year before. "And how," he asked, "is the great man?"

"Real well," I said, because it seemed that would disappoint him.

MacLunahan tapped a coat pocket, came close, and said confidentially, "I have a present he would not have shunned once upon a time." I saw the outline of a pint bottle. "Is that jigaboo fairy still standing guard?"

"Fuck off." The ladies at the information desk looked at me with surprise and didn't seem to notice MacLunahan and his bottle at all.

Out in that West Village afternoon, guys in pairs and in clusters, flushed and dazed, some of them very available, wandered back from Saturday night at the discos with tambourines around their necks. I couldn't get MacLunahan out of my mind. He lingered tiny and disturbing in the seamier byways of my memory. The first time we had met was in the aftermath of my last bender, the last time my Shadow and I spoke.

That was on my mind as I unlocked the gates of Old Acquaintance, deep in the West Village. The past had no control over the present, but somehow I was working in an antique store. It would be a quiet day. Sammi, the store cat, came over to be fed and to be scratched a bit but not too much.

Sammi had been found on the street a few years before. The mixture of fey and feral, he and I shared worked better on a cat than a person. Customers were usually pleasant but gingerly with both of us.

It was on that Sunday that a woman in her late thirties with fine features, nicely dressed in slacks and jacket, stopped in to look in the curved glasses cabinet at the front of the store. Madge kept oddments there, including some old toy figures. The customer turned and asked, "How much is that fireman?"

"Two dollars. It's a Barclay in great condition." This was the one thing in the store I knew something about.

"And the knight?" The woman had terrific brown eyes. She caught mine with them.

"Mignot. Seven dollars." She nodded and I took it out of the case. "Looks fine," she said, and my heart fell. I loved the knight, French and foolish and extravagantly painted. As I wrapped it, she said, "Sorry." And I guess I grinned, embarrassed at being so transparent. That was Addie Kemper on the first occasion that we spoke.

Toward closing that evening, Scotty, who seemed to have grown in the week or so since I'd seen him, rolled up to the door on his board and said, "Call me EZ Speed."

Sarah showed up shortly afterwards and said, "It's no joke. We're really supposed to call him EZ Speed." We walked down Bleecker Street on the way to her place with EZ Speed doing figure eights around us. After supper, she asked about Mr. Dunn and I asked about a guy she'd just started seeing. Jake was his name. EZ Speed seemed able to accept his presence.

Late that evening, as I was going home, Sarah said, "George Halle told me he met you." When I drew a blank at the name, she said. "You were with Madge at an auction." I vaguely recalled a curly-headed guy. Aside from that, Sarah and I skirted discussion of what I was doing with my life.

It seemed I wasn't doing much. Because I could sign for deliveries as well as carry things up from the cellar, Madge Hollings called me manager and paid me a little extra. She had gone through a few husbands and seen both her daughters acceptably married. In spare moments she tried to teach me the business. "Feel the grain of the carving on this armoire," she'd say. "That's hand tooled. The texture can't be faked." My eyes glazed and she sighed.

Madge's niche in decorating was handling seemingly impractical situations, outré arrangements. She had just decorated a small five-room cottage in Sag Harbor for a long-term ménage, two angles of which never spoke to each other.

Like an irregularly shaped room, my future was a puzzle for her to solve. "Kevin, you're a good-looking kid and quite bright." She was being kind. I was a kid only in the showbiz sense of having no serious credits. If I was bright, it was in no particular direction. I was too short and would be thirty-two on my next birthday. My nose was bent out of line. I had scars and several gray hairs. I debated growing a beard to hide some of the damage.

"We have to find you a wife," said Madge one day. "Or a husband." She chuckled at my expression and said nothing more. A week later, she said, "Kevin, there's an auction preview over at Glueck and Chomfrey." She adjusted the collar of my jacket, patted me on the back. "Stop by after lunch and see if anything interests you." I never spot setups until afterwards.

First, I went by St. Vincent's where Mr. Dunn sat carefully positioned to show his best angle to visitors. Kendall said, "We have him all ready to play Leo Dunn in the movie."

The most recent news seemed good. They were talking about letting him go home. "I'll be better able to rest there. Get strong enough for them to operate," he said. Then to Kendall, "Tell him who it is that's coming to visit."

"Spencer and Lettie Towns! Of Newport and Palm Springs. He owns racehorses. She writes the words for photo books about mansions. Sister Roberta reads the society pages. She knew all about them. She asked which of them had the drinking problem. She also says you are not leaving until you start eating."

Just then, a doctor in a lab coat entered. I went outside where there stood a tall and beautifully tanned couple. Mrs. Dunn introduced the Towns to me before she stepped into the room. "Kevin Grierson," she said. "Kevin worked with Leo."

They smiled their approval. I won't deny that it felt good. "Congratulations!" He shook my hand.

She said, "Meeting Leo was our greatest piece of good luck. How long have you known him?"

"Since . . . ," I began, but just then I noticed a tiny figure with a fedora and a pint bottle sticking out of his raincoat pocket.

"My God!" said Spencer Towns.

His wife looked where he did and asked, "What?" as Francis X. MacLunahan saw us, tipped his hat, turned, and was gone.

"It was that horrible little man that Leo tried to help. Mac something. That lawyer who cheated him so badly. We could never discover his name in any state bar association."

"But don't I remember him dying?" Lettie Towns obviously had seen nothing. She sounded concerned, baffled. For an instant, I caught the whole drama of a drinker and his wife. Then the door of Leo Dunn's room opened and he emerged walking slowly between Mrs. Dunn and Kendall.

Doppelgangers and Shadows were on my mind as I went east. I thought of Mr. Dunn saying, "Your Silent Partner wants to leave you just enough alive to want the next drink," and I thought of MacLunahan and his bottle.

On Broadway, just above the gentle curve at Grace Church, was a casual loiterer, a man my size and build in a filthy overcoat too warm for the day. Something in the way he stood was so familiar that my guts froze. Then he turned and revealed the dark, raddled face of a stranger.

I hurried in under the sign Glueck and Chomfrey, Estate Appraisals and Auctions. There, either Chomfrey or Glueck—I could never tell them apart—handed me a catalog with a cover that read *Household Furnishings of the Kavenaughs of Dobbs Ferry* and said, "Any questions, ask George Halle. He wrote this."

The gallery floor was a maze. Paths ran between ninety-year-old Louis XV chairs piled on tables, oak credenzas that could have stopped artillery shells, whole families of cast-iron lawn deer.

Past two gilded nymphs surprised but not displeased by their nakedness, I spotted a round, flat bronze head of Medusa. She looked like an angry sun with her serpents as twisting spokes of light. The social trick Medusa never learned was keeping her snakes inside her skull. I could sympathize.

Then I noticed a busted rocking horse, very much like one I'd had, a dusty dollhouse, a decorated chest: the toys of the Kavenaughs. In the chest were an ancient eagle bank, an armless Barbie, dozens of metal doughboys.

"Madge said she's had trouble getting you interested in any of this." George Halle smiled at me crouched on the floor testing the key of a rusty windup rabbit. Now that I knew who he was, I realized I'd run into him several times, a nice-looking guy about my height with curly hair, a mustache, and some kind of art history degree. Once he had suggested going out for a drink and I had been pretty abrupt turning him down.

"So, you've been asking around about me." I stood and just remembered to smile. "What did you find out?"

"That you have a lot on your mind." He looked concerned. "That Madge really admires the way you've gotten yourself together. That Sarah Callendar's son thinks you're cool." I wore my shirt open at the collar. He undid the next button. "You should wear it that way."

From the time I was real young, I'd always thought that my sexuality was just about to untangle itself, that someone or something would happen that would make everything clear. Recently, I had thought sobriety would do that. In fact, it made the warp and weave of human sex more than ever a mystery I looked on from the outside. "Where did you get the shirt? It's great." George undid another button.

"An old-clothes store. I had one like it when I was in high school." I'd had to abandon it on that bad day at the Y. Finding this identical one made me feel like I was reconstructing my life. "Hey?" My shirt was open almost down to my belt. It occurred to me later that someone who had been over the ground had told George I wouldn't know what I wanted until it happened to me.

"That armoire," said a man several aisles over, "is estimated at twelve to sixteen hundred."

"Step into my office," George said.

In theory nothing fazed me. In fact my experience was with a few women, a boy or two like Carl who knew my true identity, and a host of men whom I met once or twice and whose real names I never learned. This encounter wasn't going to be cloaked in anonymity. It felt like I was taking a headfirst plunge.

George had a desk in a cubbyhole behind some tall bookcases. He also had a couch. "Leave everything to me," he said.

"Every bedroom in Manhattan big enough for an armoire already has one," a woman remarked.

I heard a soft laugh and realized it was mine.

In the Village on evenings in spring and in early fall, dusk and house lights meld, living rooms seem to spill out through their French windows into the twilight streets. Once, on my way to the hospital in that magic hour, I heard a voice, quiet but clear, a woodwind not a violin, say, "Hello, Kevin." And I turned to see Leo Dunn's granddaughter, Celia, her hair like a Botticelli angel, asking, "How are you?"

"Wonderful," I said, and realized that was so. She smiled and was gone before I could even be surprised that she had remembered me.

Upstairs in his hospital room, Leo Dunn was full of plans. He was going home the next day. "I'll be back at work by this time tomorrow. Are you going to visit me, Kendall?"

The nurse smiled and said, "Of course. You have been one of my *most* interesting patients."

That's when I said, "I just saw your granddaughter downstairs." Mr. Dunn shook his head slightly and I remembered his first introducing us and his asking me not to mention her to anyone.

Kendall's eyes flickered but he let it pass. I couldn't understand why this had to be such a secret. MacLunahan too. When I asked, Mr. Dunn had refused to discuss him.

Kendall was outside as I was leaving. "I know who you were talking about. She comes by in the evening sometimes. He doesn't say anything about it. And that little man you described to me once? The one he says not to talk about? He's been around. That one is hard to spot. When you see him, he disappears. Leo Dunn has his devils, but he has angels watching over him too."

When I said I hoped to see him around, Kendall smiled. He knew we'd all be back.

With Mr. Dunn back uptown, I found myself closing the shop in the blue hour and hurrying through the West Village to George's place. Disco played on car radios, account executives dashed to their co-ops to exchange Armani suits for leathers, ancient Italian ladies trolled home with their shopping bags, on every corner couples greeted each other with huge, opened doors of little restaurants to bursts of Boccherini.

What could have been a ten-minute encounter had turned into an affair. George had a little money, charm, a wonderful apartment, interesting work, and many friends. It seemed as if all I had to offer was an attitude problem and a cloudy past. George was several years younger. But he hadn't spent a major chunk of his life in a black hole. He was an adult and I was, emotionally, maybe fifteen at best.

One link was his urge to protect and comfort. I offered a prime opportunity. One Sunday morning, he traced the path of the scar over my left eye. "They found me facedown with no ID on an elevator floor," I said. "The door was opening and closing on my head." If I told him any more, I was going to have to explain my Shadow and the Sojourners and a whole part of my life I didn't want to let touch him. So I shook my head. George kissed me, like that would make it all better.

To shake away the mood, the two of us got up and went out to a disco. There, Sunday noon was Saturday night and guys, glassy-eyed, still danced in clouds of smoke and butyl nitrate.

In November, Mr. Dunn had a heart attack and was first rushed to an uptown hospital, then transferred to St. Vincent's and his specialists. Since AIDS, I've become used to friends, loved ones going in and out of hospitals, each time weaker and more reduced. But then it was all new.

The illness came down to a physical law. Without a heart operation, he would slowly die. But with his kidneys as bad as they were, they couldn't operate on him. And, of course, the bad heart was made worse by uremia and the dialysis he had to undergo. It went around and around in my head. Mr. Dunn had shown me miracles. But not how to work them.

He was far sicker this time. I came in to find him with his hands on the sheets as if he were dead. The face behind the oxygen mask was slack. Except for shallow breathing, he was perfectly still. I made a little noise and after a moment his eyes opened. They were yellow and stood out against the white skin and white hair. They had lost the ability to light and reflect. Now they just charted the progress of the poison that weakened his body and clouded his mind. "Hi, Mr. Dunn."

For a moment, there was no recognition. Then in a voice so thin and so muffled by the mask that I had to stand close to hear it, he said, "Mac. I've had a close call. I thought they got me. Who's that Black man outside?"

Though I knew it was stupid, his not recognizing me cut like a knife. "Kendall, your nurse."

"If that's the waiter, tell him that I'm ready to go down to dinner. Every high roller in Saratoga is in the hotel tonight," he said. "Francis." His hand fluttered to beckon me closer.

Mr. Dunn thought he was talking to Francis X. MacLunahan. Suddenly, we two weren't alone. I smelled cigars and booze, caught sight of a fedora at the corner of my eye.

"There's money in the drawer," Leo Dunn said. "I saw them take it from me and put it there. You get it now and go out and buy . . ." His eyes moved as if he was afraid of being overheard. "Scotch. Talk to that Canadian we met last night. I'll be entertaining people in here later. Have room service send up ice and ginger ale."

Laughing, I tried to make this a joke. "I think they might catch me sneaking it in. Besides, someone we both know once told me that booze was a vicious mind-altering substance."

"You're right, of course," said Mr. Dunn. It seemed I heard MacLunahan snicker. But when I looked around, it was just the two of us in the room.

When I was leaving, Kendall asked, "Did he recognize you?"

"He seemed kind of confused."

Kendall's smile was fond. "Did he ask you to buy liquor and hide it for him? He does that with me too. But you are one of the lucky few he asks for when he's himself."

A day later, Mr. Dunn was totally coherent. "This is a constant siege." His eyes snapped to mine. "What happens to me, whatever I may say or do, has no bearing on your life. Don't just nod your head. Do you know what I'm talking about, Kevin?"

"Yes, sir."

He nodded, but he didn't smile. I had rarely seen him this grave. "I know you'll be fine. I knew when you first walked in the door of my house that we two would win. It's Damian I worry about. My wife does too. We don't seem to be igniting anything in him. There's no sense of the joy that has to come with release from addiction. Now, you're closer to his age and—"

"Not that close. Look, there are just too many differences between us." Mr. Dunn waited expressionless and I wanted so much to have him smile. "Your granddaughter, maybe, should talk to him." Leo Dunn's expression changed. He grinned.

Leaves fall late in New York. The gutters were still full of them on an evening when George came by the hospital with me. Damian was sitting outside Mr. Dunn's room. His hair was now neatly cut, his scraggly mustache was gone. Instead of shades and a leather jacket, he wore glasses and a gray suit. "Doctors are in there." He was bleary-eyed. "I was supposed to see him. But he's sick."

At that moment, he sounded to me like a vexed suburbanite complaining about the servants. And he looked like he'd been getting high. I felt my anger rise. "You changing your image, Damian?" From somewhere in my throat came the voice of Uncle Mike, the cop.

"For the pretrial hearings. The lawyer's got my parents convinced I have to go in there looking like a fa—" He caught himself. "Like the nerd king. I don't need this. I'm already a pariah."

"What do you do for fun?"

"Fun? Drive. A couple of nights ago, I drove all the way up into Vermont, turned around and came back."

"They suspended your license. It's going to look bad if they bust you."

"I have no one to talk to. No chicks. . . ."

He squirmed and I bore in on him. "You drive illegally. What else?"

"You mean am I drinking? FUCK YOU. I WISH I WAS!" A nurse hushed him. He stormed down the hall to a rest room.

After a moment's silence, George, who hardly ever drank, asked, "Kevin, was Mr. Dunn like that with you?"

"You don't understand this."

"No. But he's just a kid." I shrugged. "He's scared. Of the

hearing. Of the city. Of Mr. Dunn's being sick. Of this." He indicated a gurney rolling past with a patient, a woman still as death. "He's probably afraid of me. He's certainly afraid of you." He touched my arm. "Sometimes I am." That made me wince.

Damian came out of the rest room. George said, "Let me go get us some real coffee. Have you eaten, Damian?"

"No. Can I get a Coke? Please?" Damian sat down across the visitor's area and avoided looking at me. I realized his red eyes could well have come from squeezing back hard tears.

I got up and walked over. He flinched. I said, "When I stopped drinking, Mr. Dunn told me I was going to have to be braver than I had ever imagined." Damian nodded slightly. "You too? And he was right. What I didn't have to be was smart. He was there to be smart for me. My luck. Because any stupid thing you may ever have done or even thought about doing, I did." No reply. "In other words, I have no reason to feel self-righteous and my hypocrisy disgusts me. Okay?"

I was going to return to my seat when he said, "It's because of me that Kendall called the doctors in." Another long pause. "At first I thought Mr. Dunn was fine. He was smiling and joking. Then I saw he didn't know who I was and he was talking about a land deal, saying all this crazy stuff. I realized he was back in the time when he drank. He said this other name."

"Francis X. MacLunahan?" I kept my voice casual. "Yeah. Mr. Dunn does that. It's the uremia. And he asked you to get him some booze?"

"No. He kept talking like someone else was in the room. Then I saw him, this little guy with a bottle. I guess I yelled or something because Kendall came in. I mean, Mr. Dunn! Doesn't this ever stop?" Damian sounded like he wanted to cry and I felt kind of like doing the same.

He said, "I'd do anything to have it be me who got smashed up instead of that girl. I see her face every time I try to fall asleep. I wish she could forgive me." Just then, the door of Mr. Dunn's room opened. A couple of residents in scrub suits and a doctor in a sports jacket emerged. They seemed not to notice the young lady in dove gray clothes stepping lightly among them. She smiled at me as she approached. But her attention shifted to Damian, who stared at the floor.

"Damian," I said. "I'd like you to meet Celia." Moments later she sat on a chair next to him and he looked at her, open-mouthed, enraptured. I went over and looked in the room. Mr. Dunn breathed slowly with a mask on his face. He seemed to be smiling.

Kendall beckoned me in. "Leo's oldest daughter, Diana was here for the first time yesterday," he whispered. "A hard case. But Leo was at his best. They were alone maybe an hour. She came out looking teary, but like a weight was gone. Since then, though, he hasn't been well. I asked Mrs. Dunn, you know, discreetly. There is no granddaughter. Maybe there would have been, but Diana had a miscarriage. I think drinking came into it."

Something familiar lay on the floor. The cork from an old whiskey bottle. "Then there's MacLunahan," I said. "Everyone seems to agree that he died some years ago."

"And there's you," Kendall sounded a little distant. "You got a brother?" I shook my head, not wanting to hear what I knew was coming. "I saw someone on Greenwich Avenue last night when I was going off duty. Not you, because he had a bruise on his cheek you couldn't hide from me. But close."

"Real close." I looked away chilled. "Most people don't see him."

"Most people don't give terminal care. That's what I do, you know, honey. Everyone else here is amazed at how Leo hangs on. But I knew he wouldn't go until he was sure all of you children were taken care of."

As he spoke, I crouched down. The stopper disappeared when

I touched it. "At the end, I always see their souls," Kendall said. "Most times it's something gray just for a second, maybe a sound like someone sighing. Nothing like what I've seen with him. Nothing at all."

Later, George said, "Damian was aglow. He walked out like he was in a dream. What happened?"

I realized he'd had no hint of Celia's presence and I loved him for that. So all I said was, "I got him a date with an angel." He looked puzzled, but impressed. And I did feel I'd had something to do with it.

Over the next few days, what Kendall had told me sunk in. Leo Dunn had his good times. Sometimes when I came in, his face, yellow as a crayoned sun, smiled at me. A couple of times he said my name. Once, amid the thunder of garbage being picked up in the street outside, Mr. Dunn roiled in terror. And Kendall crooned, "Leo, it's all right. Don't you hear the drums in the parade?" Mr. Dunn grew calm. But he never got better.

Leo Dunn told me many times that we could not let the past control the present. But George Halle was an expert in antiques. The past was his life. Because he was my present, I felt myself being drawn toward it also. One Sunday, he took me to an auction of mechanical toys and automata that he had cataloged.

New York in early December can be fifty degrees and drizzling with people slightly itchy in those furs and trendy topcoats they've been dying to wear. But inside Masby's up on Park Avenue, it was Christmas.

A twelve-foot-high lighted tree was ornamented with cages of brightly painted, fluttering finches, Pierrots mutely serenading delighted moons, and an eighteen-inch-high Buffalo Bill puffing on a real cigar. All around it, life-sized boys in knickers, girls in lace jackets, high-hatted men, ladies in picture hats and fur muffs made gestures of wonder.

Designed as a Paris department store display, the whole

tableau was going under the hammer that afternoon. Tchaikovsky played, grand waltzes swept us onto the viewing floor. George's idea was to distract me from Mr. Dunn in this place where nothing was real.

For a while, it worked. We stood at the back of the hall as the auctioneer, a lady with Larchmont lockjaw, began, "From Maison Lambert of Paris, circa 1895, a young woman in a late eighteenth-century gown of peach and powder blue silk. The face is by Jomeau, the doll maker. A restored Lioret phonograph inside the harpsichord enables her to sing a Mozart aria and a song by Tosti."

"The silk is a replacement. The watermarks are clearly post-War," a stiff, pale man remarked to George while staring at me with exactly the same expression with which he'd regarded the silk. He seemed not to have as many moving parts as the automata. But he had made me wonder if there were any place for me in this world.

"The bidding," said the auctioneer, "is with the room. We will start at five thousand dollars." A man representing Malcolm Forbes immediately bid that. "Do I hear seventy-five hundred?" Someone on the phone from Switzerland promptly bid more money than I made in a year.

Depressed, I looked back, past the tree, out to the twilight street. And I could hear Mr. Dunn say, "Sunday evenings, as you've doubtless noticed, are one of the great times for drunks and their self-pity."

As soon as I remembered that, I knew with utter certainty what was about to happen. I jumped up, telling George to stay. But of course he came downtown. Outside the hospital, we found Damian staring up the street, still enchanted. I hoped it would be enough to see him through. Following his gaze, I saw Celia turn once, smile, and wave at us all. My own heart tipped over as she faded into the dusk on a quiet street.

Then I noticed Francis X. MacLunahan slip like a wraith into the hospital lobby. I went after him with George and Damian following. He wasn't in the elevator or on the intensive care floor.

Mrs. Dunn was crying on her son's arm. Leo Dunn had a golden glow and a slight smile as he lay still. Kendall whispered to me, "He's still within the room."

And I murmured like a prayer, "Lots of my memories are painful. Stuff I did, the years down the drain. When it gets bad, you're what I remember. You're magic and maybe the rest of my life is going to seem mean and stupid. But without you, it wouldn't be there at all."

"Kevin." Kendall pointed. I turned and MacLunahan stood at the foot of the bed with his head cocked like he heard someone calling him. Already, he was transparent. As I watched, he winked out bit by bit. In moments there was just a an antique pint bottle of Old Overholt and a battered fedora lying on the floor. Like the Cheshire Cat's smile, the fedora melted last.

TWELVE

MATT DIDN'T WAKE up until late morning. It seemed I no
longer needed sleep. I was dressed and Madge Brierly from
Masby's had me on the phone about the auction I'd proposed.
Suddenly he stood in the bedroom door on full display, hesitant,
rubbing his eyes, one foot on top of the other, his damaged profile averted. This was an act I too once played called "pity the
poor urchin." But I also remembered that waking up with no
clear idea of where you've been and where you're going next is
a hard way to start the morning. He gestured toward the bathroom and I nodded.

When Madge was through, I tried Ozzie Klackman again.
The line was still busy. All the while, the shower ran. I hung up
and brought Matt a towel. He dried his hair and rubbed a three-
day stubble. At one time it might have looked sexy. With the
bruise it made him seem down and out. He caught my reaction,
which is a talent. "There's a safety razor on the sink," I said.

"I've only used an electric." Which he no longer owned. His
life was coming apart.

"Come here." He tied the towel around his waist. "Wet your

face while the whiskers are still soft. Now the foam. A guy who picked me up when I was in college taught me." I caught Matt's reflection in the mirror with my head behind his shoulder and my arms reaching around him.

"You and Fred ran into some people yesterday night," I told him. Matt's eyes above the white mask were wary. Are we ever so vulnerable as when someone shaves our throat? "Gas heads, maybe? Did my Shadow say?" I could feel his heart beat faster. The bruise was deep, he winced when I touched it. "How did it happen?"

He didn't respond. I showed him the strokes until we came to the detail work. Then I handed him the razor. "We were leaving the place Fred lives in," he said like I'd know where it was. "They came out of nowhere. I got between them and him. One of them had something in his hand. He hit me and I went down. Fred took off and they went after him. He had said that if anything happened I should see you."

His hands shook. "Hey!" I told him. "Try not to cut off your nose. It's one of your better features."

As Matt dressed, I wondered if he'd lifted anything. Cuff links, maybe, or cologne. Some of my knick-knacks, like the children riding elephants and camels in the zoo on the mantle, were priceless. But trade never knew that.

"Sorry to bust in on you," he said when he was dressed. He trembled a bit. The kid was strung out and scared. I stuck money in his T-shirt pocket. Twenty will dent the edge of life without doing much more.

Matt told me, "I know you don't like your partner or your brother or whatever Fred is. But he said, you know, that you're okay. And I should ask you to help me."

The real help he needed I wasn't able to give him. I lacked the distance and the talent. Matt had already made it with me and with my Shadow. He knew me too well. I couldn't stand apart and demand his best from him. And I lacked Mr. Dunn's faith.

As we walked downstairs, all I could think about was how the deck was stacked against this kid.

But I knew someone who could heal. I handed Matt a card with Addie's name and number. "Try me again if you're willing to clean up. If anything happens to me, here's the number of someone real good to talk to. I'll tell her about you. Okay?"

We were on the sunlit sidewalk. Over in the park, the fountain played, a day-care center's worth of tiny kids ran and screamed. A young Latino lady in silk drawers rode by on a bike and looked our way as Matt and I hugged and parted.

A little later, I was down on Avenue A, ringing Ozzie Klackman's bell. Curiosity has killed more than cats. But I wondered what Ozzie knew. I got buzzed in almost immediately, which made me think he was okay.

As I climbed the stairs, I heard a voice saying, "IT WAS THE FUCKING BANJA BOYS! THEY SHOULD BE LOCKED UP!" A guy in a kimono and turban and full makeup stood in the hall outside Klackman's place. The apartment door was open. An ancient woman with a cigarette in her mouth stood in the living room. She could only have been an East Village super.

"Yeah?" she said.

"I had an appointment with Ozzie," I told her.

"I guess he's not here, huh?" said the super. From the door I could see that the place had been tossed. The work table was on its side, Chatty Cathy lay with her head torn off. The carousel was more than smashed; it looked like it had been ground into the floor. Every horse had been crushed. On the filthy carpet was a thick red stain. "It's wine," she said when she caught me looking at it. "The bottle was on the floor when I came in. He lives like a swine." Her accent was guttural but unplaceable.

"Any idea where he is?" My guess was that Ozzie was supposed to entice me down here. When he failed, somebody had gotten very angry.

"LAST NIGHT THE BANJA BOYS GOT RIGHT INNA BUILDING," said the guy standing beside me in the hall.

"It's 'cause you let them in, Henry," the super remarked. "The same way you let this one in." She pointed at me. "That one"—she pointed at Henry—"found the door unlocked. No sign of Klackman. The place is always a shithouse. Maybe a little worse now. Guess I call the cops, huh?"

At Half Remembered Things, Lakeisha was late. But I didn't care. I sat inside with the lights out wondering what had happened to Klackman and what the Sojourners' next move would be. As I did, I felt a distant echo of pain and was aware of my Shadow's ghostly distant awakening somewhere in the city.

I thought of the Carousel years, which is what I called New York in the late seventies and early eighties. The city was a merry-go-round. Everyone felt that as we spun through the days.

Late one night I had awoken from a dream of light and fear, looked at George Halle with his head resting on my groin, and felt as remote as a hurricane's eye. For a moment I caught the red-rimmed aura of my Silent Partner and knew we were being watched.

But when I awoke all the way and looked hard, all I could see was George, fuzzy and compact, a businesslike medium-sized bear. My legs entwined with his and my hand against his tanned shoulder looked pale. I watched him sleep in the slatted light from the street. The same thing had happened with Sarah. I'd lie there awake and marvel that my peaceful companion had a full round soul when I had only a sliver of one.

Despite all my wonder and worship, though, as it had happened with Sarah so it happened with George. We went long past those moments when my spine felt like an arrow shot at the sun or anywhere near it. In bed I paid them back with sex for the pleasure and generosity of their company. But with each passing season, the occasions grew more frequent when I felt empty and alien.

That night a cry came from the next room. Not the voice of a small child, but not an adult either. George stirred and I knew that if it happened again, he'd be awake and concerned.

Remembering to put on a robe, I went to look. For privacy George had arranged screens at one end of the living room. Behind them, on the couch, tangled in a sheet, skinny, long haired, was Scotty Callendar, fourteen. He lay facedown in a pair of the beloved surfer jams that George and I believed he took off when he showered but that he wore absolutely everywhere else.

Blanche, George's elegant and reserved Siamese dowager, curled above Scotty's head, alert, eyes scanning the dark corners, tail twitching. Since the kid had arrived for a barely announced visit two weeks before, the cat had attached herself to him like a familiar.

As I stood over him, Scott, still asleep, twisted his head like he was shaking away a dream. At the corner of my vision, I caught a spark like a firefly. Blanche's eye narrowed.

She watched through slits as I adjusted the sheet over Scott. I remembered waking up beside his mother. I remembered his father. The kid moaned, his muscles rigid. Seeing him like this, I felt, with my heart in my throat, that his life was in my hands. Carefully supervised by Blanche, I stroked his neck and whispered, "Just a nightmare," until I felt him relax.

Sarah had married Jake Bellman about three years before. George and I attended the wedding. Jake turned out to be an okay guy. Not my kind. Maybe not Sarah's. But not into drugs nor gay, not inclined to fly through the air on a flaming motorcycle. Things seemed to work out between him and Scotty. The family moved to the south shore of Long Island and Sarah opened Second Callendar Day in the Hamptons.

She and I had lunch every couple of months. As unofficial godfather, I sent Scotty birthday and Christmas presents: toys at first, then checks. I saw him rarely enough to be shocked each time at how tall he had gotten. And I waited.

The call came to me one morning. Scotty's voice was half changed. Sounding desperate and choked, like he was afraid someone might overhear, he asked if he could visit. Before clearing it with his mother, I asked George, who, bless him, said yes without hesitation. Sarah said, "Honey, thank you both. Getting rid of him for a few weeks may save my sanity and even my marriage. But if he gets to be too much is that military school they sent you to still in business?"

Too old for camp, too tough for the South Shore was my take when he showed up at the store that afternoon, scared and grim. He brought his skateboard and a duffel bag that seemed to be stuffed entirely with T-shirts. But not *A Garland Knot for Children*. Believe me, I checked.

Scotty was a little distant with me and I guess I wasn't fully prepared to deal with a fourteen-year-old. But George immediately hired the kid for a dollar fifty an hour and put him to work at Half Remembered Things preparing for the Disney sale. Scotty followed George around like a puppy. Children would have saved our marriage, I understand now.

When I crawled back into bed, George, still asleep, asked, " 'S alright?" I whispered yes.

Even if he had been awake, what was I going to say? "Georgie, the kid's haunted. His late father communicates with him through this enchanted book. Scott Callendar Senior has it in for me, by the way. Just because I contributed to his death. Some ghosts will never learn to lie down." No, the beauty of George was his being so warmly mundane. That was enough to make me snuggle up against him in the air-conditioned chill.

Not enough to keep me faithful, or even nice to him, of course. The romance dribbled out of our relationship and our partnership almost sank in ethical differences. In those years, I grew and trimmed a beard just like a hundred thousand other guys my age. We were all timeless, interchangeable, smooth as glass.

The next day maybe, or one very shortly thereafter, started with the three of us in the store. I was unpacking Three Little Pigs toothbrushes and coloring books. George and Scotty were doing a window arrangement, stringing an inflatable Dumbo so that it flew above a Mickey Mouse plate like the cow sailing over the moon. Our Disneyana sale was make or break for us.

For our partnership in Half Remembered Things, I contributed big chunks of my time and followed outside leads. George, who had put up our initial investment, handled display and promotion.

We worked like this. An old Italian woman in the neighborhood told me, dribbling it out slowly, warily, that her brother had "Mickey Mouse toys." And that he lived in Hoboken. And finally that he wanted to see what I thought they were worth.

The guy looked like the animated version of Gepetto. So much so that I thought my nose was going to start growing when I told him, "Twenty-five hundred is as far as I can go. I don't know if anyone wants to buy this stuff."

Partly this was true. That was all the capital we had available. And I didn't know how much the stuff was worth. No one did. These kinds of toys were just starting to be widely collected. But my bet right from the first was that this could do it for us.

George, who could get a little self-righteous and anal about stuff like proper ownership and taxes, flipped when he saw the windup Donald Duck, the Minnie Mouse coloring book, the fire engine with Pluto at the wheel and Huey, Dewey, and Louie, Mort and Ferd aboard. We handed over the money and grabbed the merchandise.

The pricing was all guesswork. George's book *Discovering the American Toy* got its start with his cataloging of our purchase. George got the word out. People started calling. *New York Magazine* and the *Daily News* sent around reporters and photographers. The stories were going to run after Labor Day. We spent late August getting ready.

A friend of George's gave us a two-hour tape as background music in the store during the sale. It had "When You Wish Upon a Star," "Someday My Prince Will Come," "Hey Diddley-Dee, an Actor's Life for Me," and all the rest. George and Scott played it constantly.

On the day that I remember, they were bringing stuff up from the cellar and singing "Hi-ho, hi-ho, it's off to work we go." Maybe it was the music. More likely I was cranky because I was the one Scott had supposedly come to see, but now we seemed just nodding acquaintances.

It revived my feeling that I was nothing much more than a reformed drunk, a guy who had come in off the street. I felt that if you looked at me sideways, I wouldn't be there. "I'm going to ask that 'Hi-ho, hi-ho, it's off to work we go,' be played at my funeral," I told them.

They were setting up rows of dwarves made of rubber, of metal, of plastic and paper. "Let's see," said George. "We have Doc and Dopey, Happy, Grumpy. . . . Who's this one?"

"Sleazy," I said. "Don't we have the figure of him wearing a pimp hat?" They ignored me.

Right then, the phone rang and a woman with the kind of Brooklyn accent you only hear in 1930s Hollywood movies told me, "My name is Ellen Clark. I've asked around and heard you might be interested in something we have. It's like a toy and old. Antique." When I suggested bringing it by the store, she said, "No. It's way too big. Kind of an amusement park thing."

When she told me what she had I was fascinated. But I anticipated some months-long waltz, like with the old Italian lady and the Disney toys. This one, though, said, "We can drive you to see it. Today. It won't take long." The intrigue tickled me and I made an appointment for later that afternoon.

Then I realized the time and was relieved at being able to slip out of the store. "I'm having lunch with Addie," I said. "What do you want me to bring back?" I don't remember what George wanted. Scotty, of course, would have ordered a cheeseburger, which was all he ate that summer.

What I do remember is that George nodded and lost his smile. It seemed to me ridiculous that he was jealous of Addie and me of all things. It turned out that he was right. But not in the way anyone could have imagined.

Pausing in Sheridan Square to buy hummus-and-falafel pita sandwiches and a double order of stuffed grape leaves, I watched a tour bus full of Japanese snapping pictures. Some of them focused on a hopeful but wary young man decked out in tight jeans and T-shirt, embarking on Christopher Street perhaps for the first time and oblivious to their attention.

Nothing but minor dust devils stirred on drowsy, sunny Cornelia Street. I pressed a button on a wall, said, "Kevin," in response to an oracle voice asking, "Who?" pushed open an iron gate as a buzzer sounded, passed down a narrow cobblestoned alley, and unlatched another gate.

Then, as if I had followed a ritual prescribed by a genie, I found myself in a place of trees and ivy-covered walls, where finch chirped and a black-and-white cat batted at a leaf floating on a tiny marble pool. There, across a flagstone path, was a tiny two-story house. Addie Kemper stood smiling at the worn wooden door with the quizzical owl on the brass knocker. Behind her in the office was a table with plates and a pitcher of iced tea ready.

The living space was a single big room upstairs. On the ground floor, aside from the kitchen, was Addie's office, and the blue room with the sand table and the walls lined with shelves of toys: plastic Indian villages, carved wooden leopards and giraffes from East Africa, metal knights and ladies, tiny cardboard houses, paper dragons, and silk birds—the very matter of fantasy and dreams.

Addie had bought stuff from me since my days at Old Acquaintance. She collected toys. Figures mostly. And right at the start, I learned that her instinct was unerring. If a piece came into the shop that attracted me, she showed up that week and bought it.

Gradually she told me why she was interested in them. After that she would stop by and we'd talk. We stepped out for coffee once or twice.

Then one day, I visited her house for the first time and told her about Uncle Jamey's Islands Game. She told me about a book called *Floor Games* that H. G. Wells created for himself and his sons. Or, really, for any adults and children who wanted to play together. That book was one of the bases of sand table therapy.

At lunch on that summer afternoon a few years later, I had saved snatches of the dream that had awakened me the night before. "It was lights," I told Addie, looking at her shelves. Then I spotted a small German passenger train and caught a memory. Taking it down, I told her, "It's too bad this isn't an electric number. The neat thing about them is that the windows light up."

Addie shrugged. "Imagination is better for my purposes."

And she was right, of course. Because as soon as I placed it on the table amid the plates, I remembered what had made me wake up the night before. "I had this dream about a train. It involved an old-fashioned smoker/club car, and, somehow, lights were spinning. I can't call the dream itself back, but it reminded me of something that happened when I was real small.

"When I was maybe four, my mother and I lived in this apartment house in Jamaica Plain in Boston. It probably wasn't all that great. But I loved it because not only was it near the streetcar barns, but out the back windows you could see the old Boston New Haven and Hartford tracks.

"One night I woke up, came out to the kitchen, and found my Aunt Tay reading the papers and drinking tea. Maybe she was taking care of me because my mother was away. Anyhow, she poured me some milk.

"As she did, I looked out and saw on the tracks what seemed like a single brightly lighted railway car and got very excited. Thinking about it now, I imagine it was a club car full of people, salesmen, and good timers, in that strange and distant year, 1948. The rest of the train would have been baggage cars and dark pullmans. And it must have paused for a signal on its way into Boston or before rolling through the night down to Providence, New London, and New York.

"Now, Tay was a woman with powers, and she sometimes used them. But all I remember on that occasion was her drawing me away from the window and turning out the light, saying something like 'We don't want to waste the light.'

"What I took it to mean was that all those people in the lighted car had wasted electricity. And they were condemned to a lifetime of sitting in that car and never getting home to bed."

"Sounds like a description of the West Village," Addie said and we both laughed. But expectation hung in the air, like she wanted the story to go further. I too began to wonder. Then we heard the voice of a child, her next patient, coming through the yard and I remembered the time and the Disney sale.

That afternoon, on my way back to the store, I caught a sidelong glance, turned to a guy, dark and skinny with a little mustache, six or seven years younger than I but, of course, absolutely smooth and timeless. I gave him my best profile. "You could be a cop," he said, a challenge and an invitation.

Various things made that unlikely. When I spoke, though, it was the voice of Uncle Mike the cop that said, "I could." His eyes were brown. I kept my gaze riveted on them. My eyes are blue and thus can be quite cold. Brown-eyed people sometimes find that fascinating. "You could be a punk," I told him and he sneered. The guy handed me a slip of paper. On it was a telephone number and the generic boy's name Johnny.

Later that afternoon, Scotty and I were working in the store. George had left; I have not the slightest doubt it was on business. We stuck price tags on Jiminy Cricket puzzles, Bambi teapots, Donald Duck alarm clocks, and a whole slew of Three Little Pigs items. Three Little Pigs windup toys and plush dolls, Three Little Pigs toothbrushes and cereal bowls, Three Little Pigs flashlights and coloring books.

"George is Practical Pig," Scott said, holding a Big Bad Wolf mask up to his face. I had no argument with that. "But I'm the one who builds his house out of wood."

"The hell you are! You'd be lucky to build one out of straw."

"Fuck you! I do more work than you."

Unexpectedly, that hurt. Before replying, I caught myself. "Unbelievable! I'm arguing about which of us is a harder-working pig."

Scott was laughing. He was already taller than I was. Sometimes there were hints of his mother about him, on occasion, traces of his father. "Anyway," he said abruptly. "Thanks for inviting me. You and George."

Suddenly the conversation he perhaps had come to this city to have started falling into place. "Glad to. I thought when you called and asked to stay that your old man and the book were back."

"In dreams, sometimes. A lot, actually. But mostly it was like, you know, the emergency door in planes. There's all these instructions about what to do in case of emergency. And I always want to test it before takeoff to make sure it works. Sometimes after takeoff."

"Remind me never to fly with you."

"You're the only one who understands about my father and me and the whole family curse thing with the book. My mother, I think, knows something. But she doesn't want to talk about it. With someone like my stepfather or even George there's no way to start talking about that stuff. You had no problem with it."

That was the moment to tell him why that was. "What we have in my family is a little different. Mr. Dunn, remember the guy who got me off booze and drugs? He told me addiction was like a Silent Partner. That image worked for me because since I was a kid younger than you, I had this kind of Shadow and—"

Scott was leaning forward, hanging, for once, on what I had to say. When the bell rang, we both jumped. The moment got shattered.

At the front door was a woman maybe fifty, dressed up as if for church in high heels and fake pearls, a kerchief and a short raincoat. She had on big, serious sunglasses, as close to a mask as you can wear on the street.

"I'm Ellen Clark, the one who called you earlier," she said when I opened the door. I had forgotten all about her. Something, the Village, Bleecker Street, me, seemed to make her nervous. "You said to come by and we could go take a look at it."

This, somehow, didn't feel right. In a city as ethnic as New York, with an accent like hers, a name as bland as Ellen Clark sounded fake. It occurred to me to apologize and tell her to come back in half an hour. By then, George would have returned and could tell me whether what she offered was or wasn't a good idea.

In the meantime, I could talk to Scotty about his dad and my Shadow and the bad ways they connected. But, as if he had caught my uncertainty, like quicksilver, like an autumn sky, the kid went from engaged to withdrawn. So the easiest thing was just to tell him, "Let me do this. We'll talk tomorrow before you go back." And he shrugged and an opportunity went away.

The first place Ellen took me was to a car, a Buick four-door, around the corner. At the wheel was a guy who could have been her husband, her boyfriend, maybe her brother. He wore a blue polo shirt and double-knit slacks and aviator sunglasses. I found myself noting details.

His name was Walt, that much I got, the last name was blurred. She got in back and I sat in front with Walt. Something about them made me remember an old street rule: One trick at a time; two, almost never; three, turn and run.

Out of nowhere, I recalled myself, not much older than Scotty was at that moment, racing down a commercial street deserted on a summer evening. Behind me, a car with three guys in it backed up fast. One of them hung out the window and yelled. "Stop, little boy, if you know what's good for you!"

Then a voice in my ear said, 'They catch us, they lock us up in a cage!'

So I had stretched my legs and got to the corner. Boston Common, full of people strolling, was across the way. The guys who had tried to pick me up seemed to flicker as they shifted out of reverse and drove off. The memory put me on edge.

When I say I'm from New York, I mean Manhattan. We went over the Williamsburg Bridge, of that I was sure. But the other side of the river was an unknown land. My head spun as the skyline flowed past on the left and my sense of direction deserted me. On my right were the streets and low houses of first Brooklyn and then Queens.

"You must see a lot of strange stuff in your business," Walt said and sounded like a john trying to make conversation on a date.

"You should see the store he's got," said Ellen. "All Donald

Duck and Bambi. Stuff you would have tossed out not knowing it was worth anything."

We pulled off the expressway and into a neighborhood of row houses and corner stores, of kids frantic with play in the last days of vacation. Church steeples dominated the skyline. At the end of the block, near the East River, lay warehouses and factories, piles of lumber and steel and industrial debris. In the middle of the city, the water and the street, both almost empty of traffic, evoked the feel of a quietly decaying river town.

"Here we are," said Walt as he pulled up to the curb in front of a big brick warehouse, old and closed. Getting out of the car, I looked down and saw tracks running along the cobblestoned street. At first I thought they were train tracks, then realized those would be on the other side of the building, near the loading docks and the East River. This was a streetcar line, long unused. For a moment I debated whether stepping over the rails or touching them with my foot would bring luck and decided on the latter.

"This is the guy to see the item," said Walt. I looked up to find that the door of the warehouse was open and that the forbidden third on the date stood looking at me. "Kevin, this is Al."

Al wasn't young. His eyes were hidden under the bill of a cap. He wore a big cigar in his face. Still, I caught a flash of slit-eyed recognition. Over the years, I'd learned that usually meant someone had met my Shadow. Except this guy somehow was familiar.

I was led through an office and down a hall. They slid open a big freight door and I stood at the edge of a huge loading bay. Afternoon sun filtered through cracked and dusty skylights.

The item took up most of the floor space. It was very old, but even in the dim light it was all flashing eyes and gold skin, bared teeth and striking hooves, horses that were halfway to being dragons.

Stunned, I stepped forward. The roof and platform of the Carousel were faded red and black and yellow, all covered with mystical symbols, suns and stars and hieroglyphics.

Behind me a switch got thrown, and loading doors at the back of the bay rolled open. Outside, sunlight bounced off all the glass in Manhattan, glanced over the ripples on the river, caught the gold and ivory of the Carousel. And for a moment the eyes of the horses seemed to follow me, the muscles in the legs poised aloft seemed to shimmer.

It was set up in the middle of the floor, so I walked all the way around. I was aware of the three people watching me from the door. Looking closely, I saw chips in the ebony hooves, hairline fractures in the ivory manes. I wondered if my Shadow had seen this thing and what he had made of it.

"Does it function?" I asked.

"Not yet, we still don't have it rigged." Al spoke for the first time and sounded like phlegm or voices heard underwater. Still, it sounded familiar. "You can go sit on it, if you want. It's real sturdy." I shook my head. That would not be necessary. I had visions of the machinery magically activating and suddenly whirling away with me.

"Reminds me of the old-time, carnies. Remember them? The sideshows? Siamese twins?" He stared at me with dead eyes. His hand was on the switch that would close the bay doors. But as he spoke, I turned toward him and caught sight of the edge of the scar on his throat.

"You know a guy named Fred?" Smiley Smile asked.

But I had already stepped toward the outside world. "I need to talk to my partner about this," I said. The doors seemed to lurch, but two paces took me onto the loading dock and into the warmth of the sun.

Ellen and Walt appeared not to know what was going on. Only when they had driven me back over the bridge to Manhattan did I ask about Al.

"He's a business partner," said Walt. And though he said more, things became no more specific. The only point they were definite about was the price. As I got out of their car in front of the store, I promised to get back to them.

George asked, "What did you see?"

"Something real big," I replied. "And real old and without a scrap of paper." I told him about Ellen and Walt and Al. I described the Carousel, failing to mention the rolling eyes and trembling hooves or Al's scar and what it meant. "They want twenty-five grand," I said.

George shook his head. "Sounds shaky and shady, Kev. Even if we had the money." That meant no. And I had to agree. But that didn't stop me from thinking about it. Or, it turned out, from dreaming.

Deep in the night, I felt an elevator in my chest drop a dozen stories. The fall left me awake and gasping for breath. I lay still until the pain was gone. George had his back turned to me and never stirred.

Out in the living room, Blanche lay above Scotty and stared unblinking into my eyes. The kid was going home the next day and I'd hoped he'd be awake. Scott was someone who might understand the dream I'd just had. But he slept gently, open-mouthed and vulnerable. He was still a child in most ways and it would have been unfair to get him involved. I wanted so much for things to turn out right for him.

Later that afternoon, I told Addie, "I saw him off on the train first thing this morning. George kind of arranged not to be around so that Scotty and I could talk." I shrugged. "But it wasn't the right time. His visit went okay, I guess." She made no reply.

Then I said, "I had a dream last night."

She sat across the sand table from me. I looked around the room. "You need a merry-go-round," I said. She just gestured toward a shelf with dozens of horses, high stepping wood and plastic and metal ones. I nodded and made my own carousel. Except the horses, instead of following each other around in a circle, faced out, tails toward the center, defiant and fierce.

"Remember my telling you about the lighted railway car? The one I saw from my window when I was little? Well, last night's dream started out in this bright loud place surrounded by dark. It was an old-fashioned bar car. Like one I remembered from when I was maybe three and my mother and I were getting off a train. That one had a bartender, lots of smoke and noise and cards. All of that frightened me and I held on tight to my mother's hand.

"In the dream, I noticed we weren't moving forward. We were just going around and around like a carousel. And horses powered it. They cantered outside the windows, snorted mutely, flashed their eyes, bared their teeth like guard dogs. Then I looked out in the dark and I saw a lighted window and in it this little kid my age and an old woman behind him. It was Aunt Tay and me.

"That's when I realized that the hand I held in the dream belonged to my mother's Shadow. And that I was my Shadow as a child looking up at me in the window. It was as if the dream was from my Shadow's memory and not my own. That's part of what woke me up." Addie's eyes narrowed a millimeter or two. This wasn't the first time I had mentioned my doppelganger to her.

"After I was awake, I remembered more clearly what had happened upstairs with Tay in the kitchen that night way back when we saw the lighted railway car.

"My aunt, when she saw what was on the tracks, plunged us into darkness and pulled me back from the window and not all that gently. 'It's ones like those that waste all God's light,' was what she actually said. The way she said that scared me. She brought me back to my bed and sang me to sleep with the old song that starts:

> Go brazen light,
> Come healing dark . . ."

When I was done, Addie asked, "Whose fear was it you felt in the dream?"

I thought that over without finding an answer. Then she asked, "How did you feel when you woke up from the dream last night?"

"Like a hole got drilled in my heart." Just remembering the pain made the air go out of me and left me gasping there at the sand table.

Addie took my hands and asked, "Darling, how long is it since you've seen a doctor? Not counting the clap clinic?" I fingered the scar over my eye and realized it had been the time when I woke up in the hospital not knowing who I was. Addie wanted to set up an appointment with a colleague right then and there.

That's when I remembered that without Scotty we suddenly were very busy at the store and said I'd do it later. On the way back to work, I stopped at a pay phone and made a call. The answering machine came on and I said in the cop voice that lay somewhere deep in my race memory, "Johnny, this is Detective Sergeant Burke. I want to ask you some questions."

THIRTEEN

At Half Remembered Things, early on an August afternoon almost twenty years later, I looked over the store lease and saw it had only a few more months to run. Late fall, before Christmas, would be the best time for a toy auction. Time, though, felt like it was closing in on me. When past and present collide, the future is often a casualty.

Tourists, a couple of young guys from Baden, drifted through the shop. A Haydn quartet played on the radio. The phone rang.

"Kevin? Thank God!" It was Gina Raille, breathless and tense. "That one I joked with you about, the evil twin? He was in my dressing room last night. This time we spoke."

"Hi Gina." Of all the bunch from the drama department at Mass. Arts and Science, she is the only one still acting. We see each other every once in a while and talk about Boris. She misses him too. This summer she stepped into a featured role in the musical *Gumshoe!*

"UNCANNY! He looked like you. I mean not like you look. But—"

"But the way I'd look if I'd spent the last few years face-down in the gutter." Gina, after all, had known me in my very bad days.

"Yes! Kevin, he's scary. The stuff he knows about you and me. He wants to see you. Tonight. Would you? Oh, you're so wonderful!"

As we made arrangements for that, Lakeisha came in with her headphones on, gave me a chill, dead-eyed look, and went in back. "I'm so sorry to get you involved in this," I told Gina. When I hung up I heard a rhythm like a pump under the Haydn minuet.

Lakeisha was in the stockroom, face on her arms, sobbing in great regular gasps. This would have to do with Lionel. I took out one of the earphones and said, "Men are pigs, honey."

When she looked up, her eyes were awash. "Lionel said he saw you last night up in Times Square." I shook my head but felt a chill. "You closing this place?" she asked with a hiccup.

"Probably," I shrugged. "You'll be going away to school."

"What makes you think I'm going?"

"Because if we have to, your mother and I will stuff you in the trunk of a car and haul you up to Rhode Island." I wondered if this was any different than my getting sent to St. Sebastian's. But at least Lakeisha stopped crying and looked thoughtful.

The doorbell buzzed and I jumped. A woman in her late forties stood outside on the street. It took me a moment to realize I had seen her Sunday with the man who stared, bedazzled, at the bedroom display. "My husband is in love with the Hopalong Cassidy blanket in the window," she told me, baffled. "His birthday is coming up."

I nodded, discreet and worldly, a guy who would not come between a middle-aged man and his cowboy blanket. "The price is three hundred." Her eyes widened. The past is always just a bit more expensive than we thought possible. We settled for two sixty-five.

Lakeisha boxed the woman's purchase and saw her out of the store. I felt like I was being watched. "How about lunch?" I asked. Given a choice of anything from French provincial to Szechuan Chinese within a two-block radius, Lakeisha wanted McDonald's.

We went to one over on Sixth Avenue. It was mostly empty in the middle of the afternoon. We sat near the windows and watched the world pass by. I had a salad, but I stole a couple of her fries. They were delicious.

After a while she said, "When I went to that school for orientation last month, the people in the town all looked at me like they was afraid I was going to rob them."

What I was going to tell her was that people in New England look at you that way if you're wearing mismatched socks. But Lakeisha's much too smart to lie to. "You have to try it, honey. I got sent to a place I hated. But maybe it gave me enough distance to survive." And then, like it clinched the argument, I said, "George wanted this for you."

"You going to see him tonight?"

"No. I have to meet an old friend."

"Kevin, is something wrong?" Like I said, she's very bright. "It's like you're not here. You going to be okay?"

"I've got the life habit pretty bad," I told her.

"Deep commitment!" she said. After lunch, I gave her the rest of the day off. If the Sojourners came for me in the store, I didn't want her around.

The air turned silvery and a thunderstorm moved across Greenwich Village, doing no more than settling the dust. Tourists drifted in and out. All the while, I felt my Shadow's dry heaves and throbbing spine, not pain but its evocation.

I was left to consider how the uncanny doesn't come around at magic intervals. For instance, the Carousel's second pass through my life didn't come after seven days and seven nights, or a year and a day, or a thousand and one nights, but with a logic beyond our understanding.

After my first time with the Merry-Go-Round, I didn't get back in touch with Walt and Ellen. I didn't return their calls. The incident slipped out of my mind.

When I think of the Carousel years, I recall the city through a kind of fevered haze. I woke up more often in the small hours feeling empty and alien. I recalled things that had been done to me by humans. Stuff that had happened when I was a young kid could still make me angry. Over the next year or so, I explored that anger. Some guys were turned on by the scenarios I laid out. George wasn't. I left his bedroom for his living room. Blanche watched me intently when my eyes flew open at 4 A.M.

One afternoon at Half Remembered Things, a customer was nibbling at a Robert the Robot from Ideal and I was jumpy, unfocused. Light came down the street at an angle the sun only seems to find in October and it killed me to waste the day.

George came in with Andrew, the photographer who had worked with him on *Discovering the American Toy*. At that point, I was looking for a place of my own. As he passed the counter, George remarked, "I found these in the laundry," and handed me a set of handcuffs.

"Thanks." I pocketed them. The cuffs were one of the toys for my Sergeant Burke persona. I had a rendezvous scheduled in a few minutes with the guy who called himself Johnny. It occurred to me that George and Andrew had embarked on an affair and would be happy if I got out of the way. Amazingly enough, that hurt my feelings. "I'm going to lunch if that's okay with you," I said and stalked out. I didn't return to the store that afternoon.

"With Johnny, the game is still cops and robbers," I explained to Addie at her place on a rainy evening a few days afterwards. My head spun. The night before, in the darkened kitchen of a restaurant, empty after closing, I'd made a young guy I'd never seen before stand and deliver, cuffing his hands to a pipe, yanking down his pants, and fucking him as he stood against the sink, saying not a word, making him beg to be released.

"And you're the robber." Addie watched me closely.

"No, silly. I'm the undercover cop because I'm older and wear a beard and because I can do this: 'SPREAD YOUR FUCKING LEGS, MOTHER! ASSUME THE POSITION!' I learned to yell like that at St. Sebastian's S & M. Not those exact commands. But the intent was the same."

My mouth was out of control. I'd never talked about this stuff with Addie or much of anyone else. "My dick is only average. But it's uncut. Around here, most guys are circumcised, so that makes me exotic. More real. When I was a kid, I looked too young. Like I looked fourteen when I was sixteen. Kids my own age weren't interested in that. They had just recently escaped being fourteen themselves. Certain older guys were turned on. And they were willing to pay. I had this whole other identity as Fred, a tough slum kid, close to the street. My Shadow fit in to that. Sometimes he was Fred. Sometimes I was.

"That kind of game carries over. Like, I've known for months that Johnny's real name is Stanley and he's a graduate student in film at NYU and not a street punk. That detracts from the scenario for me. But if he knew I was an antique dealer, it would kill the relationship."

"You mean he wouldn't love you?"

"He doesn't now." I shook my head impatiently and found it made me dizzy. "That's not the point." Sweat was on my forehead and upper lip. "I'm leaving George," I said. "We agreed. I'll look for an apartment. I can't go home . . . I mean I don't want to go home tonight."

Addie was shaking a thermometer that I didn't remember her having a moment before. "Open up, Kev."

"Cut it out." I turned my head away.

"In your mouth, Kev, or we take it anally. Under your tongue." Addie was well used to fractious but disoriented patients. She handed me the business end of a stethoscope. "Open your shirt and put this on your chest. A little lower. Okay. Breathe deep. And exhale. Stand up. Open your pants." She probed my groin. "How does it feel?"

"Like I'm turning a rough trick." She slapped me on the butt. "Hey! Ever think of becoming leather trade?" I asked and found I was slipping to the floor.

What I remember about the next week or two is lying in Addie's big bed, soaking in her tub, while below me, children spoke, sang, cried. I remember one night waking up, looking out the second-story window, and seeing a figure outside the gate. My Shadow stared across the silent autumn garden. Instead of seeming tougher than me, he just looked sick. And very scared.

One day George came by, bringing some of my belongings, telling me not to worry about the shop. Downstairs, I heard him whisper to Addie about a strain of very bad flu that was going around. It was the first mention I remember of the disease that was going to wreck everything. She said I had pneumonia, then murmured something to him and he thanked her.

I remember the office of a friend of hers, a lesbian doctor who did tests on my heart. I remember sitting on the edge of the bed with Addie rubbing my back and my saying, "When I was a kid, lots of my contact with guys was pretty brutal. Cops and perverts and relatives. I never felt I had any control. With Johnny and these other guys, it's like I replay all that but with me as the other guys. Like I'm looking for my childhood in all the wrong places."

"You're searching for your Shadow?"

"No. Him I have no trouble finding. The other night, I saw

him. He looked unwell. Like my pneumonia was a kind of pale reflection of what he had."

My liaison with Addie lasted a couple of months while I looked for a place to live. She taught me how to use condoms. Sometimes I thought I was a research paper of hers. Once or twice I took her out to the bars dressed in my clothes. Hers didn't fit me.

That winter I found an oversized, low-ceilinged studio apartment down on Mott Street opposite the old St. Patrick's Cathedral, the one the Irish built before they went big time up on Fifth Avenue. I awakened lots of mornings to the sound of bells. But I never went inside the place.

That winter I thought that George and my partnership, like our relationship, was over. That winter too, the Scott Callendars, Jr. and Sr., swung back into my life. One evening Sarah called, sounding tense, to say her son had disappeared.

A few days later on a gray afternoon that promised snow, I returned to the shop from an auction and found Scotty scarfing down hot chocolate and muffins as fast as George could serve them. "I'm in the city for keeps," he announced. "I thought you two were still together," he said, angry and hurt.

Walking home with Scott with his tangled hair, bomber jacket, and torn jeans with long johns underneath, I caught the glances directed his way. The admiration and longing was so intense as to be identical to resentment.

Intentionally, I led him past the Gordian knot of sneakers that hung on a lamp pole at Mott and Houston. "That's the local gang. They take the shoes off kids who violate their turf and sling them over the wires."

"Cool," said Scott with barely an upward glance.

A year and a half before, his last visit had been easy. He was basically still a child and afraid to stir too far from George and me. This time an adult was just below the surface. I asked, "Seen *A Garland Knot for Children* lately?"

And he replied, "I met your Shadow today. Uptown on Lexington."

"What were you doing there?" Is there any regret sharper and stupider than for the conversations we didn't have?

"Casing the territory. I planned not to tell you I was in the city. This guy spoke to me and, fucking Christ, Kevin, I thought he was you. In this decayed version of the same leathers you're wearing, stinking and needing a shave.

"And he kind of was you. He calls himself Fred, talked about what you and he did when you were a kid. Said he's old and savvy now and I was a great-looking boy with a lot of potential. I said I was straight and he said that being queer would just get in the way. He showed me what it's like for the kids up there." Scott looked like he couldn't decide whether to vomit or cry. "Why did you let them do that stuff to you? Fuck you, Kevin, were you that desperate when you were my age?"

"Lonely." It hurt my throat to say the word. "Things were different then. I was looking . . ." But what I'd been looking for seemed too stupid to talk about. Instead I said, "You got that much trouble with my being gay, your staying here isn't going to work."

He shook his head. "You know that's not it, Kevin. I got friends that are gay. And you and George were great together. Why did you do that, Kevin? Break up with George? Your Shadow thinks that you and he aren't gay. Or straight. Or anything human. That all you want is some little corner to be warm in. Like a reptile. That together you don't add up to one person. That you know that. But you're scared to face it."

We stood in front of my building. My mouth tasted like rust. My life seemed worse than useless. "Scott, I'm going to have to tell your mother you're here. She wants you back."

He stepped away from me then, ready to take flight. "Tell my mother I'll drop off the face of the earth and peddle my ass like you did. I figure it's that or the flaming motorcycle. Which way, Dad's way or Kevin's way? That's the question."

At that moment I felt the primal male urge to wipe the defiance off the kid's face, to put him through the same bad times and terror I remembered. But I knew that if I made that wrong move, he'd go back to my Shadow. I'd lose him forever.

Then I remembered Mr. Dunn and how, at a time when I had fucked up entirely, he had wondered if I had been sent to teach him humility. And I found it in me to say, "Maybe you got sent here to teach me patience or something. If you enroll in school and work in the store, I'll ask your mother if you can stay."

Scott nodded like he was doing me a favor. A day or two later, he came home barefoot, lips white, trembling with rage. What I wanted to do was yell at him and call the cops. What I did was make sure he wasn't actually tracking blood and order pizza with pepperoni, his favorite food that year. Next morning before dawn, Scott slipped out of the apartment wearing old shoes, with a familiar book under his arm. I heard him go up to the roof and did not follow him. Naturally, I couldn't go back to sleep.

He returned that evening with the shoes slung over his shoulder, wearing a tight grin and expensive sneakers I hadn't seen before.

"Those belonged to the guy who did it to you?"

"There were a few of them who jumped me. These were the best pair that fit. Today, they were real happy to hand over their shoes and socks and run home barefoot, crying for their mamas. Everyone saw. Their girlfriends stayed and talked to me."

"But that's all that happened to the guys?"

"Except, maybe, a singed eyebrow or two. And their blades getting too hot to handle. I kicked all the knives down the sewer."

"Okay. But I don't want to see *Garland Knot* around here again. And I'm going to give you a number. This woman is Dr. Addie Kemper. I'd like you to talk to her." And as he had years before down in SoHo, Scott shook my hand solemnly like we had sealed a deal.

Sarah, but not Jake, visited a couple of times. She didn't go into what had happened between the two of them and Scotty. She didn't need to; having him around, I could imagine. Scott was enrolled in the hip and private Elisabeth Irwin High School not far from the store. Sarah agreed to have him see Addie. I got screens to divide my place. But I had lost my privacy. I couldn't bring guys home. And I lost my peace of mind. I worried about the kid every moment he wasn't in my sight. And I mostly wanted to strangle him when he was.

George saved my life or at least what remained of my sanity by asking if Scott could stay with him the last part of each month. "That way I'll know he's getting fed half the time," he said. And, "I'm glad you're being sensible about child custody. That ruins so many divorces."

The Carousel swung back into my dreams one dismal Ash Wednesday morning. Lights twirled in the dark as I spun around and around. The barker's voice was loud and his rap was strange. As I rode past I heard him say, ". . . SAILING INTO THE SUNSHINE OUT OF THE RAIN . . ." Then he was lost in the waltz music until I came by again: ". . . WHERE WE SEE OUR OWN CHILDHOOD . . ."

On one side I passed the lighted midway, on the other I looked out onto the night and a streetcar stop. On one circuit I caught sight of a car rolling to a halt. I was pulled away as the passengers boarded. On the next spin, I saw a kid at a car window, real young, his face clenched so that he couldn't cry out his fear and pain. The car hurtled off into the dark and I was pulled back toward the light of the carnival. It was as if my heart had been torn in two, so deeply did our separating rip me.

And then I was gasping for breath, afraid to move until the angina died away, alone in my place down on Mott Street. Scott was with George. And the kid had pretty much put an end to any affairs I was having.

So, I disentangled myself from the covers, pulled on a knee-length T-shirt, and went to the kitchen area. Out the window were the worn, brick-walled yards and buildings of the old cathedral. St. Patrick's, with its Irish names on the war memorials, Italian priests and nuns, and a mostly Spanish congregation, was a few shades grander than a normal parish church. Down on Prince Street, junkies seeped in as Little Italy ebbed. But on this block, bells tolled and kids in uniform came out of the church with black crosses of ashes on their foreheads.

My chest felt as if it had a huge empty hole right in the middle, like I was a cartoon character shot through by a cannonball. Cold air bit at my heart as I sipped tea and thought about Boston and Queena Heaven Parish.

Near the parish was a streetcar line that ran from Ashmont Station through Dorchester Lower Mills along the Neponset River, over marshes, past small patches of trees and clumps of houses built on firmer ground and out to Mattapan.

Along this route, at the end of the summer when I was twelve a carnival pitched camp on an empty lot just beyond the tidal marshes. It featured nickel-a-pitch booths and cotton candy and hot dog stands, air rifle galleries, a ferris wheel, a merry-go-round with smiling horses, and a pony ride that gave a circus tang to the air.

It also had a sideshow tent closed to kids under sixteen unaccompanied by an adult. My friend Murph and I went to the fair one day, mainly on my nickels and quarters. I said the sideshow was stupid and he agreed. But it had a pull that we both felt.

Murph was thirteen and could claim to be fifteen without getting much argument. In the subtly shifting alliances of the street, he began hanging around with kids older than he was and I tagged along with him. But I was already going to school downtown, which made me an outsider. Murph and the other guys were all a good growth spurt or two ahead of me. It was 1956 and Elvis had sung. They wore pompadours and pointed shoes when I was still in a buzz cut and sneakers.

I was there when they planned to go to the carnival at night. I said nothing about it at home, just showed up at Curtis Park after dinner with all the change from my bank. There were maybe half a dozen kids, a couple I knew only vaguely. They looked at me slit eyed. Murph shrugged and whispered something. On the streetcar out, a couple of them slipped past the motorman without paying. They shouted out the open car windows as we passed over the marshes in the August twilight.

The carnival by dusk was aglow and noisy, bursts of "Stars and Stripes Forever" blending with merry-go-round music. The guys were noisy, pushing each other, laughing, looking for stuff to swipe. Admission to the tent was fifty cents. We circled around looking for a way in.

"If they say sixteen, they mean fourteen. We need money." They all looked at me. Suddenly, my jersey got pulled up over my face. "Hey, your shirt's out!" Hands were in my pockets. I heard my change hit the ground. "Depants him!" I broke free, spun away.

"Watch it, you jerk!" I had smashed into the bald, indignant father of a family. The kids when I turned were walking away laughing as Murphy counted the change he'd taken out of my pocket and no amount of squinting could keep back tears.

Then a man said, "You okay, son?" He put his hand on my shoulder. He was tall, serious looking. It occurred to me that he saw what happened and had come to help. He picked up some dimes that had dropped and put them in my pocket. He put his hand on my shoulder, which felt good. "Are you hurt?" I shook my head. What had happened was too bad even to think about. He asked me my name and I told him.

Before us was light and music, the merry-go-round. "Is there anything you want? A Coke?" Everyone seeing him with his arm around me would think he was my father. And I wanted them to think that. He guided me toward the carousel. "Let's go on this ride." And I wanted so much to say yes and be his kid.

People sailed by on the horses. Shards of dark and light made it seem as if I were catching reflections in smashed mirrors. The people looked like picture-puzzle pieces. I shook my head and tried to hang back.

He just said, "Come on," and pushed me forward. And I knew this guy saw I was broken too and was going to put me up there where I would spin away forever with all the other bits and pieces of people. Spooked, I broke out of his grasp. Suddenly, he was furious. "Hey, get back here!" He tried to grab me but I dodged him and ran to the streetcar stop. I got on board without looking back.

As I recalled that on Ash Wednesday morning, the phone rang and a woman said, "Mr. Grierson, this is Ellen Clark. A year or two ago, I showed you a Merry-Go-Round."

I managed to tell her, "There was a problem with authentication. Like who owned it. You ever straighten that out?" It wasn't that I cared. Not like George did. But the Carousel, especially turning up right when it did, scared me.

"We've got papers, Mr. Grierson. That guy Al isn't connected with the deal anymore. We found someone who says he can have it up and running."

My breath ran shallow. This could be a lot of money. Enough to make me independent of George. And it fascinated me. I couldn't deny that. "Same place?"

"No. You're still interested? We'll be in touch."

That afternoon, I sat in Addie's telling her all I had dreamed and remembered. "What happened after the night at the carnival?" she asked.

"That fall, right on schedule, pubic hairs sprouted. I practiced a new hard-eyed smile in front of the mirror. I found places where guys would tell me I was a good kid and give me pocket money."

"In return for which they molested you."

"Kind of like now."

Because I had told her about waking up with a pain in my chest, I sat with my shirt opened and Addie examining me. "Do you use butyl nitrate?" she asked.

"Poppers? No. I have a bad memory from when I was a kid. Why?"

"Because your heartbeat is irregular, which makes that a risky activity. Besides, a lot of gay men are getting sick. There's a theory that poppers might be a cause."

I shrugged. The "gay disease" was part of the background noise of the city. Then Addie said, "It's interesting that the Carousel dream evoked the memory of the carnival when you were twelve." I hadn't told her about the memory having evoked the telephone call about the Carousel.

George and I didn't talk a whole lot at that point. So when we were in the store, I didn't mention the call or much of anything else. Scott, who was supposed to be at work right after school, came in late and just stood staring at me and saying nothing. There were customers present, so I motioned him into the back room and asked what was wrong.

"I saw your Shadow again. It was interesting. He says he helped you kill my father. Which is about what my dad has always told me. Your Shadow says he knew what was going to happen, but you managed not to know. He says that you wanted to get me away from my old man. You wanted a kid. I think that's at least partly right. So, now you got a genuine reptile son and what am I supposed to do?"

What I felt was something between anger and anguish. My voice came out tight, choked. "Scott, we went through this

years ago. What I intended was to save your life. I've had to
think a lot about it since. If what I did was wrong—"

Scott suddenly turned and was gone. My heart pounded and
my head spun. I heard him tell George he'd see him at home,
then the front door slammed. I tried to calm down before I went
back out front. When I did, George was alone in the store. "That
does it," I told him. "The kid goes home to his mother or goes
out on the street."

George couldn't help himself, he looked at me with concern.
"Take it easy, Kevin. Don't talk that way. Think how Mr. Dunn
wasn't around when you still needed him. You won't do that to
Scotty."

"Listen, if I die, he's what's going to kill me. If you're so concerned, you can have him full-time. He likes you better, anyway."

"You're what he talks about, Kevin. You and the girl down at
the Bleecker Bakery who's developed those huge breasts. However he expresses it, he adores you. And, honey, I will testify
that you don't make that easy."

At Addie's, at her invitation and Scott's, I sat with her and
watched him at the sand table. He had made two small mounds.
On one he had placed a colorful toy shaman and on the other a
plastic Gandalf figure. "It's like these two wizards fight, these
spirits. Over me. And one revving himself up gets himself killed
instead, and the other lets it happen."

"I'm not a wizard, Scott. I'm just a fool who did a lot of stupid stuff," I told him when he was finished. "I've wondered,
you know, if I did it. Killed your old man. For the reasons that
you said. And I don't know. I don't fucking know. You asked me
that first day in the city how I could do all the dumb, dangerous things I did when I was your age. The reason is so stupid it's
pathetic. I was looking for a father."

Scott shrugged and turned his face away.

.   .   .

Ellen Clark called the store on a snowy day right after that. She gave me an address way downtown around the corner from Desbrosses Street and made an appointment for that afternoon. I was willing to forget how scared I'd been the last time. Mystery drew me and the idea that this Merry-Go-Round held my dreams and was worth a fortune. Carousel horses were already selling for five figures.

Scott and George were both at the store. The problems I was having with them probably made me foolhardy. Besides, the background hum of gay New York was a rising death chant. And none of the other dumb things I'd done had gotten me killed. I told nobody where I was going.

The snow fell fast and steady. Big wet flakes. Cars drove with their lights on. Taxis had all disappeared. Sound was distant, and the air smelled of ice and iron as I walked alone down the West Side, not even looking to see if I was followed.

A silver stillness hung over Desbrosses Street and what was left of old iron-bound lower Manhattan. Just to the south, new office towers rose. Here snow fell on cobblestones and on the silent river. The building at the address I'd been given might have been an old meeting house, a public hall of some kind. Not even stopping to wonder how and why they had moved the Carousel, I climbed wide, unshoveled steps and rang the bell.

Just then I had a flashback to the winter years before, to me and Smiley Smile in the backseat of the Sojourners' car. For the first time I remembered what had happened after that. The guys with the flickering heads herded us into a freight elevator. They were very pissed that Smiley hadn't been able to deliver my Shadow. Just before they came for us, my double whispered to me, 'They want to put us in a freak show like we're the two-headed boy. Straights from another dimension will pay a quarter a piece to toss peanuts to a boy and his doppelganger.'

The elevator door had opened on a cellar that stretched away like a cave. Suddenly, alarms went off all over the building. Blinding lights came on. I heard my Shadow say, 'Run!' As I started I got slammed hard. The floor came up and whacked out my lights. But I woke up in a hospital, not in a zoo.

As I remembered that, the door opened on Ellen in sunglasses and a fake fur coat. Until that moment, I could have backed off. Just then, that option got taken away. Snow muffled the pounding of feet behind me. Then Scott rushed up saying, "I'm with him."

Before I could say no, he was inside and the door shut behind us. I couldn't read Ellen Clark's expression as she led us inside. But I knew, the way one does, that there were others in the building.

Stairs to either side of the cold and dusty lobby led to a balcony. Peeling figures on the WPA mural above the auditorium doors showed something like the Sons of Labor offering the Fruits of Industry to the Goddess of Liberty.

"What the hell are you doing here?" I muttered to Scott.

"Watching out for you," the kid said. And I noticed *Garland Knot* stuck in his pocket like a pistol in a holster.

"The item is right in here." Ellen watched me as I pushed open the auditorium door. A stage with a raised speaker's platform and lectern ran along the far wall. In another time, dances, strike votes, political rallies must have taken place on the wide, worn floor. Now it supported the Carousel.

Harsh ceiling lights shone down cruelly on cracked wood and peeling paint. It could have been pathetic. But the horses themselves, eyes savage and teeth bared, made Scott whisper, "Holy shit!"

Ellen stayed near the door. I wondered how they had gotten this thing in there and if Smiley Smile was watching me. I walked over to the Carousel and Scott stayed with me like he was glued. His presence meant there was more at stake. He might get hurt or even killed because of his loyalty. And my stupidity.

Still, I couldn't help but stare. In the last year or so I had looked at lots of carousels up close and in pictures. I'd found nothing like this. Vlask, a turn-of-the-century Czech designer, had done work somewhat in this vein. But not as visceral. I calculated that broken down and sold piecemeal, this thing would be worth half a million easily.

From somewhere behind me a man said, "We have it hooked to an electric generator." Scott looked that way and reached into his pocket. The one who called himself Al stood near the door. He kept his smiling scar in plain sight this time. "You and the kid can sit up there and test it out." I shook my head. It occurred to me that I didn't feel well.

Smiley Smile gave a signal and the lights above us flickered, a low rumble began, the Carousel horses started to move. I heard a voice, alternately quiet and loud as if the barker were aboard a spinning Merry-Go-Round: ". . . life of Kevin Grierson in ALL ITS MUNDANITY AND HORROR. SEE HIS FRIENDS AND LOVERS . . . as they are and as they will . . ."

My head spun and I couldn't catch my breath.

There was George up on a horse along with everyone else I knew from Johnny to Addie. The barker continued, ". . . be, SAILING OUT OF THE FUTURE INTO THE PRESENT. SEE HIS FORMER LOVER struck down with the gay . . ." As they passed before me, everyone aged and some changed horribly. ". . . sees himself AND HIS OWN FATE."

"KEVIN!" I turned to see Scott beside me facing the door. Ellen stood back there like she was ready to flee. Smiley Smile said, "You like our Merry-Go-Round, Mr. Grierson, you'll love the rest of our carnival. In fact, you'll be a part of it, you and your friend Fred. Now that we have you, we should be able to nab him easily. Siamese twins will be nothing compared to you two. Stand aside, kid," he told Scott.

A pair of guys I hadn't noticed before moved out from behind the Carousel. The Sojourners flickered in the light. "Turn it off," Scott yelled. "It's making him sick!" He pulled out the book and said, very quietly, "If they take him, I go too."

He fanned the pages and a tiny ball of flame flew like a bullet. One of the Sojourners reached inside his jacket. The burning motorcycle hit his hand and he howled. The cycle bounced off him and caught the other Sojourner above the ear. He cried out and beat his smoldering hair.

Ellen had disappeared. Smiley ducked as Scott Callendar Sr. and his flaming motorcycle hit the transformer with a shower of sparks. As it did, I heard a voice, angry, confused, and very young singing:

> You won, sir, my son, sir,
> The prize of your fair town

The next thing I heard was a strangled scream as a giant hand squeezed my chest and forced all the air out of my lungs. Then I was flat on the auditorium floor. Electrical wires smoldered and an icicle was rammed into my heart. I was all alone as the cold spread up my arms and legs. Scott raced back into the room, threw aside the book, fell down and held me. He was crying.

"Don't die, Kevin. I called the ambulance. Please, don't die on me. I need you so much."

Snow made the sirens sound echoing and slow. "I won't," I heard myself say. And the cold stopped creeping.

FOURTEEN

THE PHONE RANG at Half Remembered Things and I let it go until the answering machine came on. "Uncle Kevin," said Miranda, "don't bring me the horse. I need a set of dishes. Not little doll ones. Ones for dogs to use. I am having a party—"

"Hi, honey," I said, fumbling to pick it up.

"Hello. Are you coming to my party? Sandy and Raz are coming, and Patsy."

"Well, no. Portland is kind of far away."

I heard her father in the background telling her, "Mirry, that's not what you said you were going to tell him."

"I just wanted to explain to Uncle Kevin," she said.

Before her father took the phone I said, "Happy birthday, honey. Watch. You're going to get the present you asked for three asks ago."

"What is it?" The greed of childhood is so simple and uncomplicated as to be refreshing.

"I guess it will be a surprise!" At two that afternoon, which would be in about half an hour Oregon time, a young woman dressed as a giant panda would deliver a Chinese doll with a dozen different costumes.

"Hi, Kev." Scotty Callendar got on. "I don't know about Patsy, but Sandy and Raz are two dogs from the neighborhood."

"Patsy is a parakeet. And Sandy is a Saint Bernard," I heard my godchild telling her father.

"Gosh, that's one party I'll be sorry to miss!" It was a long time since I'd laughed and it must have sounded that way.

"You okay, Kevin?" Scotty asked. I tried to say yes and could only manage to nod. "No. Obviously. How are things with George?"

"It'll be soon." I realized I was certain of that.

"I'm taking the next flight east. I want to be with him."

"No. Wait. Stay for the birthday. I would never forgive you if you missed the party. And George wouldn't either. He worshiped kids." It occurred to me that I had just referred to George in the past tense. "Is Mirry doing okay?" Her father and I have often talked about the chances of a *Garland Knot* showing up among Miranda's toys.

"Everything here is fine, Kevin. But something's up. What is it? The Shadow? The Carousel?" This kid knew too much. Then again this kid was in his midthirties. "I'm going to catch the red-eye."

I was about to tell him I didn't know where I'd be. But that would just have made him worry more. As we talked, I was aware that my Shadow was awakening. His joints ached with every step.

After Scotty hung up, I was oddly calm. My life has held shocks, but no surprises since my second visit to the Carousel, like watching a movie after you've already seen extended coming attractions.

·   ·   ·

When the Carousel returned for a third time it had seemed to me inevitable. In tales of magic, there is always a third time. And after that the tale is over.

It appeared in the first bloom of spring. On the plane from Boston, I saw the land grow greener as we flew south. I'd been at the funeral of Uncle Bob the lawyer, the last of my uncles, so it must have been '87. Everyone had said how well I looked. And how prosperous, as if they were rehearsing the lines to be used at my own wake.

A few of the old ones, knowing the family history, may have been searching for a manifestation of the *Faileas*, the Shadow. But even that connection to my clan seems severed. So far as I have seen and heard, no relative of my generation or the next has shown any hint of a double. Checking that out was my only good reason for going back. I wondered if me and my Shadow were the last of our kind and if the Sojourners had been right in trying to nab us for a zoo.

Younger cousins looked for the telltale signs of my sexuality and my heart trouble. The first I express in a slight alienation at these gatherings, the other by a slight stiffness of the soul, a wariness of rapture. I stayed at the Park Plaza where many years before a client had shown me how to shave with a safety razor. Next morning I went back to New York on the shuttle.

Trees were budding in Stuyvesant Park when I got home. I'd bought a co-op that winter and had just found the right place to hang the Caldecott prints. In the mail was a thank-you note from a young lady named Lise. The previous week, she and Scott had stayed with me on their way out to Long Island. From all I saw and heard they were very much in love. It amazed me that this was spring break of his senior year at Cornell.

Only after my multiple bypass in 1983 had he told me that it was my Shadow who had warned him I was in danger. "He said I was the only one who could save you. He said otherwise you and he were going to end up in a sideshow in some circle of hell."

And only on that spring break of his senior year, late one night when Lise was asleep and we were talking in the kitchen, did I tell him how his father, that time the two Scotts saved my life, had seemed so young. "He never got any older than he was when he died. Closer to your age than to mine. He seemed lost and angry the same way I remember being when I was young."

"My dad is a lot more at peace these days," Scotty had said.

A week later, as I unpacked after Boston, I wondered what would have happened if Scott hadn't pulled my attention away from the Carousel. Would the sight of my future self, my destiny, whatever that might be, have killed the curiosity and endless hope that keeps us all alive?

On my answering machine, Addie said, "Kevin, a patient felt she couldn't create an African palace. Any ideas?" I would call her later. Addie was a certainty in my life. I had already seen her riding through middle age, serene and wise on a wild-eyed wooden horse.

Since it was still early on that spring day I walked over to the store. George's *Discovering the American Toy* was about to come out in a second edition. I still took out my copy of the original and read the dedication: "For Kevin Grierson, a partner in wonder."

Slowly and by degrees I had begun to understand all that was involved when I promised not to die on that snowy afternoon just off Desbrosses Street. At Half Remembered Things, George sat at the counter doing our taxes. Details like that impressed me. If I were HIV positive, nothing else would ever enter my mind. He took every precaution, held onto his health, and waited for the cure I knew wasn't coming. I alone had seen him, defaced and broken by full-blown AIDS, swing out of the future into that old meeting hall.

"How did it go, Kev?" he asked.

"Okay. Kind of jolly. Considering it was a wake and funeral." My life, as I've said, contained no surprises. But it was a shock on a bright afternoon to glance down and spot at George's elbow photos of fierce carousel horses, stacked like cordwood in what seemed to be a cellar.

George noticed my interest. "Someone found a disassembled merry-go-round in a barn out in Bucks County. Wants me to authenticate it. The price on this stuff has gone through the roof. Maybe we can drive down Sunday and see it."

He said more, but I felt chilled. Outside the store, tourists had stopped to admire the five-story doll apartment house in our window but now were gawking at something inside the store.

I turned to tell George I thought there were better ways to spend a weekend. His head was down on the counter and he was sobbing.

"Everything scares me, Kev. When I opened the envelope this morning and saw those stupid wooden horses, all I could think about was how Larry looked before he went. And Eric. The dementia . . . Kaposi's . . . the goddamn diapers . . . oh Jesus, I feel so sick some mornings when I wake up. And I'm scared even to say it!"

And I wished we had blinds, so I could draw them and stop the eyes of the world from witnessing the misery of this gentle man. Instead, I crossed the store and put my arms around him, crooned the ancient sounds of comfort that we all know. And that we all can utter if we just let ourselves.

Over dinner the next night, I told Addie, "Then I tore up the photos. Someone else can look at the horses. It's bad enough I did it twice. I'm not falling for the bait again. I told myself that whole part of my life is over and I was too old for magic. Last night, I slept on George's couch so he wouldn't be alone. He zonked out just like always.

"And the same way I used to, around three in the morning, I woke up from a dream. I felt another presence in the room. Someone cautious and wary. But curious about what he saw.

"And I remembered the dream I'd just had. It was the recurring one where the streetcar with a kid on board rolls away from the carnival. He's ordinary enough, blond, kind of small. A real young twelve. What gets me is the pain in his eyes, the way he sits like he's afraid of being hit.

"He's me, of course, age twelve. I think of him as Kev. He doesn't seem quite as scared as he once was. He's the one who's watching me in the middle of the night. Not my Shadow. Not anymore."

"What's your Shadow up to these days?" Addie asked like she was inquiring after one of my relatives whom she'd never met.

"He's still around," I said. "Every once in a while someone sees him. I'm sure he knows about Kev. Sooner or later the kid is going to head this way. I want it to be me he goes to see, and not my Shadow."

Addie smiled and seemed to approve. It was hard to know how crazy she thought I was. We went on to talk about miniature hand-carved tribal masks, about toy columns and arches the color of sandstone with which a child could make an African palace as twisted and magnificent as a dream.

A dozen years later, I found myself alone at Half Remembered Things on the phone talking to my old friend. "Lakeisha called," Addie said. "She wondered if Lauren and I were going to see George. She wants to say good-by. She seemed to think you might not be around this evening. She's worried about you, Kevin."

"Would you take care of her, Addie? You're my executor. There's also a kid named Matt I told to call you if anything happened to me. And Scotty Callendar is coming into town. And George. . . . I'm sorry it's so sudden. But my Shadow wants to talk. I'm going uptown to meet with him tonight."

"Do you want to discuss it?"

"I don't think so. This has to happen. Thank you and Lauren so much for listening. And thanks especially for being so unprofessional over the years and not trying to have me locked up."

"Not that the idea hasn't crossed my mind. Will you come see me after you've done whatever you think you have to do?"

"You know I'll try."

As we spoke, I noticed that the air outside the window had turned silvery. Thunderstorms rattled through the crooked streets of the West Village. Tourists, passersby, ducked into the store. Once I thought I saw a head flickering across the street. When I looked again, it was nothing and I remembered I hadn't been getting enough sleep.

But when I heard the rattle and clank of steel wheels on steel tracks, I knew it was time to put on my jacket, lock the shop, maybe for the last time, hail a cab, and ride to the reunion with my old Silent Partner. On the way, a New York thunderstorm, tiny but intense, moved uptown like it was part of the traffic.

It outran us before we reached Forty-second Street. The evening sun slanted through Hell's Kitchen and into Times Square. Theater marquees, the headlights of cabs and limos reflected off the wet, steaming pavement.

Cops, uniformed and plainclothes, were out on foot, in cars, and on horseback. The city has twisted the old Square, garish, dangerous, sordid, into a Disney theme park. But between the cracks, I spotted trade and dealers, all races, all young, emerging from doorways as the rain passed. For those on the old and the new Deuce the theater crowd has always been like the nightly passage of a magic ship, lighted, loaded with riches, quick to vanish.

Gumshoe! plays the Savoy, a nicely faded old house. This isn't the show about the fall of Saigon, or the singing alley cats who go to heaven on a manhole cover. It's the one written by French people about the private eye in New York in the '30s, the one where the blimp crashes on stage.

At the box office, I gave my name and almost immediately a voice at my elbow said, "This way, Mr. Grierson." I turned to find a guy with the slightly puffy face of a retired cop giving me a slit-eyed stare. That happened a lot when my Shadow was around.

We went through a bronze door and down a few steps. Above us hung an old Manhattan skyline painted loud and flat. Spots dimmed and brightened, and from the dressing rooms, a tenor ran the scales. The property manager and her assistant readied a bouquet of roses, a vast spangled bra, and a bright silver revolver. The security man opened a fire door and I followed him into an alley where Gina, all henna-wigged and kimonoed, stood among the company smokers.

"TOBACCO ROAD!" she said when she spotted me. We embraced carefully because she was made-up. Then we stepped away from the others. "He was in my dressing room. He knew everything. What went on at MAS. That time we found you in the hospital. Things we all said and did. It was so scary. He wouldn't let me leave until I promised to get you up here. Then he was just gone."

She ground a butt under the toe of a purple sling-back. For just a moment I caught a glimpse of a twenty-year-old ingenue. "He won't bother you again," I told her and knew I had to make sure that was the case.

"Kevin, you're wonderful!" Maybe she too glimpsed that other country where we were still kids.

Then someone said, "Ten minutes, please." Security reappeared and led me to a seat at the back of the house. "When my friend shows up, we'll leave by ourselves," I said. The cop nodded, but didn't smile.

The houselights dimmed and the conductor brought down his baton. The third year of a show is when the awards are won, the original stars are gone, the audience is tourists from Iowa and Okinawa. That evening, Gina, as the owner of a Times Square nightclub, gave it her considerable best. The dancers still strutted their stuff and everything was bright and loud. The plot involved a private eye, a taxi dancer, and reincarnation. I thought of how much fun this would have been if I'd seen it with George and how all of that was over.

My doppelganger still hadn't shown in the second act when Gina and a Nazi spy had a nifty tango number. Then the blimp smashed into the Empire State Building. It was terrific. In the moment of silence before the reincarnated taxi dancer stepped out of the rubble into the arms of the detective, my Shadow said, 'I made you sit through this as punishment.' He was back and I didn't tell him to disappear.

The main theme played for the dozenth time. 'Let's take a walk west.' We went up the aisle during curtain calls. Gina got a great hand. We hit the sidewalk, mingled with a theater party from *Les Misérables,* and headed for Eighth Avenue.

'Like old times, huh, Kev?' A linen jacket that could have been one I'd had ten or twelve years before hung stained and flapping around his bones. His hair was long, disordered. His eyes burned maliciously in a pale face. 'It used to be I knew the things you were about to find out. Now I remember the things you forget.'

On Eighth, a remnant of the strip still jumps: porn shops, live action theaters, bang-and-walks for the love that just won't wait, tourist hotels for the discriminating out-of-town suit john. 'They want to call it Clinton, but it's still Hell's Kitchen and the Kitchen starts right here,' said my Shadow as we crossed Eighth and headed down a side street.

"Okay, you've been crossing my trail for the last few days," I said. "Now you've dragged me back here. You going to tell me why? And why did you set me up with Matt? You know what happened to Klackman? What about the Sojourners? And what the hell makes you think—"

'Hey, calm down. Your questions can get answered, maybe. Let's just walk around the old neighborhood, savor some old memories. What was it Mr. Dunn used to say about the past having the answers to present troubles?' A couple of bars lighted the block. He looked back to see if we were followed, then slowed. 'Your life without me was as stupid as that musical,' he said. I didn't bother to respond.

Ninth Avenue has become quite gentrified, all renovated walk-ups and ethnic restaurants, while retaining convenient clusters of drug dealers on every block. As we crossed Ninth and turned north, a bunch of Spanish guys in a doorway discreetly noted my Shadow's passing. They didn't see me at all.

I followed my Shadow into a liquor store where he pointed to a bottle behind a bulletproof shield and said, 'Daddy, buy me that.' He stuck the pint of Wild Turkey in a jacket pocket as we turned west again. Halfway down the block, we stopped in front of a flight of cement stairs. They led down a brick alleyway to a door. I remembered our first time in the city. "The site of Scarface's apartment is not exactly a big nostalgia stop for me," I told him. "He and his pals made jokes about cutting me up when they weren't fucking me. I don't think I've ever been as frightened."

'Me too. I didn't know if you were getting out alive. And that scared me plenty.' He faced the dark areaway. I heard a seal snap, saw him lift the bag to his mouth. I tasted old memory, felt a forgotten burning in my throat and chest. 'I thought seeing this place maybe would remind you that it wasn't just my bad influence. You could get in trouble all on your own. As I recall, later on you became a minor expert at terror and handcuffs yourself.'

"The ones I did it with were all adults and knew what they were getting into," I said, and heard the phoney, hollow sound the words made.

'I followed you when Scarface picked you up. The same way I did all those other times you sent me away. Like I have for the last twenty-something years. Trying to make sure you didn't come to more harm than you could handle.'

"That's because you needed to keep me alive. It took a while to figure out. But without me, there is no you." We continued west. On the blacktop of a park at Tenth Avenue, long, thin forms moved under the lights. I heard shouts, a laugh, the drum of a basketball.

"Let's get back to my questions." I said. "Why the elaborate setup with Matt and the damsel and the dwarf?"

'You're a busy man, Kevin. Distracted. No time for memories. We two have a lot to remember and not a lot of time to do it in. I needed to get your attention. Thus the damsel and the dwarf. Matt's seeing you when he did was just serendipity.'

"Nice job you did with him. What'll happen to the poor kid?"

'He's not the first to get hurt hanging around too near the pair of us. Just think of him as a test of your compassion.'

My Shadow led me across Tenth and down a block where teenage girls and their babies sat on tenement steps, past a highrise with a doorman and the old Grand Central Railway cut where far below, in pitch dark, a jungle whispered over rusting tracks.

No one else was on foot as we turned onto Eleventh and walked up a stretch of Death Avenue that was all auto dealerships closed for the night and tough topless clubs. It looked like an approach road to any American city. A tenement stood alone among parking lots. Half its windows were tinned up.

He gestured to the building. 'That's where I live.'

"Second floor front," I said, remembering my dream of the night before last.

That startled him, I could tell. But he just said, 'It's a squat. So the rent is right. It's the location that keeps me here, though.' And I knew it pleased him that I had no idea what that meant.

My Shadow crossed the avenue then and I followed him down a side street lined with parked trailers and dark loading docks. At the end of the block beyond Twelfth Avenue lay the Hudson. Across the water shone lighted apartment towers in New Jersey. My Shadow drew me behind a truck and pointed up at a building on the corner. When I looked, I was chilled. Painted on a blank brick wall was a sign reading Atlantic Shipping and Transfer.

'Where the cops found you that time,' he said. 'I've spotted Sojourners around here quite a bit over the years. Maybe they own the building as a front. There are tunnels under this place that go God knows where. I think it's some kind of gateway for them. I've kept an eye on it for years. Of course they can see me too, but I thought I was, you know, more able to dodge them than you.'

As we watched, a long black limousine glided up to the front of the place. 'Back when they dragged you and Smiley Smile in here, I rang every police and fire alarm I could find. And the boys in blue showed up in the nick of time. Weird being rescued by the law, but nice for us. Because once the Sojourner kissed you with the butt of his automatic, we were both down for the count. Of course, the medics didn't see me.'

The backdoor of a car opened and a couple of figures got out. "Smiley Smile," I said, and found myself drawing back trying to fade away. "Wasn't he in just as bad trouble as we were back then?"

My Shadow chuckled. 'Maybe old Smiley sold his soul to the devil. Maybe the Sojourners are the agents of some law I don't understand. Or they're collectors like Sandler and your other friends. Except not old toys. These guys collect freaks. Us."

My Shadow popped a pill, raised the bottle. I gasped as he swallowed. 'Anyway, that time I saved both our asses. Then, years later, you were going to walk right back into the middle of them. Until I warned Scotty Callendar. You are one lucky son of a bitch.'

Just then from blocks away, I heard the screech of a streetcar rounding a curve. "What are we doing standing out here?"

'Killing time. Waiting for the moment.' My Shadow turned and headed back toward Eleventh Avenue. 'The neighborhood is alive with memories.' We passed the parking lot on what had once been the site of the Dublin Green. 'And that's where we split up for the last time. Remember that bitch Stacey Hale? You learned more than I'd thought from her. Like Prince Hal in Henry the Fourth, when you'd had as much fun as you could handle, you knew how to send your disreputable friends packing.'

"I never thought of you as a friend."

It was late. Guys cruised for trade. A car with Jersey plates turned onto a side street. We went in the same direction, past guys waiting in a vestibule.

My Shadow seemed to ignore them. 'Ever think how many in the family used to be, what should we call it? Gifted? I don't mean just the ones with Shadows. Think of Aunt Tay. Remember those poems?

BY FELL NIGHT

I was aware we were being followed. But my double looked toward me for the next line and I said:

WITH STICK AND BONE

'Second verse!' he said, laid back his head, and chanted:

BY BLACK LIGHT

Someone whispered behind us. Instead of turning, I spoke, amazed that the words came out of me so easily:

DOWN NARROW ROADS

We went through the rest of it and when we were done, no one was following us. Out of the corner of my eye, I saw a flickering like a silver screen. And three or four guys standing on the other side of the street looking confused by how they got there. 'Strong magic,' said my Shadow.

"Have you used it often?"

'Not until this minute. I had no idea if it would work. I was surprised I could even remember the fucker.' At that point he paused and put his arm around a lamppost for support.

Along with a contact wooziness, I caught an aching deep in my Shadow's bones. "You need to be in treatment," I said, and thought about George. "Some of it even works."

'Right. Except the AIDS safety net is pretty frayed and you happen to be using the identity. Try walking into a hospital and saying, "Hi, I've got this expensive sickness and no prior record of existence." I'm tired,' he said. 'I'm always tired. And in pain too, of course.'

He headed south and I followed. "Any idea how you got sick?" I asked.

'Mostly my time was one long doze. But you weren't exactly

living your life to the full. I existed on your margins. On occasion I woke up and got real solid. Especially when you were having your heart trouble. That was what? '82? '83? People were doing drugs, screwing like it was going out of style. Which it was.

'Again, you're a lucky fuck, out of commission during the years you were most likely to get killed. I wasn't real careful. Being I was only around maybe a quarter of the time, it's taken me a long time to die. But as I got sicker, I've had trouble dozing out. Irony! AIDS made me alive.'

Then we found ourselves outside a renovated building on Tenth. Years before this was the flophouse called Mother's. 'Leo Dunn!' my Shadow said. 'He took all our sins and put them onto me. But assuming I'm absolute Evil, how come you're not exactly Good personified? You ever wonder about that?'

When I said nothing, he said, 'Of course you did!' offered me a swig, and chuckled when I shied away. After washing down a painkiller, he tossed the empty bottle in a trash can.

Trucks whizzed by and I was aware of the place and the hour. 'Yeah. It's near the time,' he said and we headed down to the Deuce.

'Mostly, I've tried to stay out of your way. But this concerns you. After Mom died, her Shadow disappeared. No one saw Grandad's double once he cooled. And it works the other way too.'

It's what I was afraid of. But I just shrugged. "You're sure about that? Substance and Shadow snuff out together?"

'Yeah. I'm sure. But there's a possible escape. One thing I know. You and I aren't exact opposites. Like, say I really am Death and Darkness. Then you should be Immortality and Light, instead of just some poor fuck scrambling to stay afloat.

'Think what we got to work with. You spent a lot of your childhood with Tay. I spent mine with our mother's Shadow. You've had Mr. Dunn and George and Addie and Scotty telling you what a wonderful human being you are. In truth, you're no more a human than I am. Just a luckier fragment of one.'

We turned east onto Forty-second Street and I was surprised to find we both knew exactly where we were going.

"I'll do my best for you." It sounded hollow and stupid even as I said it.

He grabbed my wrist and said, 'No. The time of living like fucked-up fragments is over. Tonight the puzzle we're part of gets put together. You won't even have to like me, let alone take care of me.'

On the weirdly clean and empty blocks of the new, sanitized Deuce, the theater marquees were dark. But cop cars sat ready to enforce the laws of man. At Ninth Avenue was a handful of kids from New Jersey ambling back to the Port Authority. 'Just a few years ago they'd have been in a hallway pissing their pants as they got relieved of their wallets and shoes,' said my Shadow. 'Maybe by us,' he added, and chuckled at the thought.

As we walked toward Eighth Avenue, I saw the long black car cruise to a halt on the next block. "Someone else knows where we're going. Shall we give them BY FELL NIGHT?" I suggested.

'No. That's old. Let 'em come along. Besides, what we're going to be singing is,

> JUST WE THREE GO SAILING
> ME, MYSELF AND I
> OVER WALLS AND FENCES
> THROUGH THE NIGHT WE FLY

'Tay had the answer to what we were. Probably she herself didn't fully understand it. Since she hated me, I didn't pay attention at first. But I had a lot of time to wonder. Like, if you were Me, and I was Myself, then who was I? Lately, I figured it out. With a few hints so did you, right?'

"It's the kid. I'm here to protect him."

'Protect him?' said my Shadow. 'Asshole. He's the one who's come to save the righteous and the damned. You and me, in other words. With him, maybe we're one whole being.'

We approached the Seventh Avenue subway along the north side of the Deuce. The limousine was parked on the south side. Its windows were dark. I heard the car doors slamming as we headed down the stairs. We picked up the pace. I scrambled for a token. My Shadow passed through the turnstile.

Signs indicated the 1 and 9 trains, the A, C, E, and 7 lines. Arrows pointed west for the Port Authority, east for the shuttle. With the unquestioning certainty that comes in dreams, I turned east with my Shadow beside me. People loitered. A lone cop twirled his nightstick. A beggar sat on the floor. The cop wasn't looking. The man held out his hand. I stopped and fished out all my change.

'Oh, you are such a saint!' murmured my Shadow. I could hear him panting. People were coming up fast behind us.

Only one of the four shuttles operates late at night and it was out of the station. Cars sat still and silent on the other three tracks. We went to the far end of the platform. Beyond the trains is that rarest of things in New York, a place where something actually ends or begins. And there in the wall were stairs where there never were stairs, leading down to tracks that existed only in Streetcar Dreams.

"Grierson," I heard Smiley Smile call. "You and your friend stop there or we'll drop you." The platform below was empty as we hit the bottom of the steps. My Shadow said:

> PEOPLE HALF AWAKEN
> HEAR US PASS AND PRAY

As he spoke, I heard the grinding of the wheels and I said:

OUT OF FEARING FOR OUR SOULS,
WON'T WE REST AND STAY

Behind me, Smiley Smile and the Sojourners were coming down the stairs. Lights flashed on the wires, the single headlight rushed toward us out of the tunnel. 'You got a real talent for getting saved,' said my Shadow. In the lighted windows I saw the people mundane and magical who had touched me.

The door flew open. Someone yelled "Stop!" My Shadow tripped and stumbled once, couldn't get his foot onto the steps. When I yanked him along by the arm, he felt light, insubstantial. 'Like fucking gossamer wings,' he murmured.

My parents were there on the car, Tay and my grandmother. Celia and MacLunahan sat on either side of Leo Dunn. I saw Carl and I saw George and knew he had died in the night. They all smiled at me. George winked. He was as young as he was the first time we met. Boris wasn't there. I hope that means you are alive and well, my friend.

As we pulled out of the station and into the dark, I looked and saw Smiley Smile and the Sojourners standing on the platform openmouthed. I turned back to the car and there was the kid. Wary but brave, Kev looked back and forth from my Shadow to me.

I said before that I could no longer be surprised. But since last night I've come to the end of the map laid out for me by the Merry-Go-Round. The boy stood up and before I could speak or move, my Shadow gave a long, wordless cry and collapsed weeping in the kid's arms.

EPILOGUE

AND JUST NOW, I find myself rounding the corner of my block, walking between my Shadow and the boy. Fire engines roar. The erratic pulse of the city drums. The hazy morning air is a sticky mélange of exhaust, coffee, piss, burned toast, and garbage.

In front of my building are Addie and Lauren and Scott. All obviously worried, they have come from the hospice to let themselves in and find out what happened to me. Lakeisha is with them. Sitting on the stairs, unknown to the others, Matt looks lost and scared.

He spots me first, jumps up and says, "Kevin!" Then the others turn and look amazed. And I wonder if they see just me, middle-aged and beat to hell. Or do they see that twice and this wonderful child? This life that I have led is ending. And I don't know where the new one will take me. As I come toward these friends, I start to draw deep, sobbing breaths.

I know I am lucky to have made it this far. My kind does not often survive in the world of man. And if we do, it's usually as drunks with glistening eyes, drifters and crazies, hooded figures in doorways in the rain.

This, then, is for the ones who befriended me and for the strangers, for all those who see me crying in the street this August morning and stop a moment to wonder why.

. . . written in the city of New York